Critical acclaim

'Bagshawe writes w
superior beach nove

'Even more compulsive than Jackie Collins'
Company

'A great book. A classic story of life, love and ambition in the nineties' *Woman's Own*

'Compulsive reading' *Cosmopolitan*

'Her novels are action-packed; her heroines gorgeous; and her writing punchy enough to sustain the rises and falls of these blindingly successful characters . . . I loved it' *Daily Mail*

'Bagshawe has the wonderful knack of making you love her heroines however badly they behave. A kind of sexy, grown-up *Mallory Towers*. Great fun' *Sunday Express*

'An addictive, erotic blockbuster . . . Once again Bagshawe has excelled herself' *Company*

'A fat sexy book that throbs with vitality from the first page . . . Bagshawe has produced a classic of the genre' *Daily Express*

'One hell of a read . . . funny and ultra-glam, you'll want to cancel all social engagements until you finish this' *Company*

Oxford-educated Louise Bagshawe was the youngest ever contributor to *The Tablet* at the age of fourteen. Young Poet of the Year in 1989 and former President of the Oxford University Rock Society, she worked in the record business before leaving at twenty-three to write full time. A bestselling novelist and screenwriter, her work has been published in nine languages. She lives with her husband in New York.

By Louise Bagshawe

Career Girls
The Movie
Tall Poppies
Venus Envy
A Kept Woman

Louise Bagshawe

TALL POPPIES

ORION

An Orion paperback
First published in Great Britain by Orion in 1997
This paperback edition published in 1998 by Orion Books Ltd,
Orion House, 5 Upper St Martin's Lane, London WC2H 9EA

Reissued 2001

A CIP catalogue record for this book is available
from the British Library.

ISBN 0 75280 875 3

Typeset by Deltatype Ltd, Birkenhead, Merseyside
Printed and bound in Great Britain by
Clays Ltd, St Ives plc

This book is dedicated to
Rosie Cheetham, Susan Lamb, Barbara Kennedy-Brown,
and Tall Poppies everywhere.

Chapter 1

'No! Stop it, we can't do this!'

Nina squirmed away. She kept her eyes down, hoping he wouldn't see that telltale glitter, her dilated pupils. Her face was flushed from wanting, but it was too soon.

'Come on, sugar, gimme a break,' Jeff said. His voice was rough, and she could see the outline of his hard-on through his grey flannel pants. Nina tried to be cool about it, like Judy or Melissa or any of those popular girls, and not think how much it would hurt if he put it inside her. Perhaps he wouldn't get it in, Nina thought wildly. She'd checked herself out in the bathroom mirror last night – pretty small. He'd split her in two.

'You drive me crazy,' Jeff breathed, running his hands inside the burgundy school blazer, finding her voluptuous breasts under the thin cotton of her outsize shirt. She was wearing some kind of coarse, heavy sports bra to hold them back, just like she wore her kilt a size too large, to cover up her tiny waist and full, round butt – but not even Nina Roth could hide for ever. Jeff grinned with triumph as her nipples stiffened against his palm. He'd been after her ever since he'd come off the basketball court, thought he'd like a swim, and found Nina doing twenty laps. After hours, guess she thought she'd be by herself. Jeff had hidden in a corner to watch. Christ! Who knew? Nina Roth, scholarship girl, major nerd, charity case – had a figure like Playmate of the Month! Va-va-voom, instant hard-on! When she had climbed out of the pool Jeff couldn't believe it – water streaming from her

1

hair, trailing down across a cheap black swimsuit, outlining big firm breasts, a tiny waist, a flaring ass and long, curving legs. He'd felt his cock throbbing so urgently in his pants he had to slip into the guys' bathroom and jerk himself off. That was three weeks ago.

'Not here,' she said, looking up and down the corridor, trying to back away. 'Someone might see …'

'So what?' Jeff demanded sullenly. Nina was hard work for a chick that never had a guy look at her before. Sometimes he wondered if she was worth it. He had a hundred skinny blonde cheerleaders who'd jump through hoops for the chance to lay him. 'Don't you care about me?'

'You know I do—' The bell rang for third period and she jumped aside, shaky with relief, as kids came streaming out of their classrooms. 'I have to go, I got physics. I'll see you later …'

Melissa Patton came sidling up to Jeff's locker, her arms laden with cute pink files covered in butterflies. Melissa was blonde, thin, bouncy, scraped by in most of her classes. She always talked about being an actress or a model. Real popular with the girls.

'Hey, Jeffie … some of us were going to see *Rage*, that movie? D'you wanna come along?' Melissa smiled invitingly, tossing one shiny blonde ringlet out of her eyes.

Glazer shook his head, liking the way her eyes moved appreciatively across his chest muscles. Missy and her crowd never missed a football practice.

'I'm going to hang in the park.'

'With Nina Roth?' Melissa's manicured nails curled around her gold eternity ring. He could smell Chanel No. 5 mingling with the newly washed scent of her hair; his mom would love Melissa. Jeff shrugged.

2

'I don't know why you bother. She's only into math,' Melissa snapped, and flounced away, blonde curls flying.

Right! But Nina made Melissa look like a stick of spaghetti …

Jeff Glazer slammed the door of his locker.

Inside the quiet, gleaming classroom Nina Roth took deep breaths, taking in the smell of chalk and polish and disinfectant, trying to concentrate on what Sister Bernadette was saying. Normally this was one of her favourite classes; Sister Bernadette had been a research fellow at MIT before taking the veil, and it was cool to learn from somebody like that. But not today.

The class sat hunkered down at their desks, bored and restless, drawing in their margins with one eye on the clock. Rows of smart burgundy blazers and crisp cotton shirts, tailored linen pants or neat, swinging kilts were turned towards the teacher, eyes staring glassily at the blackboard where Sister was outlining equations in chalk. They did things the old-fashioned way here: the College of St Michael the Archangel was big, impersonal and expensive, one of the most prestigious schools in Park Slope. Brooklyn's richest parents had been sending their kids here for decades, paying through the nose for the nuns, the uniform, the Catholic education. Most of the trust-fund babies ignoring Sister Bernadette were atheist or Episcopalian, but so what? St Michael's was all about *cachet*, not the Church.

The kids shifted in their seats. One or two glanced over at Nina, the nerd, the scholarship girl. Her uniform was stretched and shapeless, but everyone knew she had to buy stuff secondhand. Anyway, she never cared how she looked; she was always lost in her stupid books …

'So, the sum of the angles is …?'

Silence.

'Nina?'

3

Nina jumped in her seat, dragging her mind away from the feel of Jeff's hands on her breasts. She flushed a dark red.

'Excuse me, Sister?'

The teacher pursed her thin lips. 'Nina, what did I just ask?'

'I – I don't know, Sister.'

'I'm not surprised. You're miles away. How do you expect to get anywhere in life, Miss Roth, if you don't pay attention in school?'

Mean giggles from the class. Nina felt the familiar haze of humiliation creep over her again. They all knew she was the only one here who'd have to work her way up: their folks were lawyers, doctors and bankers; hers were a retired cop, a slob who lived for beer and *Jeopardy*, and a wasted alcoholic who ran their rundown deli between blackouts.

'Miss Whitney?'

'Ninety degrees, Sister,' Josie Whitney said smugly, shooting a look of triumph at Nina.

But Nina didn't care, not today. Because *she* was dating Jeff Glazer, the hottest guy in the school. Maybe things would be different now, Nina thought as she scribbled furiously. Maybe her luck was finally about to change.

Nina Roth was an only child, which was just as well, since her parents couldn't have afforded a second. According to her father, wheezing and complaining whenever he signed a cheque, they barely managed the first. Mark and Ellen Roth shared a dingy walk-up on South Slope and an air of bitter disappointment. They also shared a daughter, but for as long as she could remember, Nina had only got attention during their endless fights. A pawn to be squabbled over. Pop was in his fifties, fat, squalid, a major armchair jock. He mouthed off about the government and the Yankees and the weather in front of the TV, never shifting his blubbery body to do a thing about it. Pop said he was retired from the force, but Nina heard on the street he'd been canned for theft, siphoning off confiscated money and goods for himself. She never asked him about it. She knew it was true.

Then there was Mom. Nina thought she remembered a time when her mom loved her, took her walking in Prospect Park, bought her Italian ice cream on Court Street, or best of all, took her out to magical Coney Island in the summer, to ride the funfair and eat cotton candy.

But that was when she was very little. Before Dad had come home. Before Ellen started to drink.

Then things got bad very quickly.

These days Mom only hugged her in a drunken stupor, with her breath rank and tears of self-pity streaking her thin cheeks. Nina hated it, hated her, preferred to be left alone. Ellen didn't really love her daughter, Nina knew that. She took comfort solely in a bottle. Her mom was a sour woman, cocooning herself in an alcoholic fog from the misery of her life, often blacking out for entire days. She kept just enough control to staff the family store, a scuzzy 7–11 with peeling Coke ads on the door and a loaded pistol under the counter. Ellen sold cigarettes, booze and candy bars and counted the money. Matthew took deliveries, stacked shelves once a week. The important stuff, like accounts and reordering, Nina took care of. She'd asked to do it when she turned thirteen. Somebody had to put bread on the table.

Nina was sixteen years old. She knew her rich classmates despised her. She hadn't been popular at Beth Israel Elementary, either, when she was ten years old and studying desperately for the St Michael's scholarship, but she didn't give a damn, because school was the way out.

Her whole life had one blind obsession: to get out of the South Slope, away from the drugs and the garbage, the graffiti, the gangs, the stray dogs.

Away from all the dirt and despair. Away from home.

Even so, it hurt, the way the other kids shunned her, never inviting her to hang out, snickering at her patched-up uniform and secondhand blazers. Nobody ever asked her to sit at their table at lunch. Nobody picked her for their team at games. She'd gotten the reputation for being a loner, and nobody ever bothered to disprove it – at least, not until three weeks back.

That miraculous day, Jeff Glazer had actually strolled up to her locker after French, and casually asked if she'd like to go out with him.

At first Nina just stood there blinking, convinced this had to be some particularly cruel joke. Glazer was seventeen, school quarterback, the only son of very wealthy parents, and a major hunk; muscular, tall, with Viking-fair hair and ice-blue eyes, Jeff had every babe in school flirting with him constantly. He'd dated and dropped half the best-looking ones already; ex-girlfriends swore he was a stud but a user, but that never stopped the next crop of giggling cuties trying out as replacements. Nina Roth would as likely fly to the moon as be asked out by Jeff Glazer.

But he was there. And he was asking.

'Like a date?' she stammered.

Jeff gave that indifferent shrug of his. 'Sure. You want to?'

OK, so it wasn't exactly *Romeo and Juliet*, but when he'd sat next to her at lunch, Nina wouldn't have traded the envious stares of Judy Carling and her crowd for all the roses in the world.

She pinned her compass to the paper in front of her and mechanically traced out a couple of angles. It couldn't last like this, she knew that. Jeff wanted to make love to her, and if she didn't let him, he was going to dump her. Even when she said she was too young, Jeff told her that everybody did it, she was way too uptight, and if she loved him she would *make* love to him.

Nina thought of the sniggering when Sister Bernadette said she'd have to get on in the world. They were all snobs and she hated them. But it didn't matter when she had Jeff – he'd picked *her*, not them. And some of the guys on the football team, even some of the girls, had started including her in stuff since she'd been dating him. Was she going to give it up? Just 'cause I'm chicken? Nina thought. He does love me, why would he touch me like that if he didn't love me? And I know I love him …

Nina breathed in deeply, trying to stop her heart thumping so hard against her chest. She could be as good a girlfriend as Melissa or Judy or Josie … as any of those rich babes. Jeff was gonna expect an answer in Prospect Park tonight. And the answer was going to be yes …

Chapter 2

The turrets of Caerhaven Castle towered black as coal against the twilight sky, darkened from the rain and wind. The bitter storm had raged all day, churning the sea to fury against the cliffs below and uprooting two pear trees in the castle orchards. But tonight nobody noticed the weather. Light streamed from every window in the medieval walls, from the sturdy marquee set up on the croquet lawn and from the stream of Bentleys and Rolls-Royces crunching past the stone dragons on the front gates and up two miles of gravel drive.

The Countess of Caerhaven was giving a ball.

'Goddamn it, Monica. Where is that wretched child?'

Tony Savage, Thirtieth Earl of Caerhaven, tugged at the waistcoat of his immaculate white-tie suit. He hated being defied. Not only was he holder of one of the oldest titles in Wales, lord of Caerhaven Castle and seven hundred acres of rich farmland, Tony was Chief Executive of Dragon plc., the family company. Founded on blood money from the slave trade, Dragon was a pharmaceutical giant, with divisions worldwide. It was publicly held; Tony Savage had eleven per cent.

At his side Monica shrugged, offering her hand to a new batch of arrivals. 'Joanna, delighted you could come. Richard, how good to see you ...' Tall and elegant, the second Lady Caerhaven swished around in a sea-green Balençiaga, pearls looped round her neck, sapphire clips pinching delicate earlobes. She smiled dazzlingly at every unfamiliar face: Cabinet ministers, industrialists and investment bankers, along with the society set. She was charming to them all. So important for Tony's business.

The earl nodded softly to himself. Monica looked wonderful, behaved perfectly. Never gave him a second's concern. She knew her place was at his side. None of that feminist claptrap had ever sullied her brain; she just liked spending his money, hosting his parties and dazzling the *Tatler* set every season. Women envied Monica and men wanted her. She was the perfect wife.

Monica Savage had done her duty in every way. There was Charles, Lord Holwyn, and Lord Richard; the heir and the spare. And if she no longer welcomed him into her bed, that was fine too: Tony Savage had women whenever he wanted them. Monica pretended not to notice and got her little baubles from Tiffany or Garrard's as a reward.

Tony grinned. If he'd chosen the Hon. Monica Fletcher first, he'd have had no problems whatsoever. As it was, there was only Elizabeth.

Tony glanced at his sons. Charles, Lord Holwyn, thirteen. Dark and intense, he was destined to look like his father. Charles was handsome and callous, calculating like his mother and ruthless like Tony. Just into his teens and already cocky and self-possessed. It was easy to be confident: Charles was heir to a title, a castle, London property and a vast fortune. Eleven-year-old Richard would get a slice of that too, though nothing like as much. Another boy might resent it, but Richard was lazy and easygoing. Charles had dominated Richard since they were tiny boys, and Richard never complained. Richard was popular with the girls because he was so pretty; he made average grades in school; he'd be a gentleman of leisure and do very well. The kid was only eleven but Tony could tell. Richard was the image of his mother.

If only they had not had Elizabeth.

The earl checked his watch and felt rage stealing over him. Elizabeth was late for her own ball.

Elizabeth. Daughter of Louise, Countess of Caerhaven, his first wife and the only woman ever to make him look a fool. To this day Tony hated the bitch. Louise worked when he asked her not to, refused to play hostess, and cuckolded him with Jay DeFries. His former best friend. Careless whether they were seen in public, Louise made Tony Savage a laughing stock and then divorced him before he'd had a chance to divorce her. He'd hated everything about her, even his infant daughter. Louise perversely delighted in the fact her baby was a girl. And little Elizabeth was just like her mother: the same downy, dark blonde hair, green eyes and long, lean body, not a sign of her father on her. Tony was sure she wasn't even his, but admitting his wife might have borne another man's child would have been too shameful.

When Louise died, aged twenty-seven, of breast cancer, the infant Lady Elizabeth moved back to her papa. She grew up a green-eyed, rebellious minx, her mother blossoming back up in her like a flower, an almost uncanny replica, laughing at Tony even in death.

Tony ruined Jay DeFries. Dragon was powerful: it wasn't difficult. He took over DeFries's business, muddied the books, got the Fraud Squad in. His former best friend had gone down for eight years, bankrupt. Hanged himself in jail.

As Dragon grew bigger, the whispers grew smaller. Soon nobody dared mention Louise or Jay; Tony Savage, Wall Street's Robber Baron, heard nothing but flattery. But young Elizabeth, running wild, flirting with the local boys, dressing indecently, blossoming into exquisite, dangerous beauty, was in his face every bloody day. She didn't mix with her brothers or stepmother. She was her mother's kid. The cuckoo in his golden nest.

'I have no idea,' said Monica, beckoning Charles over.

'Darling, do go and find your sister. Tell her to come down here *at once*. It's *her* sixteenth, and David Fairfax has been waiting for her all evening.'

Tony Savage looked across the grey stone of the Great Hall, lit by torches flickering in iron sconces and the roaring fire burning in the grate, past the rich swirl of silk, lace and velvet, to where the plump figure of a young man stood, surrounded by toadies and cradling a glass of vintage champagne. His Grace the Duke of Fairfax, one of the most eligible men in England. Suitor for the hand of his only daughter.

'Can't think what he sees in her,' Tony said.

In her bedroom in the West Wing, Lady Elizabeth Savage leaned against the chill stone of the turret window and stared out into the night. Her eyes were used to bleak darkness and she could make out most of the landscape: the stable roofs, the black stretch of forest outside the castle walls, the low hills in the distance. She ignored the sounds of the glittering party below her and listened for the endless sigh of the sea. The cold air tasted of salt.

Granny was dead. Only two days ago she had been sitting with her in the East Wing, chattering about business, politics, and the roaring twenties. Granny never minded her talking on, her curiosity and ambitions. Two days without her already seemed like an eternity.

Despite what she said – 'Don't be ridiculous, child, everybody loves you' – Elizabeth knew Dad and Monica didn't care for her. She thought it was because she wasn't a boy.

Elizabeth grew up eager and vivacious. Scandalously careless of her station, she made friends with the servants' kids, climbed apple trees in her vest and knickers, and got suspended four times from Cheltenham – twice for smoking, twice for swearing at her teachers. A cold letter to the countess had threatened expulsion. She wasn't bookish, but Elizabeth was fascinated by business, the only thing about her dad she admired. There was an almighty row the day Tony discovered she'd been sending away for Dragon company reports.

'What is this nonsense, young lady?' he spluttered.

Elizabeth hurried to explain. 'I'm just taking an interest, Daddy. I thought I could study how Dragon does its marketing – you know I'm interested in how people sell things—'

'How people *sell* things? What are you, a *salesman*?'

'I want to work at Dragon,' Elizabeth said stubbornly.

'You have no idea what you want to do.'

'I do. I'm fifteen years old. I want to work in advertising, in Dragon …'

'Over my dead body.' Tony actually laughed. 'The *company* is going to your brother! Behave like a lady for once in your life.'

White faced, Elizabeth had turned and raced away up the stone staircase, looking for her grandmother. Flushed with anger, her father drew a deep breath and walked slowly back to his offices. With every year that passed, he was more certain Elizabeth would disgrace the family just like Louise.

But no. He would never let it happen again.

Elspeth, the dowager countess, had occupied the East Wing for twenty years since her husband died. She loved Elizabeth, although she too was convinced the girl was Jay DeFries's bastard. Elspeth's heart sank each year Elizabeth grew older, looking like a younger, prettier version of Louise. She knew Tony would never give the child a chance.

When Elizabeth sobbed out what her father had said about Dragon, the old lady coughed drily and gave her a hug.

'Never mind, Lizzie. He'll come round.'

'He won't.' Elizabeth buried her face in the stiff cotton petticoats. 'He doesn't want me to do *anything*! He said it wasn't ladylike ... and he said if I'm expelled he'll have Dolphin put down!' Dolphin was her Labrador puppy. He slept on her bed and she loved him fiercely.

'Did he?' Granny said, frowning. 'I was expelled once, dear.'

'You? When? Why?'

Elizabeth's face was blotched red and puffy from crying. Her son was going to crush this one, unless somebody stopped him. Liz was a merry little thing. She wouldn't let Tony snuff the child out.

'The year before I married your grandfather. From finishing school in Switzerland.' A wicked chuckle. 'For painting my nails red.'

'Just for that?'

'Very wanton in those days.' Elspeth smiled, slipping her wrinkled hand over Elizabeth's smooth one. 'So, you want to work? If that's what you want, dear, you shall.'

Elizabeth shook her head. 'Daddy said the company belongs to Charlie. He won't let me anywhere near it.'

'But it isn't up to him. *I* own fifteen per cent of the stock ... it was a wedding gift. It would get you a seat on the board. If you like, I'll call a lawyer and change my will. You can have it on your eighteenth birthday.' Granny's wrinkled face creased into a smile. 'I don't need to play at tycoon any more.'

Elizabeth stared at her grandmother. 'Truly? But what will Daddy say?'

'He can like it or lump it,' the old lady said crisply. 'Oh, don't worry, child. I'll speak to your father tomorrow. He can bluster away, but that never frightened me.'

She knew Daddy had called on his mother the same day.

When he went up to her again the following morning,

however, the earl found Granny stiff in her chair. Dead, from what the family doctor called a 'routine coronary'.

Elizabeth resented every smiling idiot at the ball downstairs. All she wanted was to be alone, to have a little time to mourn. The wonderful news about Dragon was dust and ashes without Granny. How can I bear being stuck with the rest of them? Elizabeth thought, blinking back tears.

There was a heavy creak as the ancient oak door to her bedroom swung open.

'I should have known you'd be hiding up here,' Charles said. His low voice was full of disapproval. 'Everybody's waiting for you. It *is* supposed to be your party, Lizzie.'

'Nobody asked me if I wanted a party!'

'You're spoiling things again, as usual. Mamma can't believe how selfish you're being. Don't you know David Fairfax wants to see you?'

'I couldn't care less about David.'

'What's that dress you're wearing? That's not the gown Mamma bought you!'

He was annoyed. Elizabeth glanced back at the plain green Laura Ashley dress with the huge bow on the bottom, lying rejected over a Regency chair. She'd known there was no way out of this horrible ball, so she'd snuck upstairs to Granny's rooms last night. Undisturbed by the cleaners, she'd unpacked the gown she wanted from Elspeth's chest of drawers; under folds of crisp white tissue, hidden away for nearly sixty years, was this vision of a dress. It was a cloud of the palest gold silk trimmed with cream lace, a whalebone corset tapering down to a billowing skirt over stiff petticoats of ivory lace, a discreet pattern in gold thread and seed pearls dusted over the bodice. It fit Elizabeth's long, lean body snugly, pushing her small breasts together and lifting them up, the skirts sweeping gracefully with every movement of her legs. She'd pulled her tawny hair up into a formal

French pleat, added topaz drop earrings and slipped her feet into apricot satin heels.

Dad could try and ignore her *now*.

'It was one of Granny's,' Elizabeth told him. 'Just go away, Charles, please.'

'All right, I'm going, but you'd better get down there. Otherwise, Father's going to come up here and drag you down, in front of everybody ...'

He would, too. Elizabeth knew that. She had to face her parents and all their vacuous friends ...

Taking a deep breath, Lady Elizabeth Savage composed herself, opened her bedroom door, and walked slowly down the winding stairs to her sixteenth birthday party.

Chapter 3

'I told you before. I can't come back early tonight, I have economics,' Nina said.

'Yeah? And what are we supposed to do? The stock needs checkin'.'

Nina shrugged. They were arguing in the tiny, cramped kitchen, standing shoulder to shoulder while Nina washed the dishes. Ellen gave them a perfunctory wipe with the towel and stashed them in the rack. She was only interested in haranguing her daughter.

'You're never around,' Ellen whined. 'You're always studyin' or out with your friends. Don't even have time for your mom.'

'Mom, I have to go to school, and I took that job at Duane Reed,' Nina told her shortly. She was too tired for this. SATs were two months away, she worked weekends and two nights a week at the local drugstore, and three evenings she had to be as fresh as she could for Jeff. The deli was just too much extra grind. They'd have to work it out by themselves.

Mr David had been right. Nina's math teacher had called her in last semester and laid out the facts.

'Nina, I have to tell you, I'm concerned about your grades trailing off.' He'd looked at the solemn little face bunched with worry under its mop of raven hair. 'Your concentration seems to be wandering, you're constantly tired, and Sister Agnes tells me you fell asleep during chemistry practical last week.'

'I'm sorry, sir. I'll try harder.'

'I don't think that's the problem.' He paused. 'Are things difficult at home?'

Nina stiffened. 'No, sir.'

Peter David gently motioned his star pupil to a chair, wondering how to handle this. He took a personal interest in the welfare of Nina Roth. She had an instinctive grasp of economics, the like of which he had not encountered since leaving Harvard. What most of the other teachers took for shyness and quietness, he knew was something very different – a blind concentration, a steely determination to master her subject. Nina might be a gangly, awkward teenager, but there was a core of iron in her soul that almost scared him. Nina Roth was destined for great things.

And now she was letting it crumble to dust. Her grades had plunged. Her essays lost their sparkle. The Ivy League scholarships he'd assumed were sure things were slipping away.

Mr David felt close to this girl. He'd asked around when Nina first came to St Michael's, knew all about the lazy father and the lush mother, heard on the grapevine that the kid practically ran the family store herself – no wonder she was so clear about basic business economics. You didn't have to be a shrink to see that Nina was compensating hard for her parents' failure, and he approved of that. But now something had changed; she was getting exhausted at school.

He knew Nina was too proud to discuss it, but everything would go up in smoke if he didn't do something.

'You work for your parents, don't you?' Mr David asked gently. 'Have you taken on any extra duties besides that? School clubs, for instance? Drama, volleyball, something like that?'

Nina smiled slightly. Drama or volleyball, indeed. He

must think she was like Missy or Josie or the rest of them.

Since she'd been dating Jeff, she needed more money. He liked her to look pretty, to have good Levi's, cool boots, whatever the other kids took for granted. And though he always picked up the cinema tickets or the beer or whatever, she wanted to spring for it sometimes, and there was no way her parents would come up with an allowance.

Before Jeff Glazer she hadn't had a social life, but that had changed, and she needed money.

St Michael's, Jeff and her parents all taught Nina the same lesson: money *was* everything. It was new uniforms and fancy cars. It was American Express cards and respect. It was a house on the North Slope and your own business, versus a walk-up on the South Slope and a rundown deli. Jeff's folks versus her parents. Hope versus despair.

People who said 'Money isn't everything' had one thing in common.

None of them was poor.

Nina Roth had known since she was a baby that the worst thing in life would be to turn out like Mom or Dad, sitting around, waiting for rescue, waiting for something to happen. She was filled with contempt when she thought about it. There was no White Knight. You made things happen yourself. When Duane Reed advertised for a junior clerk, Nina marched off to the interview, lied about her age, and was hired on the spot. First week, she'd taken her paycheque and opened an account at Wells Fargo. Each month, she checked her balance, watching the tiny green glowing numbers with intense satisfaction. She spent only what she had to, and those numbers were creeping up. They were small, but they were growing.

Money was independence, power, freedom.

Nina's eyes narrowed as she looked at her teacher. No way was she giving up her job.

'I work at a drugstore part-time,' Nina said. She sat up in the chair, determined. 'I need the money, Mr David.'

'Well, we all need money,' the older man replied, surprising her, 'but you'll be giving up a lot more money if you go on this way.'

'I don't understand,' Nina said, but she was listening. She respected Mr David; he took an interest in her when other staff hadn't bothered, just dished out good grades and no feedback. Early on, Peter David graded one of her projects a 'C' when any other student would have gotten an 'A'. When Nina complained, he told her she was smarter than the rest of the class, and therefore he wanted better results. She'd get graded by her own standards, and she'd only get an 'A' for outstanding work. If she didn't like it, she could drop his class.

Nina never got a 'C' since.

'You have your SATs coming up, assessments, reports. You'll need all that for college. Now, we both know that you're good for an academic scholarship to NYU, Mount Holyoke, Brandeis, maybe Vassar, but you can do better than that, Nina.'

'Better than Vassar?' Her eyes widened.

'Sure. Sure.' Peter David nodded impatiently. 'I'm talking Harvard or Yale. Maybe MIT if you planned to specialise.'

She shook her head, glossy raven hair gleaming in the light from the office window. 'I'd need a full scholarship for that, and they only give out a handful each year.'

'That's right. You could easily take one of them, Nina, but not the way you're performing now.' Her teacher brushed aside her protests with an impatient wave. 'No, stop giving me excuses. You are a student gifted with outstanding mathematical ability. Your economics are fluid and perceptive. You're strong in physics, chemistry and business studies, but you're letting yourself down.'

He leaned forward.

'It amazes me that someone like you would sacrifice longterm profit for pocket money. Look, Nina, the graduate market is a *market*. Maybe it doesn't matter to some of your fellow pupils, but when you come out of college, do you want a résumé from somewhere OK, or do you want to be the best?'

Nina sat there, taken aback.

'Something's got to give,' Peter David said.

She pushed back her chair, stood up straight, and offered him her hand. She's so dignified, David thought, his dry academic's heart touched by this tall, awkward teenager, standing there so seriously.

He shook it warmly.

'I hear you, sir,' Nina told him. 'I'll work something out.'

From now on, she thought grimly, Mom and Dad are on their own.

Starting that day, Nina cut back on her hours in the deli. She told Dad he'd have to check the books himself; she told Mom she'd need to spend more time behind the counters. But they didn't like it, and every day they let her know.

'You're workin' for them when we need you here,' her dad grunted. Nina looked behind her to see him slumped in his easy chair, eyes fixed on *Wheel of Fortune*.

'You don't need me, Daddy, you could do the books,' Nina said. 'You're just as smart as me.'

'*I* know that, miss. Don't you sass me,' her father said. He fancied himself a great brain, always quoting from Shakespeare and Whitman. Nina despised him all the more because he was intelligent: an intellectual, real proud of his education and never doing anything with it. 'I'm busy enough with deliveries ...'

'They only deliver once a week,' Nina tried.

'*And* I gotta stack the shelves. That's real work.'

Nina waited for Mom to wade in shrieking, but there was only silence. They were united for once. Against her.

'You spend way too much time with that fancy jock you're seein',' her mother snapped.

'He's not a jock, he's just athletic,' Nina said, her buttermilk complexion lighting up. She couldn't help it. Just the mention of Jeff was like the sun bursting through the thick clouds all round her. She'd be going round to the park to meet up with him tonight …

Her stomach felt squirmy with excitement, hungry for his touch. Sometimes she was ashamed to find how hot he could get her. Lying in her cramped bedroom at night, Nina would stare at the damp cracks in the ceiling and think about Jeff, about his smooth strong chest and the flat of his stomach with its smattering of wiry hair, trailing down to his cock, and she'd feel weird, hot and edgy, and her hand would slip between her legs, rubbing herself frantically for some release. Somehow it was better when she was imagining it than when it happened. In her dreams, Jeff's tongue was gentle over her aching nipples, his hands would stroke her butt and her back and tease her the way she teased herself … Nina's hands would start to move of their own accord under the languorous heat of her body, her mouth slightly open, panting softly as she thought about Jeff inside her, kissing her and saying soft things but somehow fucking her harder and harder all the time, until she'd lose control and her stomach would contract and expand in an exquisite, savage flash of white fire …

Actual lovemaking with Jeff wasn't quite that way and sometimes Nina thought about it guiltily when she began to pleasure herself. But it was thinking about Jeff that got her that way, after all, and she loved him so much, it just couldn't be wrong.

'He's not interested in you, girl. He's playin' with you,' her dad grumbled.

'Jeff's in love with me,' Nina said fiercely.

'Oh yeah?' Her father's pudgy face creased in scorn. 'He take you back to meet his folks yet? White trash, that's what we are. You reckon he thinks any different? Don't kid yourself.'

'You're wrong!' Nina shouted. She grabbed her coat from the back of the door.

'Where d'you think you're going, Nina Roth? You got work to do *here*!' her mother yelled.

'Sharper than a serpent's tooth it is, to have a thankless child,' Matthew pronounced.

'I'm going to meet Jeff,' Nina told them. She nodded back at the ragged pile of papers stacked on the couch. 'You should deal with those, Mom. I don't have time.'

The door slammed on its hinges behind her.

Ellen Roth stared at it. 'Little bitch thinks she's too good for us,' she said bitterly.

'You got that right,' grunted her husband.

A fresh fall wind whipped around Prospect Park, sending golden leaves dancing across the paths as Nina hurried towards the Long Meadow. She drew deep breaths, elated to be out of the claustrophobic apartment. Tantalised by the thought of seeing Jeff. A pair of joggers huffed past her and Nina flashed them a beaming smile. No matter what, when she was with Jeff, life was good.

'Hey!'

She spun round, the wind lifting her coal-black hair, and saw her boyfriend lounging under an elm tree. She felt her heart jump. God, he was so gorgeous, all those muscles huge and hard under his navy sweatsuit, picking out his cornflower-blue eyes. He was wearing the latest black Nike runners and a steel Rolex. Nina pulled her threadbare duffel tight against the chill and told herself clothes didn't matter.

'Hey,' Jeff repeated, when she caught up to him. He smiled, his eyes trawling lazily over her wrapped-up body. 'Where you been?'

'Sorry I'm late. I had some trouble back home,' Nina apologised. She knew he hated to be kept waiting. 'I got out as soon as I could.'

'No problem,' Jeff said graciously. He turned and started walking west out of the park, heading for the cheap hotel on Eighth Street they always used. Nina used to think that was so cool of him, the way he'd casually spring for a whole night although they only took a couple of hours – 'So we don't need to sneak around at my place,' he'd explain, kissing the nape of her neck. Often he'd order up room service, too, and that made her feel spoiled and exotic; waited on hand and foot, even if it was only cheeseburgers and beer. The sex was usually just OK; she always felt hot and weird when he started, but after Jeff collapsed across her with that strangled groan, bathed in sweat and looking drained, she felt … unsure. Left out. Maybe the flashes of excitement and tenseness she felt sometimes were an orgasm. Maybe that was what they felt like when you weren't doing it to yourself … She wasn't sure, and something told her there was no way she could ask Jeff. It was being alone with him, being kissed, stroked, told how beautiful she was – *that* was what Nina loved. In bed with Jeff she was accepted. Desired. That made up for everything else.

But today Nina could still hear her mother's carping voice. Suddenly the hotel didn't seem so magical … it seemed a little cheap, a little seedy.

'Hey, Jeff?' She caught up with him, putting a hand on his arm. 'Could we maybe do something else tonight?'

He stopped short, frowning.

'You don't like the Payne? Where d'you want to go?'

'I was thinking maybe we wouldn't go *anywhere*.' Nina paused nervously at the shadow that crossed over his face. 'I'd like to go to your house and meet your mom and dad.'

'Oh yeah? What for?' Jeff demanded, irritated. Nina Roth looked pretty sharp, despite the cheap clothes and lack of grooming: her creamy skin, perfect without make-up, was flushed and glowing from the fresh air; her heavy-lidded eyes glittered like polished slate and her ebony hair cut down across her cheekbones in a gleaming cap. But he could imagine the reaction if he took her home! His mother would go ballistic! She was always nagging at him to find a 'nice girl', but to the Glazers, that meant someone like Melissa or Josie ... someone like themselves. Not a Jewish checkout girl from South Slope, a scholarship kid with a lush for a mother.

'It's a dumb idea. We can't just drop in on them like that.'

'Why not?' Nina asked stubbornly. 'Are you ashamed of me? That's what my mom said.'

'She's nuts,' Glazer said warily. He didn't like that mutinous look she was giving him, though. Nina's body had nearly given him a heart attack once he finally coaxed her into bed, and there was no way he was letting her go now. 'Look, we can't go tonight, because, uh, we're having some people over for dinner. Let me talk to Mom and you can maybe come for tea, or something. OK?'

'Sure.' Nina smiled up at him, bursting with happiness.

He does love me, she thought triumphantly. He does, he does, he does!

Chapter 4

Murmurs rose from the crowd as Elizabeth descended the stairs, floating on a glorious cloud of pale gold silk. The apricot satin shoes, topaz earrings and coral necklace were perfect with her glowing skin and tawny mane.

Monica's first frown of disapproval at Elizabeth's rejecting the Laura Ashley melted into a warm smile. Her one aim in life was to get rid of Elizabeth as quickly as possible. Her husband's discreet nudge pointed out the young Duke of Fairfax, at the door to the Great Hall, gasping like a dying trout. The countess heard wedding bells.

'Happy birthday, darling. I must say you look splendid,' Tony boomed, moving to grip her elbow firmly as Elizabeth started shaking hands. He felt taken aback. His tomboy daughter looked enchantingly feminine. David Fairfax was interested, and if Love was that blind – well, Elizabeth might bring something besides trouble to the family. He thrust her forward briskly through the glittering crowd.

'Evening, David. Glad you could make it,' the earl said genially.

Elizabeth blushed scarlet. How could he be so obvious! She wanted to pick up her cascading skirts and scamper away. Anything rather than listen to Father suck up to David Fairfax while he showed her off like a prize heifer.

'Good of you to ask me, Lord Caerhaven,' Fairfax replied. His gaze swept approvingly across Elizabeth's figure-hugging bodice and lingered on the freckled swell of her breasts. 'Hullo, 'Lizbeth. Happy birthday. Smashing dress,' he added with more spirit.

Elizabeth looked at him wearily. David had had a crush on her for years. He was ordinary looking, with sandy hair and a strong jaw, graduated from poly with a spurious degree in estate management. In real life, if you were David Fairfax, that consisted of hiring a manager to run your estates. They'd met often at parties and later hunt balls and Tory fundraisers Dad wouldn't let her duck. He was OK, but pretty boring, and he was twenty-four, while she was sixteen today. She secretly thought he was a bit of a perv, chasing after a girl eight years younger.

Dad had made himself crystal clear. To him, no duke could ever be boring, but David was a young fogey: he actually wore tweeds and he listened to Cole Porter instead of Bowie or T-Rex.

Granny's spirit bubbled up mischievously inside her.

'Hiya, Dave. How's it hanging?' Elizabeth asked, grinning.

Her father stiffened, but when Fairfax laughed he just glared at her and moved off.

Elizabeth chatted briefly to David and then tried to get away. Her heart sank as she saw Monica swooping down on her.

'What do you think you're doing? Can't you see the way David's looking at you?' Monica hissed.

Elizabeth sighed and glanced back to the fireplace. Mother was right, His Grace was gazing after her with a particularly annoying sort of moony-calf expression. Like a spaniel after you refused to give it a bit of your cheese: all helpless misery and silent pleading.

'I want to dance with Richard Villiers,' she snapped.

Richard was the bluff son of Dragon's finance director, a massive Blackburn Rovers fan. She'd rather talk about

26

football than David Fairfax's gardeners any day of the week.

'For God's sake, Elizabeth!' Monica spat.

Elizabeth pouted. There was no way out of it, if she wanted to avoid a scene. She walked back across the room and watched the moony eyes light up with the enthusiasm of a border terrier spotting a rabbit.

'Smashing dress, smashing,' David repeated. 'D'you like a dance?'

She surrendered sullenly to the inevitable, much to the fury of the gaggle of hopeful debs who'd been hovering in the duke's vicinity all night.

'Sure, Dave, that'd be cool.'

David hauled her bodily round the draughty hall, stepping anxiously all over her apricot slippers. Elizabeth was selfishly furious. Why couldn't the great hulking lout take dancing lessons? He spent his life attending these wretched things!

'I say, Bessie – can I call you Bessie?'

'No,' replied Elizabeth coldly.

'You're wasted at school. Really, you know. You're very pretty. Ever thought about gettin' hitched?'

Elizabeth withdrew as far as the waltz allowed her, but was caught by David's plump arm squeezing her waist.

'Definitely not. I'm only sixteen, I haven't even been to college yet.'

The duke looked nervous but tried again. 'What does a pretty girlie like you want to bother with college for? Bet your ma and pa wouldn't mind.'

'I wouldn't dream of it,' said Elizabeth sharply. 'Anyway, I've got a boyfriend. Joe Sharp in the village.'

'Sharp? Never heard of him.'

'You wouldn't.' Elizabeth grinned again, picturing Joe, stained overalls, swearing, muscular, the forbidden taste of cigarettes in his mouth when she kissed him. 'He's an attendant at the garage, he goes to St Joseph's school.'

'Ha ha,' Fairfax chuckled, annoyingly, 'don't be ridiculous.'

Suddenly he caught her to him as they whirled in time with the Strauss, thrusting his face into her neck and kissing it. Revolted, Elizabeth braced herself and shoved him away.

'What the hell do you think you're doing? Get off me!'

She was a strong girl. Fairfax tripped and fell sprawling, and there was an agonising crack as his head hit the flagstone floor.

Around them couples stopped dancing to stare. The string quartet faltered in its playing for a second because of the commotion at the centre of the ballroom. It struck up again as the countess made frantic motions to continue, but David Fairfax lay crashed out on the polished marble, groaning in agony. Blood was seeping out of one cheek.

There was a stunned silence amongst the assembled guests.

Leaning back against the tree trunk, Elizabeth winced at the memory. Her father's face had set like granite and the ball had started breaking up as of that moment. Suddenly all the tycoons remembered important breakfast meetings and the socialites developed headaches, as the guests made polite excuses to their hosts and scurried away. David, helped to his feet by the onlookers, gave Elizabeth an embarrassed nod and hobbled towards the door. It had taken barely half an hour for the piles of fur coats and cashmere shawls to disappear from the cloakroom, and once the last guest had hastened outside the earl sent his daughter to her room, the quiet menace in his voice worse than any shouting fit.

Neither last night nor this morning had Tony wanted to hear her explanation. As far as her parents were concerned she was simply a disgrace.

Elizabeth sat under the mossy trunk of an apple tree, biting into the crisp, smoky flesh of a windfall. She loved it out in the orchard: the dry-stone walls covered with bindweed and ivy, the warm scent of mown grass, the tiny white moths that fluttered around her like scraps of lace. They kept pear, apple and plum trees, and if you didn't mind the wasps that gathered greedily around all the ripe fruit, the orchards were a glorious place to get lost in. Elizabeth discovered them as a child, to her parents' dismay. She liked nothing better than shinning up the ancient, gnarly trunks, finding a nook to sit in, and hiding there all afternoon, while the stable-hands combed the grounds calling for her.

Maybe that was the start of my rebel streak, she thought ruefully. It had been so exciting, clambering up a tangle of branches and leaves like a squirrel. If she got high enough, she could see over the orchard walls, to the red-roofed stables and the manicured green of the croquet lawn, and even past the bounds of the estate, to the clifftops and the silver glitter of the sea. She would trek back up to the castle around teatime, with grazed knees and torn stockings, leaving mud and leaves all over the kitchen flagstones, and be marched off to bed without supper.

Elizabeth smiled. Sixteen years old, and she was still in trouble.

Even the servants had been giving her stern looks at breakfast. Mother had been reduced to taking a tray of coffee and dry toast in her bedroom, while Daddy and that little prig Richard had glowered their way through the kippers and marmalade without so much as a 'Good morning'.

My God, if he wasn't already leaving everything to the boys, he'd disinherit me, Elizabeth thought, then hugged herself. Granny had put a stop to that. She needn't be afraid of Dad any more.

Even so, she had saddled up one of the bay mares as soon as breakfast was over and taken her out for a gallop across the cliff tops. It was good to be out of his way; the turrets and battlements rearing behind her seemed gloomy and menacing in the chill morning light. She'd never known Tony so furious. It was dawning on her that he had been *serious* about her marrying David. He was outraged that she'd blown her chances of becoming a duchess ...

'Lizzie!' called a reedy voice.

'Right here, Richard,' Elizabeth said, throwing her apple core into some bracken. Her brother came clumping through the trees, looking annoyed.

'Where on earth have you been? You'd better get yourself inside, sharpish. Father wants to see you in the library, right away.'

She got up, ignoring the gloating tone to Richard's voice. What an unpleasant little brat he was, he loved to see her in trouble.

She tried to ignore the nagging voice inside her that told her she'd behaved like a spoilt brat herself last night. Poor clumsy David, he hadn't meant any harm.

But no! Elizabeth thought sulkily. Why should *I* have to put up with him on *my* birthday!

When they reached the dark-panelled hall Richard turned pointedly away towards her stepmother's morning room, leaving Elizabeth standing in front of the library door by herself. She looked at the brass studs in the old oak door and drew herself up bravely. Father's bullying needs standing up to, Elizabeth told herself. She smoothed down her long mane of hair and knocked sharply.

'Come in,' the earl snapped.

Elizabeth pushed the thick door hard and it swung open, creaking on its hinges. The library was a large room, tapestries and antique swords mounted between rows of dusty, leatherbound books. A mahogany grand piano stood to one side. Behind it, his back to her, her father was sitting in front of his writing desk, a sheaf of papers laid out neatly on the green baize.

'Elizabeth,' he said icily without turning round, 'your behaviour last night was unforgivable. You disgraced yourself in front of all our friends. You made a public exhibition of yourself. Your stepmother was so ashamed she has made herself ill.'

'David Fairfax kissed me. What was I supposed to do? He was slobbering down the front of my dress—'

'Elizabeth!' Her father spun round on his seat, glaring at her. 'Not another word, do you hear me? Stop lying!'

'But I'm not lying!' Elizabeth protested, feeling the tears well up despite herself.

The earl raised a warning hand, his expression dark. 'For the sake of sheer impudence and disobedience to us you chose to assault one of your own guests.'

'That's not true!'

'Why in the name of God a decent young man like that should have been interested in you, Elizabeth, is quite beyond me, but you could not even accept a small romantic gesture—'

'There's nothing romantic about being pawed by that baboon!' Elizabeth cried angrily. 'You and Monica just want to marry me to a duke! You're nothing but a pair of snobs!'

Father gazed at her impassively. Then he reached down to his desk and picked up a piece of paper.

'This is a letter of registration, enrolling you at the Ecole Henri Dufor.'

'The Ecole Henri Dufor?' Elizabeth repeated blankly.

'In Saas-Fée.'

'You're sending me to *Switzerland*?'

Her father nodded coldly. 'Since you cannot seem to

31

behave yourself here, I am sending you to your step-mother's finishing school to learn some manners.'

Elizabeth stared at him in disbelief. 'To learn flower-arranging and deportment? This is the seventies, Daddy. Nobody does that any more. What about my A-levels?'

'You can take the Baccalaureate, for all I care.' He laid the letter purposefully in front of him. 'You have gone too far, young lady. I tell you that I will not permit you to make a mockery of this family.'

She thrust her hands deep inside her jodhpurs. 'I won't go.'

'You'll go. Or I will cut you off without a penny.'

'I'll borrow money from the bank.'

'Indeed. Do you imagine that banks take charity cases? Against what would you borrow money? Your pony, perhaps?'

Her father's expression frightened her, but Elizabeth stubbornly shook her head. 'You know perfectly well. Granny told you about her will the day she died. She left me fifteen per cent of the company.'

There was a silence, broken only by the crackle of the pine logs blazing in the fireplace.

'Your grandmother left me her entire estate,' Tony Savage said.

'No.' Elizabeth paled. 'Granny wouldn't lie to me.'

Her father picked up a tiny brass key from the green baize, reached under the desk and unlocked a small side drawer. Elizabeth felt her heart thumping as he drew out a thin sheaf of vellum, yellowed somewhat with age.

'This is Mamma's will, Elizabeth. If you doubt my word, you are at liberty to read it yourself.'

'She was making a new one,' Elizabeth said.

'She did *not* make a new one. She did *not* leave you any stock.' The earl glanced down at the parchment. 'I seem to remember there is a small jewellery bequest to you in here, but you won't inherit that until your twenty-first birthday. A bank wouldn't think much of it.'

Elizabeth stood there trembling with shock. The bequest had been her protection; she had counted on it.

'Phone her solicitors, if you like,' her father told her coolly, indicating the telephone that stood next to her on a card-table. 'They will confirm it.'

Fighting to stay calm, Elizabeth shook her head. Father wouldn't make that offer if he was bluffing, but Granny had given her a solemn promise just a few days ago.

'She can't have got round to changing it, then,' Elizabeth managed, 'but you know she intended to, Daddy. That was what she told you when you went upstairs to see her. She wanted me to have her stake in Dragon. You have to respect her last wishes!'

'Mother told me no such thing.' The earl's tone was flat. 'I confess I am sorry that you choose such a subject for more lies.'

'I'm not lying,' Elizabeth gasped. 'You know how much I loved Granny!'

'Did you? It sounds to me as though you were trying to influence a frail old woman for your own benefit. You have been a thoroughly selfish girl for far too long.' Her father leaned forward, his sallow face set hard. 'For your information, Mamma and I were discussing your brother's trust fund. The world does not revolve around you, whatever you may believe. And I notice you never mentioned this so-called bequest until this moment.' He snorted with contempt. 'You fool only yourself, Elizabeth.'

Panic and doubt washed over her in a wave as she looked at her father's cold, certain face. Did he really think she would lie about Granny? Was it possible that Granny had planned on telling her father later? And never had the chance?

The earl was holding the vellum will firmly. Elizabeth

realised, with a terrible sense of desertion, that she had lost. She wasn't a major stockholder in Dragon. She had no chance of a marketing job, no right to a seat on the board. She was just a rebellious teenager whose parents were determined to crush her.

For one wild moment Elizabeth thought about running away, but where would she go? Cardiff? London? With what money, and to do what? She was only a schoolgirl, and she'd lived in luxury all her life. She knew she'd last about ten seconds on the streets.

'You *will* go to Switzerland, one way or the other,' the earl snapped, as though reading her mind. 'If you behave sensibly, we will continue your allowance at the Ecole. If, on the other hand, you decide to cause your stepmother or me any more distress, you will receive not one centime. Which is it to be?'

At least she would get away from him.

'I'll go to Switzerland,' said Elizabeth.

Chapter 5

'Would you like some ham, Nina?' Mrs Glazer asked.

Nina shifted uncomfortably on her seat, unsure if she was being deliberately insulted. Jeff had mentioned that she was Jewish at the start of tea, and an extra chill had settled over the already icy table.

'No, thank you,' she replied quietly, taking a sip of her tea. The cup was made of bone china and rimmed with gold leaf. The cutlery was silver plate, the table made from some dark wood that looked very expensive, and the Glazers' carpets were so thick her shoes sank into them as she walked. They lived in a redbrick townhouse on Willow Street in the Heights; the neighbourhood was rich, the streets leafy and clean. Mrs Glazer answered the door in a smart red woollen suit, with gold earrings and Italian leather shoes.

Nina smoothed down her own cheap black dress. Nothing could quiet the bolting nerves in her stomach. She'd known Jeff was rich, but it was still a shock. They might both reside in Brooklyn, but he lived in another world.

Clearly his mom thought so too. Her thin, polite smile never reached her eyes.

'It's a beautiful neighbourhood,' Nina said, trying hard to make conversation. Jeff was no help; he'd spent the meal with his head lowered, pushing blueberry pancakes round his plate.

'Isn't it?' Mrs Glazer answered coolly. 'Henry Ward Beecher used to live right opposite us.'

'Is that so?'

'Nina, tell me again about your parents,' Ken Glazer said. Ken was looking uncomfortable in weekend clothes. She'd asked around and found that Mr Glazer had a job with IBM, supplying mainframe computers. The computer industry was in its infancy, but growing every year. Most people thought of the huge machines as a science-fiction fad, but Nina was certain they had a big future. Maybe every company would need a computer of its own one day ...

At any rate, computers had been good to the Glazers. She'd have liked to discuss it with Jeff's father, but every time she looked over at him his eyes were glued to the large swell of her breasts. Maybe that explained Mrs G.'s obvious dislike. Nina didn't know which was worse.

'Jeff tells me they have their own business.'

'Well, uh, not exactly.' Nina coloured. 'My mom runs a store.'

'Oh?' Mrs Glazer took a tiny bite at a chocolate wafer. 'What kind of goods does it sell? Clothes, cosmetics ...?'

'It's just a deli,' Nina admitted.

Jeff's mother gave a tinkling laugh. 'How refreshing. And whereabouts is it? I must pop in some time.'

Nina wanted to die. 'I think it would be out of your way. We're on the south side of Park Slope.'

Mr Glazer frowned disapprovingly at his son.

His wife pursed her lips. 'Yes,' she said after a moment. 'I'm not down that way very often.'

I'll bet you're not, Nina thought miserably. She gave Jeff a pleading look but he reached for another scone, refusing to meet her eyes.

It was another dreadful hour before Jeff lumbered to his feet, muttering something about football practice, and they were able to escape. Nina thanked her hostess for the tea in as dignified a manner as she could, and took her time about putting on her coat, as though it were a silver fox instead of her threadbare duffel. She felt Mr Glazer's eyes roaming hungrily over her body the whole time, but she tried not to show it. As Jeff's girlfriend, she knew she had to win his parents over. That awful woman would be her mother-in-law eventually.

As she descended the Glazers' scrubbed stone steps, Nina turned round and gave the townhouse a long, cool look. Some day, I'll be richer than you are, she thought. I'll own a bigger house, wear better clothes and have the kind of success you've never even dreamed of. I swear it.

Her small fist clenched under her cheap coat. *I swear it.*

'God, aren't families the worst?' Jeff said lazily. Outside the house, his confident swagger reappeared. 'That was lame. Come on, baby, let's go and make love.'

He admired the way Nina's glossy hair caught the light as they walked off down the street. Damn, she was a hot babe. He got turned on just thinking about peeling those heavy clothes off that dynamite body. It was worth all the shit he was going to get tonight.

Beside him, Nina dropped her eyes so Jeff wouldn't catch the contempt glinting in them. Ordinarily, she'd have laid into him for letting her down like that, but not tonight. They had more important things to talk about.

She had a sneaking suspicion she was pregnant.

'What do you mean?' Jeff asked her half an hour later. They were sitting on the bed of the same room they always used, but for once the coverlet remained straight, the sheets unrumpled. Nina could see their reflection in the dresser mirror and shrank inwardly at the sight of Jeff, his athlete's body hunched up in tension and disbelief. 'You think you're pregnant? You can't be.' He passed a hand through his gleaming fair hair. 'We've been careful.'

37

It was true that they'd followed all the current teen wisdom on sex – antiseptic douches and avoiding the middle of the cycle – but Nina had no money for a doctor and no access to a birth-control clinic. South Slope was big on coat-hanger abortions and welfare mothers instead. Jeff had tried condoms before he met her, and refused to do so again. Douches worked, he promised her: 'I've been around, baby, even if you haven't.'

'I'm late,' Nina said dully. She hadn't expected him to jump for joy – at least not right away – but this blind panic was making her nervous.

'How late?' Jeff demanded.

'Two and a half weeks.'

He shot up from the bed and started pacing the room. 'But it could be stress, right? Girls sometimes skip one for stress. You had all those college exams last week. It must have been pressure.'

Nina shook her head. As if! 'I've been under a lot of stress before, and I've never missed a period.'

Jeff rounded on her, his handsome young face suddenly aggressive. 'You don't know for sure. And anyway, who says it's mine?'

'What?' Nina gasped.

'Don't give me that weepy look. Come on, Nina, I'll bet you've been seeing other guys as well as me. It's been three months. Nobody's that saintly.'

'You know there's only you!' Nina cried, battling tears. How could he say that to her? Didn't he love her? And what did that mean, was he saying he'd been cheating on her? 'Have you got somebody else?'

Jeff leaned heavily against the window and thrust his hands into his jeans. He shrugged defensively. 'Sure. I've seen Melissa Patton a few times.'

Nina's beautiful face went grey with shock. She felt ill.

'See? I knew you'd start gettin' heavy,' Jeff sneered.

'Why the hell shouldn't I? We weren't married. I never said I wanted to go steady. That was your deal.'

Despite herself, Nina felt two huge tears well up and trickle down her cheeks. She felt like such a fool. 'I thought you loved me. I thought we'd get married,' she said bleakly.

Jeff gave a harsh laugh. 'You're kidding. You thought I'd *marry* you?' His stare was cruelly indifferent. 'OK, now I got it. You reckoned I'd fall for this baby crap and get you a one-way ticket to the good life. Huh?' He pulled out a cigarette from his jacket pocket and lit up with shaking fingers. 'Don't pull that with me, sugar. I'm not getting married at nineteen. And when I do, it won't be to some white trash.'

Nina couldn't speak. She couldn't take it in. Was this the same Jeff who had held her close all those nights, whispered sweet things in her ears, covered the back of her neck with downy kisses? Was this the boy she'd spent hours daydreaming about, the lover she'd killed herself to get time with?

Just a few hours ago she'd been eating with his parents, thanking God that Jeff was nothing like them. And he wasn't. He was worse. At least his mother hadn't been a hypocrite as well as a snob.

She'd thought Jeff Glazer was her Prince Charming: the most popular guy in school, the football hero, big and brave and daring. Now Nina saw him for what he was, as he stood scowling by the window: an immature boy, a coward, a bully, a cheat.

And she had his child growing inside her.

'I shouldn't have said that. We'll work something out.' Relieved that Nina wasn't arguing, Jeff looked away. All that white-faced melodrama, he couldn't stand it. It was kind of a shame, but there was no way he was up for this. Marry Nina Roth! She must have been out of her mind. It had been tough enough getting her invited to the house.

Sooner or later, he thought sourly, they all start whining.

'I know this guy works out of Sixth Avenue,' Glazer said, calmer now. 'Dr Fenton. He's sorted out some of the girls from St Mike's before – he's a real doctor, qualified, he'll give you anaesthetic and he's clean and stuff. It's expensive, like five hundred dollars.'

Nina was gazing at him, her face expressionless.

'Hey, I'll spring for it,' Jeff said magnanimously. 'I know my responsibilities. I'll get the money to you in school next week.' He paused. 'No hard feelings, Nina, right?'

Nina stood up slowly and reached for her coat. She let herself out of the hotel bedroom without looking round and quietly closed the door behind her.

The journey home through the park had never taken so long. The bluster of the early afternoon had given way to a glorious sunset of rose and gold, but Nina was blind to the beauty of the day. Nobody watching the tall young girl striding home, her black hair tousled and ivory complexion flushed pink from the fresh air, could have been aware of the dark thoughts racing through her. As she walked slowly home, grief gave way to furious anger, and by the time she reached Third Avenue she had started to form a plan.

'Can I see you for a moment, sir?'

Peter David turned round in the corridor to see young Nina Roth standing patiently behind him, a heavy sports bag slung over one shoulder. Not for the first time, he thought what an attractive kid she was. Her hair was swinging around her face in a shining bob, and she smelt of some delicate perfume. School uniform looked disturbing on that voluptuous body. He could feel the gaze of the boys linger on her as they streamed past. Only some heavy, dark circles under her eyes marred her beauty. He supposed a girl like Nina would be out late with some lucky boyfriend. And why not? It was the last few days of the semester. If any kid deserved a little partying, it was Nina Roth.

'Of course, Nina.' Mr David opened his office door. 'Come in.'

'How long will it be before my college results are back?' Nina asked him directly.

'About a month, but you don't need to worry, Nina. I'm sure you'll be offered a scholarship – probably several. Since we last talked, your work has improved one hundred per cent.' His smile was reassuring.

'What if I wanted to put off college for a year?'

'Delay a year?' Her tutor was shocked. 'You can't do that. We've made the applications. You enrol in the fall.'

'And what if I couldn't?'

Mr David leaned forward, his kindly face concerned. 'Is there some problem, Nina? Is it something I can help with?'

She gave him a small smile. 'Not really, sir. I just need to know.'

'Ah, let me see … I don't think that's a good idea. Competition for assisted places is so fierce. I think you'd lose your chance. Better to reapply the following year,' he said, pushing his wire glasses back up the bridge of his nose, 'but even that might be a problem. Take your place up this year, young lady.' He attempted to look stern. 'Time enough for a year's fun *after* you've taken that degree.'

Nina nodded and rose. 'Thank you, Mr David.' She clasped his hand and shook it briskly. 'Thank you for everything.'

The teacher watched her go and wondered why he felt so uneasy.

*

Nina went to her locker and opened it. The space behind the grille was empty; twice Jeff Glazer had stuffed an envelope full of bank-notes in there, and twice she had returned it. Perhaps he'd finally gotten the message. She pulled out her running shoes and one file of math notes, unzipped her sports bag and packed them inside. The rest of the space was full of the clothes she had taken from her bedroom this morning – two pairs of jeans, her boots, underwear, a few shirts and sweaters and her one good skirt. Her toothbrush, soap and flannel were packed in a side pocket from which she now removed a sealed envelope, addressed to Sister Ignatius, the principal. A similar note was tucked under her pillow at home, for her parents to find when they bothered to make the bed. She didn't expect them to show any concern for at least a day or so, which would give her ample time to do everything she needed to. Without rushing, Nina stacked her textbooks neatly inside her locker. Then she carried her tote bag into the girls' restroom, shut herself in a cubicle and changed into her skirt, a neat blouse, dark hose and a pair of flats. She emerged with her uniform folded in a neat pile, laid it on top of the textbooks and closed her locker door.

The bell rang for second period. Nina ignored the strange looks her classmates gave her as they hurried off to geography. She turned left at the end of the corridor and walked straight through the double doors, down the marble steps and out of the gates.

The bag was heavy but Nina marched down the street like she hardly noticed it. Yesterday afternoon she had gone to see Jo Kepler, her supervisor at Duane Reed, and explained that Mom had been taken ill. She was going to have to quit her job right away. She was terribly sorry for the inconvenience, but could Ms Kepler give her a reference she could use in the future?

'Sure, of course. I hate to lose you, Nina, but of course

I understand,' Ms Kepler said, shaking her head. She was really sorry to see Nina go; the girl had been one of the brightest assistants in the store, suggesting products to customers and helping them out instead of merely ringing up the purchases. She had awarded her two pay rises in two months and had been planning to offer her a place on the trainee management course next year. 'I'll give you an excellent reference, and maybe we'll see you back here when your mother gets better.'

'Thank you, ma'am. Would it be a lot of trouble if I asked you to write it out now? I don't know when I'll be able to look in again.'

'No trouble at all.' Ms Kepler stepped into the back office, slotted a headed sheet of paper in her typewriter and dashed off a reference, couched in the most glowing terms. She signed it, slotted it in an envelope and handed it to Nina. 'There you go, honey. Now you take good care of yourself.'

'Don't worry, I will,' Nina promised her gravely.

The letter was tucked safely inside the outer pocket of her purse, and now there was only one task left. Nina turned right down a side street and headed for the nearest branch of Wells Fargo. There was an empty teller window and she went straight up to the smiling clerk.

'Good morning, miss. May I help you?'

'Yes,' Nina said. 'I'd like to close my account.'

The smile was replaced by a frown, but five minutes later Nina was back out on the sidewalk with a brown envelope in her hand. It contained $627; all she had in the world.

Chapter 6

'Six thirty! Six thirty, *mesdemoiselles.*'

Elizabeth could hear the maid coming along the dormitory corridor, tapping on doors to wake up the young ladies. There was nothing so vulgar as an electric bell at the Henri Dufor, but if you were more than ten minutes late to the dining room, you'd miss breakfast.

'Six thirty, my lady,' the maid announced, opening Elizabeth's door a fraction.

'*Merci*, Claudette,' Elizabeth said, quickly swinging her bare feet out from under the eiderdown duvet before its cosy warmth could tempt her back to sleep. The beds were heavy, old-fashioned things carved from solid oak, with pretty Alpine flowers painted on the headboards, made up freshly each morning with crisp linen sheets. Elizabeth loved her bed and collapsed into it at night without a second thought. Yet it wasn't difficult to get up in the mornings, she had so much to look forward to.

'There's been a new snowfall.'

Penny Foster, her room-mate and the only daughter of a property tycoon, was standing at the window looking up at the Alps. Saas-Fée was ringed with a massive horseshoe of mountains, great stretches of shadows and brilliant white velvet bisecting each other. Green pastures full of tiny flowers lay at their feet in the summer, and the chalet school was perched low down on one of these, east of the main village. Elizabeth padded across the polished wooden floor and craned her neck past the apple-green shutters. Penny was right: even in the dark of early morning she could see a fresh blanket of white covering the upper meadows.

'Terrific!' she grinned. 'More skiing. I can do a run straight back to the village.'

'Is that all you ever think about?' Penny sniffed, pushing a lock of red-gold hair out of her eyes. Where Elizabeth had a strong, athletic body, Penny was slim and constantly worrying about her weight. She had a pair of the latest electric scales by her bed and weighed herself morning and night. She'd been taught to ski by the school instructors but preferred the ballroom dancing classes, as exercise made her even hungrier. Elizabeth thought Penny was neurotic. Penny resented Elizabeth's energy and the way she ate mountains of food without ever getting plump, but she was also in awe of her room-mate's daring. Elizabeth Savage had a wild reputation, in school and the village as well; a natural on the slopes, within months she was taking on the local hotshots, Swiss boys who had started skiing when they started walking. Elizabeth ski'd with ferocious passion, ignoring all the school rules about forbidden areas. Saas-Fée had practically year-round snow, and even after the tourists departed, admiring locals noticed Elizabeth's graceful young body in its snug lilac suit twist sharply down a mogul field or bomb down a black run, crouching into the trajectory like a brightly coloured bullet. Penny heard the other girls gossiping about Elizabeth's nickname in the village, 'Coup de Foudre', the thunderbolt. She was sure it was no accident that the phrase also meant 'love at first sight'.

Six months of Switzerland had changed Elizabeth dramatically. Her curves had become high and tight, her legs powerful. Her glossy hair had grown longer and thicker and the mountain sun had highlighted it with rich streaks of gold, the colour of warm honey. Away from Tony's constant disapproval, the sullen rebellion had

45

disappeared. There was a fresh flush to her complexion and a dancing light in her green eyes. Elizabeth would never be model-thin like Penny, but she didn't seem to care. She practically glowed with health, and looking at her standing there in her white cotton nightgown, breathing in the cold morning air, Penny felt another stab of envy.

'Come on, we've only got twenty minutes,' Penny said, and the two of them scrambled into the school uniform: ivory shirt, fitted navy blazer and skirt and knee-high black socks and shoes. Elizabeth caught her hair back in a ponytail, Penny spritzed herself with Miss Dior, and they rushed out into the corridor to join the other girls.

The dining room was laid out with long tables and hand-carved, high-backed chairs, its windows looking out towards the pastureland and the dark, scented pine forests beneath. Herds of belled cattle were already grazing, and below them the girls could see the lights of Saas Grund. After the first week, though, nobody paid attention to the view, as all the young ladies were constantly gossiping about boyfriends or rock stars. Penny's wardrobe door was covered with pictures of T-Rex and The Who; it was another weird thing about Elizabeth that she seemed totally unmoved by pin-ups, and had *her* wardrobe tacked up with ads – a pregnant man encouraging men to think about condoms, 'Go to Work on an Egg', 'Guinness Is Good for You'.

Elizabeth rushed towards the buffet and loaded her plate: newly baked bread, warm croissants, a bowl of steaming hot chocolate and some fresh apricots. Penny took a small helping of cornflakes and a cup of black coffee and they sat down.

'Hey, Elizabeth, something to interest you,' Vanessa Chadwick announced. Vanessa was a shipping heiress, a willowy blonde and a prefect, who obeyed school rules and found the Savage girl rather shocking.

46

Elizabeth grunted. 'I doubt that.'

Mornings at the Ecole Henri Dufor were spent practising music, dancing or deportment and then attending 'lectures'. These were supposed to broaden the mind but normally sent Elizabeth to sleep; Mademoiselle Charmain, the French mistress, would blather on about Marie Antoinette, or Herr Flagen, the history tutor, would drone on about the Confederation in his dense *Schweizerdeutsch* accent. Occasionally they were treated to outside guests with links to the school. These ranged from the Mayor of Zermatt to some pupil's filmstar mother. The girls still talked about the visit Yves Saint Laurent had once made.

Vanessa sighed at this sad lack of school spirit. 'His name is Herr Hans Wolf. He helped organise the Winter Olympics here last year.'

'Not Hans Wolf the skier?'

Vanessa flicked back her shiny blonde hair and consulted her lecture notes. 'He coached the Swiss ski team, if that's what you mean.'

'Yes, but he was a skier long before that.' Elizabeth tore off a piece of croissant and dipped it in her chocolate, eyes sparkling. 'Back in the twenties, when people used wooden skis they tied on to their boots.'

'That don't sound too safe,' remarked Chantal Miller, an American banker's daughter.

'It wasn't. It was incredibly dangerous. Hans Wolf set five downhill records that way during his career.'

'I'll never hear the end of this,' Penny sighed.

'How long is he staying?'

'Just to give the lecture.'

The others started chatting about the Robert Redford film showing down in the village, but Elizabeth ate her breakfast silently. Her head was miles away in a world without safety nets, padding or crevasse warnings, imagining a young Hans Wolf tearing down a mountainside on a pair of shaped planks, lashed to his feet with hempen rope. She found she was almost blushing with excitement. Perhaps she could talk to him after the lecture, ask him what it had been like. Maybe he would let her watch the Swiss team train ...

After breakfast the girls cleared away their plates and trooped into the music room for piano practice. Elizabeth was dreadful as usual but smiled engagingly at Madame Lyon; she wanted some new ski-boots and that meant Dad had to receive good reports. She plunked awkwardly at the keys, one eye on her watch, longing for nine o'clock. As soon as they were dismissed – all the girls bobbing a curtsy to the old lady – Elizabeth rushed down the corridor to the lecture hall to bag herself the best seat.

The room filled slowly with laconic, overprivileged teenagers, and Herr Geller, the headmaster, peered in to check that his flock was settled. He noticed Penny Foster and Elizabeth Savage sitting centre front and raised an eyebrow; most unlike Lady Elizabeth to take an active interest in anything.

Still, he was pleased to see it. It had been a great coup for the Ecole to land the daughter of Lord Caerhaven – titles always looked good in the pupil register – and in many ways, her ladyship had proved ideal. The earl had written him a frank letter before Elizabeth was admitted, explaining that she was a wilful girl and likely to cause trouble; on no account was she to be given business education, maths lessons or allowed to have marketing journals delivered. He wanted a young lady and not a tomboy to return from the Alps. Geller had called Elizabeth to him when she arrived and explained her father's prohibitions, expecting a storm; instead, all he got was a nod and a shrug of the shoulders.

Elizabeth had resigned herself to the inevitable. She knew the dream would have to be postponed. She wasn't

48

going to work in Dragon, and if she was ever going to escape her parents' clutches, that meant money. Tony had it and she didn't. For the moment, it was better to play along, let the family think she'd given in. She should be studying for her A-levels, but instead she was stuck in this relic from the past, learning *cordon bleu* cookery, flower-arranging and ballroom dancing. Whenever she heard Penny talk about her brother at Oxford, or Chantal's at Wharton, or Thérèse Lecoute's cousins at the Sorbonne, she felt a tight knot of anger in her stomach; no university for her – Dad only wanted her qualified for the Mrs degree. Enthusiasm was asking too much, but Elizabeth dutifully stuck roses in jars and waltzed to the 'Blue Danube'. At the end of her first term her report said, 'Modest and well behaved,' and gave her average marks for everything.

Tony doubled her allowance.

Besides, Elizabeth was enjoying herself. She thought she would loathe Switzerland, but within a week she was in love – the soaring, white-capped mountains, green Alpine slopes covered with Eidelweiss and grazing cattle, the belled goats and clear mountain air. She adored Swiss food, thick black bread and *Kaise*, cuttlefish soups, fondues and *Kirschtorte*, or cherry tart. There was spicy *Glühwein* and perfect chocolate, and the village of Saas-Fée was enchanting, with its narrow, winding cobbled streets and gabled shops.

Elizabeth made friends easily despite her reckless streak; some girls disapproved violently, but others secretly admired her. Elizabeth tried hard to sort out the real friends from the crowd of *nouveaux riches* who sucked up in the hope of an introduction to her brothers. She never trusted Vanessa since the morning she caught her doodling 'Lady Holwyn' all over her art history file.

Good behaviour and a large allowance meant she was allowed to join the termly school trip to Zurich. Penny and Chantal dived into the expensive hotel shops packed with Hermès scarves and Louis Vuitton luggage, but Elizabeth liked to stare at the towering banks, with their mirrored walls and discreet brass plaques. Businessmen in dark suits and Cutler & Gross sunglasses strode past and the news stands were full of financial journals in every conceivable language. Zurich had none of the commercial buzz of London or New York, but its sober atmosphere was impressive. Elizabeth felt she was breathing money. Finance, secrecy and power practically bled from the paving-stones. She would sit in a roadside café, sipping a glass of schnapps, and think slowly about what she was going to do about Dragon. That company was her birthright, and she wouldn't let it go.

She turned the problem over and over in her mind – in class, in her bedroom, in the village. *One day*, Elizabeth promised herself. *One day*.

Meanwhile, she toed the line. It was easy enough to turn up for classes, and it was necessary. Then she had her first skiing lesson, and her life was transformed.

Alone on the black runs from Felskinn and Langflüh, slicing down the glittering, pearl-white tracks, her blood racing, she felt more alive than she had ever believed possible. Elizabeth had two years of finishing school and from now on she looked forward to every second.

She heard the other girls rise to their feet in a rustle of lambswool and cotton as Herr Geller and his guest entered the room. Hans Wolf marched rapidly up to the lectern amidst the polite applause, with the air of a man who wants to get something over quickly. His long stride and erect back were in strange contrast to his wiry white hair and the deep wrinkles scoring his face. Elizabeth knew he was seventy-six, but he looked fifty. That's what a lifetime on the slopes will do for you, she thought, thrilled.

Sighing, Hans Wolf regarded his bored, beautiful

audience for a second. Then he reached into his jacket pocket, fished out some crumpled notes and a pair of wire-rimmed spectacles, slid them up his nose and started to read. What a waste of a morning. He resented having to do this; the young prodigy, Franz Klammer, was racing down the Lauberhorn right now and Wolf had hoped to be there, checking him out. But a banker from Geneva with a daughter at the school had asked him for this favour, and since the banker made a breathtakingly large contribution to Swiss athletics last year, Wolf reluctantly agreed. Money, after all, was sacred.

He rattled on in a dry monotone about the Olympic ideal and the healing powers of sport, occasionally glancing up at the bored faces in front of him. Most of them were examining their manicures, or staring at him with glazed eyes, except for one girl in the centre front. She was a pretty, healthy-looking child with bright green eyes and a dusting of freckles around the nose. Wolf galloped through his clichés at a rate of knots. He paused for breath and noticed the same girl looking at him as if spellbound, leaning forward on the edge of her seat. Disconcerted, the old man gave her a brief smile, lost his place, found it again and ploughed on to the end. Then he sat down, mopping his brow, and wondered how soon he could get out of here without being rude.

Herr Geller was on his feet. 'I'm sure we're all most grateful to Herr Wolf for that fascinating talk.' Dutiful applause. 'Now, *mesdemoiselles*, do you have any questions for our distinguished guest?'

The prefects duly raised their hands with prepared questions about sporting behaviour and it being the taking part that counted. Wolf answered them in an equally pat manner and waited for the attractive blonde to speak. He was slightly disappointed that she did not. After a few minutes Geller thanked him to a fresh round of applause and dismissed the school.

'Many thanks, Herr Wolf. I'm sure that was very instructive for our young ladies,' Geller was saying.

Wolf picked up his notes and thrust them back into his jacket. 'My pleasure, Herr Geller.'

'I hope I can persuade you to stay for lunch. The school maintains an excellent cook ...' Geller began obsequiously.

Wolf suppressed a shiver of dislike and was starting to decline when he felt a small tug on his sleeve.

'And what do you want, young lady?' Herr Geller snapped, annoyed at being interrupted.

'I'd like to ask Herr Wolf a question,' Elizabeth said nervously.

Wolf turned to see the girl from the front row. Close up, she was even prettier and she had a lean, fit figure.

'You had a chance during the talk, Lady Elizabeth.' Herr Geller was never too sharp with an earl's daughter.

'Well yes, sir, I know, but this isn't about the talk.'

'Don't worry, Herr Geller, I'm happy to answer the young lady's questions.' Wolf was interested despite himself. 'Go ahead.'

'Well, Herr Wolf,' Elizabeth said nervously, ignoring the annoyance on the headmaster's face, 'I was just wondering what it was like to break the record on the Hahnenkamm?'

'What?' Wolf stuttered, taken aback.

'In nineteen twenty-five,' the young girl added helpfully.

'*Ja*, I remember when it was,' Hans Wolf replied. He took a closer look at the pretty eyes and saw the pale ring of goggle-marks. 'It was terrifying. Wonderful. You are interested in skiing?' How many of his own countrymen knew he'd broken that record? It was half a century ago now.

Elizabeth nodded eagerly and Herr Geller, wanting to impress a member of the Olympic committee, added,

'Lady Elizabeth is a very good skier, I believe, Herr Wolf. Our own instructors taught her. The Ecole has an excellent record in—'

Wolf caught the scornful glint in Elizabeth's eye and was suddenly vastly amused. Maybe he could take the young *Fräulein* out for lunch at a mountain café. Good sausage, black bread, soup. A glass of *Pflaumen*. No doubt she would enjoy the chance to get out of this ridiculous establishment for a while, and it would be fun to tell war stories from his youth. The Hahnenkamm in 1925! A lifetime ago.

'So I hear, Herr Geller. I would very much like to see for myself, though.' He turned to Elizabeth. 'Young lady, will you show me what you have learned? We could take the gondola up to Plattjen.'

'I'd love to, sir.' Elizabeth glanced at Herr Geller.

'*Natürlich*, go ahead,' he said expansively. 'We have many skis, suits and boots in the games room, Herr Wolf, if you would like to join her yourself.'

'I hung up my skis a few years back.' Wolf eyed the young woman speculatively. 'Are you good?'

'Very good,' Elizabeth said boldly.

Wolf grinned. 'There are some nasty mogul fields up there. We'll see.'

Hans Wolf leaned over the rail on the restaurant balcony, wondering if he could believe his eyes. Down the steep, unforgiving slope opposite him, Elizabeth's strong young body was flying around the moguls. The stick was planted firmly and removed cleanly, she jumped high and twisted sharply from the waist. Slice, leap, slice. No mogul seemed too large, no jump too high. The teenager moved with instinctive grace and skill. The technique was unpolished, but *Gott in Himmel*! she was superb.

Ten minutes ago he'd been looking forward to an encouraging chat and a pleasant lunch. The *Engländerin*

53

aristocrat was very down to earth and warm, openly admiring of him, obviously passionate about skiing and funny about her school. He had settled on the restaurant balcony and told her to have a go at the short, steep mogul run while he ordered lunch. The first time he watched her descent Wolf thought he must be imagining things. He waved at her to do it again, to check it was not a fluke. And then again.

She was so good, it set his adrenalin flowing just to watch her. For a second the old man imagined Heidi Laufen and Louise Levier, their own World Cup hopes on the Swiss women's team. They wouldn't thank him for what he was about to do, but he didn't hesitate for a second.

He beckoned to a waiter. 'Do you have a payphone in the back?' he asked. 'I need to make a telephone call.'

'Of course, sir. Let me show you,' the waiter said, and led him into the bar. Wolf dropped some coins into the slot and dialled the number from memory.

'British Ski Federation,' replied a female voice.

'This is Hans Wolf calling from Switzerland,' he said. 'Is the director around?'

Chapter 7

Six hundred and twenty-seven dollars didn't get you very far, even in Brooklyn.

'Fifty a week,' the landlord said.

Nina shrugged and looked scornful. She was staring into a tiny, cramped little room with damp stains on the walls, a tiny chipped basin and one closet. The communal bathroom was down the hall.

'Thirty-five,' she said.

He laughed sourly. 'C'mon, sugar, we charge fifteen bucks a night.'

The Ocean Motel was in the scuzzy Red Hook area and it blended right in, catering mostly to sailors working on the docks.

'Yeah, but you won't fill this every night. I'll stay at least three weeks.'

'Forty, baby, and you're robbing me,' the landlord said. His eyes flickered hungrily across her large breasts and small waist. The kid was weird, kind of like a co-ed but with street-smarts. She was so serious she freaked him out. Not a hooker, he could tell that much. Pity, 'cause she could have made the rent in kind, any time. He'd have offered her a drink, but she had this stand-off vibe around her.

'Thirty-five.' Nina locked into his eyes and killed the fire there with an icy stare. 'It's all I got. It's not enough, I'll need to go somewhere else.'

The guy frowned. He smelled of sweat and cigarettes and Nina wanted him out of her room.

'OK. But two weeks in advance.'

She fished in her pocket, peeled off the bills from her small roll. He left. She sat down on her small bunk and put her head in her hands.

Nina wondered what her parents were doing now. Calling the police? Did they miss her? They had to miss what she could do. But even so, Red Hook was a no-go area, nobody knew her here. The cops wouldn't find her.

She felt surprisingly calm. She'd been self-reliant for a long time; the only thing different now was the circumstances. Looking back on it, Jeff Glazer had been such a stupid mistake for a clever girl. What was he? Just a good-looking jock who'd used her and then run for cover. She'd trusted him, and look where it got her. Yeah, whatever. She wouldn't make the same mistake again.

Nina got up from the bed and went to the grimy window. Outside was an alley; beyond that, the bustle and noise of dirty, dodgy Brooklyn. She had $557 and the clothes she stood up in.

Tomorrow she would go get a job. It was time to get out of here.

Nina didn't find a job the next day, nor the day after. She spent two anxious weeks trudging down Flatbush Avenue and around the Civic Centre, terrified her money would run out before she found work. Even her reference was no help.

Brooklyn was sunk in the late seventies recession. Nobody was hiring: the drugstores were full, the banks had enough tellers, even the delis didn't need a clerk. She was desperate when she had her first stroke of luck. A boy named Leon was standing in front of her in a checkout queue, bitching about the health food store that had just fired him.

Green Earth was a small Mom-and-Pop joint, a hippy-looking place. Fading paint peeled from its storefront and dusty windows, displaying an assortment of candles, vitamins and joss sticks. Not promising, but her heart beat a bit faster. Surely this place would need someone new.

A bell jangled as she pushed the door open.

'Hi, can I help you?'

The storekeeper was grey haired, maybe sixty. He was sitting behind the counter, hunched over a stack of loose receipts.

'I hope so,' Nina said politely. 'I heard you fired Leon. I'd like to apply for the job.'

The proprietor shook his head. 'I'm not replacing him. Third kid I tried in a month. All they do is sit around chewing gum and talking back to the customers.'

'I'm not like that, really. I've got experience and a reference,' Nina persisted.

'Sorry, honey. Try somewhere else.' Nina swallowed her bitter disappointment and was about to leave when he added, 'What I need is an accountant. Or a magician.' He patted the forms in front of him with a good-natured sigh.

'What are they, your records?' Nina asked.

'Uh-huh.' The old guy shook his head again. 'Never keep a store, kid. You'll go blind before your time.'

'I can organise those for you,' she said, walking towards the counter and ignoring his disbelieving expression. 'Really. My folks kept a seven–eleven. I used to –' she nearly said 'do the', but changed it to '– help with reordering and stock-taking.'

'Yeah? You good at math?' he asked, a slight interest creeping into his tone.

'Top of the class. Look, why don't you let me sit with you and sort those receipts? If you think you can use me, give me a month's trial. If not, I'll stop bothering you.' She fought to keep the anxiety out of her voice.

He paused for a second, then nodded. 'I guess it couldn't hurt.'

'I'm Nina Roth,' Nina said, weak with relief.

'Frank Malone,' the old man said, shaking her hand. 'So you understand these order forms?'

Nina started at Green Earth at six bucks an hour. She reordered stock, washed the windows, and hand-painted the storefront a cotton-candy pink. The small price list Frank kept at the counter was replaced by bold cardboard signs for special offers and discounts. Compared to the chaos of her mother's deli, Green Earth's simple product line was a breeze to keep track of, and soon Nina could tell her boss what was selling and what wasn't. Word got around fast, and more customers started coming in. Nina gave them all polite, efficient service, and made sure she learned the names of the regulars. Frank was impressed.

'How come you work so hard?' he asked her one night, as she combed through a pharmaceutical catalogue. 'You don't have to stay this late. You should be out having fun.'

'I like to work,' Nina said truthfully.

It was true, she did like to work. She had a million ideas for improvements, and Frank Malone was eager to try them all. A widower of seven years, the store was all he had left, and Nina Roth made it an exciting, friendly, bustling place to be. As they started making a little money, he gave Nina a raise; not much, but better than nothing. Nina slaved all hours, she worked like a demon. For one thing, the bright, airy store was better than her dingy motel room. For another, she wasn't the fun-seeking type. And finally, she knew she had to make herself indispensable to Frank Malone before the inevitable happened.

It took four months.

'How's my favourite girl?' Frank asked one morning, as Nina unlocked the front door.

'Good. You know, Frank, we should think about advertising. Posters round town. The local paper.'

'Too expensive.'

'It'll pay for itself in a month.' She took off her coat and hung it in the back.

'Well, I'm glad to see that.'

'What?' Nina asked, turning round.

He gestured at her stomach. 'You're putting on a little weight at last. It suits you, you should eat more.'

Nina braced herself. He'd have to know some time.

'It's not that, Frank. I'm pregnant.'

Blank astonishment. 'You're pregnant?'

She nodded.

The old man's face darkened. 'Boyfriend's not around?'

'No.' Nina's grey eyes were expressionless, and for a moment Frank Malone felt uneasy. Nina was such a serious, determined kid. Seventeen going on forty-eight. It was clear she was in no mood for arguments.

'You need any help?'

'No.' She wondered if she was being too snappy. 'But thanks all the same.'

When she'd picked up her meagre savings, Nina had just one thought in her head. She'd get a place, find a job to cover the rent, and spend her money on an abortion. It was terrible to lose her scholarships, but she couldn't stand it a second longer; she had to get out of Park Slope. Nina wanted a place of her own, away from her selfish parents, away from St Michael's and the kids who laughed at her, a million miles away from Jeff Glazer. The pain of what he'd done to her was unbelievable. Jeff said she was nothing. Her parents treated her like nothing. Nina felt so lonely and so hurt she'd thought she would die.

There was no way she'd take a cent from Jeff. In his world, money bought everything, but Nina swore she was not for sale. Once she had a job, she'd pay whatever it took to rip his bastard out of her. By next year, she'd be in control of her own life – she could reapply to college then.

It was difficult to pinpoint the moment she'd changed her mind. After she started at Green Earth, Nina meant to make a doctor's appointment, but she kept putting it off. She told herself she was settling in, but two weeks passed, then three, and she still hadn't done it. Walking down Atlantic Avenue in the summer evenings, past the Arab bakeries and falafel stands, she'd watch the black-robed mothers cuddling their downy-haired babies, and feel an unexpected tenderness. Or she'd notice a little girl trotting behind her mom in a shopping mall and wonder what her own baby might look like. Somehow she shoved the issue to the back of her mind. It was easy to ignore it, at least at first. Nina had no morning sickness, no cravings for sardine and jelly sandwiches, nothing. Her already voluptuous body didn't seem any different, except for a little tenderness around the breasts.

Two months into her job, the third month of pregnancy, Nina found herself stacking jars of baby apple-sauce. She froze as she stared at the label, showing a chubby baby with a gap-toothed smile. And she knew she'd changed her mind.

Nina *wanted* her child. No matter who the father was. She wanted someone to love. She wanted to take her to the park and buy her dolls and building bricks. She wanted to play with her. She wanted to give her all the joys, all the caring, that her own parents never bothered with. She knew it sounded selfish, but that was the way she felt.

Come on, Nina, you have to be kidding, she lectured herself. What about college? You think you can work your way through college with a baby?

But what *about* college? That was unreal, that was another world. St Mike's and Jeff's world. This was life, earning a wage and making the rent. She could survive without a college degree. She looked again at the applesauce.

A baby would be family, and that would be worth anything.

It's going to be tough, the nagging voice of reason warned her. But Nina had made up her mind. *Tough I'm used to.*

Nina always remembered the day she told Frank. It was bitterly cold, freezing grey slush on the streets, gaudy Christmas decorations everywhere, Chanukah lights in a few windows, another New York winter. She found herself looking in toy stores, full of holly and kings and neon Santas, and wondering how she'd handle Christmas with her kid. The only thing she didn't like about being Jewish was Christmas. There was no getting around it, Chanukah gifts couldn't compete with the orgy of Christmas celebrations, food and trees and lights and cards and presents, bombarding you everywhere you went. You felt guilty as a kid for feeling so left out, because even if it was all about money, lots of Jewish parents scrupulously ignored the twenty-fifth. Hers had, for sure, although Nina was sure it was more to avoid spending any dough than for God.

She decided she'd just make a bigger deal of Chanukah. Her baby would have no cause to complain.

That was when she knew for sure.

'Frank, I got something to tell you.'

'You're leaving,' Frank said anxiously. Nina had only

been around a few months but it felt like for ever. He didn't know how he'd get along without her.

'No, but I hope you won't be mad ... I've decided to keep the baby.'

'That's wonderful,' the old guy said. His face blossomed into a vast crinkly grin. 'You'll be a great mom. I guess I'm gonna have to give you a raise.'

He trundled over and hugged her. Nina almost wanted to cry. Nobody had given her such simple friendship for as long as she could remember.

Frank added, 'I been thinking about giving you a share in the profits, anyway. Five per cent on top of your wages. Since we're making some, these days.'

'Oh, Frank,' Nina said. She knew it wasn't true, and maybe she ought to turn him down, but money was so tight, she couldn't afford to. Frank Malone was a lonely man who felt paternal towards her, and she *had* made a big difference in the store. 'I shouldn't,' she said weakly.

'Take it.' Frank brushed aside her objections. 'I got a cousin in Queens, a lawyer. Did my will. I'll get him to draw up the paperwork.'

Nina hugged herself. Five per cent of one tiny store, hardly an empire. But it was something, it was her first step on the ladder. And Frank was a friend, and she was going to have a baby. The future wasn't rosy, but perhaps it wasn't so black either.

Three days later Frank Malone had a stroke. He was rushed to hospital, but there was nothing the doctors could do. He died an hour later.

'Nina Roth?'

Nina looked up from sweeping the floor as the door jangled. A tall, stocky man in a homburg and a black overcoat stepped into the store, ignoring the 'Closed' sign. She frowned wearily; there was so much to do before the funeral, and nobody else to do it.

'That's right,' she said, holding on to the broom in the hope he'd take the hint, but the stranger didn't budge.

'I'm Connor Malone.'

'Oh.' Nina blushed, wiped her dusty hands on her apron and came forwards to shake his hand. Connor would be Frank's son from Albany, the one he was always moaning never came to see him. Connor had a sister, Mary, in Texas and Nina hadn't been expecting either of them so soon. She wished she'd been wearing something more appropriate than her tatty blue jeans and red checker shirt to meet her new boss. 'Hi there. I'm so sorry about Frank, Mr Malone. He was always very good to me.'

She decided not even to mention the five per cent. Connor Malone wouldn't believe her, she could tell that right away.

'Yeah, he was a generous guy,' Connor said vaguely, glancing around the shop. 'He really pulled it together since the last time I was here.'

Nina couldn't exactly say that it was mostly her doing, so she just nodded and smiled. 'Green Earth is doing really well.'

'That's good, we'll get a better price for it.'

Connor Malone was an insurance salesman, used to sizing up assets, and he liked what he saw: great retail space, attractively laid out, nicely kept. He missed his pop but they hadn't been close for years, whereas fifty per cent of this store would be a great windfall for Cheryl and the kids. He was so pleased he missed the look of panic on the face of the small, dark-haired clerk in front of him.

'You're not going to sell, Mr Malone?'

Connor glanced at her. 'Sure, who'd run this place now?'

'Why not me?'

'I don't think so.' The salesman smiled politely. 'OK, well, thanks for looking after the place till I got here, Miss Roth. I know you didn't have a contract, but I'll see you get a full month's severance. That's only fair.'

'Mr Malone, don't you think you should keep Green Earth open? It's making a nice profit—'

'But my father's dead,' Connor explained patiently.

'Yes, sir, but I did all the book-keeping, I ran the promotions and ordered the stock. I could go right on doing that, and you could hire a junior to help me out.'

Malone looked at the earnest little face and almost laughed.

'How old are you, honey, twenty-two?'

'I'm eighteen,' Nina admitted.

'Yeah? You look older ... but still, I didn't get where I am today by hiring teenage girls to take care of business, even pretty ones,' he added with a laboured attempt at gallantry.

'But I have been taking care of business,' she protested.

Connor Malone's face lost some of its genial air.

'Nice try, Nina, but no dice. Sorry. I'll get you that cheque tomorrow.'

Nina didn't attend the funeral. Instead she stayed back and organised what passed for an Irish wake, a restrained affair with a few glasses of Scotch and some tired sandwiches, which was what Connor thought appropriate. She worked methodically in the store before the guests came back, tidying the last few boxes of pills and bottles behind the counter. Connor would be pleased to see the place straight and somehow it seemed a better farewell to Frank than a bunch of flowers anyway. Nina buffed the mahogany counter until she could see her own face and tried to figure out what Frank would have advised her. First up, don't panic.

She leaned back against the empty shelves and took a deep breath. On her own again. Well, she'd been there before.

It was scary, but she did have some options this time. The local storekeepers knew her and a couple of them had been over making probing noises. Fatimah Resaid in the large grocery across the street had even offered her a job, so she wasn't going to starve. But Nina had the baby to think of now. Even if it was frightening, she had to hold out for something better. A career with potential.

Mrs Minsky in the hairdresser's opposite, who was fond of the grave, quiet kid who'd turned Frank Malone's sorry little store around, had tried to do her a good turn just that morning. Abraham & Straus, the huge department store on Hoyt Street, ran a management trainee programme.

'My niece's husband works over there, he could put in a good word for ya,' Mrs Minsky announced. 'You got your pay, your benefits ... that's a real business, Nina, ya could go places with an outfit like that.'

'Thank you, Mrs Minsky, I appreciate it,' Nina said uncertainly.

'What, ya don't like Abraham and Straus? Ain't it big enough for ya after the empire here?' Mrs Minsky snorted, waving her hands round the empty room.

'It's not that,' Nina said.

'Ya worked in retail, in a drugstore,' Mrs Minsky pointed out. 'Now the question is, where can that take ya? In the store business, in Brooklyn? A and S is the best there is, honey, think about it.'

When the mourners returned and pounced on the whisky and salmon, Nina was still thinking about it. By the time pompous young Connor took her aside and magnanimously announced he was adding one extra week to her severance pay, Nina had pretty much made up her mind.

She was more interested in 'drug' than 'store'. Abraham & Straus *was* glamorous, for Brooklyn; a retail career could lead to Saks and Bloomingdale's, to pretty cosmetic counters and staff discounts on perfume. It would be fun and fashionable.

However, the real money was elsewhere. A year's book-keeping had taught her the kind of cash that the prescription-drug companies made, despite lazy salesmen and lousy service. New York was hooked on its vitamins and minerals, its pills and potions, and it would stay that way. There were vast improvements needed in the pharmaceutical business. She'd been a customer and she knew it. Thinking about that gave her a little frisson of excitement.

The drug business would be less diverting than a big retail store and much harder work, but it would provide better for her kid. As far as Nina was concerned, that was all that mattered.

Chapter 8

Elizabeth arched her back under the caress of his tongue. Gerard's grip was firm, one hand expertly brushing across her breasts, the other stroking between her legs as he moved down her spine. Her skin was hot and slippery, making her long, burnished hair damp around the forehead and dewing the chiselled outlines of her muscles. Gerard was so lost in lust for her incredible body he never noticed her eyes were closed. His own were fixed on the gilt-edged mirror opposite the bed, its ornate frame belying the wild scene it was reflecting. Silk sheets and pillows crumpled on the floor. A primrose satin Dior gown and evening suit flung casually over a chair. And Elizabeth's firm body curving back against him, his cock pushing in and out of her ... too hot to wait, Gerard felt himself speeding up, his breath coming shorter, starting to thrust. He gasped.

'Chérie, chérie, je t'aime ...'

She said nothing but he felt her press against his hand. In time to his thrusts, he brushed his fingertips lightly back and forwards, the way she liked it. She moaned, and his touch got faster. He felt his orgasm gathering, struggled to control it until he could make her come. Two strokes, two more, and then he pressed hard against her clitoris and heard her cry out, the flat of her stomach pulsing. Groaning with pleasure, Gerard exploded inside her and collapsed. They slumped back together on to the sheets.

Elizabeth panted as her climax subsided, coming out of

her fantasy. For a few seconds she was dizzy, disorientated. Then she felt Gerard slip out of her and remove the condom, snapping her back to reality. The James Bond sex scene dissolved into her hotel suite, Sean Connery reverted to her boyfriend, and Moscow turned back to St Moritz.

'You're so beautiful, Elizabeth. *Je t'adore,*' Gerard murmured.

'You were great, Gerard,' Elizabeth said coolly. She could never reach a climax with Gerard without fantasising. Once the pleasure had ebbed, she found she always wanted to be alone. She wondered how to get him out of her suite without actually being rude.

'You've worn me out, baby.' Elizabeth stretched out as though exhausted. 'Better get back to your own room. I need some sleep before tomorrow, and if you stick around, I'll be up all night.'

'OK, sure. I understand. The races come first.'

He was too eager to please, pulling on his clothes right away. Elizabeth couldn't stand that puppy-dog look. Gerard had seemed like he'd be different from Karl and Richard, but in the end they were all the same: knocked out by dating the famous Lady Elizabeth, society darling and starlet of the slopes.

'Well, it *is* the World Cup.'

'And you'll go home with the title, *chérie, j'en suis sûr.*'

His enthusiasm annoyed her. Who did Gerard de Mesnil want to be with? Elizabeth, or the World Champion? She knew he'd be right at the bottom of the black run that plunged down from Diavolezza tomorrow, waiting to hug her for the cameras after the ladies' downhill. It was boring. He was boring.

Elizabeth stirred restlessly. 'See you tomorrow.'

'*A demain.*'

After Gerard left, Elizabeth got up from the bed and wandered into her bathroom, a fantasy of ivory and gold.

She ran a bath, pouring a stream of expensive scented oil under the foaming taps. The fragrance of lavender and thyme filled the room and she willed herself to relax. The bathroom had a large window overlooking the lake, and as Elizabeth sank into the water she could see the spires and turrets of the luxurious Palace Hotel, where her parents would be checking in tonight. For all she knew they might already have landed. Monica could be strolling through St Moritz right now, picking up some new toys at Cartier or an extra scarf at Hermès. Dad would have gone straight to the Corviglia, the most exclusive ski club in the world. Despite a total lack of interest in skiing, her parents had bought some equipment and joined last year, skipping the long waiting list. Lord Caerhaven was old money and head of Dragon plc.; cash *and* class. The Corviglia was just another open door.

Relations with her family had changed completely. When Elizabeth was offered a place on the British ski team, Tony agreed at once. Skiing was a frightfully pukka sport, almost as good as showjumping. They could talk about Elizabeth at dinner parties again.

Soon it was clear they could do more than that. Elizabeth came second in her first slalom, actually won a downhill at Méribel. To the amazement of the Europeans, the British teenager came from nowhere to finish fourth overall in her first World Cup.

Elizabeth was an overnight sensation. The story had it all – a beautiful, sexy-looking young girl, with a strong body and cascading honey hair; a British amateur beating the Alpine nations at their own game; and best of all, she had a title. Photos of Elizabeth smiling on the rostrum in her sapphire Ellesse skisuit were splashed all over the papers. The BBC put her on the news. Reporters were hastily dispatched to Cortina to grab a quote. She was the pin-up of the moment – recession-bound Britain, with strikes paralysing the Labour government and rubbish piling up on the streets, was in need of a bit of glamour. In the 'Winter of Discontent', sexy Lady Elizabeth Savage gave people something to smile about. The press called her 'plucky' and 'gorgeous' and praised the earl and countess for letting her have a go. To their amazement, Tony and Monica found Elizabeth was an asset, her black fleece washed white by the Alpine snow.

That Christmas, Elizabeth cautiously asked her father for a favour. She wanted to spend the summer working at Dragon plc.

Instead of the curt refusal she'd been dreading, the earl calmly agreed.

'If it would amuse you, Elizabeth. I believe there's some space at head office.'

Elizabeth gaped with disbelief and stammered a thank-you.

'Switzerland has obviously been good for you, you've been a credit to the family. Is that going to continue?'

Shock was replaced by understanding. Swallowing a sarcastic retort, Elizabeth nodded.

'Good. I expect you'll enjoy it. As long as you realise the arrangement is temporary. You're bound to meet a decent chap on the winter circuit, and you'll be far too busy with wedding plans ...'

Tony couldn't have been plainer. As long as she played ball and behaved herself, she could do what she wanted, but they were still planning on marrying her off. They just liked the added extras she could bring them right now: a whole new set of parties, terrific social clout, a new sparkle on the family crest.

To underline the point, Monica gave her a diamond bracelet for Christmas, and on New Year's Day Tony quadrupled her allowance.

Elizabeth sold the bracelet. She opened a secret bank account in Geneva, and fed her allowance into it every month. The new star of the British team didn't need money. She raced as an amateur and wasn't allowed pay, but after the World Cup success companies fought to sponsor the team. Suddenly the Federation was swamped with funds. The team got aerodynamic, body-fitting suits especially made by Ellesse, and customised Rossignol skis with an extra edge. They booked suites at the best hotels and flew first-class instead of club. For Elizabeth, nothing was too much. She demanded an iridescent suit that caught the light when she hit the slopes, so she looked like a flashing rainbow against the snow. She never shared a room; she ignored the British coach; and she stayed up all hours on the circuit, partying, glittering, flirting, a butterfly playgirl in the skiing jet set.

It drove her team-mates mad. When they were getting up at six to sweat in the hotel gyms, Elizabeth was lounging in bed with hot chocolate and a croissant. When they were slamming down the practice runs, being screamed at by the coach, Elizabeth would turn up late and do her own thing. When they were ordered to bed at nine p.m. before a race, Elizabeth would be downstairs in the cocktail bar, living it up with the Austrians, swapping notes with Franz Klammer, or draping herself over the arms of the latest beau.

Janet Marlin, Karen Carter and Kate Cox, the other British girls, thought Elizabeth was a bitch. A spoilt teenage brat, she loved the limelight and rewrote the rules. It drove them nuts the way the men swarmed around her, begging for a date, drooling over the tight young body with its firm curves, the suntanned face with its big green eyes. Bad enough that Elizabeth was so gorgeous, without her showing up in sparkling diamond earrings and Perry Ellis cocktail gowns. And on top of that, she had a title. It was 'Yes, my lady', 'No, your ladyship', wherever they went. Even the press hounds called her 'Lady Elizabeth' when they were baying for a quote. Elizabeth never did what the officials told her, but nobody dared complain.

The bottom line was, on the day of the race, Lady Elizabeth Savage was a crouching she-wolf, one of the top ten females in the world. She was the best skier from Britain in fifty years. And she knew it.

Elizabeth clung to her new freedom fiercely. For the first time in her life, she had nobody bossing her; not her father, not her finishing school. Unsure of what to do, she tried to act as sophisticated as possible. The skiing circuit was full of ultra-glamorous types: billionaire Americans, old English money, European princes, *comtes* and margraves. Everybody admired her skiing and it was easy to fit in; she was rich, titled, talented. The team didn't bother her while she kept winning races. She was the *coup de foudre*, the thunderbolt, famous across the Alps. She felt edgy and rebellious, she didn't listen to her trainers. International skiing didn't have much to do with sport: the events took up one per cent of her time; ninety-nine per cent was press, publicity, planes, and parties.

In the eye of the glittering storm, Elizabeth Savage felt lonely and empty.

She got a reputation as a playgirl. Soon she accepted one of the persistent suitors: Karl von Hocheit, a male model and son of a German car tycoon. Karl introduced her to sex, and she felt defiant and wild, but they had nothing in common. Karl was handsome, but he was blond and bland. She dumped him for the Hon. Richard Godfrey, an Old Etonian, heir to a hotel empire; her parents were thrilled. Then Richard said she should win the title and settle down to child-rearing.

'Who cares?' he asked when she talked about Dragon. 'Lizzie, don't you realise you don't *need* to work? I'll take care of the cash.'

They broke up the same night.

Now there was Gerard, Comte de Mesnil. Gerard was

a good lover and made no demands. She had been with him ever since.

In her second year of competition, Elizabeth took the individual silver for the slalom, gold for the downhill and overall bronze medal. The country went nuts, but she was bitterly disappointed. She stood beside Heidi Laufen, triumphant on the winner's rostrum, and heard them play the Swiss national anthem.

Next year, Elizabeth swore. Next year it'll be 'God Save the Queen'.

That autumn, Elizabeth flew out to Davos to begin training again. She met up with Gerard and started to party. Once again, though, she began to feel a gaping emptiness inside her.

It was true that she loved to ski, but she didn't want to *be* a skier. Yet she wasn't equipped to do anything else.

All the flashbulbs, laughter and chiming champagne glasses in the world couldn't drown out the question pounding in her head.

My God. What am I going to do?

Chapter 9

'Elizabeth, you have a visitor.'

Ronnie Davis, the British coach, studied his star athlete with an exasperated expression. Elizabeth had come third in the downhill at Val d'Isère, trailing Louise Levier by a good six seconds. Shrugging, she had promised to do better at Méribel, but she'd still cut training yesterday. How could he ream her out for coming third when the media were all over her, celebrating another bronze? The kid had professional talent but an amateur attitude. It drove him crazy.

'Is it Gerard again? Tell him I'm busy,' Elizabeth said, pushing her dark glasses further up her nose. 'I want to unpack and take a shower.'

They were standing in the lobby of the Antares, Méribel's smartest hotel. Janet was already strapping up for the slopes; Kate had gone to work out in the fitness room. Ronnie knew that Elizabeth would head for a café and a paper, despite the slalom tomorrow. It was her third World Cup. You could lead the mare to water …

'No, it's not Gerard. Regretfully.'

'Hans!'

Elizabeth spun round to see a tall, white-haired figure standing behind her. She rushed to give him a hug. 'What are you doing here? I thought you retired last year.'

'It's true I don't coach, but they can't get rid of me that fast,' Wolf told her gravely. He nodded at Ronnie. 'An honour, Herr Davis. You have your country wining races again.'

'That's all down to Elizabeth,' Davis said flatly. 'I'm sure you two will want to catch up. I think I'll find Janet and run through the slalom.' He shook hands with Hans and headed for his room. Great, just great. Another hanger-on to tell Elizabeth how wonderful she was.

Hans took Elizabeth out to lunch. They rode the La Saulire gondola, suspended high over the Trois Vallées, the biggest skiing area in the world. Mountains stretched below them, vast craggy peaks covered with smooth blankets of snow, pine forests bisected with open trails. People swooped down the runs like colourful ants, but at this height the frantic activity seemed calm, minute, dwarfed by the immensity of the Alps.

Wolf had chosen the Pierres Plates, a chalet restaurant at the gondola station with breathtaking views down the valley. They sat on the sun-drenched terrace, the light burnishing copper highlights on Elizabeth's tawny hair, and watched the skiers swoop away down the black runs. Pulling on his own shades because of the glare of the mountaintops, Hans ordered for them both: soup with thick, black bread, sausage and sauerkraut, and a beer and Orangina.

'It's a beautiful view, *nicht wahr*? The top of the world.'

'Stunning,' Elizabeth agreed.

Hans waved a wrinkled hand at the scene in front of them. '*Ja*? What do you see?'

'See? Skiers, I suppose.'

'Skiers. I am surprised you recognise them.'

Elizabeth glanced sharply up at the old man, and found the pale blue eyes were narrow with disapproval. 'What are you talking about?' she protested. 'I took the bronze in the Cup last year.'

'If I was Herr Davis, I would send you home. I would not let you ski. You are a disgrace to your country.'

Hans Wolf was leaning towards her, his weatherbeaten

face angry and passionate. 'Everyone talks about you, how you do not train, you will not learn, you refuse all instruction. With these boys, always you are running around. You are not a skier, you are a tourist.'

Elizabeth dropped her hunk of black bread and pushed back her chair. 'I don't have to listen to this. Don't you read the papers, Hans?'

'*Ach*, the papers. Of course, you are a big star. *Coup de foudre*, the thunderclap, yes? A woman Prime Minister, and now a girl ski champion.' He snorted with disgust. 'You don't notice the others saying that.'

'Which others?'

'Other *skiers*. The pros. The men and women up here who are not impressed by your pretty face, your noble family. They know you are not trying. You have talent. So? Talent, you were born with. That is nothing to respect. What matters is what you do with it.' Ignoring her look of outrage, Hans Wolf dipped his spoon in the spicy soup. 'You, *Fräulein*, turn up to race like you were punching a clock.'

'Hey, I took fourth, then the bronze. I'll make gold this year.' Elizabeth tried to pretend she didn't know what Hans meant. 'Maybe I need a little polish—'

'Polish! You think taking gold is as easy as that? Yes, you took bronze last year, but only because Heidi fell in the Lauberhorn. Otherwise, it would have been fourth again. You are four, five seconds behind Heidi and Louise, each race.'

'That's nothing,' Elizabeth muttered.

'It is eternity. The Swiss girls train every day, while you go shopping. They rest every night, when you giggle with your young men. But then they are not here to catch a husband; they are here to race. And win.'

'Hans ...'

'The young Comte de Mesnil? Very rich, a good estate. A fine catch.' He shook his head contemptuously. 'Aah,

Elizabeth. When I first met you, you had the passion. You could have been one of the best. I saw a great skier, not some gilded *Hausfrau*.'

'I don't intend to marry Gerard. In fact, I'm going to break up with him,' Elizabeth said, knowing it was true. 'Hans, I'm not out here to get a husband.'

'Why do you resent the sport, then? *Liebchen*, I can't help if you won't tell me.'

Behind her sunglasses, Elizabeth's eyes filled with tears. Nobody had dared speak this way to her since she'd started racing, but it was all true. She was coasting; she was pathetic. Hans was deadly accurate: along the way, her love of the silent, plunging world of the skier had turned into a brooding resentment.

'Because I like to ski, but they're making me a *skier*. Just a skier. I want to be in business, Hans.'

Her mentor's face was a mask of astonishment. 'Is this all? You do that later, no? When you finish on the slopes.'

'No! I can't! You don't get it. My parents wouldn't let me qualify for college; they don't want me to work. I've got no degree, no experience, nothing. This is all I can do.' She gestured to the crowds behind her, and then, to her embarrassment, burst out crying.

Hans Wolf handed her a handkerchief and coaxed out the whole story. Her miserable childhood, Granny, her disastrous sixteenth-birthday ball. The showdown with Tony over the will, Switzerland, and now this.

'So. You have no way to fend for yourself.'

Elizabeth shook her head. Now wasn't the time to bring up her Zurich bank account; she'd been salting money away since the start of last year, but it still totalled only £15,000. Not enough to live on.

'Well, maybe there is other things you can do. Other firms you work for, not only Dragon. Perhaps the FIS, *hein*?' The Fédération Internationale de Ski was the sport's governing body. 'You are clever, Elizabeth. Nobody needs pieces of paper to see it. You are glamorous, well known. You might help promote the sport, but not if you continue this way – they know you are faking, they won't touch you.'

'OK, OK. I hear you.' Elizabeth felt a tiny ray of hope pierce the shadows. Sell skiing for the FIS? God knew she had first-hand, customer experience. All it would take was one post, one job where she could shine.

'What do you suggest I do?'

Wolf speared a forkful of sauerkraut. 'You stop wasting time this season and you start to train. For the first time, you work with the other athletes. You will need to sweat blood to get that five seconds back.'

'All right. I suppose I could try.'

'You will *succeed*. I will arrange for you to train with some of the men's teams – don't think of beating Heidi Laufen, think of beating Franz Klammer.'

'Klammer!'

The legendary Swiss racer had won twenty-five titles.

'You must try to be *best*. Not just as a woman – best overall. Then, you might take the gold. Anyway, this World Cup is a warm-up.'

'To next year's Cup?'

'No, idiot child. To the Olympics.'

Darkness. Panic. Elizabeth woke with a start, the shrilling of the telephone shocking her out of sleep. Semiconscious, she grabbed at it blindly.

'Good morning, my lady,' a French voice said calmly. 'It's five a.m. Your wake-up call.'

The slalom was at twelve, and she'd agreed to be ready for practice at six. Hans had arranged for her to meet up with the US men's team; there was a long mogul run down from Mont de la Challe, an unrelenting bastard of a run that would have her turning and slicing like her life depended on it.

It would be hard, hard work.

Sighing, Elizabeth hit the shower.

'Where's our princess?' Kate Cox asked at nine, when the team assembled in the lobby for training. 'Still in bed?'

'Some rich French Romeo's still keeping her up,' Janet guessed.

Karen Carter shook her head. 'We won't wait for the thunderbolt. Let's just hope she turns up for the race.'

Ron Davis joined his team, a scrap of paper in his hand.

'It's a note from Hans Wolf. Apparently Elizabeth's already on the moguls. Training. She got there three hours ago.'

'You're joking. Who with?' Janet demanded.

Davis scratched his head. 'With the Yanks.'

'Kim and Holly are training with *her*? They're letting Elizabeth see their technique?'

'She's training,' Davis said slowly, 'with the men.'

When Hans Wolf arrived at five forty, Elizabeth Savage was already waiting. He had a flash of admiration for her curvy figure, the stylish way she carried herself on those skis; he might be fifty years too late, but some guy was going to get very lucky. It annoyed him to think of a girl like that with Gerard de Mesnil. That milksop was just a snow groupie with money.

Of course, people said that about Elizabeth, but they were wrong. There was some spark about the girl he'd never forgotten; enough to make his blood boil when he saw her wasting her talents. At Saas-Fée she'd looked one with the slopes, a snow-leopard, but a year into international competition, she was a robot. Bored and cynical, lost in the glitterati.

Wolf didn't know himself why he cared. He was retired, and Elizabeth wasn't even Swiss. But it was the chill twilight of early morning, and here they were.

'How you feel? Muscles all warm and relaxed?' he asked as they jumped on the draglift.

Elizabeth nodded, adjusting her goggles.

'After four hours with Brad they will be screaming for mercy,' Wolf told her smugly.

He could see her body in front of him tensing with anticipation. Every muscle in her thighs was lovingly outlined in that shimmering Lycra; her tight, round butt sat high on her long legs.

For a second he worried that Brad would get mad at him. Brad Hinds, the US men's coach, was training for the Super-G tomorrow. The demands he made of his boys would be a shock to Elizabeth's system, but if they took time out to look at their guest, she'd have them all crashing into the mountain.

'I can't believe you're making us do this, Brad. It's a waste of fucking time.'

Jack Taylor leaned against his ski-pole, his two hundred pounds perfectly balanced, barely denting the snow. It always amazed the team, how such a big guy could be so fluid, so smooth, once he strapped his boots into the skis. Taylor was six-three, bench-pressed three hundred, refused to check into a hotel without a weights room. But get him on the snow and he moved like a ballerina.

Sam Florence, Rick Kowalski and Pete Myers had all been on the team longer than Jack, but they didn't resent him. Taylor was the great white hope for the Olympics next year. He'd taken the silver in his first World Cup, overall gold last year and was running a comfortable lead over his Austrian rival this year. Despite the overnight success, though, Taylor had worked for it. His dedication took even champion athletes aback. Taylor would be up before dawn working out, ran five miles each evening before supper, ski'd all year long to train, following the snow round the world as the seasons shifted across the globe. Jack studied videos of the competition, tested out countless pairs of skis to find a millimetre advantage for his edge. It wore you out just watching him.

Jack Taylor had his sights on next year. An Olympic gold medal for his country, nothing less. The World Cup was a practice run.

The team admired him more because he didn't have to do it. Now twenty-four, Taylor had been tapped for the US three years back, when he was skiing for Harvard at Aspen. That year he'd graduated magna cum laude in English and put off a business degree for the sport. He could only dedicate one more year to amateur competition – his one shot at the Olympics. But Taylor was never going to need the glory for a résumé. His father was a multimillionaire, one of the few Texans to make a fortune outside oil and cattle. John Taylor, Sr, had a Thoroughbred horse ranch outside of Dallas and traded Grade-A bloodstock across the world. The Aga Khan and other Arab princes made the trip across the Atlantic to buy from him.

Jack Taylor was an only child. One day he would own four hundred acres of prime Southern land, two Dallas hotels, a large stock portfolio, a colonial mansion and an exclusive stable of racehorses.

In addition to this, there was the slight matter of his looks. His mom used to say that when God was making Jack, he forgot to press the 'stop' button. Sometimes it didn't seem fair. Not only was he smart, rich and athletic, Jack Taylor's tall, muscled body was crowned with a face that stopped girls in their tracks. Women passed him on the street, paused, and turned round for another look.

Taylor had jet-black hair, so smooth and glossy it

looked like the flank of one of his mares. He cropped it close to the head in a severely masculine cut, which complemented the frank brown eyes with their dark, long lashes, the square jaw and the sensual, slightly cruel mouth. Jack couldn't help his mouth, but it was the finishing touch that broke so many girls' resistance. Set against his all-American, open good looks, the faint sullenness of the mouth, the ruthless set of his lips, spoke of a hidden darkness, a pitiless male sexuality.

Girls fluttered around him like butterflies.

Jack was selective about the ones who made it to his bed. He'd been hit on since junior high, the envy of all his friends who found it Mission: Impossible just getting to second base. Jack was thirteen years old when he lost his virginity, and thirteen and a half when his pop caught him on a haystack with his riding mistress. The riding mistress was fired, and Jack was given a lecture. Horrified by his father's lurid descriptions of what venereal disease could do to his cock, Jack was supposed to abstain. Instead, he learned everything there was to know about condoms.

His pop did nothing because he was secretly delighted. Every good ol' boy would be proud of a son who got laid at thirteen.

By the time he was fifteen, Jack Taylor was a connoisseur.

By the time he hit college, he was sexually mature. Dynamite in bed, he was dominant and skilful. Non-orgasmic women often climaxed for the first time with Jack. He learned to savour going slow, to enjoy relationships, not just two-week flings without strings. His pop boasted that if a stallion of his could sire like Jack, he'd retire ten years early, but slowly the string of cute faces were replaced by steady girlfriends who lasted four, five months at a time.

Still, Jack had never fallen *too* hard. Six girlfriends at Harvard; six broken hearts by the time he left.

Clarisse Devlin was the last candidate. Blonde, slim and pretty, Clarisse had hung on for a year post-graduation, but eventually the constant travel broke them up. Against the dream of Olympic gold, Clarisse never stood a chance, and Jack was secretly glad. He didn't need a girl hanging round right now. There were enough Identikit Euro-babes on the circuit to keep any guy happy, and being single gave him more time to train.

Taylor took practice deadly seriously. He was none too happy right now.

'It's not a waste of time. It's a favour to Hans Wolf.'

'Yeah? Why can't she train with the British guys? Or have Hans ask favours from the Canadians, not us?'

Brad Hinds shrugged. 'He wants her to train with the best. She's the women's bronze medallist. This year she wants gold.'

'Elizabeth Savage is no gold medallist.'

'I didn't know you followed the women's competition, Jack.'

'Enough to know that Savage is lazy, disruptive.' Jack's voice was ice. 'We don't need that attitude around.'

'So, not everyone's a fanatic,' Brad Hinds said doubtfully. He'd heard the same things. 'But it's only once, and we owe Hans. Come on, Taylor. He helped *you* out enough last year.'

Sighing, Jack Taylor nodded. Last year he'd pulled a ligament and might have dropped out if Hans Wolf hadn't found him the best doctor in Switzerland.

'OK, OK. But don't expect me to slow down so she can study my technique.'

His team-mates laughed.

'You wouldn't slow down for the President,' Rick Kowalski pointed out.

At that moment the draglift pulled two figures into

view and started carrying them up the mountain to the top of the mogul run.

Sam, Rick and Pete stared at Elizabeth's curvy frame with open admiration.

Jack shook his head. Sex kittens were great, but not while he was working.

'Here already,' Hans said cheerily as he slid off the draglift. 'Brad, it's good to see you. Hello, guys. Brad, can I present Lady Elizabeth Savage.'

Brad Hinds leaned forward and took Elizabeth's gloved hand. He tried hard not to show how surprised he was. Christ, the kid was gorgeous! High cheekbones, brilliant green eyes, full lips, kick-ass athletic little body. She had a tight butt, long legs, sculptured shoulders. Goggles and rainbow Lycra that clung like a second skin did a lousy job of wrapping her up. He couldn't stop his eyes flickering over her breasts. They had to be the only part of her that wasn't firm and toned. To his dismay, he felt the beginnings of a hard-on. Thank God he'd picked bulky nylon pants today.

'Uh, how do you do, my lady,' Hinds said uncertainly.

'Please call me Elizabeth, Mr Hinds. It's such an honour to meet you. I really appreciate your making time for me today.' Her small hand shook his huge paw enthusiastically.

'Hey, no problem. I'm Brad, and these are Sam, Pete, Rick and Jack.'

'Elizabeth.' Sam Florence's grin was fit to split his face. Kowalski and Myers nodded hi and undressed her with their eyes. Nothing she wasn't used to.

However Taylor's reaction was a surprise. He gave her a cold stare, shifted impatiently on his skis, and turned away. 'Brad, can we get going? We've hung around long enough.'

'Sure.' Hinds pulled out a stopwatch. 'You take the first run.' He turned to Elizabeth as Taylor settled into a crouch. 'Don't mind Jack. He's World Champion, it makes him a little excessive about training.'

'Oh, I understand,' Elizabeth said warmly. 'Jack, you were superb at Garmisch—'

She never got to finish her sentence. Ignoring her completely, Taylor pushed off with a mighty lunge and tore down the mogul run, planting his stick cleanly and with perfect rhythm, his heavy body leaping, twisting and landing cleanly and sharply.

'Jack Taylor is a real skier. He does not want to know you,' Hans whispered in her ear. 'You have not earned his respect.'

Elizabeth stood at the top of the run, her eyes narrowing.

That smug bastard. She was going to teach him a lesson.

Two hours later, Elizabeth was ready to drop. Hans had been right: training with the men pushed her to the limit. Her muscles were burning with effort, her body bathed in sweat under the suit, her head throbbing from the gritted focus it took keeping up with them. After Pete Myers sliced his way down the mogul run barely a second behind Jack, Elizabeth took a go. Swooping, turning and jumping with ferocious concentration, she made the run three seconds ahead of her personal best.

She was miles behind the men. Taylor's stare was scornful.

Elizabeth listened to Brad's comments with unusual humility, but she was biting her lower lip with rage. The second descent, she shaved off two extra seconds, but still trailed Taylor. The third time she pushed herself too hard and fell, bruising her outer hip painfully and jolting a ski out of its bindings.

'Are you OK? Maybe you'd better take a breather,' the

coach suggested anxiously. Ronnie Davis would skin him alive if the Brit's star girl was injured before her slalom.

'You made a great time for a woman, anyway,' Sam told her.

Jack Taylor caught her looking at him. She was stunningly beautiful. The type of chick who thought the world owed her a living. Or a gold medal, in this case.

'The idea is to stay upright, Cinderella,' he remarked coldly. 'Don't bite off more than you can chew. Women's training is effective for women – if they bother turning up for it.'

'I'll go again,' Elizabeth told Brad furiously.

On the fifth attempt, she managed to beat Pete Myers by half a second.

'Jesus!' Pete swore, disgusted with himself.

'Come on, Pete. You're way off today. Just concentrate,' Jack Taylor said loudly, belittling her achievement.

The girl flashed him a look of pure disdain, which Taylor pretended to ignore. He thought she was an arrogant bitch, and he wanted her to know it.

Privately, he had concluded something else.

Elizabeth was the best female skier he'd ever met.

And she was the sexiest, best-looking babe he'd ever seen.

Chapter 10

Nina was writing a job application when it happened, sitting in Green Earth in the gloom. Connor had boarded the place up, ready for sale, but Nina had kept a spare set of keys. She snuck in the back most nights and hammered out résumés and letters, a torch propped up behind her, bombarding the big drug giants until somebody said yes. At first she felt like a thief, but Nina was getting used to being ingenious. You could only ever rely on yourself. Until she landed a new job, she couldn't afford a typewriter of her own. Most of her severance cheque had been eaten by her new, tiny walk-up studio; you couldn't afford to head letters with a motel address.

She was trying ICI when the first pain came. A sharp twinge in the gut that she ignored – she was always getting pains from her pregnancy. Then it was worse. Nina pressed a hand to her taut midriff. God, it hurt, it really hurt; like the worst period she ever had. Gasping, she doubled forwards, clutching herself. There was a pause, then another wrenching, flaming stab. Nina staggered out of the door and on to the sidewalk. There was a payphone there and she dialled 911.

When the ambulance got there five minutes later, they found Nina clinging to the phone, tears streaming down her face. Her slacks were drenched. She knew what was happening. She was going to lose her baby, like she'd lost everything else.

St Jude's Blue Cross Hospital was staffed with brisk,

fatigued junior doctors. A black gynaecologist saw Nina.

'I'm sorry you lost the child, but you're OK. No reason why you couldn't have another.'

'Thank you, Doctor,' the girl said quietly.

'Got a husband?'

'No.'

'Got a job?'

'No.'

Dr Kenmore shook her head. The kid was still the light side of twenty. Most girls in that position would be pleased to miscarry. 'You're nineteen? You look older.'

Nina pushed herself up on her pillows. 'When do you think I'll be fit to leave?'

She was taken aback. 'You're fit now, physically, but you can stay and rest, that's fine. We do Medicare.'

'I have to go,' Nina said, and pushed back the covers.

'Don't you want any counselling?' Dr Kenmore asked. 'We have a rabbi here, he could talk to you.'

'No. Thank you.' Nina Roth looked up at the doctor, her face beautiful despite its pallor, heavy, silky hair ringing her face. 'No counselling's gonna change what happened. I'm alive, I have to get on with it.'

What a cold young woman, Dr Kenmore thought as she left.

Nina felt weak enough to take a cab home. She let herself into her apartment, collapsed on the bed and cried like she would never stop.

When she woke up, it was six p.m. It was bitterly cold, her rickety radiator barely blunting the edge of the chill. Her stomach hurt, but the emptiness and the loss hurt more.

Nina forced herself out of bed and went to the window. It was sparkling clean, like the rest of her tiny place. Food stacked neatly in the cupboards, rejection letters piled on the kitchen table. Total contrast to the grime and dirt outside: hookers and dealers hanging out on the street corner, sirens screaming, traffic noises and drunks. All those people, millions of people, and not one of them who cared about her. She'd lost Frank. Jeff. And now, her baby.

Idly she picked up the bottle of painkillers Dr Kenmore had prescribed. A junkie was yelling on the sidewalk below her. She could probably get about a hundred bucks for these; powerful shit, Valium mixed with opiates. Easy to get high on, easy to check out with. She would float away on a hazy, warm cloud and just never wake up.

There was a cheap hand-mirror propped against the Cheerios packet. Nina looked at the reflection inside the ugly pink piping; she was red eyed but beautiful, pale, exhausted. She saw too much experience and cynicism in her own dark eyes. She was still just eighteen years old.

Nina unscrewed the bottle and counted out two tablets. Recommended dose. She'd never seriously consider taking the coward's way out. She'd made herself a promise on Jeff Glazer's front steps, and she was absolutely going to keep it.

Two days later, she got her first positive reply.

Dolan MacDonald was the tenth drug firm she'd applied to. The position was for an assistant sales manager at $21,000 a year; a pittance by industry standards, but a fortune to Nina. She wanted the job so much she ached. Anything, anything to get her out of here.

In her first interview, she answered questions on her work experience and Dolan. Today she was meeting her prospective boss.

Nina left the subway at the Jay Street exit and headed for Dolan's offices, a functional block of grey stone behind the Borough Hall. It looked dull, but she was excited. Dolan MacDonald, with its boring pill bottles and plain white packaging, was the place to be.

Her second interview took place in a drab room somewhere on the second floor, with a bored-looking flunky who chewed a pencil the whole time, and Ivan Kinzslade, head of the vitamins division.

'You don't have a degree, but you made good grades. Why you drop outta school?' he asked without preamble.

'I wanted to get on in the world, make something of myself.'

'So why you join a tiny joint like Green Earth?'

'It was tiny, but it made a good profit,' Nina said defensively.

Her interviewer's eyes narrowed. 'Not when you joined.'

Nina sat up a little straighter, realising Kinzslade had been asking around.

'I couldn't get a job anywhere else. It wasn't such a great idea, dropping out of school.'

The Russian laughed. 'You got any family?'

'Only my parents, and I don't talk to them.'

Kinzslade called her at home that afternoon to tell her she was hired.

Nina insisted on her first paycheque in advance; she needed it for a deposit on the rent. She was surprised that demanding the money didn't hurt her image, in fact it impressed her bosses. Nina found that if she acted seriously people respected her. For the second time in a month she moved, to a small one-bedroom off Flatbush. It wasn't much, but to Nina it was a triumph. Her own apartment! For the first time in her life she had a respectable place of her own, she was doing good at work, she could pay all her bills.

It was hard, though. Nina's creamy complexion was dull with fatigue by the end of each day, even though she

was eating well. She couldn't afford unhealthy convenience meals; it was all cheap pulses, potatoes and veggies
from the local markets, fish and chicken if it was on offer.
Nina could cook, just about. Still, she was pathetically
grateful when Mrs Minsky, her neighbour, dropped
round with the odd apple pie.

'Lord, child,' Mrs Minsky said, sniffing, 'they work ya
too hard, you're white as ivory. Didn't your momma tell
ya you're too cute for this? Ya need a man to take care of
ya. I gotta grandson, Carl—'

'Thanks, Mrs Minsky, but I like things this way,' Nina
said politely, but in a tone of such finality the old lady
actually gave up.

'If those guys at your work don't ask ya out, they
should be takin' their own medicines,' was her parting
shot at the door.

Nina could have laughed. Ask her out! Like they ever
did anything else! Almost every man on her floor, from
the geeky researchers to the cash 'n' flash commission
salesman, had tried his luck already. Slowly but surely
Nina got the word out that she wasn't interested. That
might have caused resentment, but who could resent the
quiet Ms Roth, that mousy, dedicated little toiler with
her reports and calculations, always either glued to the
phone or hammering at her computer screen? Nina got a
skewed reputation. She was a major babe, but uninter-
ested in men. She was ambitious, but bored by office
politics. Nina stayed well away from the water-cooler
crowd, just doing her job, finding her feet. And soon
enough, the boys ignored her.

All except Ivan Kinzslade, who had an instinct about
Nina. The job he'd hired her for was simple, form-filling
and number-crunching. At first she seemed happy just to
do that, but after the first month, Ivan noticed her calls to
the field offices were taking longer, she was asking for
more data.

First thing one Monday morning she showed up in his office.

'Morning, Nina, you gotta problem?' the Russian asked, offering her a bite of his jelly donut.

'An idea,' Nina said, coming right to the point.

Ivan liked it. Roth was more upfront than any other young girl he'd hired. She seemed much older than her years. Ivan was an immigrant who'd escaped from Russia and taught himself English before winding up in Brooklyn. Sometimes he thought he saw a similar hardness in Nina, the look of a person who'd been through a furnace and come out tougher the other side.

'Go on, then.'

'We're wasting a lot of money in the way we sell our stuff. Look at this,' Nina said, spreading out research in front of her boss. 'We tailor journeys to our salesmen. If we paid more attention to retailers, we could focus our efforts.'

'You think so?'

'I know it. Look, Ivan, I've been the customer. I know what they want.'

Kinzslade glanced up at the grave young woman standing over him. 'I guess you can try it,' was all he said.

Over the next year, Nina crammed as much work as possible into an eight-hour day. She tried to alter Dolan's sales, organising training programmes and policy around the needs of the customers, not the company. Dolan's sales force got a reputation for friendliness and efficiency. Orders picked up, and Ivan gave her a pay rise.

Nina opened a new account at Wells Fargo, with a first deposit of five hundred dollars. Every extra cent she earned, she salted away. Waiting till she had enough money to do something.

In her second year, Nina talked her boss into thirty new computers. The expense was a black hole in the quarterly budget, but quickly paid for itself. Productivity went up two per cent; clerical expenses fell.

It was hard, grunt work, trying to change a system that had been in place for decades, but her colleagues listened when Nina talked, even the flyboys who thought any women in offices should be taking dictation.

'Nice idea you had for Ohio,' Grant McCoist, a flash Midwestern rep, told her after one strategy session. 'It'll help get our profile off the floor.'

'Thanks,' Nina said coldly.

The handsome young comer didn't take the hint. 'You know, that dress is real pretty. You should let me buy you dinner, we could discuss it some more.'

'If you want to discuss it, send me a memo,' Nina told him.

'Good morning, Ms Roth,' Ally Hendry announced confidently, turning up in her office at nine a.m. with a huge bunch of roses. 'Wanna have lunch? We could swap computer strategies.'

'I mostly eat at my desk. And they're sweet, but I get hay fever,' Nina said bluntly.

'You know, you're quite the rising star,' Jock Mac-Callister, a finance manager, told her as he leaned over her computer and stared soulfully into her eyes. 'You got some free time? You could tell me your secret.'

'I can tell you that now, Jock,' suggested Nina sweetly.

He leaned forwards.

'Hard work and imagination,' she said, trying not to laugh at the offended look in his bloodshot eyes.

'What, you're frigid? Or you gotta boy in your life already?' Jock demanded, acting like a spoilt brat. Nina regarded him coldly. That's all they were, these boys, spoilt brats whining when they couldn't get the toys they wanted. She made twenty-six grand a year now, she paid her own way. Independence that was very precious to her. Mrs Minsky might see it as natural to seek out male protection but Nina was determined never to have to. She had no respect for men and no time for romance. Jeff Glazer had bruised her heart so badly Nina never wanted to risk pain like that again.

'Yeah, I do. I have a boy in my life,' she lied.

Jock puffed up like a mating pigeon. Of course, or how could she have ignored his advances?

'OK, I guess we shoulda known,' he said magnanimously.

After that the guys left her alone. Nina was a beauty, but she was off the market.

Nina climbed quietly, seriously, relentlessly, hand over fist, without stopping for friendship or looking back for love. She didn't care. She thought that stuff was for weaklings.

The phone trilled on her desk right after one. It was Edwin Jensen, a prestigious firm of head-hunters who specialised in pharmaceuticals. She was getting herself a reputation, they said. Dragon was looking for a business development exec. Would Ms Roth be interested?

Nina lowered the soggy tuna sandwich that was her idea of a lunch break and took a deep breath. Dragon Inc. The big time. The bluest of blue chips, Dragon had pharmacies, drugstores and health food places across Europe and the States. Their executives were highly paid, with hefty bonus schemes and expensive company cars. The head offices on Park Avenue were a fantasy of marble and gold, burgundy leather and oak, exuding old-world elegance and Fortune 400 wealth.

Nina hadn't even considered the British giant. Dragon was not known for its political correctness. Just for its profits.

Dragon acted like a gentleman's club. The dress code was strict, recruitment conservative. Dragon wanted clean-cut young men, the cream of the Ivy League. Out of

Harvard via Brooks Brothers. It wasn't big on ethnic minorities, City College grads, or women.

Why me? Nina thought.

'So, would you consider interviewing, Ms Roth?'

'Absolutely,' she said. It was certainly worth a shot. At worst she'd get a little flavour of life inside a market leader.

The interview took place a week later. Uncharacteristically nervous, Nina arrived at the Dragon building on Park Avenue ten minutes early, wearing her best suit and imitation leather shoes. Dragon's HQ was a palace. The reception area was a study in burgundy leather, mahogany and marble, bustling with middle-aged men in expensive suits. The receptionist looked at Nina like she was gunge sticking in the sink drainer.

'Yes, miss, can I help you?'

'I'm here for a job interview.' Nina's voice sounded very small in her own ears and she cleared her throat. 'My name's Nina Roth.'

The woman tapped her hi-tech keyboard and unbent slightly. 'Yes. You take the elevator to the thirteenth floor. You'll be seen by Mr Gary Bellman from our Personnel division, and Lord Caerhaven.'

The back of Nina's throat dried up. 'Lord Caerhaven, *personally*?'

'That's right. He's visiting New York,' the receptionist said blandly.

Nina could feel the hostility rising off the older woman like steam. There you go, cutie, it said, how do you like them apples?

Tony Savage. The Robber Baron. She'd clipped countless articles about him at Dolan, everything from *Vanity Fair* puff pieces to *Fortune* assessments. Savage had ripped the heart out of countless small firms and research teams, invested brilliantly, fired thousands of workers, and turned his moribund family business into a global giant. He was respected but loathed. The drugs business feared him. And adored him. What the hell was he here for? Why was he attending this interview? Nina buzzed for the elevator and tried to calm herself. Thank God, she thought, I don't have too much time to think about it.

Upstairs a secretary ushered her into Gary Bellman's spacious office. The two men were sitting casually on chairs behind a long table; one, smaller chair was set in front just for her. It felt like a long walk before she could sit down.

'You're Nina Roth?'

'Yes, Mr Bellman, how do you do.' Nina shook hands, hoping she sounded confident.

The sandy-haired guy raised an eyebrow. 'How do you know I'm Bellman?'

'Because I recognise Lord Caerhaven.'

Tony grinned. He liked to sit in on odd meetings around the world; lightning visits to keep his people on their toes. Today he was inspecting Human Resources. Bellman, his new guy, liked to pick people from different backgrounds to the norm: scholarship kids, entrepreneurs, comers cherry-picked from Glaxo or ICI. This girl, Roth, had brought in some reforms at Dolan. Her file said she had a reputation already. She was clearly terrified, but putting on a good act. It impressed him; her lovely face and sexy figure impressed him a lot more.

He didn't mind the odd woman around. They cost less, they worked harder. The Dragon boys' club was no place for a lady, but then this kid wasn't a lady, she was a working-class hustler from the wrong side of Brooklyn.

And she knew who he was.

'Tony Savage,' he said.

His strong, fleshy hand gripped hers like a vice, dark eyes sweeping across her body like they could X-ray her.

Nina blushed. Savage was physically overbearing,

large and muscular. He had an air of ruthlessness that matched his reputation. She had to fight not to flinch under his stare. Next to his charcoal wool Turnbull & Asser suit, his gold Blancpain watch and his immaculate manicure, Nina felt cheap and underdressed.

'Thank you for seeing me,' she replied coolly.

'Lord Caerhaven has some questions for you, Ms Roth,' Bellman said.

Tony Savage looked Nina over for a long, luxurious moment, careful to keep his eyes expressionless. The scout reports on her work suggested some ugly bluestocking.

Nina Roth was anything but. An awesome body under that shapeless suit. A flaring bosom tapering down to a handspan waist, a tight, round ass, creamy white skin, nicely turned calves. Her body language was repressed, though. Knees pressed together. Back rigid. Clothes designed to play down that sexy shape.

Savage fired a question. Nina answered it sharply. He fired another.

Nothing seemed to faze her. As Nina talked, Savage's thoughts drifted. He wanted to see if his hands would really fit round that waist. What colour the nipples were on top of those creamy breasts. She looked uptight: great. Not the kind to sleep around.

A challenge.

Tony nodded coldly and made a small note on his pad. Nina Roth had a great future with Dragon.

Chapter 11

Nina gave herself a last check. It was her first day at Dragon and she wanted to look perfect. She'd chosen her new suit at Saks on Saturday, something she could barely afford, but it was an investment. The eighties were here.

It was a brave new world, and women executives had a new rulebook to go with it – John Molloy's *Dress for Success*. Nina had a well-thumbed copy of this bible next to her bed, and she obeyed it to the letter. Adopt a business uniform. Blouse lighter than the suit. No bright red, bright orange or bright anything. Avoid emphasising the bust.

Easier said than done, Nina thought uneasily. Her suit comprised a white cotton blouse, a boxy jacket with the latest 'power dressing' essential – padded shoulders – a skirt that hovered precisely on the knee and low pumps with natural hose. In her one concession to individuality, Nina rejected navy in favour of rich burgundy. Hopefully the jacket was boxy enough to disguise her breasts.

Nina fiddled with the floppy bow tie at her neck, and picked up her new leather briefcase.

'Let's go to work,' she said.

As her yellow cab crawled up Park towards the Dragon building, Nina read over her product marketing file. She didn't think about the oddity of her situation. A young woman with no formal training, from the wrong side of the tracks, storming one of corporate Manhattan's most exclusive male bastions ... it was unheard of. But it had happened, and Nina didn't waste time wondering why. That was the past. Her eyes were fiercely trained on the future. She'd make her mark fast and keep moving up.

She soon realised how tough that would be.

'Good morning, Ms Roth,' an elegant blonde receptionist greeted her as she stepped inside the Italian marble lobby. Nina had thought she would be early, but the lobby was full of Identikit young men striding purposefully towards banks of elevators. It was eight-twenty a.m. She made a mental note to arrive at eight tomorrow.

'I'm the new Business Development manager,' Nina explained, trying to sound like a businesswoman. 'I'm due to report to Mr Jax at nine.'

The receptionist's gaze swept across the glossy black bob, the grey eyes and ivory skin. Then she stared almost rudely at the hourglass figure only half-hidden under the burgundy suit, and the long, curvy calves that tapered down to the neat pumps. Nina had to restrain herself from checking to see if she had coffee stains on her lapels.

'Yes, ma'am,' the girl said thinly. 'Business Development is on the twelfth floor and you have offices next to Mr Robbins and Mr Daly. They've already arrived.'

'Thank you,' Nina said, but the girl had already returned to her magazine. Clearly that was it. Uncertainly, Nina picked up her briefcase and headed for the nearest elevator bank. Three young men were standing inside one car, but as Nina hurried towards it, the doors hissed shut. They didn't try to hold them open for her. She took a deep breath and pressed the button for the next one. Maybe this was just how people behaved in a big corporation, Nina told herself as she waited. After all, they didn't know her yet, and time was money. Right?

In the slow ride up to her department Nina fiddled anxiously with her buttons. The reflection in the mirrored doors showed a pretty girl, maybe a little flushed, but neatly, conservatively dressed. She examined it carefully but still couldn't see anything wrong. Shrugging, Nina shook it off. Two minutes inside the corporate jungle and already she was getting paranoid ...

At the twelfth floor the elevator stopped gently and the smoothly hissing doors opened on to a luxurious corridor. The floor was carpeted with a soft grey weave and elegantly framed prints of Dragon products. Men and women were walking in and out of various offices, but only the men were executives. The women wore short skirts, heels and pretty dresses in pastel colours, and they all hovered and smiled deferentially. Nina glanced around but could not see one other woman in a business suit.

'Excuse me.' She stopped a young redhead carrying a freshly made mug of coffee. 'I'm new. Could you tell me where to go?'

'Sure,' the girl said neutrally, giving Nina a once-over. 'The typing pool's at the end of the next corridor. You should report to Mrs Finn.'

'No, I mean – I'm the new Business Development manager. Apparently I'm going to be working with Mr Robbins and Mr Daly,' Nina explained. 'Could you direct me to my office?'

The girl did a double-take. '*You're* N. Roth?'

'Yes. Nina Roth,' Nina confirmed.

There was a second's stunned silence, and then the girl said, 'If you'll follow me, Ms Roth,' with barely concealed hostility. Making no effort to put her coffee aside, she led Nina down the length of the corridor and to the right. A small group of tiny, windowless offices nestled in a corner, with names stencilled in thin black lettering on the doors. 'N. Roth' was in between 'S. Daly' and 'T. Robbins'. You had to peer closely to read the titles and Nina was shocked to see that all three of them had the same status: Manager, Business Development. She had assumed she'd be the only one doing the job.

'This is your office,' the secretary said, showing Nina into the cubbyhole of a room. Between the desk, the filing cabinet and the trashcan, there wasn't enough room to swing a kitten.

'Tracy Jones is the assistant assigned to you. You'll be sharing her with Mr Robbins and Mr Daly,' the girl continued, her tone making it clear she felt for Tracy. 'You can buzz her if there's anything you require. All the new managers have an appointment with Mr Jax at nine and his office is on the thirteenth floor.'

'Thank you,' Nina said faintly, opening her briefcase and starting to lay out her documents.

'Uh-huh,' the girl said, and closed the door.

Gee, Nina thought wryly. What tells me they don't have many women in management roles?

Five minutes later, as she was busily setting up her computer passwords, there was a smart rap on her office door.

'Come in,' Nina called.

It swung open to reveal two expensively dressed men, both of them wearing big smiles and sombre pinstripe suits. One had a gold watch and one a steel Rolex, and Nina could see at a glance that the shoes were handmade European leather.

'Hi, I'm Simon Daly and this is Tom Robbins,' the taller one said, indicating his colleague. 'You must be Ms Roth.'

'Nina.' She stood up and shook their hands. 'I'm looking forward to working with you.'

'Ditto,' Robbins said. He had sandy hair and freckles and she didn't care for the twinkle in his eye as he took in her figure.

'Are you guys new here too?'

'Yes, ma'am.' Simon, the blond, seemed more open and relaxed. He had a slight Chicago accent and a straightforward manner. 'First day of my working life. Dragon yanked me out of my student haven and now I'm supposed to sing for my supper.'

'Goes for me too,' Tom added, eyes still roving over her jacket. 'I majored in economics at Cornell and Simon did math at Yale.'

Nina straightened up. 'I went straight into business from high school. I worked at Dolan most recently.'

'And now the big time. Well, you're a liberated lady,' Tom teased her, with an obnoxious smile.

'I like to think so,' Nina replied calmly.

'That's the reason, then. You don't have a degree and we don't have any experience. That's why we get forty-five thousand and all the others get fifty-two,' Simon grouched. He checked his Rolex. 'Ten of. Come on, let's get upstairs. We don't want to be late for our first pep-talk.'

Nina nodded and followed them into the elevator, trying not to let her feelings show on her face. Obviously, working at Dragon would be like running up the down escalator.

She'd thought thirty-five thousand was a fortune, but they'd hired two younger guys with zero experience to do the same job as her. For ten thousand bucks more.

The thirteenth floor was already pretty crowded. Around thirty people were standing in the sumptuous waiting area Nina recognised from her interview, admiring the oil paintings of hunting scenes, sitting on chintz couches, or gazing out of the stunning floor-to-ceiling windows. Nina was relieved to see four other women, but as she introduced herself, the relief lessened. Two of the girls were in Human Resources, one was a creative in

Packaging, and one was assigned to PR. As they shook hands, Nina sensed her isolation creep back. The girls had jobs that *sounded* impressive but kept them well away from the bottom line.

The door swung open and they filed in. Small, gold-backed chairs had been lined up in rows in front of the elegant mahogany desk. Nina noticed the other women automatically seating themselves in the back, anxious not to appear pushy. Squaring her shoulders, she headed for the centre front row.

Dragon hadn't hired her to be a shrinking violet.

All conversation ceased as Gerald Jax strode into the room. He was wearing a dark suit and a platinum Gucci watch. His grey hair was severely cropped and his dark eyes hard and uncompromising. The head of Dragon US, Jax was Tony Savage's right-hand man in the States. He radiated ruthless power.

'Dragon Chemical is the largest drug company in the United States. We have revenues of half a billion dollars on turnover of three billion.'

There was absolute silence as they gazed at their new boss.

'That's not enough,' Jax continued coldly. 'Lord Caerhaven wants to be the biggest in the world. We aim for radical improvements in US market share. We pay the highest salaries and we expect the best. Dragon is looking to you to implement its expansion.'

Jax surveyed the spellbound new recruits.

'We're not easy to work for. We want results fast. Those who do not deliver will be fired. Those who do – will become extremely rich. I expect to see tangible progress in the first month of your employment. Then we'll know who's intended for which fate.'

He leaned forward slightly, as hypnotic and menacing as a swaying cobra.

'We remain the best because we *never* let up. Remember this: if you rest on your laurels, they become funeral wreaths.'

Dismissed, they rose from their chairs and began to leave. As Nina stood up, Jax motioned to her to stay.

'Good morning, Nina. Welcome to Dragon,' he said.

'Thank you, sir,' Nina answered carefully.

Jax nodded at the crowd of young men. 'By now you may have realised that you're quite an exception. We haven't had many women applicants with your ability.' His tone was unapologetic. 'I hope that's not going to be a problem for you.'

Nina looked the vice-president straight in the eyes.

'No, sir. No problem at all.'

'Glad to hear it,' Jax said coolly, turning aside.

His gaze followed Nina with vivid interest as she left the room. Tony had asked for a report on this one. She didn't know it, but Nina Roth was going to be very closely watched.

The speech might have been macho melodrama, as Nina told herself once she was safely back in her office, but a part of her thrilled to the challenge. She had one month to come up with something hot. Brainstorming all afternoon, her first day, Nina fished out a dramatic idea from her fertile subconscious. Dragon was richer than Dolan MacDonald, but it followed a lot of the same practices – shipping the same drugs at the same prices right across the States. There was huge wastage, but that was 'the price of doing business'.

What if I could change that? Nina thought. What if I could get Dragon to invest in another mainframe, a computer that could track what drugs sold where? If we had a clearer picture of the market …

Nina titled the project 'Customised Response'. Her phones buzzed incessantly and the mailcart stopped by her door five times a day as data she requested came flooding back. It was a mammoth task, and even harder than it had to be.

Simon and Tom kept pretty much to themselves. Nina's trouble was the support staff. There was no sisterly feeling at Dragon Chemical. The receptionists and secretaries, far from being pleased to see a woman executive, all resented her bitterly and let it show. They called her 'Ms Roth' and made it sound like an insult. They took for ever to do her filing and often did it so sloppily Nina found herself staying late to correct things.

But the major problem was her assistant.

Tracy Jones had been assigned to the three of them. A sexy-looking redhead with wild hair, short skirts and long nails, she hated having to work for a woman. Tom's letters and Simon's charts always came before the work Nina needed typing.

Nina didn't complain at first. She was new. But eventually she had to say something and told Tracy she wanted her reports assigned equal priority.

'They are,' Tracy insisted insolently, with a flick of her rosy curls. Nina flushed, hating the confrontation, but saw all the other girls in the pool slow down their typewriters so they could eavesdrop.

She knew she had to assert her authority.

'I'm sorry, Tracy, but I don't think so. I want these letters on my desk first thing tomorrow.'

'Yes, ma'am,' Tracy said icily.

The letters were delivered to her by mailcart at nine a.m. the next day. They had two spelling mistakes and a word Tipp-Exed out in each of them.

Gritting her teeth, Nina did it herself.

Three weeks into the deadline she was seriously behind. Her proposal needed detailed statistics, and she'd have to check it before it went off to Jax. If she gave it to Tracy on schedule, Nina realised, it would be handed in late or so messy she couldn't use it at all. Gerald Jax wasn't interested in excuses.

Besides, there *were* no excuses. Nina wanted to get to management, but right now she couldn't manage her own secretary! Tracy and all the others assumed a woman had no place being an executive. They preferred flirting with the boys and Nina was basically letting them get away with it.

The bright, polite schoolgirl in Nina shrank from appearing a bitch. She remembered how hard it had been when she started at Green Earth, and she had no desire to be anyone's boss from hell. But as the deadline got closer, she had no other choice.

On Friday Nina went down to the typing pool at eleven a.m., to find Tracy sitting at an empty typewriter, painting her nails. As Nina approached, she brazenly continued.

'Hello, Tracy. I need this report typed up today. It's got quite a few statistics,' Nina told her, laying the sheaf of neatly written notes on her desk. 'Do you think you could get it done for me?'

The girl barely glanced at her. 'Sorry, I'm too busy.'

Aware of the others watching her, Nina drew breath. 'How can you be too busy? Coffee break is over and you're painting your nails. *Whenever* I need something done, you're always too busy. I think the problem is that you just don't want to work for me.'

At that moment, all the girls in the pool stopped typing.

Tracy shrugged, without looking up. Then she turned to Maria, a hard-working Spanish girl who sat next to her. 'Maria, can you do this?'

Nina tapped the paperwork sharply. She was red faced, but her voice was firm. 'No, Tracy. You are my assistant and I want you to do it. I am leaving it on your desk and I'll be back for it at three. If it isn't done by then, I am going to fire you.'

'Oh, really,' Tracy said with a sneer.

'Try me,' said Nina.

There was complete silence as Nina walked back down the corridor. Her heart was hammering in her chest and her palms were sweating, but she held up her head. She could feel the eyes of all the typists boring into her back.

Nina tried to get on with her research. It was impossible to concentrate. She didn't eat at lunch and wondered what on earth she was going to do. Nina was a new hire, very junior, and already she was making waves, but it was a matter of principle and she knew nobody else could get her through it.

At five of three Nina marched down to the typing pool to find Tracy languidly tapping at her keyboard. One look at the paper told her this was a letter of Tom's. Nina's own project was resting on Tracy's desk, exactly where she'd left it.

The typing pool fell completely silent as Nina stood in front of her secretary.

Tracy shot Nina a defiant look.

'You haven't typed up my report,' Nina stated flatly. 'I gave express orders that it was to be ready by three. Is there a reason why you haven't done it?'

'I told you. I'm too busy,' Tracy said rudely.

'And I told you. You're fired,' Nina said. 'Collect your papers from Gary Bellman in Personnel.'

The room was so quiet she could hear the other girls breathing as they watched the confrontation.

'You can't do that. You don't have the right,' Tracy challenged her.

'I've just done it. If your desk isn't cleared in ten minutes security will throw you out,' Nina replied.

Then she turned on her heel and marched back to her office.

Breathing deeply to calm herself, Nina lifted the phone and dialled an extension in Human Resources. Her palm was clammy with sweat where she gripped the receiver.

'Gary? This is Nina Roth in Business Development,' she said when he answered the phone. 'I've just fired Tracy Jones.'

'Nina, you can't dismiss anybody. You don't have the authority,' Gary Bellman said, sounding worried.

'Gary, I have fired her,' Nina told him firmly. 'And I have fired her in front of thirty-five other secretarial staff.'

There was a long pause.

'In that case, she's fired,' said the personnel director.

That night, Nina could hardly sleep. She lay on her bed and stared into space. What if Tracy had needed the money? What if she herself had been responsible for not fixing the problem sooner?

But she knew that under the same circumstances, she'd do the same thing again. Tomorrow, if necessary.

Chapter 12

Hans Wolf was right. The amount of work it took to claw back just a few seconds on each race was staggering. That first day at Val d'Isère, even with the ferocious training she'd done that morning, Elizabeth still came third in the slalom. It didn't help that Jack Taylor watched at the finish line, and left without comment.

'I can't believe it,' Elizabeth said, heartsick with disappointment.

'*Ja*. You have a long way to go. Heidi does not give up the crown just because now you want it,' Wolf replied, but then he softened. 'You were only three seconds behind.'

'For ever!'

The old man smiled grimly. 'Listen to my little snow-leopard, who yesterday is calling five seconds nothing.'

Elizabeth nodded briskly, preparing to face the barrage of cameras for her post-race interview. 'Yeah, well. Today, things are different.'

Things certainly were different. As the World Cup continued across the Alps, the British team watched her transformation open mouthed. Ronnie Davis couldn't believe it was the same girl: Elizabeth rose early in the morning to jog, practised with Karen, and turned up to formal practice religiously. She apologised to him for being so bloody minded before.

'I was a jerk, Ron. I'm sorry. I'm paying for it now.'

'No problem,' said her coach, waving it aside. Ronnie was a bus-driver's son from the East End of London.

He'd never voted Tory and despised the upper classes, but Lady Elizabeth was sweating it so hard she'd almost changed his mind. 'You're Welsh. You're stubborn. Goes with the territory.'

'*Diolch* for nothing, *cariad bach*,' Elizabeth retorted, pulling her mane of shiny honey-blonde hair back from her face.

Ronnie whistled under his breath as she plunged off down another downhill. Prolonged exercise, sun and crisp mountain air made that girl more attractive every season. They were having to lay on extra security at the hotels to keep the reporters away. Back home, Britain was slumping further and further into recession, and his dazzling champion offered a total contrast. The Ski Club of Great Britain had reported a four hundred per cent increase in membership, especially from girls. Skiing holidays were selling out. He knew several travel agents had tacked posters of her young ladyship up in their offices.

This time she wasn't letting it swell her head, but they still had problems. If Elizabeth was ever going to get that gold medal, she needed to go an extra mile. Reluctantly, Ronnie concluded that it couldn't be with him.

It was all very well, Elizabeth turning up for practice. Trouble was, there wasn't much he could teach her. Now she was making an effort, her real talent was coming through.

She was leagues ahead of his other girls. She was leagues ahead of *him*.

Ronnie called the office back home and secured some extra funding. Then he called Hans Wolf.

'We want you to come in as coach for Liz Savage.'

A dry chuckle. '*Ach*, Ronnie. You know I am retired.'

Davis swallowed his pride. 'She needs more than I can give her, Hans. What's the point of you discovering her, if you don't see it through?'

'She's the world bronze medallist.'

'So fucking what? Come on, Hans. Don't muck me about. Are you up for it?'

Hans Wolf took over as Elizabeth's coach. It was the first time in her life she'd known what real work was. To her runs, he added heavy backpacks. In gym training he upped her weights. When she studied videos of Heidi and Louise, he made her write notes. The second an event was finished, Elizabeth barely had time to shower before she was being hustled on to a plane. If they got to the next stop ahead of time, Hans explained, there'd be an extra evening for practice runs.

'Don't I ever get a break?' Elizabeth gasped, as Hans rushed her away from the press after a downhill victory in Grindelwald.

'*Nein*. Plenty of time to sleep when you're dead,' Wolf told her briskly.

Travel, train, race. Travel, train, race. Elizabeth spent day after day lost in the brutal cycle of competition. The chic bars and glittering hotels she'd hung out at last year faded from view, replaced by an endless, interchangeable set of cable-cars, black runs and slalom poles. At night she dreamed about run layouts. On planes she fantasised about sleeping till noon. But in spite of the punishing pace, she never considered cutting back.

Motivation was easy to come by. It was right there in the stocky, skilful form of Heidi Laufen, twice World Champion, and the aerodynamic crouch of Louise Levier, her heir apparent. The commentators called them unbeatable.

Elizabeth knew better. She sweated, strained, pushed her way forward, eroding the lead. Bronze turned to silver, then to gold. In one punishing month she wiped out Louise's lead. Now there was only Heidi to chase. The two girls struggled for supremacy across Europe.

Sometimes Heidi topped the table, then Elizabeth, then Heidi again.

Elizabeth found she suddenly wanted victory desperately. She was twenty years old, with nothing to show for her life. She didn't even have a degree, thanks to Tony's attitude. In the World Cup, her breeding and her bank account meant nothing. Talent was the only thing that counted. And she wanted to show she was worth something. She wanted to be the best.

Basically, Elizabeth admitted to herself, she wanted to be like Jack Taylor. She couldn't stand him, but she had to admire him. Hans forced her to watch tape after tape of Taylor's victories, pointing out the speed, the technique, the mastery.

Jack Taylor wasn't just poetry in motion. He was a symphony, an epic. He had blasted through the sport like an F-14 jet fighter. Jack might have come from nowhere, Elizabeth thought, but my God, the guy is ruthless on a pair of skis.

The Swiss, the Austrians, the Scandinavians, the French – none of them knew what had hit them. Over and over, the Stars and Stripes flew on the winner's podium.

'I cannot understand it,' the Swedish coach had shrugged. 'He is a freak. After all, there is no skiing in Texas.'

He's the best, but doesn't he know it, Elizabeth thought, annoyed. Jack bloody Taylor, with his magna cum laude from Harvard and his blatant sexuality. She'd heard the stories from some of the other girls, and tried to dismiss Taylor as a womaniser. What else could he be, with that Southern drawl like slow-pouring treacle, and that cruel, sexy mouth?

She thought about Jack Taylor a lot. It bugged her that she thought about him so much. Though she pretended not to care, his derision at Val d'Isère cut her to the quick. Elizabeth knew the American was a one-off, a once-in-a-generation kind of talent. She wanted his respect. She wanted his approval. The bastard could snub her all he liked, but she wanted him to rate her. As an equal.

When the women's and the men's events coincided, Jack Taylor turned up to the female event to cheer on Kim Ferrell and Holly Gideon, the US team. At those races, Elizabeth tried to squeeze a little more excellence from her performance. She could see Taylor watching her as she crouched forward, schussing over the finish lines. His handsome face was assessing, taking notes. But though she took three wins and a second in front of him, he never offered her a word of encouragement.

It became ever clearer that Elizabeth stood a chance, and the British media went nuts. The 'battle of the slopes' was the second favourite tabloid story, right behind the rumours that Prince Charles had a thing for Lady Diana Spencer.

Hans kept her away from the media, but that only made them chase her more.

'These people are fools,' he snorted, when he caught Elizabeth reading *The Times* at the airport. The headline 'Lightning Strikes' showed a glowing Elizabeth after a four-second slalom win at Val Gardena. 'They think you are good *last* year.'

He couldn't afford her to relax one millimetre. It was the final stage of the Cup, and things were too close to call.

'Ronnie Davis called the hotel. CBS wants the team to go on *Good Morning, America*,' Elizabeth told him, hopefully.

She wouldn't mind becoming well known in the States. Maybe it would help convince the FIS to let her do their marketing. Or be leverage to change Dad's mind about Dragon.

'The team, indeed! They want your ladyship, *nicht wahr*? Certainly not.' Wolf snorted with disgust. 'We have only two more races, and you are just one point ahead of Fräulein Laufen. The only Americans you mix with will be Taylor and Kowalski.'

Elizabeth felt her heart skip a beat under her Jean Muir suit. 'What did you say?'

Boarding for first-class passengers was announced, and they stood up, picking up their hand-luggage. Wolf glanced at his protégée, a smartly dressed young woman, beautiful, vibrant, her hair flowing loosely about her shoulders, her elegant hand resting on a Gucci purse. Her forest-green eyes sparkled like snow in the sun.

'They are already at Kitzbühel for the slalom. Thursday they ski the Hahnenkamm.'

'We've got slalom Tuesday, downhill Wednesday.'

'*Ja*, and I have asked Kowalski if you can train with him Wednesday morning. He agreed.'

'And Jack Taylor?'

'Taylor always trains with Kowalski. Rick is the American number two,' Wolf reminded her. 'He will not alter his plans for you.'

Elizabeth handed her boarding card to the attendant, smiling.

'You are excited, *Liebchen*,' the old man teased. 'Just make sure you keep your eyes on the snow. Taylor is very good looking, no?'

'No.' Elizabeth sounded dismissive. 'Jack's the best in the world. *I'm* the best in the world. Who else would I ski with?'

'*Natürlich,*' Hans said, grinning.

The final slalom of the women's World Cup was a nail-biter. Girl after girl swooped off from the summit, planting their ski-poles, turning, planting again, control and speed in brilliant balance. Kitzbühel cheered the Austrians and Louise Levier, the Swiss now certain to take bronze. But it was Heidi and Elizabeth everybody was waiting for.

Elizabeth said a prayer at the starting gate and thrust forward. Three hours of practice, days of layout study, a week of videos, all down to these few minutes. Plant, turn. Stick, slice. The cheering crowd lining the run, deafening her with whistles and cowbells and ululating shrieks, urged her forwards. Out of the corners of her eyes she saw Union Jacks, even the Red Dragon flag of Wales. She ignored it all. There was nothing registering except the flagpoles and the snow. Concentrating furiously, her technique was perfect but she lost a little speed. Elizabeth shot through the finishing line one point five seconds behind her best time on this course. She led the field comfortably.

Hans slapped her on the shoulder and Elizabeth turned to the cameras to give her reaction. She kept it short. Nothing to do but wait for Heidi.

Kim Ferrell took fourth place for the US and Kate Cox came in eighth for Britain, a terrific result for her. Elizabeth congratulated her warmly.

Finally, to roars of approval from the Swiss in the crowd, Heidi Laufen was called to the start. Time seemed to stop for Elizabeth as she reached the first gate and twisted through it cleanly. Slicing, sticking and lunging, Heidi tore through the flagpoles. White plumes of snow sprayed up behind the edges of her skis. She wasn't as exact as Elizabeth, but she was quicker. With each gate Elizabeth felt her heart sink. She didn't need to look at the clock to know Heidi's pace; she could see it in her rhythm. Laufen was letting go and she was fast.

Heidi came bombing through the finish line over a second ahead.

Elizabeth could feel the eyes of her coach, her team and the press burning into her back as she walked over to shake the World Champion's hand. Now they were level. It would all depend on the downhill tomorrow – the legendary Hahnenkamm, the fastest, toughest, most dangerous run on earth.

At the side of the ropes, Jack Taylor, looking stunning in black jeans and a sweater, was standing with the US team. Elizabeth walked across and pumped Kim's hand. 'Nice racing.'

'You too,' the redhead said. 'Bad luck. Heidi was on top of her form, right then. Didn't you think so, Jack?'

Jack Taylor shrugged, looking straight at Elizabeth. His eyes flickered over her body, but their expression was unfathomable.

'You could have done better,' he said.

Elizabeth stiffened. She pulled up to her full height.

'And I will. Tomorrow.'

Wednesday morning, Elizabeth was up before her wake-up call. She'd tried to rest but she hadn't slept much. The thought that everything was riding on this afternoon had been too exciting for sleep. She only hoped that Heidi Laufen had been similarly affected.

Quickly, Elizabeth selected a training suit in scarlet Lycra and began to get dressed. Outside the windows of her hotel suite the massive mountain peaks were jagged silhouettes against the early-morning light. A telltale brightness in the sky let her know there'd been a fresh snowfall during the night. Adrenalin pumped through her. Today would be sudden death; she was challenging the world's best skier on the world's most dangerous course. It had a hospital purpose-built at the bottom, to cater to the dead and wounded the mountain regularly claimed; victims of the Mausfalle, the sheer drop you hit just after the starting gate, or the 180° Panorama turn, or the plummeting dive of the Steilhang ...

Enough. Enough, Elizabeth told herself, selecting her training skis. Practise first.

It would be a great warm-up to the downhill, to show that son-of-a-bitch Jack Taylor just what she was made of.

Before she headed out the door, Elizabeth spritzed herself with Chanel No. 5 and slicked a dash of Elizabeth Arden over the sunblock on her lips.

Not only was she going to ski the pants off him, she was going to do it in style.

Rick Kowalski had arranged to meet her at the top of the Resterhöhe. Seven thousand feet above sea level, it was the highest ski area in Kitzbühel, guaranteeing no problems with the snow. This morning he needn't have worried, Elizabeth thought as she leaned back in the cable-car. The fresh fall in the night had blanketed the whole resort, and the peaks and valleys lay covered with a thick, unmarked blanket of soft white velvet. The forecast had been for clear skies, but she was sure there was more to come. Clouds were gathering darkly behind the mountains. She prayed no blizzard would delay the race.

The car clanked to a halt and Elizabeth stepped out, hefting her skis on to the flattened snow. She was ready for some serious training. They would be heading off-piste; apart from the Hahnenkamm there were no black runs at Kitzbühel hard enough for a world-class skier.

She looked around for Kowalski, but couldn't see him. Maybe he was out there wearing an ivory suit, or something. Elizabeth cupped her hands over her mouth and yelled.

'Rick?'

Suddenly, from behind her, a black-suited figure shot out of nowhere and sliced to a halt.

Elizabeth jumped out of her skin.

He raised dark goggles and regarded her steadily.

'Jesus Christ, Jack. You scared me,' Elizabeth said angrily. 'Where the hell did you come from? Where's Rick?'

'Good morning to you, too, ma'am,' Taylor replied. The Texan drawl was cold. 'Kowalski couldn't make it. He's in bed.'

'Really.' Elizabeth's nerves made her snappy. 'Too much *Glühwein* last night? I'd have thought even you Americans might give the partying a rest two days before your last downhill.'

Jack's eyes narrowed with anger. He paused, then said calmly, 'Actually, he has flu. He's in bed on doctor's orders, so he stands a chance of competing tomorrow.'

Elizabeth blushed. 'Oh, OK. I'm sorry.'

'He asked me to come train with you. Rick never breaks a commitment.'

'I said I was sorry.'

'And there's nothing Rick could teach you about partying, my lady. Not from what I hear.'

She bent down and locked her boots into their bindings, forcing back the reply. She was here to train, not to fight Jack Taylor.

'My name is Elizabeth, Jack. Are we going to ski, or do you prefer talking?'

Taylor studied her a moment, then lifted his stick and pointed off down the mountainside towards a dark pine forest.

'Brad found a route for me yesterday. It's got a sixty-five-degree sheer drop, a tough mogul run, some tree skiing, lots of powder on the straight.' He shrugged. 'Reasonably challenging.'

That meant white-knuckle terror, Elizabeth thought. A shiver of spine-chilling pleasure rushed through her.

'I'll want you to stick with me. There are crevasses and the new snow will have covered some of them. We'll be going close to a lot of mountain edges; concealed boulders, outcrops, stuff like that. Think you can handle it?'

'Hey. I do have a little snowcraft, Taylor.'

'You want to train with me? You *follow* me.' He was uncompromising. 'I'm not explaining to some English lord how I watched his daughter ski off the edge of a precipice.'

'I'm the best female in the world.'

'You're not as good as me,' Jack Taylor said flatly.

Enraged, Elizabeth glared at him, but Taylor held her gaze calmly, refusing to back down. He was resting his huge body on his ski-pole, dark brown eyes studying her impassively.

He was right and she knew it.

'You win.' Elizabeth swallowed her pride. 'I'll be right behind you. But this better give me a workout.'

'Hey, Princess,' Jack said, and now his look was sexual, flickering over the tight red Lycra, stripping, assessing, lingering on her breasts. 'You haven't been trained at all. After this, the Hahnenkamm's gonna look like a nursery slope.'

He pulled down his goggles and pushed off to the right, schussing swiftly down towards the forest. Elizabeth followed, gathering her body into a crouch. The snow glittered like crystal dust in the rosy dawn light, arching up behind her skis in a feathery spray. The air had the crisp, clean sparkle of high altitude. She gathered her body into an aerodynamic crouch, skis close together, picking up speed. Jack's tracks were deep tramlines on the virgin slope, their smooth, sharp angles displaying his skill like a signature. Thrusting harder, she caught up with him. His black-clad figure was aiming straight for the forest; he said nothing to her, was acting like she wasn't there. Angrily, Elizabeth ski'd closer, crowding him, until there were just a few inches between them. Taylor swung sharply left. Elizabeth followed. He immediately took a hard right. She matched him, inch for inch. Fighting. Challenging. Competing.

Without so much as a glance at her, Jack leaned forward into his crouch and disappeared. Gasping, Elizabeth found herself plunging down a sheer icy curve that had looked like an ordinary ridge a second ago. Instinctively she righted herself and hugged the gradient, while her stomach somersaulted.

You son-of-a-bitch! She was barrelling into the schuss now, beside him again, but Jack tilted away left, bringing his skis together. Why was he doing that? And then she saw it – two patches of dark shadow, bridging white ground barely two feet across. Shade like that could be covering a ravine, a crevasse. You would plunge down a hundred feet of solid ice to your death. Elizabeth broke into a cold sweat as she swung her body violently, making sure she was behind him, not beside. The broad muscles of Taylor's back, skiing without even a hint of tension, seemed to taunt her as he schussed coyly across the strip of solid ground. Elizabeth followed, dry mouthed with fear. Now she was across!

Her heart was hammering against her ribcage. Her palms were clammy under her gloves.

He wants me to beg him to ease off! she thought. Jack Taylor thinks I'll go crawling up to him, admitting I can't keep up with him! I'll die of a heart attack first, you bastard!

She settled into a racing position, chasing Taylor's handsome silhouette in front of her.

'So, how are you doing, honey?' Jack asked as she drew level. 'All warmed up?'

Warmed up? 'You said you've ski'd this before.'

'Yes, ma'am.' The Texan drawl was relaxed.

'So when does it start getting hard?' Elizabeth asked casually. Two could play that game.

Taylor looked across at Elizabeth, imagining that strong, sexy body curled up naked on the rug beside his chalet hearth. She was stunning. It was turning him on, watching her move. If only she wasn't such an arrogant bitch.

Jack didn't want to admit he was changing his mind about Lady Elizabeth Savage. He'd been determined to despise her – just a haughty British piece of ass who was squandering her talent, dissing her team-mates and turning on the charm for the cameras – but it was hard to dispute that her attitude had changed. And despite the fact that he'd rated her as competent but boring – a robot in rainbow Lycra – this year she'd been something else. Heidi Laufen had perfect technique, but Elizabeth Savage was inspirational. Fluid and fast. One of the best he'd ever seen.

This run would have beaten most guys he knew by now.

'Right about now,' Jack said, and shot over a mogul, executing a perfect helicopter spin. He plunged full-throttle towards the pine forest which now loomed up over the second ridge, shooting past a triangular sign with an exclamation mark on it. Elizabeth could only make out the word '*VERBOTEN*' as she raced forwards. Then she brought her knees together with a crash. Taylor had headed down the steepest, largest mogul field she'd ever seen. Her breath coming short, Elizabeth twisted, jumped, landed, twisted. Every muscle was shrieking for mercy. Jack Taylor was a big, strong man, and jumps he took easily Elizabeth strained to clear.

Panting for breath, she righted herself at the foot of the run. Taylor cut an S-bend between a boulder and a shadow patch, heading down the mountain. Elizabeth followed grimly as he made for a boulder, shot over it, and soared into a twenty-foot jump due south, landing cleanly and hurtling forwards.

I don't get it, Elizabeth thought as she flew into the air. Where's the break in the trees?

Jesus! Oh, Jesus! There isn't one! That maniac is heading straight into the forest!

She was going too fast to think. Jack shot into the trees and Elizabeth, terrified, shot after him, hugging his trail as close as she could. Suddenly the bright glitter of the mountainside disappeared, and she was swallowed up by green, scented gloom. Elizabeth was dimly aware of the fresh snow piled on the branches, the twigs and cones snapping under her skis. Instinct took over as she lunged, ski'd, and thrust around the trunks, ducking under branches, making the fastest, sharpest turns she'd ever done in her life. No slalom ever invented could match up to this, and you took the slalom slow, not at Warp Factor Nine! Elizabeth tried to beat back the rising panic. Follow Jack. He's got the trail. She kept her eyes on those wide shoulders, dodging rocks, bushes, branches. A crash at this speed would snap her legs like matchsticks, wrench a shoulder from its socket! Not only would she lose the World Cup, she might never ski again!

Then, blessedly, there was light. The trees thinned. She swerved right, left, right again and schussed out on to the clear snow.

Jack Taylor had pulled up a hundred yards in front of her, resting on his poles and nodding in admiration.

'Congratulations. That was some sharp skiing.'

Elizabeth sliced to a stop and ripped off her goggles. Scalding hot tears burst out of her eyes, cooling instantly against her flushed cheeks. She was sobbing, hyperventilating.

'You bastard, you absolute bastard! I hate you!' she spat at him.

'Hey, come on. You did fine—'

'Is that your idea of a joke, Jack Taylor? Your stupid macho games could have fucking killed me!'

'Honey, I wouldn't have taken you any place you couldn't handle. I've seen how you ski.' He smiled at her. 'That's why I insisted you follow me. I was going first, so if you stuck behind me you'd be fine.'

'Is that right.' She wiped the back of her hand across her eyes, furious with him, furious with herself for breaking down in front of him. Jack stretched out a hand towards her, but she was still seeing red. Angrily she shoved his arm away and pulled up her goggles.

'Elizabeth, I'm sorry. I—'

'Jack, do me a favour and get lost,' Elizabeth snarled, and thrust off violently, skiing away from him down the mountainside as fast as she could.

'Wait! Elizabeth, stop!'

Taylor's voice floated down towards her, but, still sobbing, Elizabeth ignored it. She had no idea where she was, but the lights of Kitzbühel in the valley below gave her some sense of direction. She would schuss to the next ski area and ride a lift back home. Get to the hotel, calm herself down before the Hahnenkamm.

Jack had stopped shouting, but she could hear the faint hiss of his skis some way behind. Glancing round, she saw him settle into a crouch, as though desperate to reach her. As he saw her look at him, Taylor shook one pole frantically. She ignored him. Now he could try catching up with *her*.

She was hugging the mountainside, following the steepest gradient down. Powder snow plumed around her. The world was returning to what she knew and loved – whiteness and silence – except for—

A faint rumbling sound like a growling stomach.

Nervously, Elizabeth looked up. Not thunder! A blizzard was all she needed.

The sky was still cloudy, but calm. And yet there it was again. Louder this time. Out of the corner of one eye, Elizabeth saw a rocky outcrop quiver. A pile of snow loosened and dropped heavily on to the slope.

Elizabeth slowed in an S-bend, suddenly petrified. Her face drained of blood.

There was only one explanation for that sound.

Jack Taylor was bombing after her at a speed which suggested he'd already figured it out.

Oh, Christ! She didn't know where she was! Where this slope led! If it was a precipice, she was dead! Elizabeth turned to the right, back the way she'd come, and pushed off with all her strength. She could see Taylor do the same—

And then it came! A deep cracking sound, a slow boom of breaking rock, with the ground under her feet quivering like jelly, and small pebbles and twigs falling from the cliff-face behind her!

Avalanche!

Elizabeth's body flooded with adrenalin. She pointed her skis straight ahead, crouching as low as she could safely go. Skiing for her life. Racing the snow.

Jack was heading hard right, motioning for her to follow. He knew the danger, and he came after me anyway, she thought miserably. Jack had risked his life to try and save her, and now she'd probably got him killed.

Oh, God, I'm sorry, Jack, I'm so sorry …

Her eyes were blurry with tears of terror. Sobbing, gasping, she blinked them away. She had to be brave! If she lost control, she was history.

Abruptly Taylor's black-clad figure stopped and swung round, skiing towards her. Elizabeth schussed frantically forwards. My God, don't come any further this way! she thought desperately. But he was barrelling her way, the heavy body plunging forwards.

As he reached her, another huge rumble shook the mountainside. Elizabeth's head whipped round to see a vast, menacing wall of white, piled eighteen feet high, sliding steadily down the rock face above them, gathering speed and size with every foot. Mesmerised, she gazed at the tidal wave of snow, freezing like a rabbit caught in a car's headlights.

Jack Taylor's big hand jerked her back to reality.

'You shouldn't have come for me! Jack, I'm sorry,' Elizabeth gasped.

'Tell me later, OK, sugar? Let's go. This way,' Jack said shortly, and jetted off to the right. Elizabeth followed blindly.

'This slope leads to a cliff edge!' Taylor yelled, as they bombed down the mountain together. 'We need to get to the right! You have to outrun it! Point your skis straight down and just wing it, OK?'

'OK!' Elizabeth managed. She copied him, pointing her ski-tips straight downhill, leaning into the gradient, sticks tucked under the arms. Downhill racing was instinct and gravity. If you were thinking about it, you weren't going fast enough.

'Get to the forest!' Taylor shouted.

Elizabeth headed after him, rocketing towards another grove of trees. Her body was soaking in sweat, but it wasn't enough. Behind her the avalanche had hit the slope and was cruising forwards, its mammoth weight hissing as the air rushed past the towering snow-wall. She didn't need to look round to see how fast it was gaining – a black shadow loomed over the ground in front of her, silent as death.

Jack was nearly at the trees now. She had two hundred yards to go. To her left, the slope finished abruptly, dropping down into a rocky chasm a mile deep. The avalanche was closer, closer, gently nudging her towards the precipice. She wasn't going to make it. Desperately, Elizabeth pushed to the right, towards the trees at the edge of the cliff. Jack was standing three yards into the forest, his arms wrapped round a tree trunk. The forest could resist twenty foot of snow, but she couldn't! The breath sobbed in Elizabeth's throat as she saw snow spattering across her skis, was engulfed in the shadow of the avalanche. She'd failed by a few feet, she was going to die. Air shot out of her lungs as the snow hit her, freezing, heavy, and she waited to be swept into the void—

But something held her back. A hand, *Jack*'s hand, his vast palm clamping her left wrist, strong fingers like a vice around it.

Elizabeth's body was flung forwards, her skis knocked off balance, right pole ripped from her grasp, but she didn't fall. Jack Taylor was holding on to her wrist with a mighty grip. Her arm burned agonisingly as it took the full weight of her body. She couldn't scream, because her mouth was muffled with snow. For a few horrible seconds, the avalanche trundled over her back, pressing her down into the slope. She thought she might pass out from the pain and terror, but bit her lip to keep herself conscious.

And then suddenly there was light, the weight bearing down on her slid away, and as she sucked air into her lungs the wave of snow teetered slightly and crashed slowly, unhurriedly, into the ravine.

Jack pulled her up, away from the cliff edge. Her shoulder socket screamed and she scrambled forwards with her legs. Taylor was holding on to a tree trunk with his left hand, his right hand clutching her. She could see every muscle in his arms rigid with the effort. He had been a human bridge, clutching her against the force of the snow.

Elizabeth flung herself into his arms.

'You didn't let go, you didn't let go!' She was crying, her whole body trembling against him. 'Jack, you saved my life!'

'We all make mistakes,' Jack Taylor said.

Then he tilted her face up to his, and kissed her, hard.

Chapter 13

Jack bore down on her, kissing her frozen mouth open, the tip of his tongue tracing a fiery line across her bottom lip. One arm was circling her back, pulling her to him, and one was cupping her ass and sliding up and down her thigh. Elizabeth felt burning warmth rush through her icy flesh as his body warmed hers. His chest was rock hard, his strength incredible. Jack was sucking snow crystals from her mouth as he kissed her and Elizabeth found herself flooded with a different kind of heat, a wet rush of lust that curled like smoke in the pit of her stomach.

She'd never been with a man like this. All the suave, Eurotrash men she'd ever dated with their flowery compliments and sexual proficiency had never affected her like this man who was crushing her to him. Jack was handsome, brilliant and fearless. He was also a stubborn, ruthless bastard.

Elizabeth told herself to go slow, but her muscles were melting with longing. She felt weak against such raw male strength. Pleasure fluttered across her groin. Despite herself, she moaned softly at the back of her throat, pressing herself against him.

Taylor's hand immediately slid up over the tight, cold red Lycra of her skisuit, his huge paw brushing her breasts softly, teasing the tips of her nipples. Elizabeth gasped as a burst of heat exploded between her thighs. Glancing down, she saw the outline of his erection and her eyes widened. He was massive, not just long but thick, too. It frightened her a little.

What did you expect, with a man this size? Elizabeth asked herself, but then Jack moved forward to cover her, pressing her back against the tree roots. The rough bark prickled against her back, breaking the tension just long enough for Elizabeth to gather her thoughts.

You nearly died. You're not thinking straight. You can't sleep with Jack Taylor! You only just met him!

Firmly she pushed against his chest, shaking her head. 'Jack, no.'

He leaned back a fraction. 'What's wrong, sugar?'

'We can't do this.'

'We can do anything we want,' Taylor said. His brown eyes were full of hunger for her, glittering with desire. Elizabeth dropped her eyes. She couldn't look at him.

'You just saved my life, Jack. I – I'm not clear-headed. I don't even know you!' She was stammering out explanations. 'And we have to get back to Kitzbühel! I've lost a ski-pole and I'm racing in three hours!'

Jack stared at her for a second, then sighed and stood up. He stood with his back to her and took a deep breath, trying to stamp out the fire blazing in his groin. Liz Savage wanted him. He could feel it in the hot flush of her skin, the tantalisingly erect nipples. His cock was so hard it ached. Jesus, how he wanted her. He wanted to nail her right there on the snow, peel that teasing Lycra off her and just fuck her brains out. Kiss her mouth off. Stroke her and lick her until she begged him to take her …

'Jack?' Elizabeth asked, scrambling to her feet.

'All right, Elizabeth. I'm not pushing you.'

'Thank you,' she said, hoping she didn't sound disappointed.

Taylor gestured to her boots. 'Fix your bindings and we'll get back.' He unhooked the ski-pole from her left wrist and handed her his own pair.

'I don't need these—'

'Take them,' Jack said.

She didn't argue.

When they reached the Pass Thurn skiing area, Ronnie Davis and the other British girls were standing by the gondola station, waiting for them.

Elizabeth glided to a halt and offered Taylor back his ski-poles. He hadn't said a single word to her all the way down.

'Right on time,' Ronnie said. 'We're going to head back to the hotel. So, Jack, how was she?'

'She was the best female skier I've even seen,' Jack said, without looking at her.

'Thanks for helping me practise,' Elizabeth said, blushing.

'My pleasure, ma'am,' Taylor replied softly. He nodded to the British team, turned, and schussed away down the mountainside.

'God, he's so gorgeous,' Janet sighed.

'That guy was made in heaven,' Kate added wistfully.

'I see you lost a pole, Liz. How was the training?' Ronnie asked.

Elizabeth's eyes were following Jack's tiny black figure as it plunged away to the south.

'Oh, pretty quiet,' she said.

When they got back to the hotel there was a telegram for Elizabeth. Tony wished her luck. The dry, restrained language was a message from another world. The Cup was so intense, so focused, that Elizabeth had almost forgotten about the real world below the mountain peaks. She was certain that her success this year would be enough for the FIS, but still ... Dragon was the family company. Dragon was what she wanted. It was 1980 now; maybe she could change Tony's mind ...

Just one more reason not to fail today. More pressure to perform.

Hans Wolf found her clutching the crumpled scrap of paper when he arrived in her room. He pulled it out of her grasp and tossed it on to the bed.

'Tony and Monica wrote.'

'So I see.' Wolf scowled. 'Today you do not need distractions.'

'My father will be so pleased if I win this,' Elizabeth told him.

'Child. You cannot control your father. Business is business, but skiing is life,' the old man told her, so seriously Elizabeth had to smile. 'Think about your company tomorrow, *Liebchen*. Today is for the mountain. Today is for *me*.'

'Oh, Hans, you've been so good to me,' Elizabeth said tearfully. 'What if I let you down? I screwed up yesterday.'

'The only way you let me down is if you do not try. Do your best. Not for me, for your father, even the gold. Just because you are a skier, and this is the greatest race in the world.'

The foot of the course was a zoo. Press, radio and TV crews from all over Europe were jostling for position, shouting out reports in ten different languages. Elizabeth waited with the others to hear her draw – it might be anywhere in the top fifteen numbers, the earlier the better. Heidi Laufen was drawn number three to thunderous applause from the Swiss in the crowd. Elizabeth was drawn number fourteen.

She shrugged elegantly to the BBC cameras, but she was very disappointed. Fourteenth versus third. A bad, bad position. A bad omen?

Looking graceful, polished and stunning in her signature rainbow suit, Elizabeth tried not to show her nerves.

It was always bad before a race, but this time she had eels writhing in her stomach. A few hours ago she'd been close to death. She'd lost an easy slalom yesterday. Heidi Laufen was hitting perfect form.

Her parents were watching, Hans was watching, the world was watching ...

'How's it going?'

Elizabeth jumped out of her skin.

'Jack, don't sneak up on me like that!'

'I wasn't sneaking, baby. You were miles away.'

Jack Taylor was wearing dark jeans, cowboy boots and a black windcheater with the Stars and Stripes embossed on the pocket. Goggles had been replaced by black Wayfarers. He looked just as impressive off skis as on.

The memory of his hands on her breasts sent a stab of wanting right through her. Under the sheer Lycra, her nipples tightened.

She saw Taylor watching them.

'It's cold, isn't it?' Elizabeth said quickly.

'No,' Jack said, giving her a lazy smile. The sun was blazing down on the slopes.

Elizabeth blushed and tried to cover herself. 'I got number fourteen,' she said quickly.

'I heard. But it don't matter.'

'What do you mean, it doesn't matter? I—'

'Forests, ravines, avalanches,' Jack said, cutting her off. 'Remember? This is a walk in the park.'

'For you.'

'For both of us,' Jack replied. His easy air was infuriating.

'Oh yeah?' Elizabeth snapped. 'That's just great, Jack. Anything else?'

'Yes, there is.' He touched the side of her waist, pressing her skin. 'You were lying up there, sugar. You do know me.'

132

An official marched up and tapped her on the elbow. 'You should go to the start gate now, my lady.'

'Elizabeth,' Jack said.

'What?'

He looked her right in the face. 'Just ski. Everything else is talk.'

Heidi Laufen made the run of her life. Jumping, schussing, hugging the treeline on the Stemmle stretch. It must have been perfect snow for her, Elizabeth thought jealously, as she heard the shrieks of joy, the football whistles, the ringing cowbells drifting up from below. The TV screen outside the start gate told its own story. Heidi made a textbook run. Dismayed, Elizabeth watched the spinning numbers freeze as she shot through the finish line. A new record. Position: first.

Waiting was eternity. Elizabeth took deep breaths, tried to stay calm. She studied the TV, watching the other top seeds, trying to get a feel for the course. Kim Ferrell came in second for the US. Then Louise Levier pushed her back to third. The Austrian and French champions were quick, too, but Heidi held firm at the head of the table, four seconds clear of Levier.

Then finally her number was called. Instructions, technique, layouts raced through her mind as she settled into her starting crouch, waiting for the bell. Trying to remember everything …

The countdown finished. Three, two, one …

And then, as Elizabeth thrust off down the mountain, Jack Taylor's voice drowned out the theory. *Just ski*.

The run fell away under her, a steep drop before the first two gates. Sharp swings, right, left – and now she was hitting the Mausfalle, sheer ice plummeting down, her stomach flipping over as she hit the hundred-and-fifty-foot jump. If she turned right she'd jet into the trees. Flying by pure instinct, Elizabeth ski'd straight ahead.

133

She was going too fast for thought. She hit the Panorama turn like a bullet – 180° left – throwing herself into it with her whole body, dragging herself round. The run soared over a hill and she twisted rightwards, ready for the Steilhang – hard left, then down through the forest, reaching the Woodcutter's Path. Her head rattled inside her helmet, the sounds of the shrieking crowds deafening her. Now the Stemmle stretch – if you played safe here you'd slow right down. Elizabeth swung hard towards the net, hugging the line, going 140 km per hour. A crash at this speed could maim or kill, but she felt no fear. She was soaring. Off at the Alte Schneise – nearly over, but here you could drop precious seconds if you lost position. Elizabeth held her crouch rock solid, every muscle screaming as she rode the bumps – Larcheschuss, swerve right – a huge jump by the Hausberg! Elizabeth took it high and hard. Landing swiftly, poles tucked under her arms, she could see the finish – a racing crouch down the Zielschluss, she was almost prostrate now …

She fired past the finish line, heart ricocheting under her chest, and sliced to a clean halt.

Panting, Elizabeth tore off her helmet and spun round, as the press did, as Louise did, as Heidi did, waiting for the announcement. She'd been fast. But how fast?

There was a second's silence as the dry Austrian tones announced the time.

Then pandemonium. Cameras flashing, reporters thrusting forwards, Hans fighting to get to her, and Elizabeth burst into tears.

She was twenty years old. She had just won the World Cup.

As she was swallowed up by TV cameras, Elizabeth caught sight of Jack Taylor, hanging back by the netting.

He nodded once, calmly. And then they both smiled.

Chapter 14

Tony Savage stirred restlessly in his bed. The girl in front of him looked as pretty this morning as she had last night – slim, silky legs, large breasts, glossy hair the colour of candied chestnuts – but he felt no desire. He was done, and it was six a.m.

He slipped carefully out of bed. Camilla didn't stir; he didn't want her to spoil things by waking up and starting to talk. She was a great lay, but that braying voice annoyed him. Not to mention the whining she was likely to do with it.

Tony dressed quickly. He kept one eye speculatively on the fuzz between Camilla's legs, but his mind was already elsewhere. His research team were presenting today on slimming drugs. It was the holy grail of pharmaceuticals. The first firm to develop a safe slimming drug would own the biggest moneyspinner since aspirin. Conventional wisdom was that it couldn't be done, but Tony didn't believe that. And then there was Elizabeth. Her demands to work at Dragon were getting more insistent, and this time, she had some leverage. She was World Champion; famous. If she made a fuss, the press would notice it. Run stories. Embarrass him. Dredge up the past …

A quick burst of anger sizzled through him. Blackmail, it was blackmail. Liz wouldn't let it go. Standing there in Kitzbühel, a gold medal round her neck, defying him. Like Louise …

With an effort Tony pulled his mind away and fastened his cufflinks. Nothing for it, he'd have to fob her off.

Maybe a taste of work would actually calm Elizabeth down. Switzerland had settled her, hadn't it? And there was Jack Taylor, a Texan, lots of money, Harvard. Apparently interested. He could do worse; Taylor was no duke, but then again, America was thousands of miles away. If he could pack DeFries's bastard off to the South, maybe he could forget about her. Those Southern men kept their women in line. Yes, maybe it would be expedient to keep Elizabeth sweet, for once.

Tony's elbow knocked a crystal champagne flute on to the ground. There was a dull thud on the thick carpet, but it was enough to wake Camilla. He sighed as she propped herself up sleepily, magnificent tits swaying slightly as she turned to accuse him.

'Darling, you're not leaving already! It's only, my God, it's only six.' The horsy Berkshire tones turned plaintive. 'You were going to leave without saying goodbye ...'

'I didn't want to wake you,' Tony said coldly.

'When will I see you again?'

'I'm not sure. I'll call you today.'

'When?'

'When I can,' Tony said, and let himself out of the suite. He could shower and shave at the office; there was always a freshly pressed outfit ready for him there.

Downstairs in the lobby Tony settled the bill. 'Have breakfast delivered to my guest at half-seven.' He wanted her out of there, but there was no point in being too harsh. Breakfast was a neat way to say it.

'Very good, my lord.' The receptionist's face was as blank as a discreet British hotelier's could be.

'Send up some champagne and some flowers. Not roses.'

'Yes, m'lord. Any message?'

'No,' Tony said, passing over his gold Amex.

As he strode out to a waiting taxi, the clerk shook his head in admiration. No false names, separate suites or embarrassment for Caerhaven. You had to give it to his lordship, he was a cool bastard. Flowers and champagne; he wondered lasciviously just how the latest bit of fluff had earned them.

'Where to, guv?'

Tony relaxed slightly as the cab drew away from the Ritz and headed down Piccadilly. At this time in the morning traffic was sparse; they should be on the South Bank in less than ten minutes. He made a mental note to ring Camilla before lunch and finish with her. A pair of diamond earrings, a line about feeling guilt towards Monica, that should do it. He was bored of her; she was clingy and tiresome when she wasn't performing. And good as she was, he'd had better. She wouldn't cut up rough if she knew what was good for her. Her father worked for one of his subsidiaries, her brother for another. Anyway, Camilla was pliant and nervy, another reason he'd picked her.

Tony had other business this morning. First, a quick call to Los Angeles, to check in with Jax, out on the West Coast. Get the vibe on New York; the stock was jittery on the Street and he wanted to know why. Also, to see if their latest crop of bright boys had come up with anything in the initial brainstorming period.

The Dragon building loomed massive in the pre-dawn twilight. Tony paid the cab and stepped into the deserted place, nodding at the security guard's obsequious greeting. He ordered coffee, toast, marmalade and crisp bacon sent up from the kitchen and then took the executive elevator to his private office. It was good to get in early; it added to his intoxicating sense of control. Today the *frisson* of power was particularly enjoyable. He felt lustful. Wondered about Camilla's replacement. Whoever she might be.

*

Nina walked in to work feeling nervous. She knew she wasn't alone there: every man of the new Dragon intake had submitted their reports on Friday. Jax would have leafed through them this weekend and today they got their results. Everyone was on a two-monther, so unless you got it renewed today, it was a case of clear your desk and sayonara.

She was wearing a short dress with a cropped jacket, cream cotton with navy piping, and navy pumps. She'd taken extra care this morning with her make-up, her dark hair and eyes set off with subtle shades, charcoal around the eyes, matt plum lipstick and tinted moisturiser to smooth out the skin. Her thick, dark hair had been cut and curled under at the edges in a sleek pageboy. If she was going to get fired, it would help her out to look good. She'd be stronger about it.

Nina walked into her tiny office. Her desk was almost totally clear; she'd done that Friday night. There couldn't be anything worse than standing there, maybe crying, ladling your personal effects into a black plastic bag while the secretaries watched. This way, if Jax handed her her pink slip, she could just ride the elevator down to the lobby and walk smartly out the door.

Simon and Tom were laughing together in Tom's office. She could hear the thuds as the boys lobbed paper at Tom's basketball hoop; obviously they had a bit more confidence than she did.

It's not the project, Nina reminded herself. 'Customised Response' was good, computerisation was her bag, she knew it would be effective. It was the fact that she'd exceeded her authority. Fired Tracy Jones last Friday, in public, forcing Gary Bellman to back her up. Gary Bellman, a division chief! Gary had been furious and she knew Jax would have seen what she'd done. Women in Dragon were expected to keep their heads down. Already, they'd see her as a troublemaker.

Eventually, there came the rattle of the mailcart from the corridor. Stopping at Tom's office. She heard muffled speech, then whoops of glee. New contracts for those two, then.

There was the knock on her own door. Heart hammering, Nina pulled it open to be faced with Abdul. He was handing her a small, thin envelope; didn't look like a contract.

'Is this all? You're sure?' Maybe she'd been expecting it but her heart plunged.

'Yes, ma'am. Sorry.'

Great, now the mailboy's feeling sorry for me, Nina thought dully. It was a memo envelope and she ripped it open. From Jax himself. 'Nina, please come to this office at ten a.m. sharp.'

Would Dolan take her back? God, why couldn't she have just put up with it? Now she was not only getting the can, she was going to get carpeted first. Wonderful. Simon and Tom must have realised by her silence what the score was, but they weren't exactly hurrying in to comfort her. That was business here: failure was regarded as an infectious disease.

Sighing, she looked at her watch. Best get it over with. Nina picked up her bag and closed the office door behind her, heading for the elevator bank.

Jax's secretary looked at Nina gleefully. She must have heard about the Tracy thing too.

She recognised Jack Fletcher, new at Accounts, as he stormed out of the office, his face white. Clearly, another candidate for the black plastic binliner and the cab home.

The secretary buzzed her boss. 'I have Nina Roth for you.' She listened a second, then, 'You can go in, Ms Roth,' like butter wouldn't melt.

Actually Nina was grateful for the hostility. No danger of dissolving into tears when that was their attitude; pity would have been a lot worse. She squared her shoulders under the cream cotton and marched into Jax's office.

The boss was sitting behind a heavy oak desk, his room decorated in clubby burgundy leather and dark woods. It was so traditional and masculine Nina almost expected to smell cigars.

Jax waved her to a seat. He had a file open in front of him; her project.

'This is good work,' he said.

Nina was so shocked she didn't say a word.

'Precise and focused,' Jax went on, and she carefully wiped the astonishment off her face. 'You didn't try anything too flashy, but this could save us a good lot of overhead. It's similar to what you did at Dolan, but that's OK. This isn't the movies, you don't get Oscars for creativity. We can use it.'

'Thank you, sir,' Nina said.

Jax looked the girl over appreciatively. A cool customer, this kid. She must have figured she was getting fired, but look at her. All poise and calm. A real beauty, too, in that understated way, dark hair, sharp cheekbones, huge black eyes. You couldn't tell what she was thinking, with that alabaster mask up all the time. And no matter how she dressed, she couldn't hide those curves. He felt desire ripple through him, mixed with annoyance. It would have been great to have her stay here. Under his authority.

'You fired your secretary Friday.'

'Yes, sir.' Nina's hopes sank again.

'You had no authority to dismiss another member of staff. Tracy Jones reported to Mrs Harris in Support Staff, even if she was assigned to you. Discipline is undertaken by the relevant department head and Personnel. Mr Bellman's office was furious.'

'But she defied me openly.'

'So you fired her, just like that?'

Nina squirmed. 'No, of course not. It was the end of a long line of incidents.'

'I see.' Jax's voice was mercilessly cold. 'So you had previously discussed this problem with – which one of Ms Jones's supervisors?'

'I didn't.' Now, it sounded impulsive and childish. Nina couldn't help herself, she blushed a rich red. 'I guess I thought I could handle it myself. I thought I had to, as a—'

'As a what?' Jax demanded.

Nina couldn't bring herself to come right out and say, 'as a woman'. She knew Jax knew exactly what she meant.

'Well. Your action was certainly decisive, Nina, but it was way out of line. Next time, contact somebody appropriate.'

Next time? It sank in: she wasn't getting fired. She felt almost light-headed with relief.

'Oh, yes, sir. I'll contact Mr Bellman's office right away—'

'It won't be Mr Bellman,' Jax said.

'I'm sorry, I don't understand.'

'It'll be Mr Keith Sweeney. In London.'

'London?' Nina gasped, startled out of her composure. 'I'm being posted to London?'

'That's right. The earl saw your report and requested you personally.' Jax leaned forward. 'That's not a problem, Nina, is it? You don't have any family here, or property? Nothing you can't leave behind?'

'No.' Nina bit her lips to stop a stupid grin from spreading right across her face. 'Nothing at all.'

'Good. The firm will pay rent on your apartment while you're away. You'd better take the rest of the day off to pack.'

'When am I leaving?'

'Tomorrow morning. Nine thirty out of JFK.' Jax

allowed himself a small smile at the girl's shocked face. 'This is Dragon Chemical, Nina, we move fast here.'

Elizabeth smiled and bowed for the millionth time that evening. If her calves and quads were supple and limber, the muscles in her cheeks were definitely starting to ache. At least they'd cleared out the photographers, finally, and now the athletes present were helping themselves to champagne, starting to loosen up, to celebrate.

It was the US team's victory ball. Schloss Lebenberg, the modernised castle that was their team's hotel, had been taken over. Everywhere from the casino to the pool was draped with vast Stars and Stripes and blow-up photos of the team. Jack Taylor had insisted on it; the most he would do solo was pose with the medal for the networks. The States were trumpeting their triumph from the rooftops, as usual, Elizabeth thought, amused. One individual gold, and already the TV stations, sports people, even food chains were begging to throw sponsorship at them. The British camp had its feet on the ground. After all, the Alpine nations were still skiing them off the snow in the team events.

Still, it was fun, to come out and party. She'd almost forgotten how to do it. Elizabeth's dark blonde hair hung loosely down her back; her dress was a gorgeous, slim column of white silk and gold thread, spiralling into a loose fishtail. She danced the first stately waltz with Hans Wolf, to huge cheers, then whirled gracefully round with Ronnie Davis, Brad Hinds, Pete, Sam and Rick. Everywhere she went people murmured appreciatively, pumped her hand, asked for her autograph. Elizabeth told herself she was having a good time. She wasn't going to be put out just because a certain person hadn't come to find her. After the joint photocall, Jack Taylor had disappeared. Probably with some groupie.

I'm not disappointed, I'm the World Champion,

Elizabeth thought fiercely. Who does he think he is, anyway? Arrogant bastard!

She reached for another flute of champagne and then stiffened. Someone was resting their hand on the tight curve of her back. Angrily Elizabeth whipped around to be confronted by Jack, his tall frame bang up against her. His white shirt was unbuttoned at the top, displaying a tanned chest and just a smattering of hair. He looked relaxed.

'Congratulations,' Jack said softly.

'And to you.' She was stiff with him.

'You been looking for me?' Jack asked. He reached down and made to brush some hair away from her cheek but Elizabeth pulled back sharply. God! He thinks he's God's gift, the infuriating jerk! But Jack did look wonderful, the formal dark cloth picking out his eyes, the confidence, the aggression. Stuff had already passed between them that couldn't be taken back. Even if she had skied away down that mountain, Elizabeth knew, she'd lain under him, responded to him. Her nipples had stiffened under his hands, her body had flooded with heat for him. He knew it. She knew it.

'And why would I be doing that?' Elizabeth snapped.

Jack laughed. 'Thought you might like to dance.'

'I've done nothing but dance.'

'With me,' Taylor insisted.

'Well, I've had to make do with the lesser gentlemen that were on offer,' Elizabeth answered icily.

They were standing close to the dance floor. Skiers, their coaches and families were whirling around merrily and clumsily to 'She Wore a Yellow Ribbon'.

'Come on.' Taylor held out one large hand for Elizabeth's tiny one. He was looking her right in the face with insistent, come-to-bed eyes. She felt a new flood of lust, no doubt about it. Strong arms, he had. Elizabeth badly wanted to be held by them. Pinned down again, made love to. The certainty that Jack would be great in bed mingled with the certainty that he'd done this to loads of women before, and that they'd all been eager to comply.

Her bodice was reinforced satin. Her hardening nipples would not betray her this time. He owed her an apology. Right now he's acting like he's got some *right* to me, Elizabeth thought crossly.

'I'm sorry. I'm feeling a little tired.'

Jack let his hand drop, annoyed. 'Please, girl. Stop playing games.'

'*Excuse* me?' Elizabeth said, coldly.

Jack bristled. This wasn't going the way he'd planned it at all. So he'd had a few drinks before coming to find her, so what? He'd noticed her casing the crowd. Certainly she was looking for him. They could dance, sip a little champagne together, go upstairs. Women, he hated it when they got coy.

'I booked a private suite here especially,' he said. 'There's no point, Elizabeth, I know how you feel.'

A *private suite*? He was planning on hauling me into bed? Elizabeth's brows knitted together.

'Clearly you've got no idea how I feel, Mr Taylor.' She drew herself up, took a step back from him. 'I wouldn't place too much emphasis on what happened earlier. It was a near-death experience, I wasn't thinking.'

'Yeah. I liked that,' Jack said.

They were interrupted by a waiter heading towards them with a salver. On it was a thin yellow envelope: a telegram.

'Excuse me, my lady, but it's a message from your father.'

'Thank you.'

Jack stood back, seething with irritation, as Elizabeth ripped it open. She read the message quickly, then looked up at him.

'I'm afraid I have to say goodbye. I've got to get back to the hotel. Dad wants me to come home tomorrow morning: he's going to give me a job at Dragon,' Elizabeth said triumphantly.

Jack read the exhilaration in her tone. Was there something else there? Regret? Hey, clutching at straws now, champ, he chided himself. He wanted to kick something. He was angry. Frustrated.

With an effort he made her a little bow. 'Then allow me to escort you home.'

'Thank you, I can manage.'

'I insist.' Jack took Elizabeth's elbow and steered her towards the cloakroom. Normally, when a girl got an attitude he lost interest, but right now he was dreaming up excuses to be in London.

Jack Taylor looked down at Lady Elizabeth Savage, walking stiffly at his side, refusing to look at him. Maybe she'd blown him off tonight, but only tonight. He had her down as unfinished business. He'd never lost a battle of wills with a woman, and he wasn't gonna start now.

Chapter 15

Nina looked round her new apartment and smiled. Two bedrooms, a tiled bathroom and neat, fitted kitchen, in a tree-lined Camden street. She had selected it from a list of company-approved flats, as the English called them, and eighty per cent of the rent would be coming out of her overseas living allowance. Then there was the displacement bonus, the relocation expenses scheme and her rise for signing the new contract. Dragon had locked her up for five years, but they were paying handsomely for the privilege. She'd never seen anything like this in her life. Tom and Simon and her old colleagues back in New York were probably used to it, but after years of walk-ups, living over stores and in rank motels, Delancey Street was a palace.

On the plane she had done the sums in her head. She was going to be very comfortable; the allowances, the rise, and the strength of the dollar would see to that. Britain had just emerged from years of socialist government, the country was in a mess, and the austerity measures employed by the new Prime Minister had plunged it into deep recession. Inflation was still high, but she was being paid abroad. Her dollars would go even further. She'd winced when she paid the bill on her new wardrobe – dark blue suits, smart heels, severe dresses and jackets in pinstripes, burgundy, black and chocolate brown – but then realised that it would barely dent her new monthly cheque.

The weather outside was gloomy – grey skies and

threatening rain. Nina could not have cared less. Camden was funky, full of musicians, long-haired students, stylish mod artists blasting the Jam. And Britain was full of opportunity. Nothing like the Queen-and-cucumber-sandwiches image back home – a woman could even be Prime Minister here. A woman President seemed about as likely as a man giving birth. Clive Sinclair had launched the ZX-81, a tiny home computer that played games and ran programmes off tape recorders. It was a big craze. They were wired here, they were going places. London was the city both of punk and princesses – Lady Di souvenirs from the summer's big royal wedding adorned every market stall – and the City was the financial centre of Europe.

She'd had three days to settle in. Today was the first at work. Nina felt a rush of nerves, but they were swamped in her bolting excitement. Dragon HQ, after all, was not in Park Avenue, it was right here, south of the River Thames. She was going to work in the heart of the company, directly for the earl. Tony Savage, the Robber Baron, had ordered this posting personally.

Nina picked up her briefcase and set off for the Tube. Even London's subway system beat New York: tickets and automated gates, no fumbling about with rolls of quarters and filthy tokens. A fast train would take her practically to her office door. She was over an hour early, and she couldn't wait. New decade, new city, new job. Maybe she was finally getting somewhere.

'Good morning, my lady.'

Elizabeth beamed at the receptionist as she handed over her security pass and a sheaf of company recruitment forms. They looked so official. Everything was great, even the wet, crowded streets full of businessmen barging past her, even the grey ugliness of the Dragon tower. She was used to being stopped and asked for an autograph, but in the City, nobody gave her a second glance. That was great too. They were all serious people, seriously busy. Doing real work. She had been trying to gain admittance to this world for ever.

'Mr Sweeney is the head of Personnel, and he asked if you could fill these in today.'

'Of course, thanks,' Elizabeth said.

'New Products Division is on the ninth floor, just take the lift to your left.'

Elizabeth nodded and joined a crowd of men in dark suits. They immediately parted and let her stand at the front. When the lift arrived, everybody waited until she had stepped in.

'What floor, Lady Elizabeth?' a grey-haired executive asked politely.

Elizabeth brushed back her glossy hair and told him, returning everybody's beaming smiles. Of course they all knew who she was, she was famous. Everyone was going out of their way to be nice and welcoming. She felt super-confident. Dad was wrong, she was going to fit in here just fine.

'Initial tests look promising.' Tony grinned, seeing the flash of greed lighting up Frank Staunton's eyes. 'Appetite suppressant, amphetamine base.'

'Could be big,' Staunton agreed.

Fifty-five, Frank Staunton was thin and wiry, nick-named the Terrier by his subordinates when his back was turned. He went after results like a dog after a rat, and he displayed utter loyalty to Savage, his master. Frank Staunton had run New Products for ten years, ever since Tony poached him from Glaxo. Most of his pay was stock options, so that Dragon's success was his success. Frank loved money. Self-interest made him reliable.

Tony knew Frank would never leave. The carrot had been perfectly effective, and he was also keeping the stick in reserve. Photos of Frank in drag at clubs like Heaven; arms round a fourteen-year-old cherub on Hampstead Heath; getting his cock sucked in a notorious gents' lavatory outside Waterloo Station. Not a portfolio he'd want flashed around the Travellers' Club, or the Carlton. Or mailed to his wife. Tony had never had occasion to refer to them, but the thought made him relaxed. Frank, like all the big Dragon players, had a weakness. Whereas Tony had nothing but strengths.

Frank was discussing the prospects for the new slimming drug they were developing. If toxicity and addictive problems could be ironed out, they were looking at a whole new level of power and wealth. One tiny tablet for doctors to prescribe, and the stock would be on automatic pilot to the moon.

'Your drones need to concentrate on this.'

Frank nodded. 'Including her young ladyship?'

Tony did not return the grin. He hadn't forgotten that Elizabeth was coming in today. He had to find her something to do, something to keep her quiet. The necessity ached in him like a rotten tooth; even though it was temporary, it felt too much like a victory for her. Louise's bastard, forcing her way into the heart of his kingdom. He grunted.

'And we have some others new in this morning.' The Terrier sensed his master's blackening mood and changed the subject fast. 'Joe Walsh, an analyst. Hotshot from Morgan Grenfell. Lionel White, a systems kid. The New Yorker.'

'Nina Roth.' Tony leaned forward, animated. 'I forgot, she starts today.'

'She's working in the same area as Lady Elizabeth.'

Tony didn't listen. His pulse quickened as he flashed on the girl from Brooklyn, with her strong accent and dark, grave beauty. Intelligence and drive combined with great tits, a great ass and a handspan waist. Very different from his usual blonde bimbos, she was sexy, but a scrapper. Dimly he recalled some story about her firing her secretary when she was still a brand-new rookie. And she'd known who he was. Nina was different, very different.

Beneath his sober bespoke trousers Tony felt his cock stir. Since Camilla Browning had got her marching orders he had only had Monica and one high-class hooker. He hated having to pay for it; mistresses were the better bet. His memories of the Roth girl sharpened into focus. She'd come up from the street, fast, still only twenty-one years old.

It occurred to him that was Elizabeth's age. Fucking Nina would be like fucking one of her schoolfriends. That thought sharpened the twitch between his legs into a real hard-on.

'Uh-huh.' He was casual. 'I'll take the first meeting with you. I'm going to be working with some of them myself.'

'Then you'd better come with me.'

Nina was shown into Frank Staunton's office, where ten other people were waiting: nine men and a girl. Two of the men were in their early twenties, looking expectant. New hires like herself. The girl was probably a secretary. She was wearing a pretty little dress in a Liberty print, and fashionable high heels, together with bracelets and earrings. Nina smiled at them all and began to introduce herself, but she kept one eye on the girl. There was something familiar about her, but she couldn't place her. Was she a secretary? She must be. And yet she had a soft, rich look about her, a polish. The hands were manicured, the eyebrows beautifully plucked, and now she was a little closer, the bracelets were real, gold studded with diamonds. Plus, she was sitting on a chair like the executives. Nina felt confused, more so when she caught a breath of expensive scent. Long, shiny hair worn loose, not even tied back for the office. Very beautiful, slim and delicate. Who's the bim? she thought. Sleeping with somebody?

The men were all smiling at the girl. There was a nervous deference in their body language. Nina frowned. She *was* sleeping with somebody important. Like Honor Feathers at Dolan, a talentless twenty-five-year-old piece of ass who was the managing director's regular date. Honor had gotten promotions and raises so regularly you could set your watch by them, and all the boys had been terrified of her, because she told tales out of school and got her enemies fired. Nina had disliked Honor intensely. Women like that made it harder for all other women. She had more respect for whores – at least they were open about what they were doing. This beautiful rich chick set her teeth on edge.

Elizabeth glanced up as Nina entered the room. A dark-haired, voluptuous woman, very young, wearing a tailored black suit, flat shoes and a steel watch. Immediately she blushed. The men's quick glances of approval told her that this was the right look, this girl was wearing the right clothes. She felt embarrassed. Now the woman was shaking hands, briskly and impersonally. The others greeted her as one of them. No joking or banter, they were talking business right off the bat.

The girl came closer. Elizabeth heard an American accent. And then, she glanced right at Elizabeth and gave her an unmistakable look of icy derision.

Elizabeth bridled. So she'd got the wardrobe wrong, so what? This girl looked her own age but *she'd* clearly been working for years. She hadn't had to blackmail her way into an office. Dad's company had hired her and given her a real chance. She's got no business looking at me that way!

There was only one empty chair, right at the front, by

Elizabeth. Nina slid into it and sighed inwardly. There was no getting away with it. She offered her neighbour her hand.

'Nina Roth. Just over from Manhattan. I cut my teeth with Dolan for a couple of years.'

The blonde showed no sign of recognising the name. Nina was shocked. Dolan was a big player, hadn't the cutie here even heard of them?

'I'm Elizabeth. I – well, this is my first job.'

The accent was plummy and patrician, accompanied by a little flick of the hair. The girlish gesture was out of place. What the fuck was she doing in New Products? It was a vital division!

'Oh. And what are you gonna be doing?' Nina asked politely.

'I'm not sure.' Breathy upper-class voice was accompanied with rounded green eyes. 'I expect they're finding something for me to do.'

Nina was dumbstruck. She looked down at her lap in case anybody saw how pissed off she was. Finding something for her to do!

'Elizabeth who?'

Elizabeth heard the hostility and bridled. It had been a long time since anyone had shown her contempt.

'Lady Elizabeth Savage,' she said coolly.

Nina looked at her sharply. Of course. Lady Elizabeth, the Brit skier, she'd seen her on CNN getting her medal with Jack Taylor. So, she wasn't a girlfriend, she was a *daughter*. Christ, she was just playing around on Daddy's patch. She hadn't even heard of Dolan, and here she was. No messing around with experience or education for the boss's kid.

Nina knew she should be sucking up, like all the men, but she couldn't do it. The thought of her own struggles boiled up in her like acid.

'And I'm *Ms* Nina Roth.' The sarcasm was unmistakable. 'You can call me Nina.'

One of the younger men behind Elizabeth sniggered, then clamped a hand across his mouth. Elizabeth blushed a rich red. Bitch! Who did the Yank think she was? She spun round to fire something back but at that moment the door swung open and Frank Staunton walked in. Followed by her father.

'London. Y'all have to be kidding.'

Jack reached down and patted Queen of Arabia on her sleek white neck. It was still cool enough in the early morning, but the gallop around his Texas farm had left him sweating and sore. Pop looked comfortable enough, but he lived in the saddle. Plus, he'd set Jack up on this fine, half-tamed mare, a huge beast, gorgeous but hard to control. Like Elizabeth.

'No. I'm used to Europe from the circuit.'

That was plausible. He might buy that.

John Taylor, Sr, waved a hand at the vista before them, the green lawns kept lush by sprinklers, the palm trees, gaudy flowers and rows of neat stables. Jack had loved the stud farm since he was knee high.

'But we keep the horses here. Main office, here. Major hotels. London's just an outpost, boy.' The sharp blue eyes twinkled. 'You're hidin' something.'

Jack shook his head and squeezed his knees round the mare's flank, to still her. 'I think we're wasting opportunities over there. Too many Brit and Irish stables need good studs, we're ignoring that market. Waiting for them to come to us. Plus, there are horses we never see. Meets we don't go to.'

'Y'all only have a few months off,' John said shrewdly.

'Exactly.' Jack pounced. 'Not enough time to do anything major here, but I can see if we're missing anything in London.'

'OK, if that's how you wanna spend Christmas.' His father snorted. 'This ain't about a girl, son? You got em' linin' up in Dallas! You didn't used to chase any pussy halfway round the world.'

Jack almost blushed. 'C'mon, you know me. No girl's worth making a fuss over.'

'I know you.' John spurred his stallion round to face the woods, preparing for another run. 'That's the problem, son.'

Tony listened with one ear as Frank ran through the new protocols. Most of the men in this room knew exactly what they had to do. The new kids were thrown in at the deep end.

He was watching the men take notes. Joe Walsh knew the market – he would be ferreting out info on their competitors, finding out what Glaxo, ICI and SmithKline had in the pipeline. Lionel White was already sketching computer codes for a modelling system, seeing how the numbers would affect them.

Elizabeth was writing it all down, laboriously, occasionally looking up at him and catching his frown. She seemed uncomfortable, out of her depth. He bit back a smile; her defiant streak would mean trouble unless he found her some pretence of a role.

Nina Roth sat next to her. He liked what he saw. She wasn't writing, she was drinking it all in. Leaning forwards, straining at the leash like a bloodhound, her thick, raven hair fell heavily round her high cheekbones, the young, pale skin dusted with excited pink. Under that sombre suit her body was magnificent. The breasts looked heavy, but still firm with youth. Her ankles and calves turned beautifully, her ass flared out from a tiny waist. Unlike his boyish, muscular daughter, Nina was womanly, all curves. A go-getter. Nothing ladylike about her. His imagination stripped her slowly, so she was sitting there naked. He knew she was aware of him, nervous in his presence. Her eyes kept sliding towards him, and if he caught her looking, she blushed and glanced back at Frank.

The earl was good at body language. Elizabeth sat stiffly next to Nina. For her part, Nina's eyes never even flickered towards Elizabeth's busy pad; the gesture was contemptuous, like, *I'll never need notes*.

Nina didn't know how he felt about Elizabeth. If she pissed off the chairman's daughter, she was taking a big risk. He wasn't used to females who did that.

Tony smiled. He'd made it a rule not to mess his own doorstep, but none of the pretty, blonde and bland girls stuffing Personnel or PR had ever really excited him. Not like the curvy, prickly little Brooklyn smartass.

His hard-on was refusing to go away. Rules were made to be broken.

Chapter 16

Elizabeth leaned over and pressed the button on her treadmill, pushing it up to maximum. It was already tilting at an angle, simulating uphill running. The responsive growl from the machinery blasted her ears; her space was by far the loudest in the Chelsea gym.

Several flabby ladies-who-lunch looked over, annoyed. Elizabeth was drowning out their new Sony Walkmans as they pedalled sedately on stationary bikes or trod slowly up a Stairmaster. Elizabeth was aware of them dimly, like she was clocking the admiring stares from the men's weights room next door, although she couldn't care less. Nothing mattered but the workout.

Her strong body was clothed in the bare minimum. Hi-tech sneakers, Lycra cycling shorts and a leotard in icing-sugar pastels. Blonde hair swept back and up in a raised ponytail, to keep it out of her eyes. The heart-rate monitor was flashing, but she didn't have time to look down. Sweat dewed her body, her fringe was plastered to her forehead. Arms raised for maximum motion. Balls of the feet pushing off the rubber with every pulse. Her heart beating like a roadside drill, Elizabeth Savage lost herself in vicious, punishing speed. She'd already done the weights and the crunches, training every major muscle group in the upper body. Now the endurance work.

In under an hour she'd be reporting to that utter bitch, Nina Roth. This was a pleasure in comparison.

The thought of Nina drove Elizabeth into a fury, feet

flying up the mechanical hill. They called her the Brooklyn Bomber in the office, the men, almost admiringly. She still hadn't worked out what Nina did but she sure was good at it. Phone glued to her fucking ear, barking orders and tapping out computer programs and talking science gobbledygook Elizabeth couldn't work out. Never losing an opportunity to put Elizabeth down.

Dad had given her the job she begged for. Advertising on New Products. But whatever she suggested to Nina, the cow lost no time in vetoing. It was so unfair: Jake and Richard and Dino, the other advertising guys, all loved her ideas, but Nina stopped her work from getting anywhere.

Anger burned in her face as bright as exertion. Bitch! Nina had a chance to learn; Elizabeth never would. And Nina was Daddy's bright-eyed little girl. She worked directly for him, she was his right-hand girl on the slimming drug thing. Elizabeth hated the way she smarmed up to Tony. Those two deserved each other.

She leaned forwards to increase resistance, throwing herself into the final burst. Elizabeth needed her fitness. While she was struggling at Dragon, Heidi Laufen was practising in the Alps.

Tony Savage stepped out of his car and paused while his chauffeur handed over his briefcase. Breakfast at the Connaught had been light: coffee, bacon and toast for him, enough to stave off hunger without dulling his senses. Not that there had been much danger of that. Sir Leo York, his companion, gorged himself on eggs, kippers and pastries, with a bottle of Krug. Leo called it a champagne breakfast to celebrate the deal. Tony called it a surefire sign of a lush.

He had been the one doing the celebrating. Disposing of Idun Cosmetics had completed his firesale of Loki Medicine. Leo overpaid. Now Tony was only left with the key labs division. The disposal of the rest covered his original payment. It was like getting a company for free, plus twelve million cash as a bonus.

Tony's blood sang as he walked into the building. He checked his Tag Heuer sports watch. Ten to eight.

In the express elevator Tony went over his plans for the day. Talk to New York and Sydney. Interview with the *FT* at lunch. Strategic planning in the afternoon. Tory donors do at the Opera House tonight.

He was pumped up, he wanted to celebrate.

Almost without thinking Lord Caerhaven unlocked his office, went straight to his phone and dialled the extension for Nina Roth.

Nina glanced at the scrolling text on her computer screen. The glass reflected the view behind her, the wide Thames glittering in the chill winter sun, commuter traffic streaming across Westminster Bridge, the Houses of Parliament grey and forbidding in the background. But it had been weeks since she'd noticed the view.

The earl had assigned her to his own task force. She supervised Lionel's computer modelling and found out which companies Joe should be investigating. That meant research, and lots of it. She had to find out who their most likely competitors were, and how far their slimming projects had come; what the distribution impact would be; and how it might affect their antitrust status. Nina gathered facts all day.

Because she was Tony's direct inferior, the boys at Dragon fell over themselves to help her. It was the total opposite of New York. She felt she was finally making inroads. The world drug market was coming into sharper focus, like a city emerging from a blanket fog.

If only she didn't have to waste her time with that stuck-up Sloane, Lady Elizabeth. Nina couldn't stand her: the prissy, entitled air, the super-confidence of a star and an aristo at the same time. Elizabeth kept offering stupid ideas, but all the boys here couldn't wait to tell her how great they were. Elizabeth was rude to her own father, she was bolshy with Nina, she took every opportunity of rubbing her nose in it. 'No better than you ought to be.' That was the Brit expression. Lady Elizabeth's slap in the face: you're just a piece of Yankee white trash from the wrong side of the tracks, whatever suits you wear or job you do.

The phone trilled.

'Nina?' She started as she recognised the cut-glass tones. Lord C. 'You're in early.'

'I've been at my desk for an hour,' Nina shot back without thinking, then bit her lip. Oh, God. You didn't cheek Tony Savage.

'Glad to hear it. You should be up to speed on the FDA scan, then.'

'Yes, sir,' Nina said quickly. She glanced down at her dress, a dark red cropped affair with a long, slimming jacket, by Jil Sander. Wolford tights, low Cartier heels, and fortunately, she was already made up. The earl expected all Dragon employees to look polished and pulled together.

'Then come upstairs to my office,' Lord Caerhaven said.

'Yes, sir. Right away.'

Nina carefully replaced the receiver on the hook and took a deep breath. One on one with the Robber Baron. It was the kind of chance she used to daydream about.

As she stood up she saw her hands were trembling.

Tony's office was fairly modest. It had a private bath-room off to one side which was shut, and a secretary's annexe as yet deserted. Neat windows looked north over the Thames to Soho. The décor was light and modern. It was far more impressive than Jax's clubby cavern on

Park Avenue, or Frank Staunton's expensive art; Tony Savage, Nina realised, didn't need the English gentleman look, because everyone knew he was one.

The earl was sitting behind his desk, waiting for her, wearing a dark, nondescript suit, immaculately cut. His hair was close-cropped chestnut, only lightly speckled with silver. His eyes were hazel and he had a broad, strong chest. He looked powerful physically as well as financially. There was something cold about the alert speculation in his eyes. Nina sensed a fresh, spicy scent; Floris maybe, the lightest tang, pleasant but perfectly masculine.

Anthony Savage was the best-groomed man she'd ever seen. He looked almost predatory. He wore no jewellery except a gold signet ring, stamped with his family crest.

Nina had heard all the rumours. Now she wondered if they were true. He wasn't pretty, but his sexuality was magnetic.

She blushed. She couldn't believe it, she felt a ripple of desire. Something she hadn't felt since Jeff Glazer.

Tony Savage was more man than a million Brooklyn high-school jocks.

Watch it, girl, she told herself, *you are out of your league*.

'Take a seat.'

Tony looked at the new kid. Short, but exquisite. Alabaster skin and a long, refined nose. A stylish suit that played up the coal-black eyes and hair. And close up, those curves were even more impressive.

He settled back languidly.

'I sold Idun this morning. For eighty.'

'Eighty?' Nina asked. Tony watched the wheels in her brain whirr; the very tip of her tongue touched the dark berry gloss on her full lips. 'That's twelve million more than it's worth.'

'That's what I thought,' Tony said. He was impressed:

she'd pegged the market value off the top of her head. 'Tell me about the FDA.'

Nina swallowed drily. She had news she was sure this man did not want to hear.

'They don't like drugs based on amphetamines, and even with those they sanction, you have class action suits. A single bad reaction, a good lawyer, and you have a dented quarterly or worse. The appetite suppressant has an addictive effect and suppresses various auto-immune responses. I found well over thirty landmark rulings over eight separate states, then you have Federal liability ...'

Tony watched Nina as she blasted through her findings. It was good work, well presented. She wasn't flinching; no soft soap or small talk. He enjoyed the rhythmic swell of her breasts and the sharp little hand gestures she used, long, elegant fingers tapering down to blood-red nails. Her calves slithered against each other. Despite the grown-up dressing and clever talk, she was very, very young.

'Hmm,' he said when she had finished. 'So the drug won't work?'

'Not in its present form.'

He leaned forwards.

'I want a slimming drug. One that they *will* ratify.'

'Yes, sir.' Nina didn't know what else she could say.

Tony looked at her; his gaze was hypnotic. 'And how are you settling in? Do you like London?'

'Very much, I—'

'How are you getting on with my daughter?'

Nina coloured. She felt fearful again. 'I, that is, she—'

Tony cut her off. 'You think she's a waste of space?'

Nina thought fast. Somehow, she knew that if she lied, this man would know. 'Well, Elizabeth's learning,' she replied.

Elizabeth. Tony noticed the deliberate lack of a title. She had balls, this girl, something he usually hated. In

Nina it was erotic. Maybe it was the contrast, the rounded softness of her body and the hard coldness of her manner.

'I agree with you. I don't think work is any place for a young lady.'

Nina flinched. It was like a punch to the gut. He didn't think she was a lady, then? Too common, wasn't that what the English called it?

On the other hand, he was looking at her like an equal. Giving her an amazing job for a new kid. Power and position she hadn't thought she'd get for years.

'No, no place for a lady – or a gentleman.'

Tony glanced up sharply. The girl was staring at him boldly, her pale cheeks flushed from her challenge.

'I could have you fired.'

Nina lowered her eyes. She had the thickest lashes he'd ever seen. 'Yes,' she said, 'my lord.'

He almost laughed. She was fencing with him. No female had tried that on with him since Louise. But Nina was no Louise; she was earthy, she was street, she was Jewish. Tony could handle her, easily.

'We still need to find a plan B for the drug. Do some thinking. We'll have dinner tonight at the Groucho, eight p.m.'

Nina stood up. 'Right. Thanks for the invitation.'

'It wasn't an invitation,' Tony Savage said.

'This won't work. It's flashy, consumer orientated.' Nina didn't bother to hide her exasperation. 'You keep coming to me with ad campaigns.'

'It's a good idea.'

Elizabeth burned with resentment. Her ads for their Soothex throat pastels were arresting, original. Dino loved them.

'It's not what I asked you to do, Elizabeth.'

'Lady Elizabeth,' Elizabeth snapped. She couldn't help

162

it; something about Nina's dismissive attitude made her lash out.

The two girls glared at each other. The men in the room stood stock-still; you could almost see their ears pricking up. Nina felt adrenalin surge through her.

'I don't think so. Social titles are not appropriate in the office. Not for a junior.'

Elizabeth flushed darkly.

Nina spoke up, so the rest of the room could hear her. 'If you have a problem with that, you could take it up with your father. I'll be happy to call you Lady Elizabeth, if he tells me to. Otherwise we'll keep it informal.'

There was a pause, then Elizabeth muttered, 'That's fine.'

Nina brushed a lock of black hair out of her eyes. Now she wanted to smooth things over.

'I love your bracelet, by the way. It's gorgeous.' She gestured to a thick silver cuff around Elizabeth's left wrist, covered in delicate engravings of ferns and ivy. 'Where did you buy it? I'd adore one.'

The other girl looked up at her. The green eyes were chips of ice, the aristocratic brows lifted in supercilious disdain.

'I don't buy my jewellery, I inherit it.'

Now it was Nina's turn to stiffen. 'I'm sorry, I didn't realise you were so grand.'

'Don't worry, Nina. You couldn't possibly know about things like that. Considering your background.'

Nina paled as the insult went home. For a moment, the two young women just glared at each other. Then Elizabeth gathered up her rejected work and walked back to her own department.

Nina stepped out of the taxi and tipped the driver almost absentmindedly. It had been a rush, racing home at quarter of seven, tearing off her suit, fixing her face at the speed of light. She knew the earl would not expect her to change for dinner, but she wanted to be impressive in every way.

A three-quarter black Prada jacket covered her dress, a loose, flowing sheath of Thai silk in metallic blue. The bright reds and charcoals of the day had been replaced with subtler shades: clover on her full lips, plum across her cheekbones, nails painted silver to match her necklace. The lids over her dark eyes were slate-grey, blue and black; all the colours of a dark English sky. Nina's black hair fell thickly over a grey cashmere wrap. The mirror had been kind; she was stunning, and she knew it.

Despite the long day and the rush at the end of it, Nina felt composed. Somehow, Lady Elizabeth's challenge had made up her mind. The confusion she'd felt in Tony's office had vanished long since. Nina knew what she was here to do.

The outfit she was wearing had cost over a thousand pounds. All the new money she'd thought she had was vanishing in things like this: good suits for the office, decent shoes, coats, accessories. As a Dragon executive, you couldn't shop at Marks & Sparks. You had to have an abundance of the right clothes, the stuff Elizabeth merely 'inherited'. Nina thought about that when she was dressing. How the few square feet of fabric clinging to her curves would, less than a year ago, have paid for months of food and lodging.

Elizabeth and the well-heeled young men at Dragon looked on her as nothing. An upstart, almost a child. They don't realise, Nina thought sourly, that I've *never* been a child. I've never had that luck.

Her past was a prison. Growing up in that slovenly apartment, carrying the can for Mom and Pop. Her mother a lush. The teasing she'd gotten at St Michael's for being white trash, well, some things never changed. The dizzy hope of Jeff and then the crunch of betrayal.

Rooming with drunk sailors. Passing up college. Frank dying, Connor throwing her over. Miscarrying in a dark room.

But she'd done it. She'd gotten away. Two years at Dolan, now Dragon, Nina thought, and no one to help me but me. She'd turned twenty-one a few days ago and hadn't even noticed until the evening. Birthdays just didn't seem important. Elizabeth Savage might be the same age as her, but she was younger, lifetimes younger. Even though she was untrained and inexperienced, Lady E. was drawing a salary like Nina's and getting respect and position. Because she'd been lucky enough to be born on the right side of the tracks.

Nina pulled her cashmere scarf tighter and picked up her skirts, carefully stepping across the Dean Street slush. Her coat was smart, but not practical against the biting December air. She hurried across to the nondescript entrance to the club and ducked inside. When she told the receptionist she was meeting Lord Caerhaven, the woman melted.

The Groucho was a hot place to be. Full of media executives and stars, Nina recognised a couple of famous actors, a newscaster and a pop star. There was also a division chief from Hanson and the Treasury Secretary. Every one of them eyed her up as she walked over to the restaurant.

The attention thrilled her. It was perfect, she thought cynically. Men were all the same, no matter who or what they were. Some curves and a pretty face, and they were baying for it.

So why shouldn't she take advantage? Nina felt tired of being bruised. Of being the last person on the field playing by the rules.

Tony Savage was an attractive man. She knew the gossip round Dragon was that she was his pet. Elizabeth never lost a chance to sneer about her by the water cooler. Nina respected the earl, although she didn't like him, or trust him. However, he was her boss, the ultimate power. Lord Caerhaven was known for making his favourites rich and destroying his enemies. She was sure he wanted her. Well, maybe she wanted him. Maybe it was time to do something for herself.

Tony was seated at a discreet table in a corner of the room, still wearing his work suit. He stood up when Nina appeared and waited as she shrugged off the scarf and coat, appearing in a slither of cobalt and silver.

She saw desire blaze into his eyes.

'You look wonderful, Nina.'

'Thank you, Tony,' Nina said softly.

Chapter 17

'So what do you think?'

Jack looked at Rupert Beeching and shrugged. He thought it was too cold, too windy, and too damn close to Christmas to be conducting serious business, but he'd asked Pop for the assignment, and now he had to live with it.

He was standing with a Gloucester farmer in a rundown stables, inspecting one of the finest colts he'd ever seen. Beeching was a part-timer with a useless trainer, but this one had come third in a minor race he'd attended down in Sussex. Beautifully proportioned, bursting with potential. Trouble was, his interest would spark off other buyers. Rupert wasn't so dumb he wouldn't have figured that one.

Jack thrust his hands into the pockets of his thick overcoat. The farm behind him looked out over sweeping hills; elm copses and dry-stone walls glittered under midwinter frost. In London, his secretary was drowning in messages from Paris and Galway; his book of photos and stud pedigrees was attracting a lot of interest. Jack was a good salesman, and the warm Texan accent was a help. Breeders were looking into Taylor Stud who had never considered it before. It had been a successful couple of months.

Jack named a figure, ignoring Beeching's theatrical scowl. 'Look, bud, I ain't haggling. He's pretty, but he's got no blood.'

'He *is* the blood.'

Jack laughed. 'Unplaced in three meets, third in one minor race? It ain't the Derby winner we're talking about.'

'Kerry Stud left me a message.'

'Ireland's in deeper trouble than Britain, right now. They can't match my price, and you know it.' Jack looked at his Rolex Oyster. 'Come on, Rupe. I want to take him home. I'm too tired for hassle. You think you can get a better price, be my guest, but I'm leaving now and so's my chequebook.'

The farmer winced at the familiarity, but he also looked wary. I've got you, you stupid, greedy jerk, Jack thought.

'You've got me,' Beeching said. He smiled foolishly as Jack sat down on a bale of hay and pulled out his chequebook. Coutts & Co. A lousy bank with high charges, but in England, appearance was everything.

First-class on a rickety BR train back to London, Jack sipped a watery Earl Grey and grinned to himself. Piece of cake. What should he call the animal? A funky racehorse name. Maybe Easy Money. His fledgeling operation here had been as successful as everything else in his life. It was a nice surprise to find that the business school principles he'd picked up at Harvard actually worked. Plus, it was a buyer's market. Britain was tightening its money supply, and the medicine was hurting. Jack had toasted Margaret Thatcher, strident at her party conference in a frumpy suit and floppy bow tie. 'You turn if you want to. The lady's not for turning.' Stirring stuff, sure, but monetarism was hard. Inflation fell, but recession was biting deep. Luxury, high-end businesses – like racehorse stables – were feeling it. Closing down, selling up, desperate for cash influxes. And here was the young Texan champ, riding to the rescue like Zorro. A bit of schmooze, a bit of bluff, a macho chat about skiing and sport. Amazing how all the round, red-cheeked country gents with their gin and tonics and massive girths loved that stuff.

Jack bought himself a malt whisky and soda from the drinks trolley and smiled at the ogling waitress. He sipped the drink and watched rural England slide past him, the beautiful riverside meadows and thick forests belying the turmoil the country was going through.

Old money – landowners like Beeching – was on the slide, and a new breed was on the rise. Young, smart entrepreneurs, working for themselves, clawing up the ladder hand over fist. Men just like him.

To the victor the spoils. Jack had nearly everything he wanted. And finally, he had a chance at the one prize he hadn't been able to reach. Though she'd been turning down his calls all winter and refusing all his invitations, this one she couldn't duck. An order from Ronnie Davis, the British coach, to start her training again in preparation for the Olympics. The whole British women's team to meet in Kent at the weekend. And Ronnie, bless his cockney heart, had heard Jack was in town.

'Don't tell her I'm turning up.' Jack grinned as he remembered his own words. 'It'll be good to see all the girls again, but let's keep it a surprise.'

Elizabeth tried to get her brain in gear. Skiing. The Olympics. It was important, she had to focus on it. A weekend at base camp doing fitness routines and studying videos would be a good warm-up to the new training season, but it was hard to fight the sense of failure that swamped her.

Life at Dragon had proved to be one big disappointment. She was sure her ideas for ad campaigns were good ones, but Nina Roth was having none of them. And nobody was going to listen to her over Nina, that robotic cow. Nina, with her years of experience and her in-at-seven ferocious energy. Whatever Nina was up to, in that search for a new drug, she was given total backing from everyone who mattered. With her severe suits and her humour bypass, everyone took the New Yorker seriously. Especially darling Daddy.

Constant failure had worn Elizabeth down. She stopped presenting new ideas to Nina, and contented herself with reading company reports and typing market research. At least there was enough of that to keep her looking busy, and she'd learned more than she ever wanted to know about the pharmaceutical marketplace in the UK. Which hospitals bought what, which new pills were in development. Maybe it would be valuable knowledge – if they let her do anything with it.

Elizabeth's blonde hair whipped back under her Scotch House scarf as she emerged out of the Leicester Square Tube. The cinemas flashed ads for the big Christmas movies – *Raiders of the Lost Ark, On Golden Pond*. Tinned carols bled out of tourist-shop windows and mixed with pop music from a breakdancer's transistor. It was freezing. She bought some chestnuts from a brazier stall to try and jolly herself out of it. What was Hans Wolf doing at this moment? Sipping *Glühwein* by the lake in Lausanne? Waiting for her to come back, in January, ready to forget playing shop and get on with her real job?

That was how everybody else saw it. Certainly Nina. And certainly her noble papa. Elizabeth never even thought about complaining to him. Hand Tony that satisfaction? She'd rather die. He thought the sun shone out of Nina Roth's backside. He was happy to give her all the chances of real work, real satisfaction, he'd always denied his own daughter.

Elizabeth strode briskly through the crowds down to Charing Cross. Tunbridge Wells, great. Home of rich dowagers and the biggest drugs problem outside of

Glasgow. Plus dry-skiing slopes. As if! It was like asking Picasso to practise on a painting-by-numbers book. Oh well, maybe they *were* all right. Maybe she should just try and ski.

Jack Taylor had called this morning. Again. And she'd blanked him, again. It didn't help to see that arrogant bastard doing so well, his every triumph reported lovingly in Dempster's diary, his social exploits pictured in *Tatler* for the last couple of months. When she really didn't need to feel any lower, there Jack was, staring out at her, his muscled arm slipped round some bland blonde: Violet Tomlins at the Royal Ballet do, Ursula Fane-Harvey at the Waldegraves' party, even Vanessa Chadwick, her old schoolmate from Switzerland. God, to think she'd nearly fallen for him!

Elizabeth scurried into the station, her Louis Vuitton overnight bag slung across her shoulder, and ducked into W. H. Smith's to pick up some reading for the journey. Nothing about fucking business. A Jilly Cooper and a *Standard*, that should do it. Her train was already at the platform and she secreted herself in first-class, ready to try and relax with a KitKat and the paper.

She opened it at the sports pages.

There was a picture of Jack, his warm smile beaming brightly at her through the muddy newsprint. He had his hand on the neck of a young horse, a magnificent-looking colt. The caption called it 'Another score for Taylor Stud.' Jack had named the beast Easy Money. Elizabeth flung the paper into the luggage rack.

The Alpine Hotel was primed for their arrival. A twee, purpose-built affair on the outskirts of town, it overlooked the distinctly non-Alpine dry-ski slope and was decorated with Holiday Inn-style mountains, pigtailed Heidis and cuckoo clocks. A giant Christmas tree in the lobby fought for attention over the huge display of banners and balloons welcoming 'Our Lovely Olympic Hopefuls'. Elizabeth signed in, furiously embarrassed, under a huge poster of herself, as the hotel manager fussed over her.

'Mr Davis has left a message in your ladyship's suite. Let me get a porter for your bags.'

'There's just the one. I can manage,' Elizabeth muttered, lifting her small bag.

'No, really, my lady—'

'Honestly, it's good for me. The exercise,' Elizabeth pleaded, scribbling an autograph and escaping to the lifts.

Her 'suite' was two rooms done up in tasteless pink and grey, with noisy air-conditioning that she knew would dry out her skin. Her spirits perked up for a moment as she noticed a bottle of champagne in an ice bucket and moved to pick it up, but the cork had been popped and it was empty. A small note was tucked under the neck: 'You won't be needing this. Or the chocolates, which I threw away. Meet us in the gym at six thirty.' It was signed Ronnie Davis.

Elizabeth flopped down on the bed. She wouldn't even have time to clean up. The mirror opposite showed a cross, red-eyed young woman with hair that needed a wash and skin that needed some sleep. In her futile efforts to make a dent at Dragon she'd let the gym work slide, and now she was unfit, out of condition and muscularly weak. She was tired and she looked dreadful.

'Welcome back,' she said aloud.

The gym was reserved for the team. Elizabeth could hear Ronnie's trademark growl as she arrived, in a sports bra and Lycra leggings over Adidas cross-trainers. No point trying to hide in baggy jog-pants, Ron would see right through that.

'Fucking 'ell, Karen, is that the best you can do? Pick it up, girl, gawd almighty ...'

Elizabeth stuck her head through the door. Poor Karen, Janet and Kate were racing around a circular track, sweating bullets. Tinny music, Adam and the Ants, was drifting out of a portable radio. It was no competition for the strident voice of her coach, yelling scornfully as his athletes completed their endurance tests. A group of men in BSF tracksuits lounged at the side of the track but Elizabeth didn't look at them. She was staring horrified at her team-mates. Ron didn't think any of them were up to it, and all three of them looked way, way fitter than she was.

'Hold it.' Ron switched off Radio One and and waved Elizabeth over. 'It's the nobs' answer to Anita Roddick! Good evening, milady, you've finally turned up.'

'Nice to see you too, boss,' Elizabeth said, waving at the girls who all collapsed on the linoleum.

Ronnie came forwards and cast a critical eye over her body. Clearly he didn't like what he saw.

'Flex. Biceps, triceps, delts –' Expert stubby fingers probed her cotton-wool arms. 'Quads, glutes –' Now he was pushing against her bottom, checking her out like one of Jack's horses. Elizabeth blushed scarlet. She was as soft as a marshmallow.

Ronnie frowned thunderously. He grabbed her wrist and took her pulse.

'You're jokin', aren't ya? Seventy-five beats per minute? I'm sorry, miss, you'll have to leave the gym. I'm expecting a World Champion athlete to show up any second.'

Elizabeth paled. Seventy-five? Just three months ago she'd been a steady fifty-eight. That was an athlete's rate. Joe Blow's average was eighty. Could she really have lost it that fast?

'You can't be serious.'

'*I* can be serious, darlin'. The question is, can you be?' Ronnie threw a towel at her. 'Warm up. You got five minutes. Then we're gonna see just how bad the damage really is.'

Barely forty minutes later, Elizabeth was gasping for air. Her feet hurt, her calves were screaming. The clock on the wall told its own sorry tale: forty minutes, Christ, just a warm-up session normally, and here she was, totally worn out. Her sprint speed was still OK but her endurance was shot to pieces. Fifteen minutes of vicious squat thrusts had her in tears, Ronnie screaming at her, the officials shaking their heads, Ronnie screaming at the officials. At least he'd sent them out of the room. Then Elizabeth had to endure the humiliation of a crunch routine and push-up routine in which Janet, Kate and Karen, three girls not usually in her league, outperformed her easily.

'Go and 'ave your dinner,' Ronnie barked at them eventually. 'Not you, milady. You ain't going anywhere. Drop and give me fifty.'

'Fifty!' Elizabeth gasped, wiping the trickles of sweat and dust out of her eyes. 'I can't manage fifteen.'

The coach settled himself on a gymnast's mattress. 'Fifty, Elizabeth. Hans had you on sixty for routine—'

'But that was—'

'Back when you were a skier?'

Elizabeth responded to this with such fury that she didn't hear the gym door creak open again. She tried to ignore everything; the pain in her upper arms, the ache lancing over her back, Toyah Wilcox lisping on the radio, Ronnie's cheerful hello to someone or other. *Come on!* She wasn't so bad that she had to take this shit. Surely. The floor and her upper body. Fifteen, sixteen ... now the lactic acid was burning, blazing fire around the weakness of her biceps ... Another pair of boots had joined

Ronnie's an inch from her nose. She was sweating, gasping, grunting like a stuck pig, willing herself through the red mist of exhaustion. Feeling like a tomato with the blood flooding her face. Twenty-two, twenty-three ... but there was only so much that will power could do. Elizabeth felt failure hovering over her like a vulture. She groaned. Her body simply could not cash this cheque. With an agonised moan she swayed and collapsed, her cheek hitting the dusty linoleum, gasping for air.

'We've got a lot of work to do,' Ronnie said into the silence, 'if you're gonna go to the 1982 Olympics. Let alone win 'em.'

Elizabeth nodded. She didn't have the breath to say anything.

'Oh well.' Her coach's voice shifted back into a friendly, non-business mode. 'Time for supper. You can catch up with the girls, Liz, you'll enjoy that. And your mate here.'

A sudden sickening revelation hit Elizabeth as she stared at the second pair of boots. Cowboy. Chestnut leather. She'd seen those somewhere before.

She raised her reddened, sweating face from the dust and looked up into a pair of twinkling brown eyes. The neat suit and Gieves & Hawkes shirt could not conceal the perfect strength and proportion of his iron, obviously super-fit muscles.

'Hi there,' said Jack Taylor.

Elizabeth scrubbed angrily at her hair in the pouring shower. The fragrance of lavender and thyme drifting up from her Floris conditioner, and the burning heat attacking her soreness, could not wipe away the sense of outrage. If she wasn't so mad she'd be crying. Seventy-five bpm, looking like shit, flabby, weak – couldn't even do *thirty* reps on the floor, and Jack, bloody Jack Taylor, actually standing over her, watching her collapse!

How could Ronnie do it to her? She was going to complain in the strongest language. Get the insufferable bastard thrown out. What was a Yank doing in the British training camp? What, oh God, if word of her condition leaked out? Heidi Laufen would have a very happy Christmas!

She switched off the water and started to dry her hair. Miserably she wished she'd packed a few more cosmetics. There was nothing in her bag but basic foundation, blusher and lipstick. Not much to counter the first impression Jack must have got. He was probably still laughing about it now. Vanessa and Ursula and co. had all looked like they'd spent the morning at Molton Brown. But God, she'd only packed for the girls!

Elizabeth dressed in her travelling outfit, a long, simple knitted jersey sheath from Sonia Rykiel. It was OK, but she had no jewels to dress it up with. The pale pink shade matched her lipstick and blusher and that was about all you could say. It was off the shoulder, and Elizabeth wished it had sleeves. Dinner with four athletes and a coach, it was like advertising her wimpy delts.

She didn't know which was the more humiliating – looking so ugly or looking so weak! Jack had been as polished and gorgeous as ever, and he was clearly still at his peak performance. He could race a downhill tomorrow and cruise it. Most likely he was laughing about it in the hotel bar, right now. With whatever bimbo he was here with.

That thought stopped her hairbrush in mid-stroke. She pounced on her telephone and stabbed out the number for Ronnie's room.

'Hi, it's Elizabeth.'

'Want to talk about it already? Look, Liz, it's early days. No need to panic just yet—'

'No, no.' She cut him off. 'Jack Taylor, Ronnie! What

the hell's he doing here? I want him gone by tomorrow morning!'

'He's here because I invited him. He's going to be doing a little pre-season training with us. It's just fitness.'

'Fitness, hell! He could report back to Kim or Holly.'

'Jack's hardly a spy. You didn't exactly complain about training with him before.' Ronnie's voice was sharp. 'In fact, it did you a lot of good, I seem to recall.'

'He *goes*! I'm not having it!' Elizabeth heard her own voice rise. She felt like stamping her feet. 'I'm the World Champion, it's my team—'

'Hey! It's the British team, Liz Savage.'

'Bullshit!' Some part of her mind told her to give in, but the shame and the anger wouldn't let her stop. Karen, Janet, who the fuck were they? She was the only hope they'd got! '*I'm* the medallist here! I refuse to train with a foreigner! You get him out of here, Ronnie, or I'm filing an official complaint to the Olympic Council.'

'All right, that's enough.' Davis's surprise was as obvious as his anger. 'I'm the gaffer, Elizabeth, simple as that. You say one more word about it and I'll call in the OC myself. There's a minimum fitness standard for all Olympic athletes, do you hear me? If I have you tested officially tomorrow, you're scratched.'

Elizabeth took a deep breath, frozen to the spot.

'You do exactly what you're told, girl, or you wind up a "Where Are They Now" clue on *Question of Sport*. Jack stays. You come down to dinner in ten minutes, and we never had this conversation.' Davis paused; his fury crackled down the line. 'Your attitude needs as much work as your body. You got two weeks to get both in shape or believe me, milady, you are *out*.'

Chapter 18

Nina pulled her Golf GTi sharply to the right and parked neatly. It was the black darkness of early morning in December, but the Dragon car park was flooded with light. It gave her a little thrill to see her name stencilled in white against the wall. 'Reserved, Miss Nina Roth, New Products.' Last week she had passed her driving test first time; no trouble learning the English system, because she'd never had a car in the States.

The Golf had been the first tangible benefit. The day after that long, teasing dinner with Tony, Keith Sweeney from Personnel had summoned her and shown her a range of cars. Pick one. Any colour. Red is the most popular.

Nina thanked him and took a dark blue.

She smiled softly as she left Sweeney's office. Dinner the night before had rewritten the rulebook around here. As she casually ran through chat about drugs, approvals, regulations, Nina made sure her body did all the real talking. Leaning into Tony, letting those hard eyes flicker over her bodice, her inviting smile and long legs. Tony Savage had started bringing up figures of his own. Money. Market share. Personal profits. Letting her see just how powerful and rich he really was. He was brash and obvious, but it had worked. Savage was magnetically sexual. Nina knew it was throwing her principles to the winds to flirt with Tony like that, but he was the boss, and it was what he wanted.

She tried not to think about the fact that it was what she'd wanted too.

Tony's kiss on her hand at the end of the night was slow, toying with her skin, his lips touching her hand just that fraction too long.

He wants me, Nina thought triumphantly.

She got out of the car and pressed a button on her keys. Central locking, a new invention. They were all over the place. Atari games consoles were cramming the West End toy stores, and yesterday someone at Phillips had shown them a flat, rounded metal disc, loudly proclaiming it to be the future of music. In television, video recorders were the new craze; now you could tape pictures as well as sound. Betacam and VHS were fighting it out as operating systems.

'Buy VHS. And buy stock in VHS,' Nina had told Tony last night.

He had smiled at her, a little patronisingly. 'Betacam is clearly superior.'

She had ducked her head, letting her newly waved, softly curled hair skim her shoulders. 'Yes, but VHS have more software available. Superior pictures don't matter if you can't watch any movies.'

Once more she had felt his eyes lock on hers as the finance director launched into his report. For two weeks they had been circling each other; Tony, with his diary crammed full of year-end speeches and Christmas dinners, hadn't had any evenings free since he took her to dinner. Nina, pressing her advantage, put together a file on freelance drug researchers that she hoped would blow Frank Staunton away. It was clear to her that the current slimming drug was a bust. Effective, but not safe. If Dragon put a pill out there before it was ready, the company could be ruined. Like Betacam would be.

And there was more work to do. Nina knew Tony was chasing his holy grail, but what if that was a mirage?

Right here and now there was a lot more work to do. Inefficient customer response. Poorly advertised standard drugs that were losing market share. Dull stuff, maybe, but their bread and butter. Nina made sure she had that stuff covered too. It wouldn't look good on her résumé if she spent all her time on a project that ended up a failure.

So Tony was busy and she was busy. But that was about to change.

The building was half-empty. In the last week before the Christmas holiday, many staff had taken up holiday time and gone home. Balloons sprouted from computer monitors and gaudy paper-chains looped across ceilings. There was a definite sense of unreality. In the States, Nina thought wryly, you'd get a couple of cards stood on a desk, that was it. The Brits did it differently; 1981 seemed already over for most of the drones sitting here making half-hearted calls. Partly that was because of Europe. The Swiss had packed up and gone home, retailers had placed Christmas orders long ago, research labs stocked with international teams were dispersing across the globe. Who would you call? Even the Stock Exchange was sluggish. The Brits were like a bunch of schoolchildren, watching the clock and waiting for the bell.

Nina threaded her way through Marketing. Lady Elizabeth's desk was unoccupied except for a huge pile of cards and presents. The staff sucking up. Sports fans' tributes, forwarded by the BBC. But Elizabeth wasn't here to pick them up, she was off at training camp in Kent.

Nina paused. 'This looks ridiculous.'

Dino Vincenza, senior marketing manager, looked up from his terminal. 'Lady Elizabeth is very popular,' he said silkily. 'Many people like her skiing. And her ideas.'

Nina heard the rebuke just as he meant her to. Popular, unlike you. And you're stamping on her. Technically

Dino outranked her, but she was a comer in a more important department, and a favourite of the Robber Baron.

She reached forwards and picked up an envelope at random. It was very stiff, thick card inside creamy paper. An invitation. Nina flipped it over and found a gold coronet franked on the back. What was it? A New Year's ball, Boxing Day sherry, a hunt meet somewhere? She didn't look to see whose the crest was. It didn't matter. It was another sign of Elizabeth's world, of her class, her privilege. All the things that Nina could never get.

'I'll call Maria in the postal office. Get this cleared, and future mail routed to the castle. It may be Christmas, but that's no excuse for the place looking a dump.'

'Of course,' Dino said sweetly.

Nina stormed off to her area with her cheeks flaming. She hated being mocked. Her own desk was fastidiously neat; since she was Jewish, nobody had sent her cards. Yesterday she had been pleased by this sign of respect. Now she found herself riddled with doubts. Was it respect? Or were they all snubbing her?

Come on, girl. Since when did you care what a bunch of limey assholes thought of you?

Angrily she switched on her computer and started to cross-reference. To Nina the end of the year represented opportunity. It was a chance to get her act together and her findings in order. While the rest of the company sipped sherry and stuffed mince pies, and that blonde dilettante went jogging in the countryside.

I'm efficient, Nina told herself, pulling up a new spreadsheet. I *work* during the working day—

The phone buzzed on her desk, making her jump. She snatched it up.

'Roth, New Products.'

'Tony Savage, Chairman's Office.' The dry voice sent a shiver through Nina's stomach, an electric crackle like radio static. She wasn't expecting his call until late this afternoon. 'Do you have that report on the research teams?'

'I was just tidying it up.'

'I need it now. You'd better come upstairs and present.'

'But I haven't even typed it up—'

'Now, Nina.' The earl hung up.

For a moment she sat frozen. Bastard! It wasn't ready! He'd said tomorrow, hadn't he? But repeating that to Tony Savage wouldn't help her any. He didn't like excuses; he was merciless to underlings that proffered them. Quickly she dumped her early notes out to the printer and rushed over, ripping the still-warm sheet out of the machine after it inched through. Present? To whom? The virtuous smug feeling of a few moments before evaporated.

The elevator arrived. Piped carols rang out annoyingly as Nina stood there fidgeting. 'God rest ye, merry gentlemen, let nothing you dismay ...' Which was great for the merry gentlemen, but bugged the hell out of the harassed lady.

Tony met her as she stepped out. He looked crisp as ever. No novelty Rudolph ties for his lordship.

'I have the basic gist, but it was due tomorrow,' Nina said.

Her boss frowned. 'Unlike the rest of the bloody country, we don't deal in work to rule.'

'No, sir, but I had to do the sales projections and—'

'I told you what your priority was to be.' Lord Caerhaven's angry voice had nothing of flirtation about it. 'The slimming drug. It's not for you suddenly to decide what you concentrate on. Now go in there and present it.'

Nina looked up into the dark eyes and found them unyielding. Reluctantly she walked into his office. A long table had been set up in the middle of the room and was surrounded by middle-aged men. She recognised Gerald Jax and Don Hadley, head of Finance US. Plus there was a banker from Credit Suisse whose name she couldn't place, but his jowly face was familiar – a heavy hitter.

Tony sat at the head of the table and introduced her briefly while Nina's heart flipped slowly in her chest. She didn't need lapel badges to realise who this lot were. Investment bankers, Dragon Europe heads, American management. The big boys. The guys who ran things.

Men you seriously didn't want to screw up in front of.

'Thank you, Lord Caerhaven,' Nina said faintly. 'The first thing we have to face is that Steele Ripley, our current research team, is not up to the job. Their drugs are effective but consistently unsafe. We must look for other R and D sources …'

Her throat was dry. The room seemed dreadfully bright. Not so much as a sprig of plastic holly lightened the tone up here. The eyes of her superiors were fixed on her and Nina had to fight back panic. Not a natural public speaker, without orderly notes she was flustered. She forgot company names, track records. She kept looking at her paper. She fumbled questions from around the room. Sometimes she didn't even know the answers.

Nina couldn't look at Tony. She had the awful feeling that she might be going to cry. She didn't want to cry, it was a reflex action against the embarrassment. She didn't look super-smooth now; these men were seeing just what she was, a young girl, floundering miserably, out of her depth.

'But you're arguing the allocation of massive resources. Steele Ripley are a known quantity,' Gerald Jax was objecting.

'Yes, sir. But known to be greedy and lax on safety.'

'The B-28 damage isn't as bad as you're making out.'

Heinrich Günther, Dragon Deutschland. The West German was bony and florid, anger making him more ruddy than usual. He'd discovered Dr Steele and Professor Ripley. 'Nobody has died.'

'Not yet, Herr Günther, but they would, long term.' You fucking Nazi, Nina thought, what were your parents doing in the war? 'Look, we might as well package up cocaine! You'd enjoy it, you'd get thin, at first you'd be fine. But in the end you'd be a useless junkie.'

There was a heavy silence. Jax lowered his eyes.

'Get out!' Günther shouted. 'You incompetent, you are wasting our time!'

Nina froze.

'Didn't you hear me? Get out!'

Shellshocked, Nina grabbed her sheet of notes and bolted for the door. Once she was safely in the corridor, her eyes filled with tears. She ducked into a restroom to get herself together. Christ! What had she said? Was she really that bad? Was she going to get fired?

Tony watched Nina scarper like a startled doe. Her pretty turned calves flashed out of the room, black tights with seams at the back rising up to a smart turquoise wool skirt. She'd been scrappy and scared, but she'd got the information across. He was pleased with the result. His lieutenants had something to think about. And Ms Roth had been scalded out of her complacency.

She'd been doing well, but he never liked any junior to think they were doing too well. Especially not a woman.

She was bruised now, he thought; that would soften her. That débâcle with Heinrich was wonderful. Poor little Nina, how was she to know about his longstanding fondness for a snort of Charlie? His head of Dragon GmbH thought he was being deliberately insulted.

Tony reached into his breast pocket and pulled out a folded red spotted handkerchief. He threw it at Günther.

'Here, Heinrich. Terrible sniff you've got, old man. I should see a doctor about that cold. And now, gentlemen, let's consider the points Miss Roth made.'

Back at her desk Nina typed furiously. She worked through lunch without taking a break. She couldn't afford to be caught napping twice. When the travel office sent someone upstairs with her air ticket for tonight, Nina almost told them to check if she was still meant to be travelling. But if Tony wanted her out, she'd be out soon enough. Christmas was no protection. Tony would fire someone at the office party if he felt like it.

By the end of the day her stomach was growling and her fingers were cramped. She filed everything into a briefcase and set off for Heathrow. She guessed she was still going, since nobody said otherwise.

London and its suburbs slipped by her in a cold drizzle. The sky was already black, but there were too many clouds for stars. Nina drove as fast as she could without breaking the law. She didn't want a ticket or a delay; no more black marks, please, Lord.

The Human League, Madness and Diana Ross blared out of her car radio. When Haircut 100 came on Nina switched off. Shitty music, shitty weather, stuck-up old-money pricks! she thought. I hate this fucking country!

But did she want to go home? After today, maybe she'd have to. All the money, the allowances, the car and nice clothes, vanished. The thought made her sweat. Back to Brooklyn? No job, no references ... when you were in with Dragon, great; when you were out you were usually dead. People who pissed them off didn't work again. At least, not in the drugs business.

At the airport she checked in for Dublin with British Midland and was directed to the VIP lounge.

The earl was standing to one side in the middle of a knot of men. With a start Nina recognised Harry Cohen from Planning, Joe Bould from Strategic Accounts, even mousy, capable Maggie Stevens from Customer Relations. For the second time today she was taken aback. She'd thought she was the only one Tony was taking to Dublin, to attend a Europe-wide conference on distribution routes. But there were at least seven others!

Trying to hide her discomfiture, she walked over.

'Miss Roth. Good. I thought you were going to delay us,' Tony said coolly.

Nina smiled lamely. She didn't dare say a word. Tony wasn't smiling at her or glancing over; he seemed deep in a discussion with the Cohen boy. Clearly she'd got it very wrong. She was just one more junior exec; nothing special.

From Dublin airport they were ferried in limos to the Shelbourne Hotel. The hotel was old fashioned, with art deco nymphs at the gate looking out on a small green park; it was bustling with delegates in evening dress, packing the Horseshoe Bar and talking shop. The Dragon contingent filed into a packed conference room to listen to speeches; they would be changing for dinner later.

Exhausted and upset, Nina tried to force herself to listen. She saw Maggie taking notes but this was kids' stuff for her. Stuffed shirts from ICI, SmithKline Beecham and Glaxo droned on about healthcare providers. The room was warm from the packed audience, and Nina was fighting to stay awake, to fake some enthusiasm, and to avoid the besuited assholes all round her trying so obviously to catch her eye.

And then it was his turn.

Tony Savage stood up at the podium and noted the immediate response. The packed room jerked to life. Heads lifted. Whispers ceased.

He was the Robber Baron.

As he talked – with enough gravitas for a Lord Chancellor, rather than a takeover pirate – Tony felt the pleasure of it all flood through him like adrenalin. His quarterlies looked great. Recession? What recession? Look at these pricks, he thought: drab, plump, soft-bellied losers, the lot of them. He knew they'd all heard the rumours: the debauchery, the vengeful streak. They loved it. They wished they were him. Like Machiavelli, Tony thought, I'd rather be feared than loved. And nobody said a word. He took his pleasures like a City barrow-boy, but last July, he'd been there with Monica in Westminster Abbey, a sombre and dignified peer, watching Diana Spencer waltz off with the Prince of Wales.

Louise and Jay DeFries were the last people ever to make him look a fool; and look what happened to them.

As his speech raced to its conclusion, Tony let his gaze find his own people. The boys and Miss Stevens were watching with appropriate awe, but it wasn't them he was looking for. And then he saw her: a flash of light blue in the drab browns and greys; pale face framed with that thick cloud of black hair; a dragonfly amongst the midges. Nina. She was watching him, and Tony was amused again. Because even though she quickly dropped her eyes, it wasn't fast enough to hide the blazing anger, the rage in them, burning in her dark pupils like fire on coal.

Chapter 19

After Tony's closing address, the room broke up to prepare for dinner. Nina rushed upstairs, feeling stressed out. She knew she'd glared at him, knew he'd seen it. The misery and rage would not be held back. He had lectured her and humiliated her. God knew how she was going to get through tonight.

Her bedroom was decorated with genteel, faded charm: Victorian prints and a radiator whose age could not be disguised by its new coat of paint. But it was luxurious, after a fashion; the bed made with heavy Irish linens, fresh lavender and roses scenting the air, the wall mirror mounted in an antique brass frame. Nina unpacked her overnight bag quickly. She wished she'd been smart and brought some Pro-Plus. If the rumours were true, Joe Bould across the hall would be refreshing himself with a quick line or two of fine Peruvian marching powder right now. But Nina didn't do drugs. Loss of control equalled weakness.

In the pretty mirror she repaired the damage to her exhausted face. Concealer under the eyes, white pencil along the bottom lid for that alert look. Light turquoise shadow with sea- and dark greens at the edges, a bronze slash of blusher painting the colour back into her cheeks, berry lipstick with a neat matching liner, her dark hair curled gently into her face. It took less than five minutes; Nina planned everything in advance now, it was a habit. Even her make-up. She pulled on a pair of dark-green velvet mules by Ferragamo and grabbed her dress from the hanger. Full-length, bias-cut jade crêpe, layered thickly enough to be opaque, it was a creation by a hot new Manhattan designer, Donna Karan. Looked nothing on the peg, but when Nina slipped it on, adjusting the thick gilt clasp on the left shoulder, it clung to her curves then fell from the waist, making her look like a Greek goddess. And it moved like a sea wave.

Nina smiled softly. She looked beautiful. On nights like this one, you could put on your beauty like armour.

Downstairs the Dragon party had assembled already. Maggie Stevens's jealous scowl – she'd picked a boring black velvet number, probably from Next – reassured her.

Harry Cohen coughed. 'Shall we go in? They've set our placings.'

Nina followed her colleagues. The conference had set out tables back to back, dispersing delegates from different firms around the room. That was the point: you swapped business cards, made contacts. Nina was cynical. She didn't believe real work got done at these places. Conference jaunts were an institution, an excuse for a booze-up and salary-swapping, comparing your status. Whatever.

The menu plan had Nina on Table 1. She checked it again just to be sure. Table 1 was surely for the MDs and directors, wasn't it? But there she was, so she mounted the wooden steps at the end of the room.

'Nina Roth,' she told the hovering waiter.

He glanced at a list. 'Yes, madam. Just over here.'

Nina followed the man right to the head of the table. She was two places down from the Chairman of ICI. To her left was the Finance Minister of the Republic. The chair to her right was empty. Trying to hide her surprise, she smiled and shook hands in complete confusion as she sat down. And then a shadow passed over the table and the waiter was seating her other neighbour.

Tony Savage.

He looked great. Tony had been born to black tie. The other bigshots here were grey and bespectacled, nerdy, or plump. The earl was lean; spare and muscular, his hair dark, his eyes glittering as he sat. Nina couldn't help but notice the table's reaction, how these gentlemen smiled at her boss with their eyes full of envy, curiosity, and loathing. The alleycat was among the tame pigeons.

She had to say something.

'I'm – I – good evening, Lord Caerhaven.' She didn't dare call him Tony, not after today. 'Aren't the delegates supposed to be sat separately?'

'Umm.' The arrogant tilt of his head looked down on her. 'They are, but I ordered that you be sat next to me.'

Nina swallowed.

'Is that a problem?' Tony asked. His eyes were dancing, observing her discomfiture. 'Would you rather be down there, with the others?'

'No, sir.' She was blushing. Although everybody at Dragon called Tony sir, in a work situation, there was something disturbing about it right now. The formalised submission. The sense of his power. And his closeness. Nina took refuge in a belt of champagne. 'I'm sorry about this morning, sir. I should have been ready.'

'Yes, you should have,' Tony said. 'I set the priorities. You follow them. Is that clear?'

The rest of the table were talking amongst themselves while the starter was laid out. Nina knew they were being rude, but Tony clearly didn't give a fuck. She swallowed the rest of her glass. She was a mess of fear and desire.

'Yes, sir.' She couldn't help it, she blurted out, 'Am I fired?'

He grinned. His eyes flickered down the bodice of her dress. The look burned a wash of fire across her skin, like the alcohol was burning down her throat. Under the silk, her groin tightened.

'You're good. I can use you. You're just not as good as you thought you were. Don't act on your own initiative, act on *my* initiative. Dragon is not a democracy. You're not at your five-and-dime store in Brooklyn now.'

The reference to her past jerked Nina's eyes back up to his. The earl was looking at her in that superior, maddening way Elizabeth had. Don't forget who you are, it said. I took you out of there and I can send you back.

With an effort Nina nodded. Bastard, she thought, he's got the whip hand and he loves it. She turned to the Minister for Finance and made some desultory conversation, pushing her oysters round her plate. She couldn't eat. Tony Savage, on her other side, was lording it over the rest of the table; sometimes their eyes slid over her dress, but then it was always back to Tony. That was his magnetism, and anyway, for guys like these, sex always came second to power.

Nina drank champagne for courage, enjoying the icy, bubbling sting in her mouth. I might be white trash, she thought angrily, but I'm *smart* white trash. The best. I got here myself, asshole, and you were born in a goddamn castle!

She forced herself to take a little of the *entrée*. Grouse and roast parsnip. The earl was still watching her. She felt his gaze on her shoulders, the curve of her waist. The champagne was buzzing round her bloodstream. Despite herself, Nina felt herself tense again, moisten between the legs.

The Minister turned to Tony. 'Lord Caerhaven, Miss Roth does you credit. She's got a better grasp of EU regulations than some of my officials.'

Tony smiled. 'Nina's got a top-drawer brain, Minister. That was my first reason for hiring her.' When the old buffer reached for more cranberry jelly, he grinned down at Nina.

The alcohol made her brave. 'And what was the second?'

'The packaging,' Tony said lightly. Then he turned to his neighbour, and didn't speak to her again for the rest of the meal.

Once the plates were cleared the room broke up.

'I'll go and mingle.'

The earl was shaking hands, but he broke off to put one on her shoulder. 'No. Wait in the lobby. I'll be right out.'

Nina picked her way through the crowd, weaving and smiling. She was dizzy and carefree. Maybe she should have gone easy on the wine, with an empty stomach, but what the hell. She wandered out and stood by a dusty palm in a large brass pot, refusing to meet the hungry male eyes that followed her.

Tony was out less than a minute later, striding through a crowd that seemed to part around him. Nina noticed how tall he was; even with her heels, he towered over her. He beckoned to her curtly and they walked into the Horseshoe Bar together. Nina found she was backed into a corner.

'I like your dress,' Savage said.

'I'm glad you like something.'

He laughed softly. 'Prickly. Let's see how good you really are.'

Nina caught her breath. The dark eyes and predator smile were fixed on her, and the desire in them was naked. So blatant she felt herself tighten some more, the downy hairs of her belly lifting in response. Jeff had never looked at her that way, with such expertise, such pure confidence.

'Are you asking me on a date?'

'No. I'm asking you to bed. Don't tell me you're surprised.'

'I guess not,' Nina murmured. She kept her voice down, afraid people would hear them. Caerhaven didn't seem to care about that; or anything, she thought. She stared back at him. 'And what if I say no? You sack me?'

He moved a step closer. Crowding her. Bending slightly, so his face was close to hers, so that when he spoke, she was looking at his mouth.

'You're a clever girl, you know what I do for my friends. And you want me. So let's not play games.' Savage held out his hand to her. 'Come with me.'

'We're going up there together?' Nina whispered. Tony smiled; he liked the way the kid kept blushing, eyes darting about, like a hare looking to bolt. 'But what will people think?'

'Who gives a damn?' Tony Savage said.

They rode up together in a stately, creaking elevator, joining some suits and a couple of dowagers. When the last of them left at the fourth floor, Tony turned to her, casually, and reached for her breasts through the silky crêpe, feeling their heaviness, palming them deftly, feeling the sharpness of her nipples. Nina gasped. Her knees weakened. He didn't say anything but he smiled, letting her know he could feel her response. Nina felt ashamed but also flooded with heat. Experimentally Tony moved one hand down to the flat of her stomach, resting it there, feeling the warmth of her burning through her gown. The other came up to cup her chin, and he slowly pushed his thumb into her mouth.

Nina started to suck it. She didn't know what he was doing to her. She was light with lust, almost collapsing, pressing herself against his hand.

'Steady,' he said. Like he was laughing at her.

The elevator juddered to a halt. Nina tried to pull herself together. Tony waited politely for her to walk out first.

The penthouse suite was to the left. Nobody passed them. Tony reached for his key calmly, without hurrying, but Nina could see his hard-on outlined through his pants. His desire was as strong as hers, he was just more used to it. How many women has he had? she thought. A hundred? More than that? Every touch, every look of his was assured. Business and society whispered about him. His girls, his Teflon romances. Not one of them had ever breathed a word. For a second that made her uneasy; how could that be? Was it a Brit thing, a code of silence? Or did Caerhaven use the carrot and the stick?

Come on, girl, you're not afraid …

The key connected with the lock.

Tony held the door open for her as he flicked on the light. Nina looked round a gorgeous suite, crammed with flowers, baskets of fruit and nuts and chocolates on a silver tray. The furniture was mahogany, Georgian antique, including a full bookcase. There was a white damask chaise-longue and armchairs in navy-blue leather. A huge mirror dominated one wall; oil paintings the others. The bed was a double, pillows heaped on a snowy coverlet; lambswool blankets and broderie anglaise.

Tony shut the door.

'Are you nervous?'

'No,' Nina said boldly.

He came over to her and steered her into the centre of the room, at the foot of the bed. Facing the mirror. Then he tipped her face up to his with both hands.

'Liar,' he said.

Then he bent down and kissed her. Nina breathed in cigar smoke, light, sexy masculine sweat, that expensive aftershave he used. His lips were brushing hers softly, not gentle so much as exploratory. Tasting her. Pushing on her. Getting a feel for her mouth. Then he was rougher, kissing and breaking off, using his tongue, biting her, his hands slipping round her face, yanking her to him, and then his hands moulding the roundness of her butt, stroking her breasts, her belly, pushing down between her legs. Tony was strong: he wouldn't let her force the pace, holding her back when she squirmed under his touch, closing her mouth with his when she wanted to speak.

When he broke off, Nina's breath was ragged.

'Have you ever had an orgasm?'

She blushed. 'Of course.'

'With a man? No, I thought not.' Tony broke away from her and reached for the clasp on her shoulder, unpinning it. 'Let's have a look at you, baby.'

Nina just stood there as her gown slithered to the floor. The dizzy, squirmy mixture of embarrassment and excitement was almost too much to bear. To want a man like this and have him know it. A man you didn't even really like. But the antagonism made it better ... carefully she stepped out of the dress and kicked it aside.

She stood naked in front of the mirror except for a tiny scrap of lace at the groin; full, firm breasts, a sleek waist, and a high, rounded ass. Soft upper arms, sweetly turned calves, small feet. She saw the light in Tony's eyes burst into flame. He groaned and pulled her to him. Nina felt his hands everywhere, tugging her panties down her thighs, his fingers sliding into her, feeling her arousal. The rough cloth of his suit brushed against her everywhere. His erection was larger and harder now. She wanted to undo his belt but her fingers wouldn't work, they were shaking.

Tony reached for his shirt buttons. He broke two ripping them open, he couldn't get naked fast enough. His cock was throbbing in his pants, he was a teenager again, fighting to control himself. The girl was light headed from the champagne, but even so, magnificently responsive, and naïve at the same time. Passionate but clumsy, clearly not used to it. If not her first, he'd be one of the first. The thought was exquisitely exciting. She'd been worth waiting for. Check out that body, those incredible breasts with the gorgeous, dark-fleshed nipples, tight as raisins, waiting for him. He could get his hands round her waist and her ass was out of this world, he could fuck her all night long. He'd been with no really clever woman since Louise but Nina didn't turn him off. Her brain would make her inventive. She thought she could get round him, but as he'd shown her today, he had her future, everything, right in the palm of his hand. He had her where he wanted her, and that was just how it'd stay.

'God, you're beautiful.' He pulled her on to the bed. 'I could fall in love with you.'

'Bullshit,' Nina said sweetly.

Tony reached for her.

Chapter 20

The phone buzzed. Elizabeth's left hand reached out to grab it while her right hand flung back the blankets and her feet swung down to the carpet.

'This is your wake-up call,' the recorded voice intoned. 'The time now is ...'

Five forty-five a.m. She dropped the receiver back on the hook and bounded towards the bathroom, flicking on all the switches. Light stops the production of melatonin, the body's natural sleep hormone. After frustrating months of reading, Elizabeth knew her biochemistry back to front. Anyway, the morning routine was conditioned now. Quickly she washed her face and showered briefly, dried herself on an ugly peach towel that looked like a reject from BHS, and pulled on her running gear. Four days in Tunbridge Wells had tightened her butt and strengthened her legs. Ronnie's threat hit home; whatever else happened, she had to be fit. The team had followed a set training routine, but that wasn't enough for Elizabeth. When Karen, Janet and Kate had finished, Elizabeth would change suits and head back out the door. Five extra miles every night, then team dinner, then free weights. Seeing the other girls with better physiques than her fired Elizabeth's competitive edge.

And it was a good way of avoiding Jack Taylor.

Elizabeth pulled on her sports bra, ignoring the little thrill of excitement and anger Jack always provoked. Sitting there at dinner, pretending to discuss business with her. Ronnie refused to get rid of him, and Elizabeth just had to take it: Jack lying next to her in the weights room, bench-pressing three hundred, his chiselled muscles contracting, sliding back and forth, his jaw clamped tight in ferocious concentration. She hated him. His perfect body. His peak conditioning, his fucking business success.

Elizabeth flung herself into a warm-up routine, lifting her heels up to her butt to get the blood flowing round the hamstrings.

'He's got the best body I've ever seen,' Karen had gasped last night. Ron had put them all through a second fitness test. Jack joined in, and Elizabeth was forced to watch. Jack's powerful quads tensing as he ate up the squat-thrust routines. His back muscles knotting and sliding in the press-ups. And his bicep curls, God, the weights he could lift. Elizabeth felt her team-mates' eyes just eating him up.

'He's nothing special,' she muttered.

They'd gaped at her in disbelief.

When Elizabeth hit the machines, Jack was watching her. She was clamped in place like a prisoner. And flexing, clamping her legs open and shut for the inner thighs, Jack had hung back and just blatantly stared between them.

'Open.' Ronnie yelling at her like a sergeant major. 'Close and open. Come on, Elizabeth! Open. *Open*. Great ...'

Elizabeth pushed up from the soles of her runners, swinging her arms, blushing furiously. Remembering the betraying, ridiculous rush of sexual heat as she sweated and struggled, forcing her thighs apart, trying not to let that arrogant fuck see what effects his little games had on her. It was killing her, that was a plain fact. If Ronnie didn't get him out of here, there was a terrible danger Elizabeth was going to crack. She'd lain awake for an hour last night, dizzy with longing, not daring to touch herself in case that made it worse.

She took a swig of water from an Evian bottle, stretched out her calves and hamstrings, and opened the door. The hotel was just stirring, waiters setting out places in the awful buffet dining room, papers being shoved under doors. Outside, the roads were still quiet in the morning darkness. Elizabeth's blood was flowing now and she was looking forward to her run. For forty minutes she was alone with her body, nobody hassling her. She was hungry to get back out there to the snow. Louise and Heidi would be practising on World Cup courses, while she had to muck about on nylon fibres in distinctly non-World Cup Kent.

She jogged out of the lobby and stopped dead.

Jack Taylor was standing there, wearing pro Adidas runners and a US Olympic tracksuit.

'What the hell do you want?' Elizabeth demanded.

Jack gave her a lazy smile. 'To go running, Sherlock.'

'Who told you? Ronnie?' She stopped herself. 'Actually, I don't care. I run by myself.'

'Well.' He shifted on his feet, a movement that reminded her of his skiing. 'I know you're scared of me, sugar, but—'

'Scared? Don't be ridiculous.'

'Sure scared. You've been avoiding me ever since I got here. Which I think is kind of unfriendly, for a guy that saved your life.'

Elizabeth flushed. 'You provoked me into skiing off.'

'Provoked you?' Jack shrugged, his handsome, cruel mouth twisting a little scornfully. 'Because I took you on a hard run? I thought you could handle it, girl, but maybe I was wrong. I guess you've always been afraid of real competition.'

Elizabeth gave him an icy stare. 'You're heavy, Taylor. You're not built for speed. Your muscles are all wrong.'

'Try me,' Jack said.

'OK.' Already she was turning the local roads round in her mind, rewriting the course. 'We'll start by the station, then up the High Street.' That was two miles of solid uphill work.

'Fine by me, Princess.' Jack didn't flinch.

She turned away from him and loped off to the right, heading for the pool of neon orange under a far streetlamp. Her feet were lifting off the asphalt, rising to the challenge, flying away from him. Behind her Elizabeth heard Jack's grunt of surprise and the heavy thud of him on the ground as he raced to catch her. It took him four or five seconds. As Jack pulled up beside her, Elizabeth effortlessly increased the pace.

'Come on, Taylor,' she said coldly. 'Let's see what you got.'

Thirty minutes later she was covered in sweat. Straight hill running, then hill running on a curve, with small flat stretches to keep it aerobic. Elizabeth was working at the top of her range but she could feel Jack really suffering. He *was* too strong for sprinting.

'It's called muscle memory,' Jack gasped when they finally hit the Pantiles. Royal Tunbridge Wells was a ghost town at this hour, its prosperous red-brick houses and pretty Georgian streets deserted. He watched Elizabeth fly past countless gift shops and antique dealers, her long neck lifted, her haunches in front of him tight and fluid.

'What is?'

'Your fitness. How fast it's coming back. Even if you lose it, you're not starting from scratch. You should be ready for snow work in a couple more days.'

'Well, thanks, Coach,' Elizabeth snapped. She was annoyed that Jack hadn't cried off yet, the stubborn bastard. 'Let's see if *you're* ready for this. Toad Rocks. Half a mile up this curve.'

Four minutes later she turned into a dirt track off the main road. The prehistoric rock formation thrust out of thick woodland, surrounded by sand; a giant beachhead hidden in the middle of Kent. Elizabeth usually ran there in the mornings, via a much softer route. Overhead the sky was lightening, the pink and gold streaks of dawn creeping in from the east. She forced herself to bounce on her feet and breathe regularly.

Behind her Jack Taylor caught up, hit a rock, and collapsed, gasping, tearing the air into his lungs. Unbelievable. That exhaustion was all the reward she was going to get. He'd taken everything she could throw at him.

Petulantly Elizabeth ignored him and started some deep stretches. Jack said nothing, so when she was done she turned to face him. He was still lying prostrate, clutching his ankle.

'What's wrong?'

'It hurts. Christ, I think it's fractured,' Jack muttered.

Guilt surged through her. Who'd been playing macho games now? If Jack's ankle was fractured, it was highly unlikely it would heal in time for the Olympics. He was the favourite for gold. She'd have robbed him of that just to make a point.

Elizabeth gasped in dismay and sunk to her knees by Jack.

'Oh! It's all my fault, I'm so sorry.' She reached out and touched his lower leg but Taylor flinched away from her. Elizabeth's eyes prickled with tears. 'Can I test it, Jack? I'll be very careful ...'

He nodded, biting his lip, and spread his legs a little to make room for her. Gingerly Elizabeth draped herself across him, her breasts brushing his thighs, and reached forwards with both hands. His ankle was lying in a pool of shadow from the rock. She couldn't see if it was discoloured.

'Gentle,' Jack murmured.

Elizabeth took his foot in her hands like it was made of eggshells and massaged it lightly, expertly, her long fingers working the muscle and bone, probing for any swelling.

'You seem OK to me—'

Suddenly Jack pounced, slipping one arm over the small of her back and tipping her into the sand. His legs kicked underneath her and his mouth fastened against hers in a deep, rough kiss.

'Bastard,' Elizabeth snarled.

'You play rough, sugar. You nearly killed me.'

He tasted of sand and sweat. He kissed her like he knew what he was doing. His arms were thicker than her upper thighs. She was back on that mountain, lifting her body into his, remembering herself dangling into space, hanging on to life by the strength of that arm. There were no men like Jack in her father's office.

'I came to England to find you,' he said, looking right down into her eyes.

'What, you can't live without me?' Elizabeth asked, trying for sarcasm and failing.

He grinned. 'Sure I can live without you. It just wouldn't be nearly so much fun.'

Then he kissed her again, and again, covering her face and her neck and ears with downy, butterfly kisses, till Elizabeth gasped and pressed her body into his.

'Come on.' Jack hauled her easily to her feet. 'We'd better get back, or I'm gonna take you to bed right here.'

She trained that day in a fever of anticipation and happiness. Partly to prove something to Ronnie, partly to show off to Jack.

'I can't believe it.' Ron was fulsome in his praise as

they lined up in the Alpine View buffet restaurant for lunch, Elizabeth heaping her plate with pasta salad, baked potatoes and tuna. 'You're almost at race fitness.'

'Cow.' Karen's joky insult had a slight edge to it. She could sense that the antipathy between Jack and Elizabeth had gone. As had the other girl's fantasies of displacing Lady Liz as number one.

'Umm, I must admit, I didn't think you'd be ready.' Janet had a dig too. It wasn't fair. Ronnie's threat had leaked out and she'd hoped Elizabeth might just be dropped. Now she was going to waltz off with a medal and maybe Jack Taylor. None of them could miss the way his eyes had fastened on her all day.

'It's called muscle memory,' Elizabeth smiled sweetly. 'My body just needed reminding.'

'You've worked hard.' Ronnie grinned as they all slotted into a table. He liked the resentment crackling round the room, it would make them more competitive. 'I think you're ready for snow training too. Hans Wolf called from Lausanne today. He wants to get you back on the snow, mid-Jan.'

That would mean giving up on Dragon. But then, thanks to Nina Roth, I'm going nowhere fast anyway, Elizabeth thought. Maybe it was time to cut her losses.

'Great,' she said.

Jack called for her after dinner.

'Let's go out for a drive.'

Elizabeth looked up at him in surprise, but Jack gestured to her tacky room. 'We can do better than this, don't you think?'

They passed Janet in the lobby. 'Training starts at six tomorrow,' she said, staring jealously at Jack's arm threaded through Elizabeth's duffel coat.

'And she'll probably be there,' Jack replied. Elizabeth

bit back her smile, but Janet's eyes glittered with dislike anyway.

A hire car was parked in the forecourt, a sleek Mercedes. Elizabeth slid into the passenger seat while Jack jumped in beside her. A set of keys were resting on the dashboard.

'Where are we going?' Elizabeth asked.

He smiled. 'You'll see.'

They drove out of town towards East Sussex, dipping up and down country hills. Jack drove smoothly, unfazed by the narrow woodland roads and sharp corners. The night was crisp and cold, the stars brilliant in the clear sky. Rabbits scurried away from the headlights, and once she saw a white owl's wing ghosting up out of the trees in front of them.

He parked outside a cottage on the edge of Frant village. 'My country retreat. I stay here when I'm going to meets.'

Jack jumped out to open the door for her. His Texas gallantry made her nervous.

What's wrong with me? Elizabeth thought. Suddenly she cared desperately about the kind of impression she was giving him. It had never been that way with Gerard de Mesnil, or Karl, or any of the others.

'Come in.' Jack flicked on lights and ushered her into the cottage. It was beautiful, with timbered ceilings and wooden stairs curving upwards. Elizabeth hung up her duffel on an old-fashioned coat-stand and followed him into a tiny drawing room. A careful pile of kindling, coal and logs was all ready in the grate. Jack took a box of Ship matches down from the mantelpiece and lit a firelighter. It crackled into flame at once.

'Cheat,' Elizabeth teased.

Jack turned his head and gave her a wicked smile. 'I'm not that rustic. Want a drink? Port, sour mash, champagne?'

Elizabeth shifted on her heels as he drew the curtains. She wanted to drink herself brave. 'Maybe a little champagne.'

While he rummaged in the kitchen Elizabeth snuck upstairs. The bathroom was painted a child's blue with yellow ducks in the basin, and the single bedroom was papered with a Laura Ashley burgundy sprig. A pair of dumbbells lay at the foot of a large bed covered in a pretty eiderdown. Something about the place made her happiness tighten around her heart.

She went downstairs. 'It's lovely, but it doesn't seem very you.'

'How do you know what's very me? You don't even know me,' Jack said.

Elizabeth felt shy. 'I'd like to,' she said.

Jack leaned over and kissed her very softly on the lips. Then he handed her a chipped stone mug, half-full of champagne.

'No glasses. At least it proves I didn't take you for granted.'

They drank the champagne by the fire, Elizabeth nestling her head in the crook of Jack's arm. He didn't make any move on her, and slowly the nerves started to fade. When he finally started to stroke her, Elizabeth wanted it, she was light with desire for him. They started to kiss, gently, then more urgently.

'Are you ready?' Jack whispered.

Elizabeth nodded, even though she was still scared.

He took her head in his two hands and kissed her again. 'Sugar, I was dying for you the first moment I saw you. It's not an audition. I won't do anything you don't want.'

She smiled and held out her hand to him.

'I got a better idea,' Jack suggested. Then he scooped

her up in his arms like she was made of cotton wool, and carried her slowly up the stairs.

Chapter 21

Snow lay thick on the ground in her tiny scrap of garden. Outside on the street it was already turning to slush. Nina let herself out and set the burglar alarm. It was still a thrill to do that; the two-bedroom, three-storey house in Tufnell Park, ninety grand, her first piece of property. Tony had recommended her to the Hong Kong & Shanghai for a wonderfully low mortgage, and the smart Camden flat went to somebody more junior. Her Christmas present had been a diamond necklace and earrings from Asprey's, which Nina was planning to sell after a decent interval.

'I don't celebrate Christmas,' she said when he handed over the box.

Tony was unabashed. 'You do now.'

Despite the glorious chill fire of the jewels, Nina thought how easy it would have been just to say, 'Happy Chanukah.' But that was Tony, he didn't move an inch. For anybody.

Nina climbed into her Golf and swung out into the traffic. January was a buzz; maybe it was Britain's long, booze-soaked holiday, but once New Year's was over, the capital seemed full of fresh vigour, as though desperate to make up lost time. Nina spent the holidays in Companies House and the library of the British Medical Association. She knew Frank, Carl and her other colleagues thought she was a crazy workaholic. They also despised her once the rapid promotion came through. Senior manager, that young? Nobody said anything to

Caerhaven's new piece of ass, but the frostiness was there.

She flicked on the radio as she turned past King's Cross Station. The news was dolorously announcing flooding round the city of York and a passenger train marooned in a Welsh blizzard. The Americans were stalling over the Falklands. Unemployment was up again.

Anger doesn't bother me, Nina thought, it's the other thing. Junior pricks of the type that always sucked up to Liz Savage had started to suck up to her. That was branding as bad as any scarlet letter. The irony was that she *deserved* the new slot. Busting her ass all vacation, she'd found an answer, to both of Tony's problems.

The last time she'd seen him was Christmas Eve, in a suite at the St James's Club. He was taking a lunchtime Intercity to Cardiff to be ferried back to his castle, and he wanted to see her before he left. Nina was flattered by his hunger for her, but unsettled by the Christmas present. She took it and then him, straddling him on the bed, riding him almost violently. Tony provoked her. He was good in bed, very expert in his moves, and his power was a turn-on, but it wasn't like it had been that first time. It hadn't been that good again.

Dublin was the climax of a lot of things, she saw that now. Fear, and greed, and anger against a world from which she was permanently barred. Anger at Elizabeth, making her feel once again that she was just white trash. Nina lifted her chin and flicked the dial to Radio One. They could all go to hell. She deserved this promotion, even if that was not why she'd gotten it. The Police were yelling, 'We are spirits in the material world!' Nina tapped the steering wheel in time. Yeah, brother, Amen to that.

Tony had his problems too.

'They involve you,' he'd said, reaching across her breasts for the Cristal, his green eyes bland.

'How?'

'My darling daughter isn't happy. She thinks we are stifling her creativity. Or more to the point, that you are. Ever since she came back from her bloody training camp she's been making merry hell.' The aquiline face was tight. 'She's aggressive. Insistent. She wants me to fire you.'

Nina sat bolt upright, the silk sheet slithering to her waist. 'What?'

'That's right.' He was amused at her outrage. 'She says you never consider her work—'

'That's because she never does any. I ask for market research on hospitals, she turns up with cut-and-paste adverts for aspirin.'

'Do you look at her stuff?'

Nina seethed with resentment. 'Fuck no. I'm New Products. I want market research. Facts. She reports to me, she should do what she's asked. I'm not looking for the next Charles Saatchi.'

'But you may have to humour her, I'm afraid. She's making good skiing times and she's in the Olympics this year. She's talking about making a fuss in the press. Giving interviews.'

'And you don't want that to happen?'

'And that isn't going to happen,' Tony said, his voice light as silk round a blade. The darkness in his eyes made Nina shiver. 'Make her happy, darling, would you? Smooth things over. She is my daughter, after all.'

Nina slipped out of bed as Tony pulled a cigarette from his silver monogrammed case, heading for a shower. She'd been furious. She relied on him to block Elizabeth's moves in the office, and now the snobbish little cow was going to win? She didn't understand Savage. He talked about Elizabeth with passionate dislike, but now he was ordering Nina to roll over! Maybe blue blood was thicker than water, after all.

Nina spun her car into its new slot, closer to the building's entrance. The paint was still gleaming. She knew she was making a lot of enemies here, and Lady Elizabeth was just at the head of the queue. They would tear her apart like a pack of rabid dogs if Tony ever took his protective hand off her shoulder.

She took out her slim dossier from the back seat. To hell with them all. If she couldn't be liked, at least she could be good. And that would have to do.

'Catch!' Jack spun the box across the room and Elizabeth's hand shot upwards to grab it. He thumped the table. 'Reflex like that, you should be in baseball.'

'Cricket, please.' Elizabeth smiled as she ripped off the wrapping. 'Garrard's! What's this, another present? Christmas is over, don't tell me you haven't noticed.'

She flicked open the small box to find a pendant, a platinum ski on a long chain. 'Jack, it's so cool ...'

'It's not cool, it's romantic. Look.' He fished the matching ski out of his pocket. 'I'm keeping this half. Thought it was better than a split heart or a sixpence or something corny like that. It's a goodbye present.'

Elizabeth jumped on the eiderdown to kiss him. 'I love it.' She wanted to say, 'I love you,' but didn't dare. When you said, 'I love you,' men heard, 'I've got meningitis,' they ran away so fast. 'But what do you mean you're going away? It's nearly a month to snow training.'

Jack took the chain from her hands and looped it around her neck. He was quick with the clasp; it still amazed her, the guy was so big and yet so graceful. 'I got to go back to Texas. Check on my studs, check on the new orders.'

'Oh.' Elizabeth frowned. 'Can't that wait? Don't you want to be with me? We're going to be so busy once training starts, they'll have the national officials all over us ...'

'It's business. I have to go.'

'You don't have to, you want to. Whatever.' She was really pissed off. They'd waited so long, and now all she got was a few days snatched before and after Christmas. His business success was waved like a flag in her face, and Elizabeth felt miserably conscious that her own grand scheme had come to nothing.

'Hey, you'll want time at Dragon, right? You made your old man take you on, you might as well make it count for something.' Jack dropped to the ground and began a fast set of stomach crunches.

'You're right,' Elizabeth said. It was true. She had made Dad take her on, and the power she'd had then she still had now. If that bitch Nina Roth was going to block her, she could have her fired. What was the point of leverage, if you didn't use it?

Nina went up to see Tony as soon as she arrived. Mrs Perkins, his secretary, tried to brush her off.

'Are you down in the book, Miss Roth?' She made a great play of consulting her diary. 'Oh dear, I'm afraid there's been a mix-up, you're not here.'

'I didn't make an appointment.'

'You didn't *schedule* an appointment? Then it won't be possible to see him now.'

'He said I should drop by any time,' Nina said, trying to smile. Mrs Perkins was giving her a superior gate-keeper's look that said, I know what you're all about, you hussy. She probably had a huge crush on Tony herself. Casually Nina fiddled with her cuff to flash her gold Cartier tank watch, set with diamonds, another Tony bauble she could never have afforded on her salary.

Mrs Perkins went white. Bingo, thought Nina maliciously, and he probably sent you out to buy it for me, you uptight old bag.

'Lord Caerhaven is very busy. He doesn't see anyone without an appointment.'

'Mrs Perkins,' Nina said sweetly, 'I don't have much time. I'm afraid I must insist you buzz him for me.'

She faced the older woman down. Nina knew she was an insolent Yank brat to her, but still, she was a senior manager and Mrs Perkins was a secretary. Nina had earned her status and she was never going to be put down or blocked off again.

Mrs Perkins's whiteness blossomed with rage, two red spots blooming on her cheeks like berries in cream, but she icily depressed her intercom.

'I'm sorry, my lord, but Miss Roth *insists* on my disturbing you.'

'Nina? Terrific. Send her in, Mrs P.'

'He'll see you now, Miss Roth,' Mrs Perkins said unnecessarily, her voice thin with annoyance. Nina gave her an insolent wink as she opened the door.

Tony was standing facing his windows, gazing out over the river that glittered in the weak January sun. He turned to face her, his eyes assessing her pale blue suit and green silk shirt, her expensive Patrick Cox mules and sheer Wolford stockings. Looking her over with sensual possessiveness. Nina found it arousing but disturbing, the way his eyes stripped her, like a boy appreciating a favoured toy.

'You like your new parking slot? And you're wearing your watch.' He smiled. 'What about the earrings?'

'Too much jewellery's not appropriate for the office.'

'But I like to see you in them. Wear them tomorrow.' Tony gestured to the notes she was carrying. 'What's this?'

'I think I've found you some answers. To the slimming drug problem. And to Lady Elizabeth, too,' Nina said.

'Good girl,' Tony said warmly.

*

Elizabeth got into the office to find her friends genially welcoming her back. She smiled and asked them all about their Christmases, but she felt empty inside. Jack had actually flown off and left her, and she wouldn't see him for weeks. Then there would be a hard haul to reach Olympic Champion skiing level, then the Games themselves. Elizabeth felt sick with nerves. It was '82 now, the Olympic year, and the bloody rings were appearing everywhere, on Mars bars and Coke cans and in the papers and on the telly, with endless profiles of herself. Along with Jayne Torville and Christopher Dean, the ice skaters, Elizabeth was apparently Britain's other dead cert for gold. She thought Heidi and Louise might have a few words to say about that. Heidi was three times World Champion and only beaten by a nanosecond last year. Plus, she was Swiss, she'd have been skiing all winter. Cabbies, socialites, and now the rest of the office, everyone was wishing her luck, cheering her on, treating her with a kind of awed respect that felt like a vice crunching her skull, the pressure was so huge. It was incredibly difficult to focus on anything else, but she knew she had to. If she couldn't wring something out of her bastard father now, she never would later. Win or lose, by Easter the Olympics would be over, and she wanted some kind of role to go back to.

She picked up her internal phone directory and skimmed the pages, looking for Nina Roth's extension. It had been changed. Now it began with a five. Elizabeth frowned; five was for people with their own offices.

'Hey, Tom, has Nina Roth moved departments?'

Tom pointed at the ceiling. 'Only upwards. She got a promotion while you were away. She's got her own room now, her own assistant. It's some kind of record.'

No way, Elizabeth thought angrily. 'You're kidding, she only just got here.'

Tom nodded. 'Umm, and the boys in New Products aren't too happy about it either.'

'But why? What on earth did she do that was so great?'

Elizabeth saw poor Tom suddenly blush and look down. Then it hit her.

Of course. She was always close to Daddy. So now she's a bit closer; another tart for the harem. Sleeping her way effortlessly up the ladder. Well, that was the only thing Daddy ever rewarded women for, or in the case of Monica, for not making a fuss. Was he bored of the girls in pearls now, Elizabeth wondered acidly, and moving on to career women? What did a hard-nosed robot with breasts do for him?

At any rate, she wasn't going to let either of them stand in her way.

The phone on her desk buzzed loudly. Elizabeth picked it up.

'Elizabeth, is that you, darling?' She tensed at the sound of Daddy's voice; the nice words flecked with sarcasm, the way he always spoke to her. She'd spent the whole Christmas break riding out over the freezing Caerhaven fields, or going for long hikes along the clifftops, just to get away from that utterly bloody tone. 'Could you come up to my office? Nina Roth and I have a little suggestion for you.'

Elizabeth checked her reflection in the mirrored door of the lift. Her hair fell loose and glossy over a Jaeger jacket in butterscotch cashmere and matching tweed skirt. She wore low brown heels and eight-denier tights, the thinnest wisps of nothing she could find for her legs. The pre-training session had got her back into shape; she fit the same size twelve now but she was half a stone heavier, her weak legs and buttocks firmed into muscle, her taut upper back making her look taller. A gold cuff bracelet fell over her left wrist and Jack's long platinum ski glinted against a cream silk shirt. She had no make-up but she didn't need it. The healthy athlete's glow was back in her skin.

The lift doors hissed open and she stepped out to face Mrs Perkins, who gave her an obsequious smile. 'Lady Elizabeth, how nice to see you, you look beautiful ... did you have a nice Christmas? Lots of exercise, I expect?'

Elizabeth smiled graciously and chatted but her heart was thumping loudly in her chest. She could feel the adrenalin surging through her bloodstream, like it did before a race. Nina and Tony. Together. Was she going to need it? Was there going to be a fight?

'No, no, go in, Lady Elizabeth, of course he's expecting you,' Mrs Perkins was twittering. Elizabeth stepped through her father's lobby, unconsciously rubbing the signet ring he'd handed over at Christmas. All Savage children got theirs at twenty-one, the heavy gold circle cut to fit, stamped with the family crest. I've got a bloody right to this, Elizabeth thought, summoning up her anger. He can't shut me out any more.

She walked into Tony's office.

Nina stood by the desk, listening to Elizabeth and Mrs Perkins murmuring outside. Mrs Perkins sounded remarkably friendly and deferential; but then Elizabeth was quality, after all, and I'm just the help, she thought cynically. Tony got up when his daughter entered the room and walked across to kiss her on the cheek. Nina pasted a smile on her face as she watched them. Christ. Look at the stuck-up little cow. This was the girl who wanted to take her job away! A castle. Swiss finishing school. Hunt balls and tweed skirts!

The earl and Elizabeth said hello and kissed the air by each other's cheeks. The words were friendly, but the ceremony was stiff. Nina forced the grin off her face.

They're as screwed up as me and my loser folks, in their way.

Tony waved both girls to a seat.

'Elizabeth, darling, Nina's had an idea.'

Chapter 22

'Lady Elizabeth.' Nina nearly choked on it. 'Do you recall that New Products was working on a drug, B-28?'

'The slimming pill,' Elizabeth said.

'Yeah. That drug was a bust, but the research on it turned up some interesting side effects.'

'Part of the pill components were vitamins,' Tony said, 'intended to replace lost nutrients if the appetite suppressant stopped the punters eating. B-28 failed toxicity tests, meaning it poisoned the system—'

'I know what toxicity means, Daddy.'

Daddy! Speaking quickly to cover her annoyance, Nina ploughed on. 'Vitamins may be the next big thing in retail. Along with bottled mineral water and keep-fit, we think they're going to be the craze of the eighties. We were hoping you could help.'

'So was I, but every time I came up with an idea – for anything – you refused to look at it.'

Elizabeth held the American's gaze and saw the dark pupils flash, Nina's lush beauty spiced with anger.

There was a pause. Elizabeth saw Nina glance at Tony, but her father looked blank.

'Yes, Lady Elizabeth. I realise I may have been too hasty,' the dark-haired girl said slowly. She dropped her eyes. Clearly furious.

'You can be a special help to us with a new pill we're launching,' Tony said smoothly. 'People want one pill for everything. It's been difficult in the past.'

'And we've got one?'

'Well, we've found a way to combine iron and calcium,' Nina Roth said. 'Usually, calcium blocks the absorption of iron. So our new pill will be the most complete thing out there. And you are the perfect person to sell it. You could combine the campaign with your skiing career. You see, we're thinking of calling it Dragon Gold. As an Olympic hopeful, a World Champion already, you would be the perfect face for the brand.'

'You want me to be in adverts?'

'Only print ones, Elizabeth. I'd find television ads a little vulgar,' her father said. 'But you would also be in charge of the campaign. Designing it. Selling it. You can create copy, oversee the agency account, everything.'

Elizabeth found her fist had curled into a tight ball. Amazing what a little blackmail could do. It sounded like a good product, and she would have total control. She was careful not to betray her elation.

'Is the pill gold?'

'Yellow, from the beta-carotine,' Nina explained. Elizabeth hated her patronising air. She might not be a lab rat like Nina Roth, but she wasn't stupid. Nina thought she had a monopoly on anything needing a double-figure IQ.

'What do you think, darling?' the earl asked lightly. 'Right up your alley, isn't it?'

'Right up my alley,' Elizabeth agreed. 'If you mean it, about my having total control.' She leaned forwards, looking at Tony challengingly.

She's ignoring me, Nina thought.

'Of course,' Tony said.

'If I'm to control this line, I shouldn't have to report in to Nina.'

Nina sat perfectly still, anger blazing through her like fire through petrol. She had no doubt at all that Tony would cave in. All he wanted was the quiet life. And if that meant humiliating Nina then that's what he would do. She looked over at her young ladyship, the girl so poised and polished in her upper-class clothes, and her eyes were flint.

'No. Nina will be out there, supervising the actual launch, but your work will be overseen by Dino Vincenza. He's in charge of marketing, after all.'

'Suits me, Daddy. Although maybe it would be better if I reported in to Dino on everything. In the future.'

Nina bit her bottom lip. Caerhaven had tensed, and she sensed he was very angry, but he was the consummate pragmatist.

'If you like,' Tony said.

'Then that's fixed.' Elizabeth stood up, pushing herself up on the soles of her feet, perfectly balanced. It was a strong movement. She gave Nina a barely perceptible nod, then shook her father's hand.

'Well, that's all,' Tony said, dismissing the meeting.

Nina got up, unable to look at father or daughter. She followed Elizabeth's stiff back out into the corridor and waited by the elevator bank with her. She wondered if Mrs Perkins had been listening in to that exchange, thought about the look of triumph that would greet her next time she entered Tony's office.

Elizabeth stepped into the lift. Nina followed her.

'You know, this works great for me,' Nina said. 'I really have so much work to do already, one less job will be a relief.'

Lady Elizabeth's green eyes fixed on hers. 'Nobody asked you if it would be great for you or not,' she said.

'That's right.' Nina couldn't help herself. 'I didn't go running to Papa to ask him to fix things for me. But then I'm not a part-timer. I really work for a living.'

'Yeah, you don't bother having a life. I heard that,' Elizabeth Savage mocked. 'Except when you go running to your boyfriend's bed. *That's* why he lets you do real work, sweetie. Daddy's not big on women, except the ones he wants in his bed. That's the only reason you made the grade.'

'You silly, spoilt little cow,' Nina snarled. 'You've got no idea how I made the grade. I'm the smartest person in this goddamn company.'

'Certainly the best at Daddy's *special* assignments.' Elizabeth reached out and slammed the pause button. 'But don't get any illusions, Nina. You'll never replace my stepmother. You're nothing special. Girls like you come and go, you're just a toy to him.'

'He doesn't give a damn about you. He's only doing this to shut your stupid little Sloane mouth up.'

Elizabeth smiled. 'You think I need you to tell me that? And you think I care? I've got a right to this company. I'll get my chance any way I bloody well can. Although I expect you'll be blabbing all this to him next time he takes you to bed.'

'No chance, bitch,' Nina snapped. 'I can look after myself.'

'Ditto.' Elizabeth let the lift slide downwards. 'And I can handle you. In fact I just did, didn't I? I'll be trotting off to Dino now, since he's my new boss.'

'Watch your back, kiddo,' Nina said.

Elizabeth laughed. 'I don't think so. I'm more than a match for you. And give it a rest with the melodrama, would you? You're in England now, you know, not a bit player on *Starsky and Hutch*.'

The lift slid smoothly to a halt and the doors hissed open.

'After you, milady,' Nina said softly.

Elizabeth turned and gave her a brilliant smile. 'Oh, you can call me Elizabeth, Nina. I like to encourage familiarity from the staff.'

She walked off towards Marketing in a soft swish of cashmere and tweed, her long, honey-blonde hair gleaming neatly down her back, her elegant walk giving Nina visions of deportment lessons and private dances. Fury balled like a fist in Nina's stomach.

I might be in England, she thought, but I'm still playing by Brooklyn rules. And girl, you just had your first and last warning.

Nina sat down at her desk and tapped into her computer absently. Her mind was already in Switzerland. And on what it would take to bring Lady Elizabeth down.

'So. Tell me more about these *Wünderkinder* you've discovered,' Frank Staunton said.

Nina crossed her legs and leaned back in her chair. Lady Elizabeth had flown off to Switzerland, and no one else around Dragon dared to give her a hard time. She was wearing a navy suit with white piping, a *prêt à porter* from Chanel. Gucci heels gave her an extra inch of height and Tony's diamonds glittered on her lobes. The Swiss team she'd found were a slam-dunk. Right now she could face Heinrich Günther, Don Hadley and the rest without a qualm.

For a moment Nina remembered the frightened, desperate teenager she'd been barely three years back. Well, that girl was dead. She'd killed her. The power she felt right now was worth any amount of catty looks from Tom, Elizabeth and the rest of them.

'I've found a primary research source I think should replace Steele and Ripley.' Nina passed folders around the table. 'Dr Henry Namath, Dr Lilly Hall and four technicians under their employ are currently operating in Zurich. They're freelancers and have supplied specialist work to pharmaceutical giants and bio-tech companies. They work on complex computer modelling systems. Dr Hall's the biochemist, Dr Namath the computer expert. Their ratio of success to failure is very good.'

'But slimming drugs, Miss Roth,' Heinrich Günther

objected. 'Your folder refers to cardio, respiratory, anti-inflammatories ...'

'If they already *had* a slimming drug, we wouldn't be taking this meeting.' Nina risked insolence; she saw the amused gleam in Tony's eye. 'The reason I propose we annex them is that they have recently done some interesting veterinary work. A drug called Leptate has helped to slim pigs.'

There was silence. Pigs weren't humans, but they were mammals; they were close.

'And why has not ICI jumped on them already?'

'Only because they aren't scanning the breakthroughs in animal medicine, I guess. It occurred to me to cross-check over the vacation.'

There, Nina thought. Under the table her manicured fist curled softly in on itself. Now they'll stop despising me, she thought. They'll have to. That kind of lateral thinking is what's lacking over here. And with one brainwave I just got them closer than they've ever been before.

'We should move fast, though. Somebody else is bound to notice soon.'

'I agree.' Frank Staunton was looking at Tony, nodding.

'And I.' Seeing which way the wind was blowing, Herr Günther had decided to jump in there too.

'My daughter will be out there supervising a new product launch. As she's skiing in the Olympics, it will be perfect cover. Meanwhile Nina will be in Switzerland, essentially to cover sales and shipping, but actually talking to Doctors Hall and Namath.'

'Terrific, sir,' Gerald Jax said admiringly.

'*Ja*,' Günther agreed. 'Nobody will think twice about it.'

'Then that's settled.' Caerhaven smiled softly.

The meeting broke up. Nina noticed that the soft

murmurs of congratulation were all headed Tony's way. Heinrich Günther gave her a sharp look of dislike, which was the best compliment she was likely to get. She glanced angrily at Tony. Why did he want to steal her idea?

The earl looked over from his crop of courtiers and caught her staring. He frowned slightly and Nina dropped her eyes. He didn't appreciate the protest. *I'm still the boss*, his dark eyes warned. *Don't fuck with me.*

Nina walked through to Marketing at five p.m., carrying a folder on Dragon Gold. Ad executives and their secretaries gave her nasty glances and stopped talking when she passed by their desks.

She stopped in front of Elizabeth's little cubicle, expecting to see it plastered with pictures of Elizabeth holding medals or grinning out of the pages of *Tatler*. Maybe some shots of Jack Taylor; she'd heard the rumours they were seeing each other. One rich-kid jock screwing another, just perfect. She knew Tony thought so. And she was with him there: Elizabeth married and in Texas meant Elizabeth out of her hair, giving dinner parties and throwing charity balls like little ladies were intended to. But the walls were covered with ads. Saatchi's pregnant man, the Honey Monster, some apes throwing a tea party. Nina recognised each one of them. Maybe looking up at other people's triumphs was the closest her little ladyship would ever come to work.

Elizabeth looked up. Her long hair was caught back now in a velvet clip. It looked ludicrously fresh faced and boarding-school-ish.

'I've come to bring you the notes on the new product, Elizabeth.'

'The notes? Oh, thank you, but I have them already. Mrs Perkins is making sure I'm up to speed.'

Nina shrugged.

'I'll get everything I need direct from my father,' Elizabeth said, 'so you needn't concern yourself.'

'OK,' Nina said, through gritted teeth.

'And I've just heard that you'll be out in Switzerland too. Do you like skiing? Maybe you could come out and watch the Olympics.'

'Thanks, but I find *work* keeps me busy. I prefer to concentrate on the job in hand.' Nina dredged up some murky names from her memory. 'I guess I'll just keep my fingers crossed for Kim Gideon and Holly Ferrell, those are our girls, right? Or if not, Louise Levier and Heidi Laufen. The Swiss. If you're neutral, it's nice to support the host nation.'

Lady Elizabeth's green eyes regarded her with maddening coolness.

'How silly of me. You're the total professional. Just work, work, work, but then of course that's how you've been getting all your wonderful promotions. Pretty earrings, by the way. They look rather expensive.'

'I earned them,' Nina said.

'So I hear,' Elizabeth replied.

Nina turned on her heel and walked away. She didn't want the rich bitch to see her riled. She wanted to slap that silly, smug little face until the ears bled. Goddamn, I've been working since I was seven years old, I don't need to come to England and have some no-nothing blueblood call me a whore to my face.

Nina's office was a haven of silence. She looked round: soft, dove-grey carpets, an orthopaedic chair, a kidney-shaped desk and top-of-the-range computer. She was a senior manager now, with her own secretary and two fax machines.

I earned this, she thought fiercely, I did, I did.

The wall opposite her desk was decorated with a large square photograph. Nina had chosen a Patrick Demarchelier shot, a black and white showing a grimy

Brooklyn street scene. It was nowhere near her old neighbourhood but so what, poor was poor. As Nina stared at it her heart hardened up again, shaking off the insults and misgivings.

Jeff Glazer. The laughing kids at St Michael's. Her fat fuck of a father slumped on the couch in front of *Jeopardy*.

Never, never again. She was sitting here wearing Chanel. It was gonna take more than a few dirty looks to faze her now.

Chapter 23

Tony Savage lay back in bed and watched Nina. He felt marvellously relaxed. The ultra-modern, Japanese décor of the Halkin Hotel matched his mood perfectly; soothing, with no fuss or bother. He congratulated himself as Nina dressed. The girl had been quite a find; an off-the-wall thinker, with relentless ambition. And the best piece of ass he'd ever had.

He thought of Camilla Browning, with her horsy voice and clingy manner. Looking back on it she seemed as exciting as a lowing cow. Nina was in another league. She turned him on like a light switch. Nina Roth would die before she'd cling on to anything. Tony casually studied the soft creamy flesh at the top of Nina's thighs as she pulled on her panties, plain white cotton from Marks & Spencer. Nina had the best pair of breasts he'd ever seen, she was all soft curves and hard-assed Yank attitude. Tony knew it was one more source of jealousy around Dragon that he was laying her. Heinrich, for example, looked at her when her back was turned like a slavering dog. He'd even caught the bellboy tonight with his eyes on her butt like he could see through her dress. Tony liked that. He loved lesser men drooling over what he had.

'My flight leaves at noon,' Nina said. 'I'm going home now. To pack.'

'Are you taking your bracelet with you?'

Nina picked up the trinket he'd bought for her tonight. It was a light twist of silver set with opals and sapphires.

'I don't think so. I don't plan on going to many parties.'

'I want you to take it,' Tony said.

Nina stiffened. She hated it when he used that tone. The jewels she'd loved at first were now beginning to annoy her; she couldn't say why.

'I went to a lot of trouble to get it for you. Why won't you take it?'

'I guess,' Nina agreed after a pause.

Tony smiled. Nina was too prickly for hearts and flowers, fine. But he was still in charge. That was the best thing about this little one: she was smart and driven, but still too young to really see things straight. When she got a good idea, she came right to him. Women did that a lot, he noticed. They picked up silly romantic ideas about work, they invented spurious loyalties and clung to the idea that hard work would be rewarded. People worked hard in quarries, but rarely got rewarded. Results. It was all about results. Nina would give him her best work, she would be comfortable, she would wind up a middle manager and be grateful for it too. The jewellery made a nice point: he didn't want her getting too independent.

Recently she'd been hanging back a little in bed. Initially she'd been passionate; lately it was like the bloom had gone for her. But Tony was skilled, he knew how to ride over that first reluctance. His desire for her was still at full throttle. He had no intention whatsoever of letting her go.

'Good girl, that's the ticket. You'll want something to wear to the Olympic parties and launches that Liz dreams up.'

'Yeah.' Nina's dark mood blackened further. She reached for her bra and dress and pulled them on quickly.

'You must send me reports on her. See that she's keeping out of trouble. And what the story is between her and the Taylor boy,' Tony said.

'Of course. I'll keep you updated.'

'I knew I could count on you, darling. We'll rush forward with wedding plans as soon as he pops the question. Throw her a spectacular bash, and then it'll be off to darkest Texas.'

'But never mind.' Nina walked forwards and perched on the end of the bed. Tony's wallet was laid open on the side-table; there was a prominent photo of the countess, Monica, with two teenage boys. Elizabeth was noticeably absent. She watched her lover as she added, 'You won't be so much gaining a son as losing a daughter.'

Lord Caerhaven gave a short bark of laughter.

God, you really do hate her, Nina thought drily. How interesting.

She took a taxi back from the lobby of the hotel. The receptionist kept shooting her sidelong glances, until Nina turned dark eyes towards him and stared him coldly in the face, at which the man dropped his eyes at once.

The cab took her up to Tufnell Park. It was only two a.m., but the roads in the city centre were already deserted. Nina stared out of the windows; a thin drizzle was lashing little beads on the windowpane that sparkled in the lamplight. Her new bracelet sparkled too, twisting between her fingers. It was a wonderful piece; expensive but not overpowering, impeccably tasteful. Just what you would expect from the Robber Baron.

The house was deserted and still. Nina had shoved most of her furniture into storage and switched her bills to Dragon. The answerphone was blinking furiously: six messages from New York and Europe that had missed her in the office; one from Anita Kerr, her secretary, inviting her out for a goodbye drink. Nina was sorry she'd missed that one. Anita, who knew how hard she worked, was the closest thing she had to a friend in the office. Anita and Brian Kane, her neighbour, who she sometimes jogged with on a Sunday, represented her non-Dragon social life. But I don't need one, Nina told herself. I don't need to be a butterfly like Elizabeth. I have things to do with my life.

She went into the kitchen and pulled out the last Tesco pizza from the freezer. Then she started to fix a pot of coffee. She drank so much caffeine these days, she could drink coffee right before bed without any problem. Coffee and pizza was a small pleasure, a solitary moment in a day filled with people she didn't really like. Take the function last evening, a stuffy Caerhaven party at the House of Lords. Senior Dragon people went. Why had she been asked? Because Tony wanted to impress her? Or his cronies? It was the eighteenth birthday of Charles, Lord Holwyn, Tony's eldest son. Charles was a miniature version of his papa, striding through the crowd, being heartily congratulated by obnoxious schoolfriends and bluff business associates of Tony's. Lord Richard, his little brother, seemed blond and bland, like his mother. Nina watched Tony's wife curiously. She seemed sexless, almost faceless, despite her inoffensive prettiness. Yet she moved through that crowd with a poise Nina would never have, looking bored but charming at the same time. There were more titles and money together in that room than Nina could get her head round, and she hated every last second of it. An attractive but stupid girl named Camilla Browning kept bumping into her all night long, showering her with clumsy insults and cutting remarks about Americans. Eventually Nina escaped with a glass of bourbon to the terrace, to watch the Thames roll sluggishly by. When Tony wandered out and casually suggested the Halkin as a rendezvous, Nina was relieved. But by the time she met him in the lobby, her attitude had hardened. She disliked Tony almost as much as the rest of them.

The microwave pinged.

Even if it meant more run-ins with Elizabeth, she was looking forward to Switzerland. That country was all about money. And Nina knew money. Maybe in Zurich she could make the deal that would gain her respect once and for all.

Before she ate, Nina picked up her new bracelet and dropped it in an envelope, addressed to Anita Kerr. Her note asked Anita not to wear it around the office. It might be a foolish gesture, Nina thought, but it felt good. If rather dangerous.

The plane dipped towards Kloten airport, overlooking Lake Zurich and the snow-capped mountains around the city. Nina watched the scenery with idle curiosity. It was her first time in Continental Europe but she couldn't spare much interest in picture-postcard views. Her mind was racing through the biographies of Dr Lilly Hall and Dr Henry Namath.

They were a strange pair. Dr Hall had been a full professor of biochemistry at the University of Western Australia. She was a holder of the Order of Australia for her breakthrough work in disease-resistant crop genetics. Lilly was a practical woman, she didn't take time to publish her work. Her college demanded more name recognition, there was a spat over tenure, and Dr Hall left for the private sector. Her work since then was ambitious, and often failed, but the scores she did make were serious. Lean pigs! Nina could shiver just thinking about it. Her photograph in the file was ten years out of date; it showed a jowly woman in her forties, short, squat, with leathery skin from too much exposure to the sun. If there was a romance, nobody knew about it.

Dr Henry Namath. Pictured four years ago, nothing to write home about in the looks department – Buddy Holly glasses and facial hair that would do credit to Chewbacca the Wookie, but a razor-sharp mind. Between the lines of his file Nina read him as your classic nerd. As a teenage boy from a cold northwestern suburb outside Minneapolis, Harry Namath had been twice expelled from school for crashing a mainframe computer. Later he had done two months in juvenile detention for doing the same to a state mainframe, causing all the lights in Pennsville, MA, to stick on green for a full day. Namath had been writing code and programming machines for ever, since that meant feeding strips of paper with holes punched in them to metal behemoths working the binary system. He'd maxed out his SATs, but with the criminal record, only scraped in to University of St Thomas, a Catholic college, where he'd barely cruised through. Nina grinned when she recalled that. Maybe UST didn't have any computers.

Now he was writing programs as a freelance. Picked up an easy doctorate at the London School of Economics, hired by IBM, fired in six months. Clearly a maverick. Bumped into Lilly Hall at a hospital fundraiser in London, when she was completing a project for the Ministry of Agriculture. They'd been together ever since. Lilly did the pharmacology; Harry wrote programs for companies, showing how her drugs and genes could be used.

Both of them were arrogant, rebellious and probably as greedy as she was for the big score.

Just the kind of hustlers I can do business with, Nina thought.

After Customs she picked up her baggage and jumped in a cab. Tony had personally selected her apartment off the Storchengasse.

'Very nice,' the cabbie said pleasantly when she gave him the address. 'Very good area, you will like.'

They drove through the jazzy Niederdorf area, past outside cafés, tobacconists and bookstores with slanted roofs. After London everything seemed very clean. Nina watched an ancient *Kirche* slip by, then banks with brass nameplates. It was very cold and the sky was a dazzling blue. She could see mountains in the distance. It felt like an alien world.

The Storchengasse turned out to be a major shopping thoroughfare for the seriously rich. Hermès, Chanel, Cartier; it was thronging with women in silky-looking furs. When the cab drew up outside a smart, flat-fronted building with a uniformed doorman, Nina stepped out with a sigh of pure satisfaction. She gave the driver a generous tip.

Her apartment was fully automated. Nina punched a combination into a wall panel and the front door slid open. Doubtless Dr Namath would approve. It was decorated in white and cream with touches of gold, very Swiss and baroque. The refrigerator was fully stocked; a basket of fruit was laid out on a small ebony table by her bed. The card was a sterile, printed welcome message from Luc Viera, MD of Dragon Switzerland. Tony kept a skeleton office in Geneva. Mostly Viera and his gnomes kept abreast of the gossip floating out of the banks. Nina imagined the Robber Baron's orders coming through, how annoyed the career suit Viera would be to be told he was point man for a kid. That idea pleased her almost as much as the apartment.

Money and power, that's what Tony Savage was dangling in front of her face. Nina selected a bitter Swiss chocolate from the open box in the kitchen and bit into it carefully. It was sublime. Maybe she should wear his jewellery, next time he told her to. After all, wasn't this everything she'd always wanted?

'So.' Elizabeth dumped her skis down in the boot room for waxing and pushed her goggles up over her face. Her skin was stung red from the cold; white wax was smeared clown-like over her lips but right now she wished she'd done her cheeks too. She clump-clumped her way into the hotel foyer. It was so ironic: good boots anchored your turns like rocket boosters on the slopes, bombing you forwards with perfect weight precision, and yet the second you unclipped the skis you were crippled, tripping and lurching like astronauts on the moon. She sat down carefully on a step and unstrapped them, ignoring the stares from the tourists and sports groupies. 'At least I haven't forgotten how to ski.'

'You could have fooled me,' Karen Carter sniped. 'Still four seconds off your best. And five off Louise's – she did that course in two-twenty over Christmas.'

Elizabeth shrugged. 'I'm improving every session.'

What the hell was your time, loser? she wanted to snap, but bit it back. She was coming in for unexpected stick from the press. Slagging a fellow Brit would only make things worse. Karen or Janet Marlin would be bound to leak it. Jealousy over Jack Taylor had soured the team spirit, and the Olympic setting made things a lot worse. Everywhere the team trained they were greeted with huge five-ring banners, cheering Swiss and multinational officials, sports journos and television crews. The World Cup felt like a local gymkhana in comparison. Big stars were wandering round every venue: Torville and Dean, Robin Cousins, and the rest. Since it was Switzerland, the bobsledders would be tackling the Cresta Run. Glamour and glory were in the air; deadly rivalry and the weight of history. You couldn't escape the atmosphere. Adrenalin crackled around like electricity up the cablecars. The élite were here for Olympic gold medals. Nothing less.

Karen Carter, Janet Marlin and Kate Cox were not here for Olympic gold medals. Or for Olympic medals of any description. They had no chance. Martin Bell in the men's team had no chance. Lady Elizabeth Savage was the UK's only real contender. All the other girls got asked was, what was it like to ski with her, didn't they feel privileged watching such a great talent emerge? Des Lynam contented himself with Karen, because Elizabeth was too busy to speak to him. And the stuck-up cow had somehow waltzed off with Jack bloody Taylor, after pretending for months and months that she hated him. Janet told Karen Elizabeth was a proper little madam, and Karen had totally agreed. Ronnie Davis kept his distance, because Ronnie would soon be training only the main team. Elizabeth would zoom off again with Hans Wolf, the genius coach they'd all have given their eye teeth to work with. Elizabeth was just too good for the rest of them.

'Did you take a look at the *Sun* this morning?' Janet asked.

'Yeah, but it doesn't bother me.' The tabloids were all running nasty pieces about Elizabeth's lack of commitment, commenting on her Alpine rivals' current times. 'I'm heading out to Klosters with Hans tomorrow to start the real work,' she said lightly.

'Well, hold the back page,' Karen sniped.

Elizabeth smiled softly at her. What was the point? Did Jack get this crap from his team-mates?

'Will you be packing all your pictures with you?'

'Yes, I will.' She grinned as she thought about her piles of ad mock-ups. Elizabeth had been spending every moment she wasn't skiing working on Dragon Gold. Nina Roth was due in Zurich soon and Elizabeth wanted to have something to show her.

'I don't think you should be doing anything but skiing, Elizabeth,' Karen lectured. 'It's not proper.'

Elizabeth squeezed her feet into trainers and eased into some deep stretches.

'England rugby players work in banks. Sally Gunnell's got a fulltime job. So have Jayne and Chris. It's supposed to be an *amateur* event.'

'Amateur is right,' Karen muttered.

Elizabeth rounded on her. 'Yeah? Think you can do better? I don't *need* to train as hard as you, Karen, because I'm twice as good. You can stick to opening supermarkets and writing columns for *Cosmo*. I'm out here to do something for Britain. You don't have a prayer, not if you spend every day of the year on the snow. So get out of my face.'

Karen's mouth dropped open as Elizabeth stomped off to the elevator bank.

'Snobby cow,' she said.

Kate Cox moved closer. 'Don't worry, she'll get hers. I heard Louise Levier's been training with Franz Klammer. She'll be lucky if she scrapes a bronze.'

Janet glanced down at a ski brochure franked with the Olympic rings. Jack Taylor's bronzed, square-jawed face.

'Can't think what he sees in her.'

'Not that much,' Karen said gleefully. 'He hasn't called her once, not at this hotel. I checked with the operator, pretending to be her.'

'You never.'

'I did. And you know his reputation: find 'em, feel 'em, fuck 'em, forget 'em. He fancied her, she dropped her pants, end of story.'

'You reckon?'

'She's had it far too easy for far too long,' Karen muttered. 'She's got it coming, that girl.'

Chapter 24

Nina shivered and looked at her watch. Quarter of nine in the cold morning light, no sign of life. The bell on the fading pistachio paint buzzed insistently; the grubby steel plaque read Hall/Namath Consulting. She was in the right place at the right time, representing Dragon's global power and wealth. And nobody seemed to care.

This was the sleazy part of town, facing away from the lakeside. The main rail station was a few blocks away, the *Straßen* packed with dull, shabby apartment blocks full of unskilled workers. Maybe this was the only low-rent street in Switzerland. The shuttered stores used Chinese letters; the wrappings dropped in front of the delis were Turkish and Polish. It was almost like being back on Flatbush, except the air was clean.

Nina shifted from foot to foot. The neighbourhood wasn't stirring yet from whatever trouble it had seen last night. Otherwise she'd have been scared to be stood here, wearing an expensive, tailored suit of dove-grey cashmere, a silver cuff bracelet and prim little studs. Her make-up was pulled together, a pale foundation, clover lips and cheeks. She'd made sure she dressed as formal and old as possible. In her experience, mavericks liked to keep all the craziness for themselves. If executives showed up in jeans and T-shirts they panicked. No, Nina wanted to look dull and trustworthy. And rich. As much like a nice Swiss banker as she could manage.

She picked up her briefcase and depressed the buzzer

again, a long, hard push. Namath's deep, warm voice had said eight thirty. Real insistent.

'Are you sure?' Nina had asked, surprised.

'Eight thirty's good for me, Ms Roth. Best time of day. Clear head, you can think straight.'

Now she'd been stood here for fifteen minutes. It was freezing, but little midges were already buzzing around. This quarter had been built·on former swamps. Fuck, she was going to have to leave and get to a phone, rearrange.

Angrily Nina took her finger off the buzzer and kicked hard at the door.

It swung open, yanked back by a tall man with a broad chest, a square, clean-shaven jaw and handsome brown eyes. He was wearing a robe and not much else. He was very tanned. He looked furious.

'*Gott in Himmel, was ist geschah? Was ist los?*'

Nina swallowed hard. 'Dr Namath?'

He straightened up. 'Yeah. Who the fuck wants to know? Are you from the embassy? I sent the visa papers over last week. Don't you people have phones?'

Nina flushed scarlet. She didn't dare look at him, he was almost naked.

'I'm Nina Roth from Dragon. I – don't we have an appointment?'

'You're who? Oh, sure, the drugs people.' He was still pissed off. 'What the hell do you want now?'

Nina was miserably confused. 'Sir. It's quarter of. I've been here since eight thirty. That's when you told me to turn up.'

Dr Namath paused, then shrugged his shoulders and grinned. 'You're kidding. You thought I meant eight thirty as in a.m.?'

Nina had absolutely no idea what to say. If it hadn't been for the voice she'd never even have recognised him. She was expecting a bearded geek with bottle glasses she could sign up on the spot, a poor researcher who'd be grateful for her attentions. Not this big hulk standing here in his robe, laughing at her.

'I meant at night. When we're done. Lilly doesn't even open her eyes till ten, kiddo. Go have some breakfast and come back then.' He gestured to the thin Paisley robe covering his bronzed chest with its wiry black hair and cutting off above stocky legs. 'I'd ask you in for coffee but I'm not exactly dressed for it.'

'Yes. Sure. Uh, I'm sorry I got the time wrong. In Dragon we tend to—'

'Eleven,' Namath said firmly, and shut the door in her face.

Nina went to the chrome and glass temple of the Container design centre for breakfast; something ludicrously expensive to charge to her platinum company Amex. Spending money would help her feel back in control. She was still blushing with embarrassment and annoyance when the coffee came, a large espresso so thick and bitter she could almost rest her spoon on it. The restaurant was full of businessmen. Nina ordered a *Wall Street Journal* and *Financial Times* sent over and breakfasted on croissants and a bowl of wild strawberries. She buried her face in the *Journal*. Kiddo! He'd wrongfooted her, dressed her down whilst nearly naked, then called her kiddo! How frustrating was that, to be all revved up for the big poaching operation, and then …

Namath had made her blush. Not just because she'd gotten the times mixed up, either. Whenever he'd lost the shrubbery and got himself the lenses he'd unwrapped something pretty special. That was no nerd. He looked like Sean Connery with an American accent, when she'd confidently been expecting Pee-Wee Herman. And her Swiss banker look hadn't taken him in for a millisecond. It was just like being back at Dolan in her first week,

238

when she'd got everything wrong and stumbled round with her face permanently set to strawberry.

Nina began combing through the financial reports. Boring stuff about interest rates and EC budget quotas. But Dragon stock was up significantly. That must be Tony's latest raft of disposals; he was getting sharper and deadlier every day.

A small heading in the Marketing section of the *FT* caught her eye. A nice photo of Dragon Gold, the new vitamin pill, in new packaging. The revamped label was bold even in black and white, and showed a Dragon sitting on a hoard of vitamin pills. A raft of slogans jumped out of the text: Dragon Gold – Go for It; Ill-Getting Gold; Gold not Cold; Golden Wonders. Despite her mood, Nina started grinning. Then she stopped.

The next picture was very familiar. Too familiar. Lady Elizabeth Savage, posing her lean, hard body in a new skisuit, black with gold detailing. Skis resting against her shoulders, holding up a bottle of pills and smiling that arrogant smile.

'British Olympic hope Elizabeth Savage launching Dragon Gold in Kitzbühel yesterday. Breaking her training to supervise the launch, Savage has commissioned a bold ad campaign that seems to have been an instant hit. UK retailers' advance orders are high, and with Savage also personally involved, Dragon Gold looks set to become an important retail line for the UK giant.'

Nina felt a thin coat of ice settle on her heart. Elizabeth's launch plans had been faxed to her last week and ignored. Who cares what the princess does with her stupid pill? But this looked good. Amazingly so. She reread the piece and stopped dead at the order figures. Goddamn, that was terrific. There was no denying it. It's got to be a massage by the sales department, Nina thought, then shook her head. No. There was no way Tony would hand Elizabeth any extra credit.

She made herself look carefully at some of the follow-up slogans, due to be wheeled out next month. After novelty, Elizabeth had decided to use the pill's medical advantage, calcium and iron together. Again, the line was short and sweet – 'Blood. Bones. Brilliant.'

Nina called for the check and pushed the papers away. She didn't know anything about advertising, but she trusted her instincts. They were screaming. Underestimating your enemies was a dumb mistake, and clearly, Elizabeth had hit paydirt.

It doesn't bother me, Nina thought. So she's got some talent? Great. It takes more than talent to survive out there. Assuming she doesn't scamper off to Texas with the playboy.

If Elizabeth was more of a danger than she'd thought, Elizabeth would be more fun to bury. Simple as that.

Nina glanced back at the grinning picture before she threw the text away. She longed to wipe the grin off that rich-girl face.

'Come in,' Namath said grinning, opening the door for her. He was wearing a grubby white lab coat and tinted goggles, but she could still see the faint trace of mockery behind the eyes. 'Lilly's just in the kitchen, waiting for you.'

Nina followed him inside, taking a deep breath. They'd probably been laughing at her all morning long, but she had to be in control here. As far as these people knew, she was an angel from heaven bearing gifts: secure funding, top equipment, fat salaries. Namath and Hall were fly-by-night researchers, hawking their projects round hospitals and drug firms; they had to be up for this. She wasn't going to be shaken just because Namath had opened the door semi-naked.

The kitchen was clean and functional. They'd converted this building themselves; the table looked through a reinforced glass window over the lab, where pigs and rabbits were crouched in wire cages and computers perched on tables strewn with messy notes. Dr Lilly Hall *did* resemble her picture, short and squat. She was wearing blue slacks and a red shirt, sitting at the table sipping an Orangina.

'Dr Hall, I'm Nina Roth,' Nina said confidently, leaning over and shaking her hand. 'I'm with Dragon. We'd like to talk to you about a joint venture.'

'So take a seat. We're listening,' Harry Namath said. Nina sat.

'You look pretty young to be a pharmaceutical exec,' Lilly Hall commented. She was unimpressed by Nina's expensive suit. Nina also guessed she might be irritated by her looks. 'How old are you?'

'Twenty-eight,' Nina lied.

Harry Namath snorted. Quickly she moved on. 'Doctor, we're aware of your recent biochemical work on pigs. We're very impressed and we'd like you to come and work for us, exclusively. We have a heavy package on offer including your own lab and guaranteed non-interference in your research. We understand how Hall/Namath do things.'

'Done your homework, yeah?'

'What do you want us to work on?' Harry asked.

'Same area.' I don't want *you* at all, flyboy, Nina thought, but I gotta kiss your butt to get Lilly here. 'We don't like to get too specific before you're actually on board.'

'Well, I wanna know,' Dr Hall insisted. The Aussie accent was as thick as sourdough.

'Slimming pills, Lil.' Harry regarded Nina. 'That's what they all want. Especially Dragon: they hired Steele and Ripley—'

'Strewth!' Lilly laughed rudely. 'Is that right? That what you're after?'

Nina's fingers balled into a fist under the table. 'Yes, ma'am,' she said calmly. 'You've seen the benefits we're offering. Plus autonomy. You'll get full funding and remuneration but be free to do things your way. All the other big firms have tried to stuff you into suits and ties.'

Lilly Hall looked up at her partner. Harry shrugged. 'I want to go back to London,' she said eventually. 'You cover relocation as well?'

'Yes, ma'am.'

'Then if we can work it out, legally, I'm game.'

Nina froze. Just like that? She had them? Could it really be that easy?

'But we'll want more money. And a legal guarantee, we're in charge, you just own the results,' Harry Namath said.

'There's no more money,' Nina said authoritatively. 'You already have our absolute best offer.'

Dr Namath stood up slowly and looked her up and down. Then he opened the kitchen door out of the hallway.

'OK, well, thanks for dropping by,' he said.

'What?' Nina said.

'Come on, kid. We've both been around the block a few times more than you. You'll go, best guess, fifty per cent higher than your "absolute best", and believe me, you'll need to. Or I just get right on to Glaxo.' Namath picked up an imaginary phone. 'Yeah, hi, is that legal? 'Cause Dragon are lying in front of us with their skirts up and their legs open, but they're only offering a quarter mil ...'

'OK. OK.' Nina knew she was scarlet. 'It's negotiable.'

'And I want to deal with a lawyer on the cash,' Lilly added, 'no offence, kid.'

This is about the deal, it's not personal, Nina told herself, biting her lip. 'Sure.'

'That's better.' Harry Namath's face was straight but Nina heard the laugh in his voice. 'If we're gonna work together we've got to be able to trust what you tell us. Like, for example, how old are you?'

Nina couldn't believe it. She swallowed hard. 'I'm twenty-two.'

'Really,' Lilly Hall said, rather coldly.

'But I went into work straight from school. I've worked in retail, at Dolan MacDonald and now Dragon. I have years of experience.' Nina knew she was justifying herself but she couldn't stop. 'My computerisation programmes at both Dolan and Dragon were instituted across the whole of the US. I'm a senior New Products manager, and,' she added with an acid stare at Namath, 'it was my research that discovered the breakthrough pharmacologies you've been working on.'

Dr Hall nodded. Nina got to her feet, leaving a couple of business cards on the table. She'd done it, she'd got them. That was what she should focus on, not the fact that the good-looking cowboy in the goggles and white coat had just utterly humiliated her.

'I'll see you out,' said Harry Namath.

He walked her to the door. Nina offered him her hand.

Namath shook it. He had a dry, firm grip. 'Brooklyn, right?'

'Right,' Nina said flatly.

He shook his head. 'Twenty-two. Pretty funny, but then it was a good save.'

She smiled slightly. 'Maybe it was.'

'I'm an American too, kiddo. You can't put it past me.'

'My name is Nina, Dr Namath.'

He fielded the rebuke easily. 'Only if mine's Harry. So, your lawyer will be in touch, we'll talk again.'

'Right.' She glanced up the street, looking for a cab.

'Hey Nina,' Harry said, 'great suit.'

'Thanks,' Nina muttered.

He closed the door.

Tony Savage picked up his phone with a shiver of pleasure. Sex rippled through him now whenever he heard any mention of Nina's name. She'd been away for a week. He wanted her to get through her deals quickly and get back. He was missing her softness and prickly ambition; lays like Nina didn't grow on trees.

'Go ahead, m'lord.'

'Nina? I read your fax. Good work.'

'Thank you, sir.'

Tony grinned. She wouldn't use his first name on a company phone. Whether it was paranoia or her stupid pretence that she separated business and pleasure, he didn't care. He liked Nina to call him sir; for her he was great God from whom all blessings flowed.

'How long is it going to take for you to wrap things up? You're missed around here.'

'A while yet. Legal is on it, but I want to get to know them. Dr Hall is thorny, but she knows exactly what she's doing.'

'And Henry Namath?'

There was a pause. 'Harry's real interesting, sir. No bullshit. When we talk about computers, he's … intense. He'll go with us if he thinks it's right for Lilly.'

'You like him.' Tony was surprised. 'Good. It'll be helpful in getting them to commit. Just don't like him *too* much, there's a girl.' Nina said nothing, so he ploughed on. 'Maybe I should come out there, Nina, get a sit-rep,' Tony added, silkily.

'I can fax you detailed reports. You don't need to come out.'

Tony glanced down at the receiver. 'No. You don't understand. Maybe I *want* to come out. And how's Elizabeth?'

'I don't know, sir. I'm seeing Lady Elizabeth next week. Where she's training.'

Tony grunted. 'What about her and Jack?'

'As I said, I don't know. I've been busy with Harry.'

'It's important to me to know the state of that relationship, Nina. It's a priority for me. Remember? Namath can get on just fine without you. My priorities are the ones that count. Don't forget it. Do you understand me?'

'I understand you perfectly, Lord Caerhaven.'

Tony flipped through the thick, gold-leaved pages of his desk diary. 'First Saturday of the month. I think I'll come over. To your apartment. We can have a chinwag before I fly out to Elizabeth. You'll enjoy that.'

There was a small silence. 'I might not be free on that Saturday.'

'No, you're not free. You're tied up with me,' Tony said.

He hung up. The pleasurable *frisson* had vanished completely. Tony glanced at the phone, then across his desk to the latest bunch of reports from sales. After the success of Dragon Gold, his wretched daughter had started taking matters into her own hands. They were small things, both of them, but not to be tolerated. Tony had learned early on that rebellion was there to be stamped on. In London, Switzerland, or anywhere else.

And the natives were getting restless.

Chapter 25

'Yeah, the response is fantastic.' Jake Ansom's voice crackled down the hotel telephone. 'Boots just put in another major order. Central buying says they're thinking of stocking it as standard.'

'Brilliant.' Elizabeth grinned. 'What about the independents?'

Village chemists were important too. She wanted her pill to be flying off shelves everywhere, right now, while it was still hot. They wouldn't allocate advertising money for ever. Elizabeth had spent months going over boring sales projections and histories for lots of their past brands. Now it was paying off. Once Dragon Gold was a household name, half the battle was won.

'You've got a real instinct for this stuff,' Jake said. 'Everybody's talking about it.'

Elizabeth laughed. 'Look, I want to launch in France. And put a major push into hospitals.'

'Hospitals? But—'

'Trust me, OK? Then we need to talk to water companies. Vittel, Evian ...'

Jake snorted. 'Bottled water? That's never going to catch on. Why should anybody pay for *water*? You get it free out of the tap.'

'Just set it up, Jake.' Elizabeth didn't mind his teasing, she was brimming with confidence. The years of reading trade magazines and pinning up Clio award-winning ads on her walls were all bearing fruit. Ideas were tumbling out of her like water bursting through a dam. And

Elizabeth knew what the stakes were. She had something to prove. By the time she was through, not even Daddy would ignore her any more.

Jake was still fretting. 'If you *insist*, but Liz – you can't launch in France, just like that.'

'Why not?'

The line to England gave a crackle as though amazed. 'Because it costs money to set it up! Lots of money! You don't have the authority—'

'I do. I've got total authority for Dragon Gold. But you're right, it's a waste to set up distribution in just one foreign country.'

Jake sighed with relief.

'We need to go across the whole continent. No, it's OK. I spoke to Father this morning, he wants me to go ahead.' That was a lie, of course, but Jake wouldn't know it. Everybody at Dragon assumed Tony adored his only daughter. 'You can check with him, if you need to.'

'No, that's fine,' Jake said hastily. 'I'll get our people in the local companies—'

'To call *me* direct. Father's very busy, he doesn't want to be bothered. That's why he gave me sole responsibility.'

When Ansom rang off she smiled. Maybe she was taking a risk, lying about Tony, spending millions, but someone else would soon discover how to link calcium and iron. Right now they had a USP, as Procter & Gamble would say, a unique selling point.

I know how this company works, Elizabeth thought, her heart quickening with excitement. As her father's daughter, nobody would question her. And with the power and wealth of Dragon right behind her, she could launch her product and make a success of it Europe-wide before anybody had time to stop her.

Elizabeth launched herself into her warm-up routine, flexing, stretching. Outside a new blanket of snow had covered the mountains and she was late for meeting Hans and Jack. Oh well, they could talk theory for a bit. It was going to take some doing, supervising Gold and training hard, but she was sure she could handle it. Like they said round the office, if you want something done, ask a busy person.

Surely this boldness would win Tony over. That was the way he worked: jump first, ask questions later. Tony was always saying that the person swearing it couldn't be done was run over by the person who just did it. It was daring, ruthless daring, that had made the Robber Baron – why shouldn't it make his daughter?

She grabbed her lilac skisuit with the iridescent stripes. Success made her feel romantic. The skintight Lycra was what she'd been wearing during her first battles with Jack. It hugged her tight butt and chiselled quads, and it shimmered thousands of rainbows as she plunged down the slopes, flashing bright as a starling's wing.

Elizabeth was annoyed with Jack for not calling, but she shoved that feeling aside. Today they'd be skiing again, skiing together, for the first time since she got to Switzerland. She twisted her glossy hair into a neat ponytail and picked up her goggles. No forests, no avalanches, God, this was going to be fun.

Elizabeth smiled softly at the bowing concierge as she left the Hotel Möller. It was one of the most exclusive in Klosters, unmarked from the outside, at first glance just another gingerbread-gabled townhouse in the heart of the old town. Places like the Möller did not advertise for guests. Hans knew the proprietress, so Elizabeth got the best of both worlds: as much privacy as you could get in the Olympic capital, stately courteousness and old-fashioned elegance, but also a first-class suite wired with faxes, three phone lines and even a small Quotron terminal, linked to the markets via Zurich. That was for the gnomes, rich Swiss financiers who used the Möller regularly. And despite the apparent rustic nature of the receptionists, they were ruthless on the phone. No journalist had scammed his way through to Elizabeth yet. The first night she arrived they camped outside the door; but when one tabloid hack tried sneaking into the lobby two gigantic bouncers had appeared silently from nowhere. The press let her alone.

It all came at a price, of course, but Elizabeth didn't worry about that. She charged it as a business expense and used her Dragon corporate Amex. Well, she couldn't ask Ronnie Davis to fork out for it, and the other girls were still sulking in St Moritz.

She caught the cable-car up to Gotschnagrat. Klosters dropped away beneath them, and Elizabeth's heart lifted along with her stomach; the sun was brilliant in crisp blue sky, new snow on the mountains glittering like powdered glass. Skiers were out in force, neon specks blazing over the runs, hundreds-and-thousands spattered on ice cream. This was skiing, this was coming home. Rocky crops and plunging walls of ice vanished below them as they moved on. Everything was so vast in the roof of the world; the sky so close you could touch it, crevasses that would drop you straight into hell.

Elizabeth moved among the tourists. She kept her dark goggles on so she wouldn't be bothered. Now Klosters was some brown speckles on the snow, they were passing Davos, with its dreary purpose-built blocks and endless lift queues. Traffic was toytown cute from the cable-car windows, bright sun flashes sparking from tiny windscreens. She felt an edgy knot in her gut as she looked down. Funny, you really felt how high up you were in one of these, whereas a plane seemed clinical and safe. Sometimes a car would stop for a few moments, and hang creaking over the void. That always scared her. Maybe it was too many Bond flicks: they made you expect a wheel failure, a lurch southwards, sickening drops into a fireball death. Chairlifts were worse. Years out on the circuit, and Elizabeth still thought that was a dodgy idea, park benches that flew. She never told Hans about her little phobias, he'd have teased her unmercifully. And as for Jack …

Elizabeth grinned at that thought as she stepped out at the Gotschna station, selected a flat patch of snow and buckled on her skis. Rossignol had custom-made these for her; they slid and turned, almost weightlessly, slicing and twisting in motion like part of herself. The snow was good, well packed but not icy, and the air at altitude had a perfect champagne sparkle. Just a few brave souls were pushing off towards the start of the Gotschnawang, and she recognised Hans straight off; you couldn't mistake that ramrod stance, nor the incongruous shock of white hair under the ancient goggles.

She glided over with one effortless push. '*Güten Morgen, mein Herr, wie geht's Ihnen?*'

'Elizabeth!' Hans smiled, clapping one mitt on her shoulder. 'You are well? Good!' He glanced her over critically. '*Ach*, not bad. It almost seems that you are fit. But fitness in the gymnasium does not equal speed on the slopes. All winter Heidi Laufen has been practising, and you are dabbling in business. What have you to show for it?'

Elizabeth grinned. Same old Hans. 'Maybe something big, in a couple of months.'

The old man's face creased. 'In a couple of months, *you* will see something big. Heidi Laufen with an Olympic Gold.'

'I don't think so. You don't get them for second place.'

'So,' Herr Wolf was sarcastic, 'you think Louise Levier will beat her to it?'

'I'm not that bad, boss, I'll show you,' Elizabeth said cheerfully. She waved down the plunging drops of the

Gotschnawang run with a ski-pole. Ski-instructors scared tourists with tales of this one; the Wang route to the south was unmarked, full of stomach-lurching dives and vicious mogul fields. If you were trying to crunch your way back into contention, there was no time for easing into it. Elizabeth's nipples tightened pleasantly from more than the cold. She'd been looking forward to taking this on with Jack, the adrenalin, bobsled-speed, his hard quads and glutes straining and pushing beside her ...

'OK. We go.' Hans pushed off.

'Wait! Where's Jack?'

'Jack?' Wolf blinked; his mind was already locked into the run. 'You were late.'

'You mean he's *left*?' Elizabeth asked. 'He can't have done, Hans, I'm only fifteen minutes—'

'*Ja, ja.*' Hans was impatient. 'He is by now halfway down. He said, this is too important to waste time, he does not like waiting. Maybe at the bottom he stays for you, maybe he takes the gondola to Parsenn.'

'I see,' Elizabeth said coldly. She couldn't believe it. Son-of-a-bitch, selfish, arrogant bastard! Fifteen bloody minutes! First he didn't ring her, now he wouldn't wait for her ... As she followed Hans over to the lip of the first schuss, Elizabeth ran over all the moments they'd had since he presented her with her little platinum ski. There weren't that many of them, really. Phone calls in the office, mostly brief news updates on their lives.

Jack's platinum trinket pressed against her collarbone as she thrust off from the top. Instantly her reflexes took over as her body hugged the ice, her stomach floating fifty yards behind her as she flew behind her coach. Elizabeth flicked into ski mode like she'd turned on a light, keeping her eyes a hundred yards in front, turning to the left cleanly. The slicing edges of her skis threw up a small arc of ice. She barrelled left again, then right, hugging Hans's tracks so perfectly you could hardly tell there were two people on the track. But Jack was still in the back of her mind, even while she concentrated on her technique. Resentment lay clammy over her heart. Maybe she'd been right the first time. Jack Taylor just lived for the chase, and now he'd had her, he was going to—

Elizabeth swung right a fraction too late in an ugly turn, the angle was huge. Hans glanced behind him and frowned as Elizabeth ducked her head, abashed. Bloody Jack had put her off. A howler like that could lose you a third of a second, maybe more, if it happened on race day. Her annoyance intensified. Maybe Vanessa, or Clarisse or all Jack's other groupies put up with it, but she wasn't going to.

You'd better buck your ideas up, mate, or else—

'Elizabeth, *lieber Gott*!' Hans grumbled, as she smoothly fell in beside him. 'Horrible, you ski like a farmer's wife, and slow as a cow.'

'Sorry,' Elizabeth mumbled.

'Sorry won't save you.' On a small flat patch Hans carved to a full stop, Elizabeth just fast enough to match him. Her coach was shaking his head. 'Come, show me something, *Fräulein*, the World Champion I ski with! Where is your head? Not on the schuss.' The bright old eyes watched her clearly. 'Heidi pines for her *Jungen* only *after* she skis. Forget him for now.'

'I wasn't thinking about Jack!' Elizabeth protested hotly.

'No?' Hans said shrewdly.

Elizabeth flung herself into the next barrelling drop before Herr Wolf saw the blush on her face. Was she really that obvious? It was embarrassing. And he was bloody well right, Taylor wasn't worth it.

With a wrench she turned her gaze to the plummeting white track before her, settling her body lower towards the ground, feeling the gradient in her belly. She hurtled forwards so fast it seemed her skis barely grazed the snow, flying over the ice crystals until the horizons were bleeding into each other. Hans dropped behind her, and all the world was whiteness and freefall, angles and sticks, her strong muscles twisting and leaping. The Wang run fired her downwards to its finish like a bolt from a crossbow.

No posts announced the end of the piste. The kind of skier that tackled the Gotschnawang runs didn't need them. Elizabeth simply ground to a halt, a vertical wave of powder pluming up behind her like the tail of a giant white peacock. She ripped her goggles from her head and stood there panting, still recovering when Hans zoomed the last schuss a full nine seconds behind her.

'*Ja*,' Wolf gasped, breathing hard himself. His eyes twinkled. 'That is the girl I remember. You are now fast. But reckless.'

'Overcautious, undercautious,' Elizabeth grumbled.

'Speed *and* skill. That is what we need. But with much work we shall have it.' Hans brightened and waved at the café. 'A schnapps? We will celebrate, but it will be the last before the Games.'

'What?'

'No alcohol. Also early bed, strict diet, no caffeine,' Hans said happily as Elizabeth unlocked her boots.

Great, Elizabeth thought glumly, trudging up the wooden steps behind him. Skiers sipping their *citrons pressés* or *Glühweins* gawked at them, whether it was recognition or just the speed of their arrival she didn't know. As Hans led her inside, the familiar waft of frankfurters, soup and cheese with black bread hit her. A pine-log fire crackled in one corner and her heart rate dropped steadily. That was good; real fitness meant quick recovery, and—

'Hello, milady,' Jack Taylor said. He was perched on a barstool, drinking mineral water, wearing the red, white and blue suit of the US team. Obviously the recognition thing is not too much of a problem for *you*, Elizabeth thought, swiftly clocking at least five Swiss girlies with their eyes constantly flickering Jack's way. Hell, why not? He looked great, as usual: bronzed, huge, the dark hair cropped a little tighter than when she last saw him, the cruel mouth set in that maddeningly confident way. Maybe it was the snow. Or the suit. In a Savile Row three-piece Jack looked a real babe; but in a skisuit, out here, he looked like a champion. A world beater with the gold already reserved. How great it would be, Elizabeth thought a little sourly, if *I* had no competition.

'Jack,' she said. What was he expecting, a fucking ticker-tape welcome? 'Are you coming up to the Weissflujoch? We're just going to have a quick schnapps.'

'You're drinking alcohol?' Jack asked.

'Yeah.' She heard herself get curt. 'I'm not a Muslim.'

Jack put some money on the bar and waved at Hans. 'No, I want to do some Strela blacks. You were late, Elizabeth.'

'It was only a quarter of an hour,' Elizabeth said angrily. 'You were rude, Jack, you should have waited for me.'

Jack shrugged. 'Sugar, I wouldn't ask *you* to wait. You want to drink schnapps, relax your schedules, ski tramlines like the Weissflu? It's the Olympics. I never screwed up a schedule in my life for anything, especially not for manners.'

'Nice to see you too.'

'Hey. I'm thrilled to see you. Look, if it was anyone else, I'd be on the gondola right now, but I gave you guys an extra five minutes to get here.'

Elizabeth was furious. 'Look, Jack, don't do me any favours, all right?'

'What's your problem?' the Texan demanded, brown eyes narrowing.

'I don't have one.'

'I'm letting you train with me, Elizabeth,' Jack said softly. 'Wouldn't do it for any other female. This is—'

'The Olympics, yeah, so I gathered. And I know what you think of females. But you needn't bother yourself,' Elizabeth snapped. 'I'm skiing a tramline run right now.'

Jack looked at her for a few seconds. Then he said, 'OK,' casually, waved at Hans and stood up. 'I'll call you tonight.'

Elizabeth turned away to pick up her schnapps. 'Like I said, don't do me any favours.'

She picked up her glass and sipped it slowly, listening to Jack's heavy footfalls as he clumped out to the terrace.

'Problems?' Hans asked, but Elizabeth shook her head. She started to talk techniques with the coach, while glaring at one of the adoring Swiss girlies, who was irritatingly staring at her as if she were mad.

Chapter 26

'Great, so we'll complete next week.' Nina was filing more notes as she talked to Luc Viera. She rubbed her aching temples; it was the end of another long, busy day. She'd been setting up contracts and offices and new administrative structures; she dreamed of figures, she woke up with crunching migraines and rows of accountant's print swimming before her eyes.

A shadow fell over her desk. Nina looked up.

Dr Henry Namath, Dragon Inc.'s latest contractual supplier, was looming over her. He wore a pair of jeans and a Yankees sweatshirt. Behind him Frau Bierhof, Nina's new assistant, was looking outraged. Obviously Harry had barged past her. As usual.

Nina sighed. 'Hold on, Luc.' She looked at him, exasperated. 'Harry, what's wrong with the phone?'

'Nothing. If you answered it.' Namath pointed to the pile of message slips on her desk.

Nina shrugged; if it was Tony, legal or a vital call, Steffi Bierhof let her know, otherwise, sure, she ignored them. Who had time? 'Can't it wait? Guess not. OK. Look, Luc, Dr Namath's here, I have to go. You know the fax in my apartment, right? I'll check the details tonight.'

She hung up. 'OK, Dr Namath, I'm all yours.'

'Great,' he said, pulling her coat from the rack. 'Let's go find a restaurant.'

'We'll discuss it here. I have too much work to do, and—'

'Nina.' Namath bent over her, his black hair and blue eyes seriously distracting. 'Let me tell you something. Biochemical principle. The human body needs food.'

'Really, I—'

'And mental agility suffers without it. Come on, it's an investment, it'll stop you screwing up from low blood sugar.'

Nina couldn't stop a tiny smile as she accepted her coat.

'That's better.' Namath looked her over with a forty-watt grin. 'Come on, I got a table. Best place in town.'

Well, she *was* hungry, Nina rationalised as she followed him out.

The cab pulled up off the Dörfli and Nina stepped out, looking at the narrow Gothic houses, antique shops, cafés and bookstores mingling with underground night-clubs. That was Zurich, if you had time to enjoy it. Grimm's fairy tales by day, Soho by night. She felt too exhausted to be appreciative, wondered what Namath had in mind: another fancy Swiss eatery, full of bankers and ladies in furs, unpronounceable dishes and alcohol strong enough to fuel rockets. If she ate one more lamb and dandelion salad she was going to explode.

'So, we're going somewhere ethnic?'

'Very ethnic.' Namath pushed her to the right and pointed. 'The Hard Rock Café.'

Nina laughed.

'Well, American is ethnic,' Namath said, grinning, 'and I felt like Bud and a cheeseburger, I hope you don't mind.'

They were shown to a small table in the back. It was cramped and in sight of the kitchen but Nina couldn't have cared less; it was dark, busy, full of American babble and waiters carrying trays piled with fries and ice cream. A girl materialised right away and Harry asked for a cheeseburger, beer and fudge melt chocolate cake. Nina went for grilled chicken and Diet Coke, with a fruit salad.

'That's really going to do your cholesterol a lot of good.'

'So now you're worried about my cholesterol?' Dr Namath asked.

Nina blushed. Harry had been a hellish pain in the butt; he ran their lawyers ragged, he insisted on supervising all the lab details, wouldn't buckle on a goddamned thing. Once the ink was dry, Lilly Hall had gotten the best terms any Dragon contractor had ever had. She had to admire Namath, he knew what he was doing. Impressive for such a young guy, but like Harrison Ford once said, it's not the age, honey, it's the mileage. Young kids were coming up everywhere. The eighties was the decade of the entrepreneur. Even if Namath didn't fit the red-braces-with-dollar-signs stereotype. For a man who'd be a millionaire in less than two years, Harry dressed like a workman.

But face to face he was real attractive. The logician's brain came gift-wrapped: short hair, raven black, and sharp azure eyes. He had none of Tony's powerful elegance. Namath was brutish to look at, stubborn, annoyingly light hearted; getting his own way while refusing to take life seriously. Nina thought about him often, caught herself, and tried to stop. She told herself it was her scientific side, how could she not admire a man who thought in code, a mathematician who could read numbers like a language?

'Well …'

'I can handle it. Or maybe you think I'm too fat.'

Nina was forced to glance at his body under the loose shirt. Nice, very nice. He was big but lean, well balanced, one of those naturally strong guys who didn't need the gym.

'What did you want to discuss? Lilly's bonus? It's being credited to her tomorrow. The lab? That's ready to inspect Monday. Or was there another contract problem? I hope not because we've moved on from that ...'

'None of the above.' Namath dipped a handful of fries in barbecue sauce. 'I wanted to talk about us.'

'Us? I thought we'd straightened those problems out, Harry. I know you think I've been harsh but—'

'Harsh? You're a nightmare. I buckled in to you more times than I want to think about.'

'Like hell,' Nina said.

Harry smiled. 'I mean *us*. Now it's a done deal. You and me. Dates.'

'Dates?'

'Dates. You remember them,' Harry said maddeningly, 'not the dried fruit or the calendar kind, you must have had some. Girls like you don't get away without them.'

'Girls like me?' Nina repeated stupidly. It was dumb, but with those clear eyes looking right at her she felt silly, like an idiot teenager. Somehow she'd never expected this. Namath was mildly flirtatious with every female, and they'd fought so much, and she was the corporate enemy ...

'Girls who are so radiantly lovely,' Harry said.

Nina blushed deeper. She had no idea how to react. Nobody had ever said anything like that to her in her life – it was always catcalls, or 'babe', or Tony's explicit praise. She was used to Tony making her feel like an erotic sculpture. Did he really call me radiant? she thought, and felt strange, different. Vulnerable and shy.

'I don't have boyfriends,' she said flatly.

'Good. I don't want you to have boyfriends, I want you to have me,' Harry said, taking a bite of his cheeseburger. He looked like he was loving it. Nina flashed on Tony, eating and drinking with perfect restraint. In public the earl was always totally dignified, the Robber Baron, impeccable and ice cold.

'No. It's nothing personal, but I tried it once and it didn't work.'

'Some guy treated you bad?'

'You don't want to know.'

'You're wrong there, toots, I want to know everything.'

'It's private,' Nina said coldly. 'Happened a long time ago.' Yeah, when I was a different person on another planet. Nina brushed the beautifully cut cotton of her moss-green Martine Sitbon jacket, matched with a white silk shirt. Her strength, her hardness, had taken her from that girl to this one. Tony Savage she could handle. She wasn't scared of him. But right now she was very, very scared of Harry Namath.

'OK.' He accepted that, but wasn't put off. 'So that means what? You're going to punish every other man you meet for the rest of your life?'

'I'm not going to punish anybody, I just don't want to deal with it.' Nina stabbed defiantly at her chicken. 'I have enough on my plate. I'm trying to build a career.'

'Surprisingly enough, I had noticed that. But that's no way to live, you can't take a computer to bed with you at night. Do you read Kipling? The *Just So* stories?'

'No,' Nina said, smiling faintly at the thought of her ever having time to read fiction.

'You should do.' Harry looked across at the young woman in front of him, groomed, self-possessed, lifetimes older than her age. There was something in that beautiful face he couldn't read, some veil those dark eyes were pulling down. God, but Nina was so lovely, dark hair round her face like a thundercloud, cheekbones like knife-slashes in her pale face. He had ached for her since the second he first saw her, then his lust had mixed with something else; he'd never known a girl like her, breathlessly efficient, such a worker, so organised and pushy and quick. It was easy to tell she'd never been educated, but she was vividly smart. Nina was *it*. Weird and obsessive, but she was it, she was the one for him. And vice versa. Harry wanted to rip all that armour off and make her see it too.

'There's one about you. The animal who doesn't need anybody, just sways around all day, going, "I am the cat who walks by himself." '

' "I am the cat who walks by himself"?' Nina smiled despite herself. 'I like that.'

'Even cats need company. It'll be wild, we can discuss Turing machines and Church's lambda calculus under the stars.'

'Don't tempt me.'

'See? You're laughing,' Namath said triumphantly. 'Come on, try being happy for a while, what could it hurt? If you don't like it you can always go back to being miserable.'

He winked at her and Nina felt a warm flush of desire lap around her belly and tighten between her legs. Oh God. She should never have agreed to dinner. She wanted him now, wanted him pretty badly. But of course, that was impossible.

'I can't go out with you.'

'You're in love with somebody else?'

'No!' That idea was so off-base she really did laugh. 'Definitely not. I just need my independence.'

'Independence, hell. You're terrified of me,' Harry said shrewdly.

Nina tilted her head. It was such an arrogant, lovely movement he wanted to reach over and kiss her.

'I'm terrified of nothing. But I don't want a man, Harry, it's not compulsory.'

'Then a friend. I could do with some company.'

'You've got Lilly.'

'Lilly? No, we're just professional partners. She likes classical opera and shit that bores the hell out of me. And she's nuts about her work, whereas I like to switch off.'

Nina weakened. What could that hurt? Could it hurt? She'd never had a real friend since Frank Malone. Now he was making her think about it, she *was* lonely, she did feel ... 'But you don't mean *friends*. You'll just try and take advantage.'

'Nina.' Harry reached over and grabbed her hand. His fingers felt rough and calloused, covered in tiny scars and burns from acids or Bunsen burners. 'I swear to you, I won't do a single thing to you you don't ask for. In so many words.'

Tony rang Nina a week later. 'Getting on OK, darling?'

'Fine,' she said. She launched into a summary of the new division she was setting up, a restructuring of all their research projects. It was Nina's idea to have their various teams – human, medicinal, animal and supply – all report to the same people. That way knowledge would be pooled. It was already starting to pay off: a useless side-effect in a Dutch team's experiment was the clue their coronary people had been looking for. And Lilly was a landed fish now. Nina was confident.

'I know all that.' Tony was brisk. 'Stock's up two and an eighth. I'd like you to knock something out for the quarterly newsletter.'

'Sure.' Nina was pleased. Their newsletter for analysts was important to Dragon; it led to big orders from the pension funds and institutionals. Now she'd really get noticed. 'I'll get a promotion for this, and a rise?'

'You just had one.'

'Come on, Tony, Dragon's about results, not tenure!'

There was silence on the end of the line. 'Where were you last night? I got the machine. Same thing on Wednesday.'

Nina looked down at the phone she was holding and felt a soft chill dance across her spine. 'I was out.'

'Really?' Caerhaven's voice was measured. 'With whom?'

Never complain, never explain, Nina thought. 'With Harry Namath.'

'Of course, the charming Dr Namath. You went to the ballet, or the theatre? How delightful.'

Nina's heart thudded against her ribcage. 'Uh, we went to the movies. *An Officer and a Gentleman*.'

'Maybe we should get you home, darling. He sounds like a bad influence. Just as we were getting you civilised, you start watching drivel like that.'

Nina said nothing. She'd loved the movie. Maybe she was meant to identify with Debra Winger, although she felt like Gere instead; she knew what it was like to have a worthless lush of a father and grow up feeling like dirt. Something in Savage's voice warned her not to say that, however.

'I spoke to Lady Elizabeth's coach yesterday. She's moved up to Klosters, away from the team hotel, so she can train with Jack Taylor.'

That was a lie. She'd been too stretched to give the Sloany bitch a second thought, but Tony would explode if he thought she'd ignored his orders.

'That sounds promising, but you should go yourself. I'll call her and tell her you're coming.'

'OK.'

'You don't sound too enthusiastic, darling, but I think I can cheer you up. Tell you what, knock that newsletter into shape for me and we'll talk about it.'

'Why can't we do that now?'

'No. I mean face to face,' Tony said warmly. 'I actually found some space. I'll be in Zurich next Friday.'

Harry picked her up on Wednesday night, late enough so

263

Frau Bierhof was gone and she didn't have any excuse to hand. Night was falling outside the office window, the phones had stopped trilling and even the fax machine was silent. He found her crouched over her IBM, tapping away obliviously, her face lit up in a ghostly pallor by the light of the screen. Namath recognised that Nina sunk-in-my-work look. It was easy enough to sneak up behind her, lean over the keyboard, punch a few buttons and shut it off.

'What the hell—' Nina shouted.

'Calm down, kid, I haven't lost your work, it's saved.'

'Are you sure? You better be.'

'Hey, this is Dr Henry Namath, remember, fluent in processor, computers are my friends.' He yanked her up from her chair and started waltzing her round the darkened office, humming the *Doctor Dolittle* theme. 'Oh I can *walk* with the monitors, *talk* to the monitors ...'

'OK, OK,' Nina said, smiling. What the hell, it was nine p.m., and she was taking a morning train to Klosters. She let Harry throw her her coat and pull her down the stairs. 'Where are we going?'

'To my apartment.'

She pulled back. 'Hey, Harry ...'

'Where is the trust?' Harry asked rhetorically. 'I told you, you needn't expect anything from me until you ask for it. Maybe not even then.'

Nina gave him a suspicious look but climbed into the cab. She could always brush him off if he decided to try it on. She tried to ignore the half of her that was longing for him to do just that. So far he'd been as good as his word: fun to be with, great company, but nothing more. A peck on the cheek was all she got when he dropped her home. Did he really think she was going to ask for more? Was she going to?

Stop that! Come on, girl, you know he's out of bounds.

He's a prize asset, he's business, you can't risk it, you don't want to get involved …

She was wildly curious to see Harry's place. A neat penthouse on the Niederdorf, a one bedroom with *Sports Illustrated* on the couch, a mess in the drawing room, functional black and white. Thick books on pure mathematics and piles of computer paper everywhere, not much luxury apart from a huge TV. But he'd set it up for her: two chairs in front of the widescreen, home-popped corn, chilled Millers, nachos, a large bowl of M&Ms …

Nina burst out laughing as Harry reached for the remote and pressed play. The screen flickered into life, the CBS commentators started yelling, goddamn, it was the Superbowl, last year's final she'd complained to him she missed.

'Have a beer,' Harry said, 'I got chilli dogs waiting to be heated up.'

'Oh, this is great,' Nina said, smiling, 'this is so great—'

Harry walked up to her and kissed her full on the mouth.

Nina melted. Instantly. It was thermonuclear melt-down, weak at the knees, her lips parting, his pressing, her back arching into his arms, his tongue—

'No!' She pushed him away, breathing hard, fought for control. For time. 'You said you'd wait till I—'

'I lied,' Namath said.

Nina forced herself to sit down and crack open a beer. 'Don't spoil it, Harry. Let's just watch the game, all right?'

She refused to look back as he went into the kitchen. She was so turned on, just from that. Oh God, help me, Nina thought. She wasn't in control any more, she was out of control. He was so gorgeous. And so smart, and so sweet. Regret stabbed at her like a dagger. Harry liked her, because he didn't know her. He just had no idea what he'd be getting himself into.

She wanted him so badly. She wanted to cry.

Chapter 27

Nina checked in to the Fluela at noon. She hated Davos. Huge cinder-block hotels, roads clogged with traffic, gawking Eurotrash tourists lumping skis and boots on their way to the endless lift queues. This was town as theme park: skiing, skiing and more skiing. Snow, fondues and ugly nylon suits. Elizabeth's world.

She got her room key and went right upstairs. Last night with Harry had unsettled her, she felt nervous and edgy. She wasn't *like* this, her confidence gone and her armour dented. Tony was turning up tomorrow, and she didn't even know how she felt about that. Soon it would be time to transfer back to London, with a promotion. More money, more status ... I'm writing a section of the *analysts'* report, Nina reminded herself, staring out of her window at the icy massifs in front of her. I'll see less of Harry, I'll get back on track, it'll be great.

She thought about Tony as she dialled Elizabeth's hotel in the valley below. He seemed to miss her. That had to be a plus.

So why was she wishing so hard that he wouldn't show up?

'Hotel Möller, *güten Tag.*'

'Can I speak to Lady Elizabeth Savage? This is Nina Roth.'

A few seconds before Elizabeth picked up. 'Nina! Daddy told me I might have the pleasure.'

Nina's confusion vanished in a hot surge of anger. She

said politely, 'I wonder if I could have a few minutes of your time? Tony would like a progress report.'

'But of course.' Silky limey tones, sounds just like her papa. 'Would three o'clock suit?'

'Not really. If we meet then I can't get on a train until—'

'That's the only time I've got today.'

Nina bit her lip so hard it hurt. 'Then three o'clock it is. I'll come to you.'

'Wonderful. I'll look forward to it.'

She got to Elizabeth's hotel at ten of, after twenty fruitless minutes tramping Klosters' fairy-tale streets trying to find it. She was cold and exasperated, her Jimmy Choo boots probably ruined, her ass freezing off under her primrose Galliano skirt. Nina wanted to show up for the bitch wearing Levi's and a sloppy Joe, Harry-style, but Elizabeth might have reported her to Tony. Nina knew they hated each other really, but she didn't understand them any more. And she didn't trust either of them. As well as the cold, Klosters oppressed her with its huge Olympic rings everywhere, TV crews on every corner, the Games paraphernalia limbering up. A picture of Elizabeth herself, green eyes limpid, gazed out from an import cover of a British sports magazine.

Jealousy flashed through Nina. Elizabeth had all this, but it wasn't enough, she wanted her playtime in Daddy's back yard as well, all the trappings of the businesswoman without doing one thing to earn them. In Klosters Nina was forced to think about the loathsome prospect that Elizabeth actually won an Olympic gold. Then she really would be famous, she'd be a heroine to the Brits. World Champion was good, but those things came and went. The Olympics had that magic. What would Elizabeth do with leverage like that?

It made her sick just thinking about it. Today she was

here, wasting her time, freezing her butt off, playing a stupid game – Elizabeth thought Nina was taking a report on the vitamin pill but all Tony was interested in was Jack Taylor. Nina smiled grimly as her new boots scuffed on icy cobbles. Jack, another rich kid, another snow jock. What was there to admire in skiers, anyway? Only rich kids *could* ski. You wouldn't get many competitors from the Bronx or the East End, not like running or soccer or something. That must cut the competition pretty good. Probably ninety per cent of potential champions would never even see a goddamn mountain.

Lady Elizabeth's hotel was right next to the Walserhof, where Charles and Di had stayed last year. It looked rich but utterly discreet and secure. Nina picked out the guards right away: burly 'guests' who didn't quite fit in by the elevator, reception area and front door. One of them caught her assessing look and turned away, not used to being identified. But I'm not like the press, *paisan*, Nina thought. We can spot muscle in Brooklyn.

The receptionist showed her to an anteroom and Nina settled down to wait. And wait. Her anger grew as the minutes ticked by, her mind on the trains, rearranging her travel plans. This selfishness was gonna get her home at nearly midnight.

The door opened and Elizabeth strode in. She was dressed in some kind of sexy, clingy rainbow-suit with black sneakers. Goggle-lines marked her tanned face. She was glowing from exercise, tawny hair pulled back in a girlish pigtail and her gold signet ring glinting on her left hand. Elizabeth looked like a convent girl on a school outing, and this, *this*, was the kid who fancied herself as Charles Saatchi, that tried to have Nina fired?

Elizabeth smiled defiantly and dumped a pile of fax papers on the table.

'Sorry I'm late. Got caught up in a crash on the Strela.

Really vile, one of the Spanish girls twisted her ankle. She's out, most likely.'

'Oh.' Do I care? Be polite, Nina, be polite. 'Was she a contender? They can't have much skiing in Spain.'

Elizabeth smiled. 'I suppose you didn't do much European geography. Spain's got a lot of decent spots – Sierra Nevada, Formigal, Baqueria-Beret ... and anyway, most people would say I couldn't have much skiing in England.'

'Unless you'd been to Swiss finishing school,' Nina said, unable to resist.

Elizabeth inclined her head. '*Touché*. How's Zurich?'

'Busy. We have a lot of ground to cover, it's like setting up a new business.'

'Just like me, then. Why don't you have a look at my stuff, tell me what you think?' Elizabeth asked.

Nina reached over and took the pile of faxes she was proffered, pretended to look through them. The ad slogans seemed snappy enough, there was lots of butt-kissing from France and Germany. She'd check this rubbish on her way back tonight, just in case, by some fucking fluke, there was anything interesting in it.

'It's doing very well back home, the sales are still holding.'

'Yes.' Elizabeth nodded proudly. 'Did you realise that's almost three weeks since our last TV slot ran, and they're *still* selling?'

'I'll admit, you seem to have a flair for advertising.'

'I do indeed. A talent you could have used.'

'I needed you to work on other things. Market research matters, Lady Elizabeth.'

'Yes, I realise that now,' Elizabeth said coolly. 'As you can see from my work, I've managed to use what you made me learn. Now I know more than most account executives about what our market *wants*. And when we tailor the work to that – bingo.'

Nina pressed her manicured fingers deep into the table mat. *Oy, I can't take much more of this, with madam sitting there condescending about geography and telling me about the market!*

'Well, that's about it. How's the skiing coming along?'

'Why do you care?'

Nina flushed. 'It could be good for the product.'

'I suppose that's true. Pretty well, so far, but we'll have to see,' Elizabeth said vaguely.

'Are you training with your boyfriend?'

Elizabeth seemed to freeze for a second. 'I don't have a boyfriend.'

What? 'Isn't Jack Taylor your boyfriend?'

'No, Jack's just a friend,' Elizabeth told her. 'We do ski together. Sometimes. But if I get any free time I spend it on work, not socialising.'

She flashed Nina a brilliant smile from perfect white teeth and stood up, extending one hand. 'I must dash, meeting the coach on the Weissflujoch and the queues are horrible! Will I see you at the Games? Or maybe in London. Give Dino my best. And say hello to Father for me.'

Nina picked up Elizabeth's notes with a sinking heart. *Just a friend.* Was that a cover, or did she really mean it? Had they busted up? There were a lot of papers here, it looked like she was taking it seriously. Maybe in that bimbo's head she was involved in Dragon for real.

Tony wasn't going to like it. And neither did she.

Elizabeth watched Nina leave from her bedroom window, the dark hair immaculately styled against the designer clothes. Roth looked as professional as always. She could scarcely believe they were the same age. Were all career women like that, or just the Americans? Nina Roth had that low-class tough-guy attitude, a real don't-fuck-with-me type. Dad had surrounded himself with those men; Elizabeth recalled hundreds of them over the years, guests at the castle, tennis-tournament partners, padding the crowd at Monica's receptions. Faceless stormtroopers with that jungle vibe underneath the sombre suits, she'd called them 'the piranhas' when she was a kid. The big difference being that all those lackeys were male.

While she snapped on her boots and reached for her racing helmet Elizabeth thought about Nina for a while. She was sleeping with Tony, but there was something else there. I have to face up to it, Elizabeth thought, she hates me, and she's *good*. She's really good. It made her edgy when Nina asked about Jack. There was something behind that – Nina Roth wasn't interested in her love life … or lack of it – but she'd have to worry about it later.

Elizabeth arrived at Drostobel feeling tense. The sky was slate blue, thick, pregnant clouds lumbering over the sun, dappling the slopes with shade, and creating small pools of vertical beams where the light broke through, like medieval paintings of divine grace. The air was thick and close as well as chilly. Hans had been pleased with her progress so far, she could tell because she spoke fluent Hans, although to anyone else his endless lectures on angles and crouches and now we try once more, *Fräulein*, would seem unbearable. Hans only cheered you once the medal was won. Or lost.

Her fitness hell in Kent had worked. Cross-training had given her extra strength and flexibility. Her records showed that she'd shaved almost a second off her World Cup time for the Davos meet. Trouble was you couldn't count on that – the rumours were that the Swiss team had also come up with new routines.

Heidi and Louise were skiing the course in Verbier. The Austrians were in Grindelwald and the French in Flims, the main contenders spreading themselves out amongst the courses by mutual consent. Hans and she would rotate as well. Heidi and Louise had real good fortune; every meet was home base for them. And there was more that upset her. The Strela crash she'd nearly skied into, Grace Cortez lying there, her foot twisted, back arched in agony, every skier's nightmare. Poor Grace, she'd nearly made the top ten last year. Now the dream had skidded away along with her skis, for these Games and maybe for ever. Elizabeth's mouth dried up thinking about that. They were all just one fall away from oblivion.

Focus, focus, Elizabeth warned herself. Hans was taking her down the Drostobel, less scary than the Wang but about as steep. Difference was, he'd had it fenced off and poled up. She sighed. Slalom and Super-G, her weak points, but they needed work.

At the top of the lift she slid on to the snow and tightened her helmet strap, looking round carefully. Where is he? I should be able to pick Hans out of the crowd by now ...

Somebody rapped on the Union Jack emblazoned over her visor. Elizabeth looked up crossly. 'Hey, cut it out! Oh, Jack, hi, I was looking for Hans.'

'He couldn't be here.'

'But we've got a session. He never misses training.'

'I'm sure he's got his reasons,' Jack said lightly. 'Wouldn't share them with me, which is something I purely hate.'

Suddenly she was glad she was wearing the helmet. Didn't want Jack to see the silly, puppy-like longing probably written all over her face. It was the warm Texas sun in his voice on this gloomy day. Or maybe the matt-black suit, no goggles, that made him look like a thug from a spy movie. It was awesome on that body, moulded to his chest and quads, with just a discreet Stars and Stripes over the heart, US training colours.

273

'Thanks for the message. See ya,' she said, but Taylor clamped a massive paw on her gloves before she could push off.

'He asked me to help out.'

'Hans asked you to train me?' Elizabeth repeated.

'I guess,' Jack said, shrugging, his dark eyes fixed on her. 'I'm polishing Super-G this afternoon. I don't mind showing you what you're doing wrong.'

Hans, you bastard! Elizabeth thought. This would be good for her and Hans knew it – he didn't give a damn about anything except her skiing. It was murder to have to take it from Jack Taylor. 'Show you what you're doing wrong!' And she *would* have to take it, because Jack's Super-G was outstanding. Possibly his best discipline – and with Taylor, that meant a hell of a lot. She had no choice here at all.

'Thank you. That'd be great,' Elizabeth muttered. She'd been avoiding him since the day she arrived. It occurred to her that this would be the first time she'd seen him ski since the World Cup.

'OK,' Jack said evenly. He cursed Hans Wolf silently under his breath. He owed Wolf too many favours to turn him down, but the old guy just didn't know what he was asking. Elizabeth, he must have been out of his brain, thinking he could make a future with the spoilt, stuck-up little brat. First she got on his case about leaving England to train, like the Olympics didn't matter, like her dumb-ass job at the drug company really meant something. Her pa was never giving her a shake, and she should have seen that.

She should have been *here*, like I was, he thought. Then when she does turn up she's foolin' about in the hotel, she ruins my schedule, snaps at me ...

Jack took his skiing seriously. It took the last World Cup for Elizabeth to get his respect. Now the rumours from the British camp were she was back to her old ways, her prima donna mode. This time her distractions were 'business', quote unquote, and not boys, but it was all the same thing. Toys. Games.

All that time I pined for her, Jack thought, but I wasn't with her. Wasn't seeing how she acted. She turned up to team camp looking like cotton-candy, she was so weak. It killed him to see her, weeks before the Games, being late, temperamental ... it wouldn't matter but Savage was a world-class talent, she had the potential to be one of the true greats. Jack just knew it, he smelt it in her like a fox scents a vixen. For her to throw it away like this was disgraceful. If a kid of his acted that way he'd tan her hide. She made him mad.

But then there was the other little problem, the one he'd brought on himself. It was real, real easy to get pissed at Elizabeth. Not so easy to ignore her. Or forget her. Why should I care if some limey chick doesn't take my calls? Jack thought angrily. It bothered him that she was blanking him again. He couldn't forget that kiss on that freezing winter morning in England, the waiting for her sharpening the pleasure, feeling her resistance melt, and then the cottage, and everything he'd imagined – but better. Elizabeth's long honey hair drifting over his chest, her flat stomach fluttering under his hands, her endless legs and sinewy body writhing over him, those little bud nipples taut on her pale breasts ...

Elizabeth was looking at him from under that biker's helmet. Impatiently. That tilt of her head bugged the shit out of him.

Come on, Jack, that was it, she's a great piece of ass, but there are lots of those. Now you gotta train with her so let's get on with it.

Well. He *would* train her. He'd show her exactly what standard was required to be an Olympic champion, what she'd forfeited with all her stupid games and scrappy practice. What sweat bought you.

I'll show you, sugar, Jack thought.

'I'll watch from the top the first time. We'll do the three slalom courses, then the Super-G, then you follow my instructions. Just holler if you want to drop out.'

'I won't want to drop out,' Elizabeth said, glaring at him.

Jack smiled coldly. 'We'll see. On my mark, left gate ...'

Chapter 28

The doorbell buzzed. Nina jumped, startled. She was still tugging her brush through the ends of her hair, she'd only gotten to the tinted moisturiser stage of her make-up. Her watch said eight a.m. It couldn't be him, it had to be a mistake. She ignored it and rubbed pale concealer under her eyes; God, she was so tired. Up at five to wash her hair, but she'd gotten in at midnight and been forced to stay up till two, trying to think of some way round the Lady Elizabeth problem. Her body had broken through some kind of barrier. Being tired like this gave you a jittery false energy, like the kind you get on too much caffeine.

The buzzer again. Shit. Nina slipped her feet into the Stèphane Kelian stacked mules and stumbled to her entryphone.

'Tony! Sorry, you're so early – come right up.'

She rushed back to the bathroom, frantically scooping up last night's underwear from the tiles and shoving it into the laundry basket. No time for make-up now, she might smear it. Tony, oh God. Her heart started hammering, she felt a nervous sweat break out across her back. Flung open the window to the freezing morning air to lose the steam from her shower. The mirror cleared and she caught a glimpse of herself as the doorbell trilled: dark hair damp and sleek, her body-hugging Chanel number in navy and white over a crisp Prada shirt. The most expensive suit she owned. There could be none of the casual pants and jumpers she wore out with Harry;

for Tony, nothing but the best was acceptable. You had to be it and look it, for the greater glory of the Robber Baron. Her face was bare, but there was no time to put that right.

'Coming, Tony, just one second!'

She spritzed herself with Joy, his favourite, and sprinted to open the door.

Harry Namath stood there, holding a video and a packet of Butterkist.

'Oh.' Nina gasped with surprise, then recovered herself. 'Er ... Harry! Come in, sorry, I was expecting someone else.'

'So I gathered.' Harry stepped into the apartment, looking her over. He was wearing jeans, runners and a sweatshirt, with a battered khaki rucksack slung over one shoulder. '*Tony?* I thought it was always "the earl" or "Lord Caerhaven", some feudal bullshit like that.'

Nina wanted to die. 'Well, I usually refer to him that way to outsiders – I mean, other people. He's the boss, I have to be respectful.'

'But privately you're friends?'

'I wouldn't say *friends*,' Nina said evasively. 'Not strictly friends ...'

'That's good.' Namath's handsome, open face curled a little with dislike. 'He's sharp, but I hear bad things about that guy.'

'Successful people always have enemies.'

'OK, OK, if you like him ...' Harry handed over the cassette and the popcorn. 'Brought you the game and some supplies. In case all this culture gets too much for you. It's a goodbye present.'

'It's a what?' Nina said. She clutched the video to her chest. She couldn't believe the dismay she felt. 'Where are you going?'

'To England, honey, remember? To London.'

'But I thought—'

'So did I, but Lilly's found a place she wants to be. Says she's seeing some interesting results on the latest batch of mice.'

'But why does she need you with her?' Nina pushed her hair back from her eyes. 'You run the computers ...'

'She's real insistent. I don't like to let her down,' Harry said. He moved a little closer. 'You look upset, don't tell me you're gonna *miss* it. All those fights and screaming matches ...'

Nina dropped her head so he wouldn't see the look on her face. He was grinning, teasing her, but she didn't feel like laughing. A big wave of loneliness and loss rolled right over her. It dawned on her like a flash of lightning, what a lifeline Harry had been out here, how she was already relying on him, how fucking miserable it was going to be without him. Yesterday she'd wanted him gone, and now he was going, so why wasn't she thrilled?

Namath walked up to her and cupped her chin in his hands, gently tipping her face up to his. She looked so beautiful, trying to be polished but rushed instead. Her hair was damp. He breathed in the faint scent of her shower gel. Desire and frustration clamoured inside him, he felt himself stiffen just from getting close to her. He wanted Nina so much. When she'd pushed him away the other night he'd found it hard to sleep. Yesterday evening he'd picked up a tourist in a bar, gone back to her hotel and banged her mercilessly, but it hadn't helped. A one-night stand wouldn't do it any more.

'Like I'll miss a migraine,' Nina smiled weakly. She knew she should prise his hands off her face, but she didn't move.

'I guess I'll see you in a month.' Harry was still looking right into her eyes. 'Do I get a goodbye kiss?'

'Do you want one?' Nina whispered.

Harry looked at her for a second. Then he bent his

head, very slowly, touched his lips on hers, just brushing them, lightly, drily, an echo of a kiss.

'Is that it?' Nina whispered. Harry was hovering there, his mouth close to hers, she could feel the heat of him, hear his breathing. Lust crashed over her like a wave, and she couldn't stand it, she lifted herself up to him, pressing her lips against his. Harry pulled her to him, kissing her over and over, biting, licking the inside of her lip, kissing her neck wildly, his hands moving up to her hair, tousling it, not giving her time to think.

'God, you're so lovely,' he murmured.

Nina felt her knees give. She was arching against him, totally, helplessly responsive. His fingers flickered at her waist and then his hand was on her, pulling her shirt out, his palm moving upwards to the wire and lace of her bra, brushing over her nipples.

God … Nina gasped. She felt a sharper tug of lust shoot right down her body.

'Baby.' He was cupping her breasts now, groaning softly with pleasure, his thumbs stroking, just the right pressure. Nina forgot about telling him to stop. She couldn't say a word. A spasm of pleasure exploded across her groin, she felt herself moisten, he was almost too slow, she wanted this, *needed* it now, and there was none of that squirmy, ugly undertone she felt with Tony, it was real straightforward.

Harry's other hand slipped down from her waist, past the tweed and gilt buttons and up her skirt. He was tugging the silken waistband of her hose, twitching off her panties. Tony's due at ten, what if he's early? flashed through Nina's mind but then right out again. She felt herself part her legs slightly, involuntarily, and then his hand was on her, covering her, two fingers tracing the slickness, unbearably softly, Harry's breathing rough and unsteady, and then he pressed his whole hand on her and she shook, a light, sweet orgasm rippling through her.

Nina's cry was muffled by his kiss, her legs gave, she was dizzy from the pleasure of it but still hungry, still tight with desire. They collapsed backwards on to something, the sofa, Harry pulling her up almost harshly, climbing on top of her, lying against her still dressed, kissing her, his fingers darting over gilt and silk.

'Your flight …'

'Screw my flight. I'll get the next one.'

'We can't,' Nina managed.

Harry bent his dark head to her ear and shoved himself against her. He was hard, really hard and thick. Nina felt herself move against him, beneath him, she couldn't think straight, she felt an animal longing to have that in her, filling her, plugging her.

'How wrong you are,' Harry said, and then his hands tightened round her again, circling her waist, lifting her up as easily as a rag doll, flipping her on to her stomach. Nina turned her head around, sooty hair tumbling in a thick curtain over her face, to see him unstrapping his belt, dragging the shirt over his head, tearing at his jeans. His chest was paler than his face, smattered with wiry curls, the muscles wonderful, tight but not huge, natural and perfect. His powerful thighs pinned her legs down, she felt denim brush the back of her thighs as he threw off his jeans. Nina's stomach clenched with longing. Harry grabbed the hem of her thousand-dollar skirt and shoved it unceremoniously up round her waist, exposing her butt, the lean, tapering line at the back of her thighs, Nina's rounded softness. She inhaled sharply and pushed up on her elbows. Harry wanted to shout out loud from the glory of it, how perfect she was, he could almost see the blood rushing to his cock, he was so hard for her now it hurt. His fingers trembled a little as he unsnapped her bra. In the gilt mirror opposite he saw her, totally disarrayed, her face flushed with heat, her incredible breasts lifting out from the unbuttoned shirt, the nipples dark and tight like black cherries in cream, tiny waist and round ass lifted towards him. So many girls these days didn't eat. Harry had taken a few home, gotten them undressed and found an ironing-board backside, sexless and boring. But Nina, his Nina, she was all girl, the way her ass flared out from that tiny waist, goddamn …

He had to get inside her or he was gonna come. As gently as he could he made to open her thighs, but Nina thrust back, impatient, she wanted it too, and Harry pushed in and took her, first time, right there, feeling her tight and hot around him, moving with him, urgently …

'You like that?' Harry whispered. Nina's breath came in sobs, she could feel every thrust, she could see herself in the mirror, Harry moving behind her, taking her, his hands gentle on her tits but still teasing, moving over them so that the intensity of the thrill spread right across her body, a neon web, lighting up wherever he touched her now, even her legs where his thighs were pinning them down, her back when his chest rubbed against it, wiry hair brushing her spine and making that wall of pleasure bigger and closer.

'Yeah …'

'You know, this is how we used to make love. Humans.' Harry was talking low and fast because he found it hard to breathe. His arousal poured over Nina's skin like a caress, like downy kisses. Every atom of her felt suffused. 'It's the best way.'

'Why?' Nina choked.

Harry thrust again, picking up the pace, going harder and faster. Perfect rhythm. Slamming into her.

'Because it goes in deeper.' His breath was hot on her ear, he felt hot blood surging into her belly, she was pressing back into him, writhing under his touch, abandoned, God, she was passionate, she was so beautiful. He pushed again. 'Like that.'

'Harry!' Nina said, and there was a note under the

heat, something strange, almost sad, but she wanted it because she was moving with him, Harry felt sex overwhelming him, Nina grabbed his hand and grabbed it to her mouth, kissing it, he felt her tighten and stiffen, saw her eyes close and her lips part ...

Nina couldn't think or move, the pleasure, the wanting was so huge now and she felt the sweet pressure filling her and blocking her, like a tidal wave rearing up, building, and then Harry's arms were hooking under her armpits and pulling her closer and he was taking her stronger and harder and the wall exploded, white light behind her eyes, and she came, sobbing out his name.

Harry's orgasm burst from him like Nina had ripped it out of his heart. Which maybe she had. He collapsed against her, relaxed and perfectly happy. He wanted to stay there for ever.

'You've got to leave,' Nina panted.

Harry reached over and kissed the side of her neck. She was warm, soaked with sweat.

'Really,' Nina insisted. She pulled her clothes away from him, got unsteadily to her feet. Namath stared at her; black hair was falling over her pretty face.

'Is that all I get?'

'It was great,' Nina said softly. She padded over to him with her shoes in her arms and kissed the top of his head, but reticently. She's holding something back, Harry thought uneasily. 'But really, I have a meeting, and I can't wear this.'

'We'll do this again. When you get to London.'

'Sure.' Nina dashed round, picking up her stuff, as Harry pulled his clothes back on. 'Look, you can still make your flight ... call me when you find a place.'

She pecked him on the cheek as he left. Taken aback, Harry found he was standing in her hallway, his sneakers unlaced.

'Gee, thanks for stopping by,' he muttered.

*

283

Nina waited until she heard Harry's footsteps on the stairs. Then she sat down weakly on the floor and started to cry.

Chapter 29

Tony stepped into Nina's apartment with a smile. He enjoyed travel. Flights in first-class were never too dreadful; Mrs Perkins organised his drivers, hotels and suites with military efficiency, he was always checked in automatically, and grovelling staff greeted him wherever he went. That hardly registered; the earl barely thought of them as people at all, they were part of the wallpaper. What he enjoyed was the barometer his travels gave him. How he was doing. What the rumours were this week. Each flight involved some waiting in a VIP area, some mingling with other first-class travellers when one boarded, usually last, and the common or garden businessmen filed past. Tony pretended supreme indifference to the whispers, the recurrent glances and nudges, the occasional obvious stare. But he loved it. They reacted to him like schoolboys to a football striker, drama-group actors in front of Robert de Niro. He'd noticed it gradually, years ago, as his empire started to build and his strings quietly started to jerk. It got more pronounced as Dragon took off, building to a crescendo as he became England's foremost takeover shark. When Jay DeFries was ruined and dragged off to jail, perversely, the whispering stopped for a short while. They were too scared to say anything at all. He sometimes thought he'd enjoyed that period most of all.

Today, of course, he was famous. The Helmers buyout had been concluded last week, a perfect hostile raid that left the stock in Tony's hands and the chairman in tears, or so the City whispers had it. On this morning's low-key flight they had chattered like starlings. Lowered voices, naturally, and pretend-casual looks in his direction, but it was wonderful, the sense of jealousy and curiosity all those losers were giving off. Satisfaction had lined his stomach as pleasantly as the warm croissants and coffee he'd breakfasted on. If they thought he had it good now, Tony wondered, what on earth would they say once the latest newsletter went to the number-crunchers?

Nina's find was looking exceptionally promising. He'd called Lilly Hall in for a meeting; frightful harridan, but she knew what she was about. The photographs of slim mice and svelte monkeys were exquisitely dramatic. Human trials would take a long time. It was hard to get permission to experiment on human beings in the West, which was nonsense, of course, how could science ever improve that way? Tony reflected calmly on his methods of avoiding that problem. Quiet little research centres in Africa and South America, where indigent adults would fight each other for the chance to earn twenty US bucks a day. And to think, they'd all get slim as well. Whilst the real beauty of the thing was that Nina's reorganisation of his research divisions would prop up the share price all by itself. Delicious rumours of his new bombshell would leak out, and then, by God, it was open season. Dragon Inc. would be on automatic pilot to the stars, and he, Tony Savage, would be lifted along with it into orbit.

Tony was tired of being a big fish in a small pond. He was an hereditary peer, and since the Queen had legendarily proclaimed there were to be no more duke-doms created – apparently she was very relieved when Churchill turned down the chance to be Duke of London – he wasn't likely to get bumped up, a gong could have no meaning. He had a perfect social life, the respect, or better, the fear of his fellows. Charles and Richard were shaping up nicely, Monica was an asset. There was no further to go in the UK, he needed to set his sights a little higher. In the States he'd still be a minor figure, not like those slick bastards Hanson and White, or the half-Frog Sir James Goldsmith. And that was what Tony desperately wanted. Success on a global scale. He wanted to hear that muttering at other airports besides Heathrow. Hanson, White and Goldsmith were up there with the oil owners and the finance boys like George Soros. There were only a couple of hundred men like that, it was the world's most powerful and exclusive club. Tony hungered for admittance. And he felt he was just about on the brink of it.

Nina's grace-and-favour company flat. White and gold, modern and automated. He'd been here before years ago but forgotten all about it. She was probably overwhelmed by the luxury of it, Tony thought. *She has no idea what she's doing for Dragon. Not the first clue what she really deserves.*

'My dear girl, you look wonderful,' he said warmly. She did. His dick was stirring pleasantly right off the bat; Nina Roth wearing a fluid suit in creamy pink, the colour picking out the lush blackness of her hair and the purity of her pale skin. Tony's experienced eye identified the cut, that was a Ralph Lauren, one of her more demure numbers. It hovered just below the knee and buttoned up past her magnificent cleavage. He grinned. So unlike Nina to be prudish. Her make-up was minimal, a little blusher on the sharp cheekbones and a clover lip-gloss. Tony breathed in but scented no perfume. How amusing, she was being so businesslike. It was almost as if he hadn't fucked her.

'Thank you. I hope you had a good flight?'

'Quite acceptable, darling, thank you.'

'Great ...' Nina pushed a stray lock of hair out of her dark eyes. 'Shall we get right to it?'

287

'Fine with me,' Tony said, making to slip off his cashmere overcoat.

'No.' Nina put her hand on him to stop him. Tony looked down and saw that she was bright red. 'I didn't mean that ...'

He looked at her sharply. 'What's the problem?'

'No problem, we just have a lot to discuss first, about work, and your daughter, and I think we should do it right away.'

'Right you are.' Savage shrugged himself back into his coat. 'We'll go and have some lunch; business before pleasure, I suppose.'

Tony took her to the Merci Hotel. Nina felt the fear gripping her heart squeeze a little tighter as the staff recognised him at once. There was an orgy of bowing and scraping as they were ushered to a discreet table overshadowed by an ornamental tree. She wondered if they were expecting him to take her upstairs and bang her after the meal.

While Tony confidently ordered for both of them Nina opened her file. Her mouth was dry and she felt her heart palpitating. Maybe she'd always known, in her head, what manner of man the Robber Baron was. But when he was sitting in front of you it was different; the aquiline face, the hawk's eyes scouring the room, like he was permanently scoping for targets. She knew he had always watched her in the same way, the powerful rajah stripping her with his eyes, assessing her like a farmer at a cattle market. In London she'd enjoyed it, but that was before she'd met Harry. The jewels, the callous sensuality, started to rankle. Sitting here while the waiter wheeled over their champagne Nina saw clearly why she'd sent Anita that opal and sapphire bracelet. What looked like generosity was something very different. Tony knew it and she'd known it, but she'd been too cowardly to admit it. He forced her to wear those jewels because she didn't like to; because they marked her out as his property. His plaything.

She could put a label on that uncomfortable feeling now. It was the way Tony made her feel like a high-class hooker.

Tony leaned over her as he poured the Cristal into cut-glass flutes. Nina breathed in his aftershave. She had to fight the impulse to shrink back. Oh, God, she thought, nervously. She was going to have to tell him it was over. She wondered how he was going to take it. She felt petrified.

'To Dragon. May she spread her wings and fly,' Tony smiled, touching his champagne flute to hers.

Waiters set a starter before them, braised veal and truffles in a white wine sauce. It was delicious but Nina could hardly taste it. Nervously she handed her boss the notes for the quarterly report, the piece she'd been sweating over all week.

Tony scanned it quickly, glanced up at Nina, nodded. Then he leaned back and read it more slowly.

'Very good.' The patrician tones were smoothly pleased. 'Very nice, exactly what the institutional boys are looking for.'

'And will I get a promotion?' Nina screwed up her courage. She'd delivered for Dragon: once in finding Lilly and twice with the reorganisation.

'Nina.' Tony looked faintly amused. 'You've just had a promotion. What will your colleagues think?'

'Only to senior manager. That's nothing. And since when did you give a damn about what your employees think?'

He nodded faintly to that. 'You're doing very nicely.'

'I've set up a whole new division, sir, it's going in the newsletter—'

'Sir? We are being formal today.' Tony speared some

veal and truffles and made a cutting motion with his left hand, his gold Rolex flashing in the sunlight, ending the discussion. 'It was a very simple idea.'

Nina didn't push it, but she was annoyed. Simple idea it might have been, but none of his gilded flunkies had ever thought of it. And it was on simple ideas that business empires were built.

Oh well. Once her report was published, and credited, to her, Nina knew she'd be in a much stronger position. She had no doubt this was going to send Dragon stock to the ceiling. At that point, headhunters would start calling with tempting offers from other firms. Tony'd have to give her her due, pay her for her results.

Patience is a virtue.

'We'd better talk about Elizabeth.'

The tiniest cloud settled on Caerhaven's forehead, a minute frown as her name was mentioned.

'Yes. She's getting rather ubiquitous at home. There are too few British athletes in with a chance at these Games.' Tony shrugged. 'So give me good news, tell me when the Taylor boy's going to pop the question.'

Nina breathed in. 'I'm afraid I can't. I don't think they're together any more.' She watched Tony's expression darken. 'It's impossible to check on that relationship right now, with the Games so close. Elizabeth isn't training with her team, she doesn't socialise, she just skis and works out.'

'I don't believe it,' Tony said angrily.

Nina shivered. Oh God! 'There's something else. It's about Dragon Gold.'

'What? Oh yes, her little pill. Managed to make a go of it, a few orders from Boots.' Tony took a belt of champagne, then another, refilled his glass. His flirtatiousness had vanished. It was amazing, the way you could almost see the little cogs whirring as his mind worked, analysing, planning, hovering round the problem like a vulture round a corpse. 'Maybe I can give her a few UK products to play with until we *can* get her married off. At least she'd be content.' He almost spat out the word. 'And unnoticeable.'

'I'm afraid not. Not if I read the figures she's been giving me correctly. She's tried to bury what she's doing, but reading between the lines ... Lady Elizabeth's trying to launch Gold in Europe. She's dealing direct with the national offices, she's talking to German and French ad agencies, and she appears to have got herself a budget from central funding.'

There was a crashing silence. Tony Savage lowered his knife and fork and stared at Nina.

'I could have it wrong,' Nina muttered.

'I see.' The earl's voice was ice. 'And with what authority is she doing this? How could she unlock our monies like that?'

'I believe she's doing it with your authority. She refers to you a lot in the correspondence I've seen. She's just giving orders, and they're assuming she has the right to do it.'

'You're serious.'

'Yes, sir. Dragon is a family company ... Lady Elizabeth is your daughter, and she has sold a lot of pills. Maybe they thought it was natural to expand – nobody would dare challenge a Savage. It is fairly ... unorthodox. And bold.' Nina had to admit it, she loathed the princess, but you had to give it to her, it was gutsy as hell. And with someone less sussed than me, she might even have got away with it; presented Daddy with a Europe-wide success as a *fait accompli*. She tried to smile at Tony. 'Like father, like daughter, I guess.'

The earl's head jerked up. His eyes stared right through Nina, the fury in them blazing like coal, so fierce she shrank back in her chair.

'I don't have a daughter,' Tony Savage said.

'No.' Jack's voice was impatient, almost disdainful.
Elizabeth smarted under it as under a whip. Bastard!
She'd been dropping and twisting for hours, trying to
follow Jack's bawled instructions, till her waist was sore
and her butt ached and the whole world was a blur of
flying snow and flapping flagpoles. '*Left* a little, then
right, lean into the curve for extra room!' He was
shouting as she screeched to a halt, skis digging into the
ice. Elizabeth was panting, red faced under the helmet.
Fucking bloody Jack, if only he had been a little less good
at the Super-G and she'd got something to throw back at
him. But whenever the arrogant jerk sliced down in front
of her his sodding technique was perfect. Elizabeth had
watched in dismay. Next to Jack's grace and precision
she felt like a fat builder trying to dance *Swan Lake*.
Taylor was so big, such a burly git, where the hell did it
all go? He took those turns like he was computer
controlled. Jack Taylor, the skiing Texan android.

'I'm doing the best I can,' Elizabeth shouted back.

Jack shook his head and pointed to her helmet. 'Say
what, milady? You're gonna have to do better than that.'

Elizabeth's Lycra gloves fumbled with her straps,
ripped off the helmet. Her scrunchie came with it and a
great cloud of tawny hair tumbled down round her
shoulders. Her green eyes were sparkling; Jack fought
back the surge of desire lapping round his groin.
Goddamn, he wanted to trip her up, right here, right
now, and just—

'Christ! I *know* that, I'm trying my best! Can't you be a
little encouraging?'

'I could. But I won't.' Jack shrugged; his handsome
face was glowing gently from exercise, like he'd just
completed a few pleasant strolls. Elizabeth knew she was
a wreck and that made her crosser than ever. 'I'm not

British, sugar. I'm not here to fly the flag and get your autograph.'

'What the hell's that supposed to mean?' shouted Elizabeth.

'It's supposed to mean that you need a lot more work.' Jack lightly lifted his ski-pole and touched her on the chest. 'You need to quit being late, quit skipping practice, quit playing shop.'

'I'm doing something real—'

'Oh, like hell.' Jack was too annoyed to take this bullshit any more. 'You got no future there and you know it. You've got some ego thing going on with your Dad, you're letting it waste the best chance Britain's got for a gold.'

'Jack, I don't know where to start.'

'Then don't.' Jack's dark eyes were uncompromising. 'The world doesn't owe you a living, Princess. You got no degree, no experience, but somehow you think you can barge in and take over from day one.'

Elizabeth said nothing.

'You got the talent, you should stop fucking around, or you're not going to win, sister, and that's the bottom line,' Jack said harshly.

'You know, you sound just like my father,' Elizabeth said.

Jack was angry. 'Fuck you, babe.'

'I don't think so, Jack. Once was enough.' Elizabeth strapped her helmet back on and lifted the visor. 'Thanks for the workout.'

She lowered her poles to the ground and pushed off southwards, disappearing in a flash of iridescence down the Strela black that led down to Davos.

Jack Taylor watched her go. He'd made her sweat it, he'd made his point, and he'd also spoken his mind. Those things needed saying.

Damn it! he thought.

Chapter 30

Tony stepped out of the limo at the airport concourse and motioned for Nina to get out.

'Sorry I can't stay, darling. I must go back and sort this out.'

So I gathered, Nina thought. Tony had called for the check right away and bundled her into his waiting car. On the drive to Kloten he'd made her go through the figures over and over. 'Why don't you just call everybody and tell them it's all off? If you want to do that. I mean, it's not such a bad idea ...' Nina stopped herself mid-sentence. What was she saying? That was her practical streak speaking, she wanted Elizabeth Savage to get busted, and brutally.

Tony looked at her blankly. 'You don't understand. I'll deal with it, and not a word to anybody, or you can kiss Dragon goodbye.'

'I won't mention it.' Nina drew back from his intensity as their car pulled smoothly over to the kerb.

Tony's expression softened. He lifted one hand and tucked the wind-blown hair back behind Nina's ears, looking her over pleasurably. 'Really, darling, so sorry we've been interrupted. But you'll be home very soon, we can take up where we left off.'

Tony bent to kiss her, but Nina turned her head, so it landed on her cheek instead of her lips.

He pulled up sharply. 'What's the matter with you?'

'Tony,' Nina said, and her voice suddenly sounded like it belonged to someone else, someone a lot calmer than she actually felt, 'I'm sorry, but that side of our relationship has to finish.'

Caerhaven looked down blankly at her. 'Don't be ludicrous. We're perfect for each other, we enjoy each other.'

'It doesn't feel right any more. I'm sorry, Tony. I'll return all your jewellery,' Nina said.

Tony almost laughed. The luminous dark eyes locking on to his were so serious. As though she had any idea, as though there was any way he was actually going to permit this.

'Nina, Nina.' The fingers stroking her hair suddenly moved on to her cheekbones, tracing their line. 'You don't understand. *I* enjoy *you*. We stop when I get tired of it.'

'What?' Nina whispered.

'You heard me.' Tony checked his watch. 'Now, I don't have time for this, I'm on the two thirty. Don't send me back the jewellery. Wear it the next time we go out.'

'I'm not going to see you socially any more,' Nina said.

Tony's hand cupped her face and tightened. He spoke softly and smiled deep into her eyes.

'I gave you everything and I can take everything. You'll be reasonable, darling, or it will be the worse for you.'

Elizabeth's feelings were mixed as she stepped out of the courtesy bus, its new gold paint emblazoned with the Olympic rings hoping to compensate for the ramshackle suspension. Monica would have had kittens, negotiating the winding Alpine roads in that, but she was used to it. You had to be, if you were skiing for Britain. Apparently not even the thought of a glorious women's gold could persuade the BSF to part with hard cash, so the team arrived at Flims in a nicely painted old banger, courtesy of the Swiss Confederation.

'Did you see the French coach?' Janet Marlin asked as

she grabbed her bags and dumped them on to the snow. 'It passed us driving up to Davos. Madeline de Lisle showed me around. It had Ataris and bunk beds and everything. Just like rock stars use.'

'How would you know what rock stars use? Been in the back of the bus with Duran Duran?' Kate teased her friend.

Elizabeth leaned forwards and grabbed her purple hold-all.

'Careful, milady, don't strain yourself,' Karen said nastily. 'Carrying your own bags? Is the butler off sick, then?'

'Sod off, Karen,' Elizabeth snapped.

'Forget about the French coach, did you see the American one?' Kate added, with a sly glance at Elizabeth. 'It's a bloody palace. Ford are sponsoring them and they've got a lounge area, a video …'

'What, don't they have their own mountain?' Elizabeth replied sarcastically.

'You should know, love, didn't Jack show you around?'

Elizabeth stiffened. She'd walked right into that.

'Why should he? I hardly see him any more.'

'Yeah, I heard something about that,' Karen said. 'Or maybe he just didn't want you to bump into Holly Ferrell. The US team travel together, they just sleep on separate floors. Bad news if the ex bumps into the current, ain't it?'

'Holly?'

'Yes, Holly. Didn't you know? He's been skiing with her day in, day out since they went to Grindelwald. Doing the Lauberhorn and the White Hare …'

Elizabeth couldn't help it, she paled. Hans and she had just done that area, the best in the Bernese Oberland, skiing the legendary runs around Wengen and the Eiger. Gradients that were so steep, runs that turned so well they were pure motion, a champion's dream, like the mountain's own gift to the skier. Her heart did a slow flip in her chest at the thought of it. Jack skiing the Lauberhorn with someone else! Charming Holly Ferrell, a blonde society babe who had never greatly troubled the timekeepers nor the sports writers. A meat-and-potatoes athlete, a richer, prettier Karen. Holly would not fight with Jack. All she would do was watch him in dewy-eyed wonder, Elizabeth thought viciously, and they could hum 'The Star-spangled Banner' as they schussed back to their hotel at night. Holly, yes, Holly would be Ms Perfect, a nice wholesome Miss America with white teeth and no personality …

The other girls were watching her.

'Why should I care? I've seen Jack ski, I don't think I can learn anything more from him.'

'Sure. It's all about skiing,' Karen said.

Ronnie Davis arrived from the back of the coach and the girls fell silent. He glanced from one flushed face to another.

'Catfights again? Just cut it out! We've got a couple of weeks until the start of the bloody Games. None of you has trained on Crap Sogn Gion yet, yes, Janet, ha ha, very amusing … wait till you're halfway down to Murtscheg. And Elizabeth – don't even think about skiing off-piste from Cassons.'

Elizabeth's head lifted, startled. She had been planning exactly that tomorrow, once Hans Wolf settled into his chalet on the slope above them.

'But Ronnie, it'll be perfect practice …'

'Perfect for you to schuss off the edge of the cliff. No way, girl, you're back under my orders for the duration.'

Elizabeth nodded sulkily. He was taking away her drug. Nothing but the hardest, harshest white slopes, peppered with moguls and virgin powder, could distract her from all the stress. And Jack. She wanted to forget

297

him but that was easier said than done, with all the US media out here on a feeding frenzy. Taylor this, Taylor that, it was the gossip that leaked out from the Olympic Village, it was the profiles in *Newsweek* and *Time* and the *Herald Tribune*.

'I've already spoken to Herr Wolf.' Ronnie's rough voice spoke the name deferentially, you couldn't deal with a legend any other way. 'He agrees with me. From now on, it's Olympic courses only. You ski them till you can see them with your eyes shut.'

'Ronnie.' Kate spoke up winningly. 'If Hans is coming up here tomorrow, why don't you have a word with him, see if he'll take us for some training too?'

'Get lost, Kate!' Elizabeth exploded. 'Hans is *my* coach, he doesn't waste time with fifth-raters—'

'That's *enough*!' Ronnie rounded on Elizabeth. 'Christ almighty, this is supposed to be a team.'

'So the papers are right about you,' Janet said to Elizabeth, pink faced from being called fifth-rate. 'The things they're saying.'

'What things?' Elizabeth demanded.

'I said that's enough.' Ronnie's bark was sharp enough to scare them all into silence. Elizabeth saw him give Janet a death-stare. 'You're sharing a chalet, Janet and Kate, and Karen, you're in with Elizabeth. One more word from anybody and I'll report in to the Sports Council and FIS. Nobody talks in bars, and nobody,' he added with a sweeping look, 'speaks to the press. There are all the home comforts you'll need in these chalets, including a weights room.'

'Are there the papers? I'd like to see how we're getting on in the Falklands,' Karen said smoothly. Elizabeth looked at her; she wanted news from home as well, but there was something in Karen's tone that made her edgy.

'I can tell you that, love. We're winning. There'll be *no*

298

papers, no radio, no distractions. From now on we're just here to ski.'

Elizabeth unpacked her hold-all in her room. It was soulless and functional, maybe the best way for an athlete's quarters to be; a hotel-style uniformity could be Zen-like in calming the brain. There was nothing here to make her nervous, except the view from her pale blue blinds. When you opened them up you saw Mount Startgels looming over you, the vast rocky outcrop blanketed with snow, spearing the deep clear blue of the sky. When Elizabeth slept under mountains she felt them as a presence, frozen giants who could almost breathe if you had the spell to unlock them. Startgels was the site of an Olympic slalom. She would be out on it soon, in the red, white and blue. The downy snow that looked so virginal covered so many things: abysses, crevasses, cliffs, soul-searing pleasure, death and glory.

'Horrible, isn't it?'

Elizabeth jumped; Karen noticed the long, glossy hair shimmer as she moved, the expensive burgundy cashmere dress, the Italian shoes. As well as the sports hold-all, Elizabeth's clothes cases were at the end of her bed; moss-green leather, embossed with some heraldry thing in gold. They looked antique. Fucking hell, she was so posh you could wonder if she ever used the toilet, Karen thought. Dislike seethed in her stomach. Pictures of milady were all over Flims, usually grouped with Louise and Heidi of Switzerland. You didn't have to speak the language to get the idea – they all thought Lizzie was the only threat. Karen had felt it keenly when Elizabeth jetted off to Klosters with Hans; the press that stayed with the official team had only asked about Elizabeth. The rest of them were a Mickey Mouse outfit, and nobody bothered pretending otherwise.

Karen was the best, though. She'd held the UK record

before bloody Hans Wolf called up from Saas Grund and suggested they give the stuck-up cow a trial. Karen wouldn't have creamed off any World Cups but without Liz she'd be the UK champion and she'd have respect.

'What do you mean?'

'That.' Karen pointed at the Alp. 'Oppressive, makes you want to see pubs and cherry trees.'

'We get enough pubs at home, don't we?' Elizabeth asked mildly. She thought about Jack with a sharp ache. He felt like she did about mountains. He loved them and lived them, but they were still strange enough to enchant him; to Franz Klammer and Louise Levier they were everyday.

'Can't think your sort ever sees much of a pub.'

'You'd be surprised.' Elizabeth looked away, partly because she didn't want to fight, partly because she'd just flashed on Jack again; drinking with him in the White Swan at Frant, watching the firelight crackle shadows across his face and hearing how strange he sounded under all the horse-brasses and dried hops hanging from the timbers. 'How was Verbier? I heard you did the mogul field at Mont-Fort in record time. That must feel great.'

Karen flushed. Condescending bitch, she sounded like the Queen asking what you did for a living. Karen had squeezed everything she had to shave one second twenty off that run, a tough mogul field, relentless and very steep. And she knew she was still three or four seconds off Elizabeth's average.

'Hardly a record. Heidi Laufen has that and you have the British.'

'English, then, you'll have the English record.'

Yeah right. Karen shrugged and left the room.

Elizabeth flopped down on her bed and stared out at the pistes. What the hell, it was good to have the hostility. Something other than Jack to occupy her mind.

*

At six p.m. sharp Elizabeth appeared in the drawing room for supper, a tasteless fish and pasta thing cooked up by the team nutritionist.

'Protein, carbs, bit of fat, the boffins know what they're doing,' Ronnie Davis said cheerily, thanking God he could go down to the Little China in the village later. 'Here are your schedules, girls. Elizabeth, here's yours. Hans has called and he'll be meeting you tomorrow.'

Elizabeth dutifully wolfed her food while the other girls chattered. Teams and times and who was going to get busted in the drugs samples, the Spanish team's new skis and who was screwing who. Janet had been asked on to *A Question of Sport* and Karen thought a sponsorship deal with Nike was in the works. God, as if any of it mattered! Elizabeth thought. She said nothing after Ronnie went to go and check the weights room, eating her tasteless food and trying to rehearse the courses in her mind. She was trying to become a race machine. Maria Peraña's new skis and Freyja Gundstrom's drug test, so what? If it was Louise Levier, now …

Elizabeth took her plate to the kitchen and washed it up. None of the others said a word, but she didn't give a monkey's. They could try and send her to Coventry like a pack of bitchy schoolgirls; she was going to work out and then head straight for bed.

On her way through to the chalet gym Elizabeth paused in the TV room. There was a bunch of papers strewn prominently over the sofas. She grinned as she saw they were English, great! Ronnie's censorship hadn't worked that well.

Elizabeth flopped down and leafed through them. *Sun*-speak doggerel about Our Boys in the South Atlantic, but it was good to get news from the outside world. If only to remember that there *were* other things in this world besides the Olympics. Shooting in El Salvador, John de Lorean had gone bust and some English cricketers were banned for busting sanctions to tour South Africa. There were no ads for Dragon Gold, maybe they'd all run yesterday. Elizabeth flipped to the back pages. Nice snaps of Christopher Dean doing a faultless double-axel. She hoped the rumours about those two were true, that they could skate both Yanks and Russians right off the ice ... her green eyes flicked determinedly over the story topped by an unsmiling Jack Taylor, his cruel mouth set hard as a gladiator. Then there she was: big picture, her ski-poles in one hand, goggles round her neck, hair pulled back from a chiselled face. Elizabeth recognised the shot, her triumph after a personal best Super-G in practice, back at Davos. At that moment she recalled the mix of triumph and annoyance, because it sunk in how much Jack's training had helped her. She looked gorgeous. She couldn't suppress a thrill of pride.

She soon stopped grinning.

'SNOW HELP TO BRITAIN,' sniped the *Sun*. 'TEAM SPIRIT SAVAGED,' screeched the *Mirror*. 'SELFISH, SECRETIVE, SAVAGE,' screamed the *Star*.

The articles were pure acid. Elizabeth was a playgirl who insisted on luxury hotels and refused to train with the team. Not a word about the fact that her training was agreed by Ronnie, that the hotels were to keep her away from the press ... if you read this you'd think Elizabeth was betraying her country, taking a skiing holiday at the nation's expense.

'We hope Lady Elizabeth knows what she's doing,' said the *Sun*. 'If she gets the gold – terrific. If not, we'll need some answers, Lady E – England expects, you know.'

'What the hell's this?'

Ronnie Davis reached down and tore the papers out of her hands. 'Don't pay any attention to that crap, love.' He stuck his head into the kitchen. 'Ladies, get in here *now*.'

'What's the problem, Ronnie?' Kate asked innocently.

Ronnie shook the crumpled sheets of newsprint. 'This. English papers I told you we weren't having. Somebody must have ordered them up here. They've been printing crap about Elizabeth I didn't want her to see.'

All three denied it, Karen shaking her head like butter wouldn't melt.

Elizabeth made a real effort and shoved the lump back down her throat. Somebody had not only wanted her to see that, they'd been feeding the media those lies in the first place.

'It's OK.' She looked at the girls with measured calm. 'After all, I *am* World Champion. I don't let fish-and-chip wrapping put me off my stroke.' She paused and looked directly at Karen. 'I can promise you, it'll take a lot more than that.'

Chapter 31

Nina's heart lifted as she stepped out of Swissair Flight 223. There were no soaring mountains as you came in to land at Heathrow. The sky was overcast and the plane was full of grumpy passengers carrying their Lindt selections and cuckoo clocks, all wishing they were still out on the slopes. But not Nina.

A Dragon driver, mercifully untalkative, had been sent to pick her up. You had to give it to Tony. When you were with Dragon, life was smooth.

'Home or office, madam?'

'Home, please.' Nina was still young enough to get a kick out of being called 'madam'. She settled back into the soft leather seat and watched the motorway slip past. She thought pleasantly that soon this would be normal for her, once she was promoted. A Golf GTi wouldn't cut it then. And hell, why not? It happened to the young Turks in the City and Wall Street all the time. Nobody could say she didn't deserve it.

There was a minibar, a TV and a copy of the *Financial Times* on the back seat. Nina flicked to the share listings. Sure enough, Dragon was up, a real big jump – two and an eighth – and if she was right, this was just the beginning.

She poured a glass of mineral water with a slice of lime. It was good for the skin. She didn't want to be all dehydrated when she saw Harry again. Once she'd talked some sense into Tony, they could start dating. Nina shifted a little. Harry still left an echo, that sweet crunch she thought she'd never get without shame. Wow, kid, what a discovery, Nina teased herself, there's more to life than work.

Namath had made her less hard but more alive, like somebody unthawing after an age in an ice-box. It was better than triumph or satisfaction. It was simple happiness and hope, because maybe, at last, things were going to be different.

Her place was perfect: furniture replaced, radiators on, warming the house against the March chill. Anita had even gone to M&S to stock the fridge.

Nina rushed upstairs and took a long, blissful shower, then phoned the office.

'Coming in today? Surely there's no need,' Anita protested.

'There's lots of need.'

'You could take the afternoon off. Nobody expects you in. Maybe you could go shopping.'

Nina chuckled; she hadn't changed that much. 'No, I'll be there in an hour. Could you possibly call Frank Staunton and let him know?'

'OK, I'm sure the boss'll want to see you.'

True, Frank Staunton was her boss. Well, not for much longer.

'And somebody else will want to say hello, I expect. Friends of yours from Switzerland: Dr Hall and Dr Namath, they've popped in to see Frank.'

Even though there was nobody around Nina blushed. 'Er, great, sure. See you soon.'

The Dragon tower on the South Bank loomed forbiddingly into the grey sky as Nina stepped in out of the drizzling rain. She'd changed into a Donna Karan tweed, with Manolo Blahnik heels and a thick silver cuff bracelet, one she'd bought herself from Mappin & Webb. Tonight she was going to send Tony a thick parcel of jewels. If he refused to take them she'd send them to charity. She was never going to wear them again.

'Good morning, Miss Roth,' the receptionist said. Nina clocked the quick flash of hostility from one beautiful girl meeting another. She was pleased, that meant she looked good. Men she recognised smiled and waved. A good sign. They thought it was worth kissing up to her. The quarterly report must have made quite an impact.

The elevator hissed smoothly to a stop and Nina stepped out, smiling and glad-handing her way to her office. Anita greeted her with a mug of coffee and a mountain of notes.

'Just to get you up to speed on recent developments. The Helmers acquisition went through, Clophramine has been approved for beta-testing. Frank Staunton wants to see you in twenty minutes. I'll buzz you, OK?'

'Fine.' Nina sat down and leafed through the head-lines. Only one page got her attention: a curt memo from George Gage, in Production, copied to New Products.

'Owing to quality control concerns, company product no. 87569 is being temporarily discontinued. Sales are to be withdrawn until further notice.'

Memos like this were the kiss of death. Advertising was immediately stopped and further orders not accepted. The last time Mr Gage's clammy spectre had fallen on her division was with Protaxin, their hotly tipped anticoagulant, when one final batch of tests had shown delayed side-effects – two chimps became impotent. Nobody in pharmacology liked the word 'lawsuit'.

Nina lowered her coffee and tapped her computer keyboard. Interesting – normally products didn't get out there unless they were super-safe. The cost of recall was huge.

Her IBM flashed up the name: 87569, product,

Dragon Gold, executive in charge, Lady Elizabeth Savage.

She gave a low whistle. Goddamn, he really knew how to bear a grudge. Elizabeth's strategy had been groundbreakingly successful. Nina knew it could have opened the door to the vitamin market. Three billion dollars a year's worth of trade, parcelled up between three of their rivals – Hoffman LaRoche, Eastman Kodak and Pfizer. Caerhaven had wanted a way in for years, but he'd rather throw it away than take it from Elizabeth.

For a second she almost felt sorry for Elizabeth. Tony was a hell of an enemy.

Not my problem, Nina thought.

'Come in, come in.' The Terrier gave Nina a thin little smile, his eyes sliding over her suit without seeing it. 'The traveller returns. Good work, by the way.'

'Thank you, sir,' Nina said, as Staunton ushered her in. Harry and Lilly were sitting on his burgundy leather couch.

'A great achievement, the liaison with two of our prized assets.'

Liaison? I *found* them! Nina smiled as neutrally as she could at Harry and his partner. Lilly looked at Nina coldly, said, 'G'day, kid.' Harry sprang to his feet. He walked over to her.

'You look gorgeous,' he murmured. Nina flushed and shook hands. Harry traced a small line on her palm, one fingertip stroking the soft flesh between her thumb and forefinger. It was too sensuous. Nina yanked her hand away.

'Hello, Harry, I hope you're settling in OK.'

'No complaints,' Namath replied. His tone was grave but his eyes were dancing.

'Dr Hall was just going through her latest results with me,' Frank Staunton said.

'Then I won't bother you,' Nina said with relief.

'I'll drop by your office when we're done,' Namath said.

'That would be fine.' She smiled briskly.

Frank Staunton turned back to the dumpy woman on his couch. How delicious, her attempts to hide it were pathetic. Nina had something going on with Namath. He was sure that would interest Tony. It was just the kind of thing the Terrier loved to ferret out. For the daughter *and* the girlfriend, things were going to get a little hot around here ...

In her office Nina pressed a cooling hand to her brow. Oh God, Harry, you shouldn't have let anything show ...

Anita poked her head round the door. 'I've got the priority mail for you, and your copy of the quarterly report.'

'Great! Let me see it,' Nina said. Anita handed the newsletter over; the Dragon logo stamped in gold on thick vellum, charts and projections at the front, new business at the back. She found her piece right away: 'A New Approach to Drug Research'. Nina felt victory flood through her. She settled down to read.

Two minutes later, her heart stopped.

For a few seconds she felt dizzy, so stunned and betrayed she didn't know what to do. Then Nina lifted her phone and tapped out Mrs Perkins's extension.

'Chairman's office, can I help you?'

'Yes you can, Mrs Perkins. This is Nina Roth. I'd like to speak to Lord Caerhaven.'

'I'm afraid that won't be possible.'

'Mrs Perkins, I must speak to him. It's urgent.'

'I'm afraid it's still not possible,' Mrs Perkins told her smugly. 'Lord Caerhaven isn't in the country. He can't be reached. I can take a message—'

Which he'll never get. 'I see. Where is he?'

'He's out in Switzerland, Miss Roth. Cheering on Lady Elizabeth.'

'It's going to look bad,' Ronnie Davis warned Hans. 'The papers are eating her alive.'

'*Ja*, and now she knows this!'

Ronnie quailed a little before Hans's fury. Amazing how the old man could screw with your head.

'That wasn't my fault.'

'I know, Ronnie. But look at her.' Hans pointed to Elizabeth, sweating bullets as she peeled off her goggles. 'What says your stopwatch?'

'Five-forty on the Cassons. Two-ten on Nagens-Start-gels,' Ronnie agreed. 'And her Super-G's picked up almost a second and a half. She's making amazing times.'

'She can do better. We have but two days. No more distractions and envy.' Hans glared at the silhouette of Karen Carter. '*Bitte*, Elizabeth leaves the team chalet and moves in with me.'

'OK, guv.' Ronnie threw up his hands. 'If it's right for the team ...'

'For the team? *Ach!* I do not know, I do not care. For Elizabeth, it is right.'

Both men glanced back at Elizabeth. On the wooden slats of the cool-down room, her long, lean body was twisting itself backwards and forwards as she bent into her deep stretches. Elizabeth wore the geometric slashes of the red, white and blue, a mobile Union Jack. Hans had deliberately delayed the time she would put this on; when she wore the national colours it had to be significant, like donning armour for battle. Suddenly it was about more than times, rankings and rivals. Fräulein Laufen was not just Heidi, she was Switzerland; Marie Le Blanc was France; and for these few weeks, Elizabeth would be Britain, taking her country's flag into battle.

That was the magic of the Olympics. For yourself, you could get tired and weak and jaded. For your country, you would fight till you dropped.

'So what's the story?' Ronnie Davis asked. 'She will get a medal?'

'Of course.'

'And what colour?'

The old man gave him an incredulous stare. 'She will get the gold. I am surprised you even ask. I have never been more certain of anything in my life.'

'Lovely,' Monica said. She reached over and gingerly unwrapped a whisky silk scarf from its layers of tissue. Their suite at the Park Hotel was the best Flims had to offer. Every place in town had been sold out for weeks. TV crews swarmed over the resort like ants, besieging the skiers' chalets and the Olympic Village. Spectators arrived every day, a polyglot crowd packing everything from the Park to the lowliest rented chalet. Even if you were the parents of a medal hopeful, there was no room at the inn.

Unless of course you were Tony Savage.

'We'll stay for Elizabeth's races, then we'll go straight back,' Tony said. His face was expressionless as he stared up at the mountains. The competitors' chalets were fenced off; some common little man named Davis had curtly told him he couldn't speak to the little bitch. But words were being had in London right now, and that would change.

'Oh, really, darling?' Monica murmured, admiring herself in the wall mirror. The Nicole Farhi in orchid lambswool clung to her concave stomach and slender shoulders, swaying below the hem when she moved. And Tony's latest offering, a necklace of diamonds and lapis lazuli, just this side of vulgar, would set it off beautifully. She knew she'd photograph wonderfully tonight. And tomorrow night. And every day that the cameras asked for comments from the proud parents. 'I think we could stay, don't you?'

'If you like,' Tony agreed absently. The fax machine in the drawing-room was spewing out confirmations of everything he wanted to hear. Elizabeth's pill, all her sales routes and advertising, had been withdrawn from every region like it was toxic. His word had gone down, and her work was snuffed out like a candle.

The phone rang. Monica picked it up.

'Monica Caerhaven ... oh darling, it's you, how thrilling. Yes, he's here.' She languidly handed the phone across to her husband. 'It's Elizabeth, dear, for you.'

'Thank you.' Tony cupped one hand over the receiver. 'Darling, why don't you find Charlie and Richard and go out shopping for a while?'

It was a clear dismissal, and Monica didn't hesitate. Smiling blandly, she nodded and left the suite.

'Hello Elizabeth,' Tony said. 'I've got some rather bad news for you.'

Chapter 32

Outside the chalet windows it was still dark, the deep blue shadows of the Alpine massifs blocking the rising sun. There had been a snowfall last night. Elizabeth could tell from a faint scent in the freezing air, and from the way the sky was brightening, the streaks of dawn lighter than usual. She'd slept fitfully, tossing and turning in the hard orthopaedic bed. She'd tried to sleep but it was no good. The conversation with Tony had filled her with a white-hot rage that just refused to simmer down.

He'd torn apart her work, her baby. No consultation, nothing. Sure, she'd expected him to be a bit annoyed, but nothing like this. To stop her having any success, Tony was prepared to wipe out all their market gains and take thousands in losses. She felt the bitterness as strongly now as she had last night. Once the Games were over, she was going to have to decide what to do. Father had buckled in in the first place, why? Because he was scared she'd make a scene. Not such a strong reason, Elizabeth thought, but it was to him. So what would Tony do once she was gold medallist? She'd be famous back home. Like they said, you were World Champion for a year, but Olympic Champion for life.

The desire for revenge. It was incredibly strong. It was blazing up in her. She started to march on the spot, swinging her arms and heels through the warm-up she could do in her sleep. Hot blood started singing round her body. She hadn't needed more incentive, but there it was – the gold would give her the means to get back at

Tony. And Nina Roth. How could she figure it out from the notes I gave her? Elizabeth wondered, but clearly she had, and she'd shopped her straight to Daddy. Oh, the delight Nina must have felt, bringing her down—

She stopped herself as she lifted one leg on to the windowsill, bowing into the stretch. Come on, girl, not now. You've got exactly one day to the start of the ninety-fifth Olympiad.

There was a sharp rapping on the door. Hans poked his head round.

'Hey, I didn't mean to wake you.'

The old man waved that aside. 'Only in the morning you ski, you must rest all afternoon.'

'OK, boss.'

'Where are you going?'

'Sogn Gion this morning.' The men's World Cup run was a women's Olympic downhill for the first time. Tomorrow afternoon Elizabeth would be out there for real.

'Some others are also there.'

'No kidding, it must be a regular traffic jam,' Elizabeth said wryly. Everybody would want to get last-minute dry runs in.

'Do not be distracted, *Liebchen*,' Wolf lectured her sternly.

'Don't worry.' Elizabeth turned her head to him. It was amazing, Wolf thought, how she could be covered with streaks of sunblock and goggle-lines and still look so beautiful, so dignified. The blonde hair had lightened two shades in the mountain sun and her green eyes sparkled with fierce determination. 'Nothing is going to distract me now.'

Elizabeth ski'd down to the first lift areas. Hans was right, it was busy. Practice suits were out, national flags were in; unless your suit was stamped with an official

313

number, you didn't see snow in Flims today. She waved cheerfully at Robin Cousins, walking past her to the ice-rink; Martin Bell was queuing for the cable-car up to Cassons; the Swiss hero Pirmin Zubriggen was chatting to Alte Skaardal from Norway. The women were busier around the Murtscheg gondola. Most were clutching their skis to them like shields. French flags, Swedish, Norwegian, Austrian, Swiss. Elizabeth's heart gave a sick little flip when Louise Levier passed her; there were six girls in the blood-red suits with the white crosses, but she knew Louise by the tight waist and lean, mean quads. The Swiss turned her head and nodded politely. Neither of them felt like small talk.

Somebody tapped her on the shoulder as she shuffled into the line. Karen Carter.

'Shall we ride up together?'

'Sure,' Elizabeth said blandly. She breathed in, the chilly morning air stinging her nose. Steam was rising from their breath like cows standing in the farm back home.

'You might as well. The press heard Hans moved you out of the team chalet.'

'I wonder how that could have happened,' Elizabeth said mildly. She wasn't rising to it. She gestured over at the queue for Cassons. 'Look at Martin and Graham. Martin was top ten in practice yesterday. Wonder what they're talking about?'

'Most likely Jack Taylor,' Karen said, glancing at her with nasty pleasure.

Elizabeth shrugged. Maybe it was. The rumours of Jack's total dominance in practice surprised nobody. If he won his gold as easily as they were expecting him to, he'd be a legend, the new Franz Klammer. To Karen she only said, 'Look lively, dear, or we'll miss our spot.'

The gondolas swung round, scooping up the athletes. Elizabeth and Karen climbed in with some French officials and half the Spanish team, two hefty girls ranked twentieth and thirty-first in the world. They stared at Elizabeth most of the way up, whispering in awe. Karen was really pissed off.

Elizabeth smiled at her serenely and turned her attention to the crisp new snowfall on the Olympic runs beneath them. The gondola swung upwards and onwards, into space, flying them to the cold, white roof of the world. It was the last session before the Games, and skiing, thought Elizabeth, would be the *only* thing on her mind.

At Sogn Gion Karen got out, strapped up and ski'd off without another word. There was no way she was going to follow Elizabeth and be shown up. Elizabeth smiled at the Spaniards and some others pressing round the top of the run. She felt warmly about the lower-level girls; kids for whom it was the thrill of a lifetime just to be in the Games, to march out tomorrow in their national blazers. When she saw the threats – the Austrians, Louise, Heidi or any others – Elizabeth looked away. It was like an electric shock. Those super-fit, super-skilled she-wolfs stood between her and the dream. There was no point in false friendship when the piste was the arena, and the skis on your feet were swords.

Elizabeth pulled her dark blue helmet on and clicked her Rossignols into place. This run was straightforward. Long, almost 3,500 feet vertical, with spectacular views. Not that she had any time to look at scenery.

She took a deep breath and pushed off. Straight away she was picking up speed, leaning into the first left. Elizabeth was skiing by reflex, her body adjusting, leaning, pushing, her weight shifting on the skis, mingling with the mountain's slope. Fresh morning snow plumed up around her, downy as feathers, flying back from the slicing cut of her edges. She was threading her way through other girls, diving and leaning through them with precision that left them gasping. Over a stomach-flipping ridge, Elizabeth's strong back flattening almost to horizontal, perfect lift as she landed. Exhilaration flooded her like oil round an engine, she was hot, she had it! There was Karen, Jesus, look at her, boring textbook skiing. Elizabeth flew past her. Now the run was clear for a little while, she could see the red and green of the Italians towards the finish. She turned to hug the treeline, she felt weightless, the speed and gravity had dissolved her mass. First past the ridge and then through this glade ...

There was another figure on the course. Skiing in the blind spot under the forest, so she hadn't expected anyone there. Far too big and fast to be a female. Wearing the starry costume of the USA.

Jack Taylor.

Elizabeth reacted fiercely. Her heart was pulsing, it happened in a millisecond of real time, but this was ski time, parcelled in half seconds and point two-fives. She barrelled slightly to the right, her skis shooting across the diagonal, arcing powder up behind her and all over Jack as she jumped the ridge in front of him. She had faster momentum, it bombed her right in front of him, flying over the jump and landing. Point, plant, lift, slice to the right and fly down the home straight. He was coming after her. She didn't look behind her, but his shadow was on the snow, dark on the crystals glittering sunrise pink. Furiously Elizabeth ski'd from the gut, her waist crunching as she whipped in to the final turn, close by the orange nets. It was silent out here, their blades just skimming the snow, but the fury of her competition was totally real. Jack was gaining on her inexorably, he had too much muscle, he was going to win ...

No! Elizabeth's body screamed. No! No! She thrust violently with her poles and willed herself forwards as

Jack arrived beside her, every tendon in her legs blazing, and shot across the finish line, first by less than a head.

Elizabeth unhooked her helmet. Jack Taylor ripped off his goggles, glaring at her. She turned and pushed off without a word, skiing on to the start of an easy red.

Jack schussed down behind her, both poles tucked under one arm, his balance perfect, fluid and controlled. He grabbed her by her arm.

'What the hell was that all about?'

'You were in my way,' she snapped.

'No, ma'am, but you sure got in mine,' Jack said. The dark eyes flicked over her body-tight suit. Elizabeth felt herself respond, an involuntary twitch between her legs, her nipples hardening under the thermal fabric.

'If you can't take the competition, Jack ... I hear Zubriggen's looking good this year. It must be nasty, to get beat out by a girl.'

'You moved pretty fast.'

'Fast enough to ski you off the snow, Taylor,' Elizabeth snapped, 'and you must have made a damn slow time from the top for me to catch you like that.'

'Well now. Wrong again, sugar. I stopped to tighten up a clip. I'd just started up again when you came tearing down with a bug up your ass.'

'Yeah? But you took me on, and you lost.'

Jack snorted. 'Because you had a fifty mph start, girl. You couldn't beat me if I was skiing on one leg.'

Elizabeth glanced up to see a small crowd of girls pretending not to watch them fight. Angrily she flattened her edges and slipped down into the trees. Jack tilted his skis in perfect harmony, so they moved with each other like synchronised swimmers.

'Bullshit. It's all macho bullshit, Jack,' she taunted. 'That what Holly Ferrell tells you when you hold her hand down the Lauberhorn? Oh, Jack, you're so good, nobody in the world can touch you ...'

'Cut it out. Holly's a good skier.'

'Holly's a moose,' Elizabeth said, recalling a school insult, 'she brays in the forest.'

'You want to put up or shut up, baby,' Jack said angrily.

Elizabeth fought down the desire. Inside her catsuit she was slippery with perspiration, and not just from the run. She rounded on him.

'I beat you a minute ago, I can do it again.'

For a second she thought he was going to laugh in her face. Then the brown eyes narrowed. 'Princess, you're on. Right after the Games. You get ten seconds' start on the Lauberhorn.'

'Five will be fine.'

'Sure, if you really want to embarrass yourself. We'll ski for a wager. If I lose—'

'You endorse my next Dragon product. Free of charge and for as long as I want.'

Jack's face clouded. 'I'm not a goddamn used-car salesman.'

'Afraid you're going to lose?'

'Then if I win, you fly out to Texas, you spend the night with me.'

Elizabeth flushed. 'What, you'd have sex with me?'

'Till you could hardly walk,' Jack said slowly.

She said nothing.

'Scared?'

'Drop dead, I'm not frightened of a bet I won't be paying. You're on.' Elizabeth thrust out one gloved hand. Jack took it in his bare one and shook it, squeezing hard enough to let her feel his strength.

'See ya, honey,' Jack said, then reached down and patted her on the butt. Elizabeth whipped round but he was already a hundred yards in front of her, skiing back down to the village.

She pushed forwards and laboriously started to step up

the slope. Boring, but good work for the thighs. The morning sky was bright from the snow, sunny and rosy with promise. Above her, she looked up and saw Christy Lansch, the Austrian number one, turn in tightly at the end of the piste. She looked good, but Elizabeth knew she could do better.

She took a deep breath of crystal-cold air and joined the chairlift queue, rank-and-file skiers staring as she passed. She was going to do the Sogn Gion until she could ski it blindfold.

The Arena Olympique was packed out. Waiting in their tunnel, the British teams fidgeted, listening to the hubbub of the crowd, watching the flash of television lights. The president of the IOC droned on about the Olympic ideal. The nations would march out in alphabetical order.

Ronnie Davis, wearing the white trousers and navy blazer of a UK official – 'Makes me look like a soddin' bellboy' – smiled encouragingly at his girls. Opposite them stood the giant Olympic torch, dull now, waiting to blaze up the sky like a bonfire.

Elizabeth was trembling. She didn't want to cry but she was fidgeting, easing her nerves away. Right now she was just one of the crowd, until the BBC cameras closed on her face. Lucy Mansfield, a bobsledder, was carrying the Union Jack, how must she be feeling?

Out there were her family. Tony, that selfish bastard, flighty Monica and two half-brothers she hardly knew. They'd have Frank Staunton and a bunch of corporate types in their box, but she wasn't going to worry about them. More to the point, there was Hans, somewhere in the stands, unofficial. He had declined to march as a British official; he was Swiss, he said firmly. Elizabeth wondered if Hans would cry, then dismissed that idea. Hans Wolf never cried. Not even when was he born, most likely.

Karen, Kate and Janet stood around her but didn't bother making conversation. She almost smiled. Family and team, it was just the same; surrounded by people but on my own, Elizabeth thought.

She wondered how Jack was feeling right now.

Over her blazer her tawny hair lay long and glossy. Under the TV lights it would show up almost platinum. Maybe it would—

'*Royaume-Uni!*' bellowed the announcer. '*Great Britain!*'

Elizabeth straightened up as the column began to walk forwards, Lucy tilting the flag just right so it fluttered free. She thrust back the butterflies squirming in her stomach, smiled, and waved like the Queen.

After all, the world was watching.

Chapter 33

Nina sat in her office and considered her future.

Her options were very limited now. She had to believe that Tony had some explanation. Without the newsletter giving her credit, it looked like this was just another success for Dragon's team. She wasn't even mentioned by name.

After a lot of pushing, Mrs Perkins had admitted that Tony was due back in England tomorrow. He couldn't spend a whole week in Switzerland glad-handing his cronies when Dragon's stock was rising so fast. She knew the Robber Baron. Buy something fast, before all that extra cash sloshing around becomes a homing beacon for a takeover shark even bigger than him.

'Could you try and reach him in Flims, Mrs Perkins? I need an urgent meeting.'

'About what?'

'I'm afraid that's really between me and Lord Caerhaven,' Nina said smoothly. Stick it up your ass, she thought sourly. Whatever Tony was playing at, she was still *persona grata* at this firm. The airport limo, the obsequious doormen, the very fact that Mildred Perkins was taking her calls; these things only happened to Friends of Tony. In fact Mrs P. would probably assume Nina wanted to arrange a rendezvous, and it would be more than her job was worth to stand in the way of any pleasure of Tony's.

'Certainly, Miss Roth,' said Mrs Perkins thinly, then hung up.

When Nina came back from lunch there was a message on her voice mail. Tony telling her to meet him at the Halkin at nine p.m. He sounded pleased, like she had finally seen sense. And he had nothing on the agenda but sex.

Elizabeth stood at the start of the Lauberhorn, quietly flexing her quads and calves, waiting to be called. First in Super-G and the two Flims downhills, second in the slalom to Levier. Best of all, Louise had crashed in the Cassons race and Marie Le Blanc came second in Super-G, so right now, her competitors were spread out. The British tabloids were reserving judgment, but they'd stopped slagging her off.

Hans was icy cool. He let her give one-line statements to ITV and *Olympic Grandstand*, that was it. After Flims all he said was that she needed to work on the slalom. Good old Hans; Elizabeth knew he'd be down at the bottom right now eating his heart out.

This was the Blue Riband race. Women had never been permitted to ski the Lauberhorn before in any World Cup. People died on this run, their skis tangling in orange netting, shooting into trees in the fog, taking too much speed after the endless right-hand bend; men broken like dolls under the shadow of the Eiger, looking out at the Schilthorn valley. The safety officers were screaming in protest, but the girls wanted to ski it, and TV wanted the ratings. There was no women's record for the Lauberhorn, so Janet Fraser of Great Britain had set the first; three minutes fifteen, the first and last record she'd hold in her life.

Louise Levier made three-eight. Heidi Laufen three-seven. Marie three-ten. All blazing performances. Ingmar Lystrom, the Swede, crouched in the starting hut in her blue and yellow suit, heard the gun and slipped noiselessly out into the descent. The crowd went nuts, yelling and ululating, shaking their cowbells and football rattles. She was next.

'Number eight, representing Great Britain, Lady Elizabeth Savage!'

Elizabeth stepped up into the starter's hut. She was the favourite, the noise was deafening; a few boos were mixed in with the bells and whistles, the home crowd were for Heidi and Louise. The countdown began, she felt strangely calm. Nerves that seethed minutes before you ski'd sort of evaporated once you were actually up there. Out of the corner of her eye she saw the crowd packed behind the nets, Union Jacks waving brightly against the snow. Behind them and the Olympic media towers the Schilthorn loomed up, white snow and craggy black rock. It was settling; the Alps were uncaring, unchanging; the Olympics would blink in and out of this valley and leave no trace behind it.

She pushed off.

The schuss, leaning as low as possible, feeling the speed pick her up like a bullet and fire her down the track. Plant, slice, she had it covered, she saw the jump, soared clear and landed smoothly. The crowd shrieked but she was hundreds of yards on already. Now hug the trees, careful, careful, lower with the body – Elizabeth's tight quads steering her. Through the tunnel, bombing over the snow, the other girls had already packed it a little lower, squeezing out some air, the surface was faster that way. Long, long right, Jack's instructions flashing up and she shifted left milliseconds before the turn. For a moment she thought she wasn't coming back up, her gravity was too low, but then she tilted, righted herself, she was upright again, too fast to see flags or register cheering. There was the gate! Low, if you were thinking you were too slow ...

Elizabeth thrust through the gates, couldn't slow down

fast enough and tumbled over under her own tidal wave of powder. She felt like an idiot, scrambled to her feet.

For a moment they all just waited. Elizabeth hated this: your racing heart stopped, you couldn't breathe until the time flashed up. Hans walked over, put his bony hands on her strong shoulders.

Three-six point five-five. A roar went up from the crowd, Ronnie Davis jumped three feet in the air. 0.45 of a second faster than Heidi Laufen. The Swiss team turned away in disgust, the camera crews rushed forwards and Hans gave her a dry little nod. Her lead was extended yet again. Less time than a heartbeat, but it said, Britain one, Switzerland two and three.

'Lady Elizabeth – CNN—'

'Lady Elizabeth, can ITV have a few words—'

Camera lights shone brightly into Elizabeth's rosy face; microphones like fluffy marrows hung suspended over her head and hand-held ones were thrust under her nose.

'How does it feel to win the first women's Lauberhorn?'

'I wouldn't know, I haven't won. Christy and other great skiers have to go yet. It was a thrilling course to race, and I'm just going to concentrate on the next slalom.'

'That's it, ladies an' gents,' Ronnie said, beckoning to officials to get the rat pack off his girl. 'Liz, that was brilliant, you were flying down the fucking thing, I thought you were going to take off!'

Hans Wolf gave him a reproving look. 'You lost control at the end.'

'Yeah, but only after I was through the gate.'

'It's not good, it shows you lose control. If it happens on the run, *glaub' mir*, you can die.'

Elizabeth lowered her head, annoyed. She was burning with triumph, she thought Hans might have been a bit more upbeat.

'Elizabeth, your dad's flying home today,' Ronnie said. 'He wanted you to give him a call before he leaves.'

Elizabeth smiled. 'I don't want to talk to him. If he asks again, tell him I can't be bothered, simple as that.'

'Right,' Ronnie said uncertainly.

Elizabeth reached over and took a yellow flask of isotonic squash from an official. Tony could go screw himself. Once she had the gold in her pocket, she could make his life a misery.

'Still we have more work to do,' Hans said, like he could read her thoughts.

Elizabeth nodded and smiled. Behind them Stars and Stripes were waving, the crowd cheering Kim Gideon's competent three-eleven.

'I know. It's not over yet.'

The words sounded blissfully unconvincing. Bring them on, Elizabeth thought, Heidi, Louise, Tony ... she was going to blow everyone away. This was her moment.

She was invincible.

Nina arrived at the Halkin at nine precisely. Tony had avoided her calls all day, but he was going to have to deal with her now.

She checked herself out in the elevator mirror as she rode up to his suite. Her raven hair was twisted up in a formal French pleat; her suit was Comme des Garçons, chocolate brown piped with cream. Low mahogany heels from Pied-à-Terre, opaque silky tights, no jewellery. Her make-up was shades of brandy, berries and gold. She looked five years older in this rig. Beautiful, but serious too.

The elevator slid noiselessly to a halt and discharged her. Nina stared to feel a little scared. God, she wished she'd been able to get hold of Harry. They'd had just one Chinese together, the first night she got back, then he'd jetted off to France with Lilly. The dinner had not been the slam-dunk Nina wanted. She was tired and edgy from the flight and the shock of the report, and mad at Harry for coming on to her in front of Frank Staunton. Harry was loose and she was wound up like a string ball. They hadn't fought, exactly, but Nina left early. Nina's fortune cookie told her to beware the dark forces lining against her. Harry's said he would be successful in all he did.

She wished she'd been a bit softer with Harry. She could have done with a friend right now.

Nina pressed the doorbell outside the earl's suite.

Tony opened it and ushered her in, smiling softly. Inside the expensive Japanese minimalism of his suite someone had laid a table laden with extravagant dishes, vintage Krug chilling in a silver ice-bucket and warm bottles of saki next to plates of sushi and vases of purple orchids. Nina's glance swept to the single bed. There was a large, royal-blue box laid out on it, stamped with the gold crest of some jeweller or other.

She wanted to laugh. That was his answer to everything.

'I don't buy it any more, Tony,' Nina said harshly.

He lifted an eyebrow. 'What don't you buy?'

'This bullshit.' She pointed to the table and the box. 'Whatever it is, I hope you got a receipt.'

'Nina.' Tony Savage sat down calmly on a cherry-wood-backed chair and looked her over. 'What are you talking about? Come on, darling, I hope you're not going to be difficult. You're a clever girl, you know how stupid that would be.'

'Are you threatening me?'

'Threatening you? Don't be idiotic. Think about who I am and who you are. Sounds like you have delusions of grandeur, Nina. You're really not that important.'

'I'm the reason Dragon went up five points in two weeks,' Nina said fiercely. 'That work was mine. My words in the report. But you didn't credit me, you didn't even mention me.'

'Why should I?' Tony said, and there was an edge to his voice. He reached for the champagne, popped the cork and poured out two glasses. 'It wasn't *your* work, it was Dragon's work. Done with our funds, achieved with our name. We did struggle along quite nicely before you arrived.'

'You have to give me credit for the work I've done. Nobody else in this company managed it. You owe me promotion and—'

'I don't owe you a bloody thing,' Tony said, standing up and walking towards her. He didn't shout, but there was a quiet menace in his voice that made Nina shrink inside. 'I rescued you from Nowheresville, Brooklyn, I made you a wealthy young girl—'

'Out of the kindness of your heart.'

'Nina, this is silly,' Tony said silkily. 'I think I've been generous to you. Come on, darling, I can't remember a woman I've enjoyed more.' He leaned down and stroked the black satin coverlet on the bed. 'You want a promotion, more money – that can be arranged, I'll dream something up. Providing you stop all this nonsense about credit.'

Nina stared at him. 'You think I'd sell myself to you? My God, is that the kind of woman you think I am?'

'It's the kind of woman I *know* you are.' Now his eyes were black pinpricks of cold rage. 'You proved that in Dublin.'

'I wouldn't touch you again if you were the last man alive!' Nina snarled.

'Of course. You prefer something a little more basic. Like Harry Namath?' He laughed to see her pale in front of him. 'You know me, Nina, I like to have my finger on the pulse. But I wouldn't put too much store in that one, darling, he's not interested any more.'

Tony's aquiline mouth was twisted in amused contempt, watching her reaction eagerly. She felt sick.

'You told him,' she said dully.

'Of course I told him. In some detail,' Tony said lightly. 'We had a long chat over the phone while I was in Switzerland. I like to keep on good terms with the staff.'

Nina said nothing. She could almost hear him doing it.

'It was a pity. He seemed rather put off, didn't have much to say. You Americans can be so prudish ... a shame, I'd have liked to swap notes.'

'Go to hell, you bastard,' Nina spat, her eyes flooding with tears.

Tony reached up and traced his finger round her jaw. 'But angel, you still have me. As long as we understand each other, I can make life very sweet for you.'

Roughly Nina pushed him away. 'Yeah, we understand each other. I got your number. I would rather fuck a leper with syphilis.'

'I don't think you understand. I'm not asking you for this, I'm telling you. Otherwise,' Caerhaven said blandly, 'it's over for you. You'll be fired. You won't find work at any other drug company, once I put the word out. You're an alien in Britain, you have no friends here, as you so correctly put it, no credit outside. And I don't think you've got many friends *inside* the company, Nina, in fact I gather you're rather unpopular. People will assume that you're just another tramp, this time one who worked for me and whom I've now tired of.'

'I do understand,' Nina said, quieter now.

'Good.' Tony ticked the points off on his fingers with a maddening smile. 'You're fired. You're kicked out of the country. You have nothing to show for your time with us. Word will go out loud and clear that you're a bimbo with an attitude problem. And you won't have your boring little boffin to run to either. He had you all wrong, sweetheart; he doesn't want used goods.'

He picked up a flute of champagne and held it out to her.

'Or we can forget this unpleasantness, and you can look forward to a very pleasant life and a bright little future.'

Nina hesitated for a second, then took the glass.

'You were wrong about Dublin. I didn't sell myself; I used you for what you could do for me.'

'See? We're so alike, Nina, we're two sides of the same coin.'

Nina smiled back. She moved closer to him.

'Wrong again, my lord,' she said. Then she flung her chilled champagne right in his eyes, and walked out of the suite.

Chapter 34

The alarm went at six as usual. Nina was halfway to the shower when she realised there was no need. She wouldn't have to be in the office today.

She got up anyway, washed and dressed. She put on a butterscotch suit, Wolford hose and flat heels. There was no way she could feel comfortable in jeans on a Friday morning.

Her head ached but she was dry eyed. She'd done all her crying last night. Tony was gone, all her work had vanished like a puff of smoke. Harry was gone too, and maybe that was the worst thing. She wondered why it should matter so much; it was stupid, a few meals, a movie and one good lay. She wanted to batten down the hatches on her weak, leaky heart. Wasn't this why she'd sworn never again? Namath had snuck his way in there and now she was hurting, really hurting, a fresh burst of that soul-searing pain she thought had gone for ever.

Nina put on a little make-up. She didn't feel like it, but it was about dignity. Tony would love to picture her sat here crying, red nosed, with suitcases under her eyes. She felt hollow with grief and loss, but she wasn't going to put it on a billboard.

Outside her window the sun rose into a balmy spring sky. Nina fixed herself coffee and listened to the *Today* show on Radio Four. She was never home this late. Outside her kitchen window Nina saw scrappy little flowers bobbing under the fence, crocuses next to wilting snowdrops and a couple of waxy yellow daffodils bobbing cheerfully. She stared at the flowers and wondered how they'd got there. She'd never had any time for gardening.

At nine a.m. Nina rang Dragon.

'Can I speak to Anita Kerr in Nina Roth's office, please?'

'One moment.' A brief pause, then, 'There is no such office registered here, madam. Anita Kerr has been transferred to another department.'

God, that bastard works fast. 'Which one?'

'Label Production.'

Nina felt a chill run over her forearms. Labels – that was worse than getting fired. Anita would have to spend her days double-checking tiny E-numbers and drugs and RDAs. And it was based in Slough.

'But she's on vacation for a week.'

'Then Personnel. I need to discuss collection of my personal effects.'

'You've been terminated? Whom am I speaking to?'

'This is Nina Roth,' Nina said, as calmly as she could. The scorn in the girl's voice was something else. She knew exactly who it was, but she was loving making Nina jump through all these hoops.

'I'll see if Mr Sweeney can talk to you. Hold please.'

She put her on hold for a full five minutes.

'I'm sorry, but he's not available.'

'Then his deputy.'

'Nobody in Personnel is available. Would you like to leave a message?'

Nina left her number and hung up. She had personal notes and research papers, phone numbers for the scientists she'd talked to, project studies on all the rival companies. Invaluable when she was looking for a new job. She decided to wait until lunchtime for Keith Sweeney to call her back. The blazing humiliation was bitter as raw sloes; she paced around her drawing-room, restless, her mind racing as she tried to seize on something, anything, she could do. She came up with zero. Nina Roth, mid-twenties *putz* from Brooklyn, versus the Earl of Caerhaven? Dino, Tom, Luc Viera, they'd be lining up to deny anything she said.

At nine forty the doorbell buzzed. Nina opened it to find a spotty kid in a grubby T-shirt clutching a cardboard box.

'Nina Roff? Delivery for yer,' he said, thrusting the box into her arms. 'Sign 'ere. If that's your car out front, someone'll be round to collect it in a minute. And the furniture.'

'The furniture?' Nina said blankly.

'Yeah, it's all in the papers,' he said indifferently. 'See ya.'

She slammed the door behind him and sat down on the couch. The small box contained her pens and pencils, a pad of W. H. Smith writing paper, and three postcards from Zurich. Her notes and notebooks were nowhere to be seen. There was also a thick envelope franked Berman, Graves & Bowler. BGB were Tony's front-rank legal firm; they were the ones he used for serious shit, the real heavy-hitters. She ripped it open. A pink P-45 form from the UK government, a 'you're history' form, fluttered to the ground. She ignored that and went straight to the letter.

Dear Miss Roth,

You are hereby advised that your employment has been terminated for cause, as verbally advised. You are prohibited from entering the premises of Dragon Chemical. Your work and contact notes are proprietary intelligence and will be retained. Your car remains the property of Dragon and you are required to return it immediately or face legal action. Other personal items, purchased for you on the 'Settlement' company allowance, are also to be returned (see itemised list attached). You will not be receiving a reference from the company. The Home Office has been notified of the change in your residency status ...

There was another sharp rap on the door. Nina jumped to her feet and opened it, to be confronted with five burly men in red and black Dragon Security outfits. A white van was parked outside her fence.

'Owright?' said the team chief, pointing to the letter in her hand. 'We've come for the stuff. You got the car keys?'

Nina stood aside to let them in. Silently she fished in her pocket for the keys to the Golf and handed them over as the other men filed past her and started to carry off her furniture.

'That's it,' the foreman said approvingly. He handed her a small receipt. 'Best to get it over with quickly, like. I knew you wouldn't make no trouble.'

'No.' Nina was quick to reassure him, if it would get these baboons reeking of curry out of her place. 'I won't make any trouble.'

At least, she thought in silent fury, not yet.

Friday morning dawned crystal clear over Verbier. The sun shone brilliantly over the rocky mountains. Snow had been patchy, and the piste at Veysonnaz had been thickly blanketed overnight with artificial snow.

'Suits me fine,' Elizabeth remarked to Hans over her creamed porridge and lean ham. 'Artificial packs down those little air pockets, it'll be faster.'

'*Ja*, and that is not so good. Veysonnaz, only a red, but very fast. Maybe now too fast.'

'Too fast? That's like too happy, there's no such thing.' Elizabeth smiled, her teeth white against her golden skin.

She had the tight, healthy glow of the peak-performance athlete, and confidence dripped from her like jewels from Monica's neck. Three days of events and she had built up unstoppable momentum. Hans had never seen her ski like this. It was like she had reached down right into her guts and pulled up her last reserve of speed and skill. He had to struggle to keep her away from the media, in case the things they were saying went to her head. Her nearest rival was Louise, with Christy second and Heidi third, but they were way behind Elizabeth. Hans had never seen a female like her. And he knew she knew it. She was so confident she reminded him of Jack Taylor.

'You have two more days of races. You *can* be caught, *Liebchen*.'

'Yes, Chicken Licken, and the sky might fall down.'

'I don't understand …'

'Oh, don't worry, Hans. I promise I won't be complacent, not till I'm wearing the gold. Louise's really hot on this one.' She shook her head for a second. 'What do I do if she skis a perfect run?'

'You want to beat someone, there is only one way,' Herr Wolf said drily. 'Ski it faster.'

Elizabeth took a final slug of her freshly squeezed orange juice, jumped up from the table and poked her head out of the kitchen window. 'I'm going to go out for a quick run down the Savoleyres.'

The speed-skiing course. Hans knew better than to forbid it, she was just crackling with energy.

'Elizabeth, only once, *verstehst Du*? Or it can take the edge off your run this afternoon.'

Magic words. The green eyes were instantly grave.

'You got it, Coach, just one trip.'

Stepping off the draglift at the top of the run Elizabeth wondered if this was what it was like to get high. She felt beautiful, invincible. The electric lifts were running for the benefit of the Olympians alone on several runs, but spectators on neighbouring pistes stopped to cheer her and wave at the Union Jack suit. The icy *couloirs* of the speed-skiing run were fenced off and almost deserted, apart from two or three athletes with some adrenalin to burn. Savoleyres was a real speed kick – leave your stomach at the start and rocket to the bottom, the skiers' version of bungee-jumping. A plunge on this baby would fire her up. Elizabeth knew her brain was mainlining serotonin, the happiness hormone you got from perfect exercise. And victory. And the high, desert whiteness of this mountain.

She unhooked the metal circle between her legs and schussed forwards.

'Lucky seat. I sure wish that was me.'

Elizabeth jumped out of her skin. Jack Taylor was standing there, wearing a USA practice suit in subtle navy. The men were skiing the Tortin downhill today, a tough customer full of moguls. Elizabeth scowled a muttered hi.

'We must stop meeting like this,' Jack said easily. 'How's Holly bearing up? She's making real good times, you be sure and tell her how proud I am.'

'Give your messages to your girlfriend yourself, Jack, I'm not AT&T,' Elizabeth snapped. 'I have other things on my mind.'

'So I see. You're skiing pretty hot as well.'

'God!' Elizabeth exploded. 'You are the most arrogant man I have ever met, Jack Taylor! Don't you dare patronise me! I have this gold in my pocket, and *you're* getting caught up by Zubriggen.'

'I tripped on the last race.'

'Always some excuse.'

'No excuse, Lizzie, I'm going to win this with a ten-point margin,' Jack said angrily.

'I'm skiing as well as you are, Jack, and I've had to

335

with your putdowns. You're only faster than me because you're a man.'

'You noticed, how sweet,' Taylor said icily.

'Don't flatter yourself, Jack, you were five minutes' fun,' Elizabeth said, hissing like a bobcat.

'Well, baby, you sure gave me a real *quid pro quo*,' Jack said slowly, his Southern drawl crawling over her like his eyes. 'And I'm lookin' forward to my next piece, when you lose our bet. Though be warned, it'll last a lot longer than five minutes. I'm going to collect in full.'

'Ooh, what would Holly say?' Elizabeth taunted. 'Except she doesn't need to worry, because you won't be collecting anything. Now excuse me. I came here to ski.'

She snapped up her visor and pushed forwards, disappearing in a flash of primary colours.

Jack glared after her. He'd chased halfway round the world for that?

'Jesus fucking Christ!' he said.

At the top of Veysonnaz the athletes stood around, shifting on the snow and not talking to each other. Most were silently following the monitors rigged inside and outside the hut. There was nothing to say.

At the starting gate Elizabeth was ready to go. Her heart was racing as though she were halfway down already. Two minutes to triumph or defeat.

The news wasn't good. Her championship lead just narrowed. Heidi had led until Louise ski'd, two girls before Elizabeth. A bravura race; less than two-hundredths of a second slower than the world record. The race of Louise's career. And the only thing between the Swiss girl and the podium was Lady Elizabeth Savage. The crowd thought it was sewn up. Obviously so did Louise, thrusting both fists skywards in a victory salute and hurling a pole into the air like a cheerleader's baton.

There was no more time to think. The klaxon sounded

and Elizabeth settled forward, as low as she could go. Within the fifteen-second start time she could choose when to push off and she composed herself, keeping Hans's words drumming through her head, settling low, low as she could to the ground …

Elizabeth shoved herself forwards, violently, launching due south like a rocket, the packed snow hurtling beneath her long skis, the edges turning nicely as she soared over a hill, a mini-jump taking her twenty yards ahead. How do you top a perfect run? You go *faster, faster*! Her muscles burned as she forced herself down for the vertical plunge, hugging the netting line for greater velocity. Wind howled past her helmet, the crowds near by shouting and clanging bells behind the rope. From the blurred red, white and blue of the Union Jacks Elizabeth knew she was ahead. Yes! Yes! She'd beat Louise, she just needed to keep it up, to get that speed – run a sharper angle by the netting …

As she headed into the final furlong Elizabeth saw the Brits jumping up and down, hysterical with joy, waving flags and yelling. *She must be ahead!* But she couldn't take chances, had to clinch it. Elizabeth thrust herself forward, taking the last turn at a dangerous tilt, her chest inches from the ground, right by the netting as she—

Suddenly she was out of control! A small, sick lurch she tried to steady but was going too low and too fast to stop, and Elizabeth slammed into the side netting, screaming in pain as the tips of her skis thrust through the woven nylon, halting instantly as her body travelled forwards at over a hundred and twenty miles per hour. Her legs were spreadeagled, flung against the solid grip of her boots, the world was a white and blue tumble of sky and snow, then cracking bone, her own distant screaming, and a warm red stream of blood on the icy ground before pain washed everything away in a terrible darkness.

Chapter 35

All she wanted to do was crawl away and die, Nina thought. The young, beautiful woman who gazed back at her from the mirror seemed a mirage. Surely she was a raddled old hag of seventy; she had to be, feeling so weak and so exhausted. All the years she'd been working, at Green Earth, Dolan and Dragon, Nina had kept up the pressure, climbing hand over fist up the ladder with blinkered determination. Now the sweep of events had hurtled past and left her behind, and she felt drained. Dragon was rewriting her history as ruthlessly as the KGB; she had been a nothing, a non-person. Every day she saw the upward march of the stock. Little articles about Dr Hall's research appeared in the bio-tech sections of the papers. And big, commanding photos of Anthony Savage, Earl of Caerhaven, the Robber Baron, dapper and collected as he ramraided yet another three companies while bravely coping with the tragedy in Switzerland.

That was the thing that saved her.

No matter how lifeless she felt, there was still a core of strength buried deep inside. Too much pride to look at those charming pictures and just take it. Nina clipped the photos of Tony and pinned them everywhere – above her kettle, on her mirrors, by her bed.

It worked like a voodoo charm. Soon grief was only her second emotion. The first was rage.

The first thing to do was sell the house. Knight Frank & Rutley gave her ninety-five thousand, a profit of five grand on the purchase price. Then there were the jewels. Since Tony had refused to take them back, Nina wasn't going to offer twice. She needed the money. Every penny of it. You had to have funds to go to war. A place in New Bond Street, the leathery old tortoise behind the counter fairly drooling over the quality of the carats and the filigree workmanship, offered six thousand. Nina laughed and started to walk out. She left with fifteen.

Then she checked into a cheap hotel for a week to try and figure out what to do. Flights home were cheap, money went further in the States. Plus she had right of residence there.

But I'm used to Britain, Nina thought. I know the European market. And this is where Tony Savage operates.

It might be ridiculous, she knew, but she wanted revenge.

If the authorities didn't know where she lived, they couldn't serve her with any nasty letters. Nina knew about English bureaucracy – she figured she would have some breathing space. She rented a cheap flat in Highgate for cash, using a false name – a nasty shock, when she'd got used to luxury. The clothes hanging in her tatty wardrobe were thousand-dollar suits, she had silk shirts and Italian leather shoes and a Patek Phillipe watch, but a tiny table, a creaking bath and paint peeling off the door frames. The TV was secondhand and she didn't have a kitchen, just a fenced-off little enclosure that was part of the drawing-room, but Nina had been in worse dives than that.

She bought a used computer and fax machine from *Exchange & Mart*. That ate up a thousand pounds but she needed those things for survival. Once they were set up in her cramped little bedroom Nina's spirits lifted just a touch.

Now she was ready to go to work.

She couldn't find a job.

Glaxo, Wellcome and ICI turned her down flat. At Hoffman LaRoche, Eastman Kodak and Pfizer she talked her way to a first interview but that was all. She was trying to explain her 'upset' at Dragon, and as she sat there fumbling the shutters came down in the interviewers' faces. Nobody was listening.

Tony Savage had been as good as his word.

He was clever, very clever, Nina thought bitterly as she left SmithKline Beecham. He let her have a few interviews. Even a couple of job offers. She could never prove any blacklisting, but she knew just what was going on.

The jobs she was offered were suitable for an entry-level executive without a degree. Procter & Gamble's science trainee programme, Johnson & Johnson's marketing course. She got five or six offers like that. She turned them all down. They would mean years of working her way back up; the same frustrating struggle for promotion and recognition. It would be like starting over.

Nina couldn't live with that. She was going to have to find another way.

Elizabeth blinked dizzily, her mind struggling to the surface through pain and fatigue. She was desperately thirsty and there was a wrenching ache in her left ankle. Her body felt wrong. Unbalanced.

'She's coming round.' A clipped English voice, a grey-haired doctor leaning over her bed. 'Lady Elizabeth. Do you know where you are?'

Elizabeth whispered, 'Pain. Water.'

The surgeon lifted a beaker of water to her mouth and motioned to a nurse. 'Give her ladyship some pethedine.' He gave her a brisk, impersonal smile. 'I'm Dr Jopling, one of your father's regular consultants. He had me flown out here to attend to you after your accident.

You're in the Clinique Reine Catherine, outside Geneva. We'll be flying you home as soon as you're fit to travel.'

The nurse silently injected something cold into her side.

Elizabeth stared at him, groping for meaning. Images flooded back into her mind: the race, her fall, agony and blood.

'I fell.'

'I'm afraid so. We removed your spleen. You had a serious accident and underwent several operations, but you're all right now.'

'No.' Elizabeth shook her head. The pethedine was working, making her dizzy as the comforting warmth flowed through her body, washing away the pain, but something was very wrong.

Dr Jopling's face was professionally reassuring. 'We can discuss everything later, once you've had a chance to adjust. I'll call your family; they've been waiting for you to recover consciousness, and I'm sure you'll want to see them—'

'Doctor.' Elizabeth's voice was a weakened croak. 'I want to know what happened. Please tell me now.'

'Very well.' Jopling came closer to the bed and looked like he might be going to take her hand, but then thought better of such familiarity. 'You suffered a severe fall – at intense velocity – sustaining serious internal and external injuries, including haemorrhaging, broken bones and fractures.' A beat. 'The worst damage was done to your left foot, which was broken by your fall and then sliced to the bone by your right ski. This injury was further compounded by your ski boot. It crushed the severed portion of the foot.'

He paused. There was no way to soften the blow.

'Every effort was made to reattach, but the nerve endings were beyond repair. I'm sorry to have to tell you that we amputated your foot at the ankle.'

Blood drained from Elizabeth's face as she glanced

down to the end of the bed. Two feet seemed to point upwards under the blankets, but she only had sensation in the right one.

'A prosthesis,' the surgeon explained. 'It's plastic; attached to your leg with a metal frame, jointed on the ball of the foot to simulate as normal a walk as possible. The best on the market; your father insisted.'

Elizabeth quietly said, 'Thank you, Doctor.'

'You won't be crippled, Lady Elizabeth. Recovery will take a while, but you should be able to manage a medium-paced walk eventually.'

There was a deathly silence.

'I'll never ski again?'

'I'm afraid not.' Jopling's words were measured, but his tone was final. 'No running, no skiing. Apart from possible gentle swimming, no athletic activity of any kind.'

He pretended not to notice as tears filled Elizabeth's eyes and trickled silently down her cheeks.

When she felt she had control of herself she buzzed for the doctor.

'I'd like to see Herr Hans Wolf,' Elizabeth said.

The name seemed to shock Jopling. His face creased just a fraction. 'Herr Wolf was refused permission to see you.'

'Refused permission? Don't you know he's my coach?'

'Of course, Lady Elizabeth. It was precisely because he was your coach that it was felt he would upset you – considering how you received your injury.'

'Hans had nothing to do with this. Accidents are risks we take every time we strap up.' She pushed herself up on her elbows and glared at Jopling with fiery eyes. 'Who refused him permission? You?'

'Not at all, my lady,' Jopling said hastily. 'It was Lord

Caerhaven. He has control over all the arrangements here.'

I'll bet he does, Elizabeth thought. 'OK, Dr Jopling, please call Hans and ask him to come and see me.'

Jopling nodded. 'I believe Herr Wolf is staying in the city. Despite your father's ban he refused to leave. He has called to check on your condition every day.'

Elizabeth started to cry, she couldn't help it. She brushed back the tears. 'Has anyone else called?'

The doctor spread his hands. 'Hundreds. The officials, the British team coaches, your team-mates, many other competitors, and the media ... I have a roomful of flowers waiting for you, now you are recovered.'

Am I? 'Did ... did Mr Jack Taylor ask to see me?'

'He rang to ask after your condition, and he sent flowers, but he didn't request an appointment, no.'

'I see,' Elizabeth said dully.

'Do you want your flowers?'

She shook her head. 'I don't think I'm in the mood. Give them to other wards.'

'Certainly, Lady Elizabeth, and I will call Herr Wolf.'

'Thank you. Doctor, who won the medals?'

Jopling looked at her with a certain amount of pity. 'Louise Levier took the gold, Christy Lansch the silver and Heidi Laufen the bronze.'

'And Jack Taylor took the men's gold?'

'Of course,' Jopling said absently as he checked the charts at the foot of her bed. 'There was never any doubt about that.'

The door opened at three p.m. Elizabeth sat up, hoping to see Hans, but it was her father.

Tony thanked the nurse and waited until she had vanished before closing the door. He walked over to Elizabeth with a vast bunch of blossoms in his arms, and laid them on her bedside table. White roses, the roses for mourning.

Elizabeth flopped back on her pillows. She knew disappointment was all over her face but she didn't have the strength to care.

'Darling, you look terrible. Are you feeling OK?'

'I've lost my foot, I'm never going to ski again,' Elizabeth said flatly, 'and I've lost an Olympic crown I had sewn up.'

'We don't know if you had it sewn up. There were lots more races to come.'

'I tell you, it was sewn up,' Elizabeth repeated angrily.

'Well.' The earl perched himself on the edge of her bed. 'Never mind about that now. I've come to discuss your future. Clearly you're not going to be skiing, and I gather Mr Taylor is out of the picture.'

'Who do you *gather* that from? Your girlfriend?'

'I don't have one of those, Elizabeth, but if you're referring to Nina Roth, she's been dismissed. For insubordination.'

'You're breaking my heart,' Elizabeth said bitterly. 'You get good information, though. Jack was never *in* the picture. So I'll have to come and work at Dragon.'

'Yes.' Tony leaned forward and spoke softly. 'I've thought about that. I have some terrific openings for you.'

He reached into his jacket and handed Elizabeth a sheet of paper. Her eyes flickered quickly across it, then rose disbelievingly back up to his.

'You have to be joking. Corporate Hospitality, Events Organisation, Promotional Literature – why don't you just assign me to the typing pool?'

'Why, can you type?' Tony asked urbanely.

'It's not a joke, Dad!' Elizabeth shouted. She jerked her leg under the covers. 'My foot's made of *plastic*! I know

344

you were angry I did Dragon Gold without your permission—'

'Angry? Yes, I was angry. What you fail to understand is that Dragon is *my* company. Nobody does anything without my approval. Nobody is going to make me look a fool, Elizabeth, you least of all.'

'I won't do those two-bit dressmaker jobs.'

'Then I'll give you a small allowance, as long as you behave yourself and keep out of the spotlight. Don't think there's a third option. There never was.' Tony's smile was full of malice. 'Do you know, I thought of you just yesterday. I was talking to Dean Bradman in the Sydney office, and he told me the most marvellous Australian proverb: you've got to cut down the tall poppies. You were a tall poppy, Elizabeth, you and Nina both.'

Elizabeth looked right into his eyes. She couldn't believe it. She was lying here with her foot shorn away, and this was what he was saying.

'I—'

Tony held up one hand. 'Don't spoil things, Elizabeth. You don't have the same power to embarrass me now. You're not quite the national heroine you were. It seems the press are blaming you for reckless skiing, and apparently you were rather disliked by your team-mates … nothing official, of course, but that's what's leaking, and that's what they're printing. One can't trust the press. And none of them will be too eager to print any muckraking stories about me, considering the source.'

'You *owe* me,' Elizabeth said fiercely. 'I'm your *daughter*. Don't you owe it to my mother?'

The earl sat up as though he'd been stung. He looked at her again, more carefully, a musing expression on his face.

'You look so like her,' he said absently, then, 'Those

345

are my offers, Elizabeth. Take them or leave them. To be honest, I don't give a damn either way.'

He tapped the paper again.

'In fact, Elizabeth, I'm doing all of this *because* I owe your mother.'

Elizabeth had nothing to say. She watched him as he left the room.

He hates me, she thought. My God, he actually hates me.

Chapter 36

Hans came by to see her. Despite his stiff manner, he was brokenhearted and it showed. A light had gone out in those clear blue eyes. Elizabeth had sworn she wouldn't cry but it was no use; Hans Wolf's grief, contrasting with Tony's casual cruelty, opened the floodgates.

'*Ach, est ist unmöglich ...*' He rattled off a torrent of bitter *Schweizerdeutsch*, cursing the mountain, the course, the weather, everything. 'It should have been me. I am an old man, but—'

'But you can still ski? No, that's how it should be. You lived for the snow long before I was born and you'll live for it till you die. I was careless.'

Hans's bony hand gripped hers fiercely. 'Never again do you say that, Elizabeth. Never have I seen you ski that way. You had wings, you were an eagle. You had the gold in your pocket.' He snapped his fingers. 'Mademoiselle Levier was a dairymaid next to you.'

'You didn't say that at the time.'

'*Liebchen*, you know your old Hans. I was only being cautious ...'

'Wish I had been,' Elizabeth said. She struggled for a brave face in front of him, but despair was squatting over her heart like a toad. Every day she forgot it when she was medicated to sleep, then when she woke up there were a few cruel seconds of not realising before it clicked back in. Her prosthesis was cleverly made and fitted to her ankle, no expense spared, a thick metal cuff covering the join between flesh and plastic. But the basic fact was still there. She was a cripple. Right now, her strength was flowing away. Her muscles were softening as she lost her appetite and couldn't exercise. Her reserves of energy were draining, her heart rate speeding up. But what does it matter, when you'll never need to be fit ever again?

Memories were torture. The crash, the Veysonnaz run, she hardly thought about. It was her supreme, immortal confidence. Elizabeth died when she remembered what she'd said to Hans, and worse, to Karen and Kate, and Jack Taylor. All the people she'd fought with. She'd thought that gold was in her pocket like a Swiss franc. Well, her enemies could surely laugh now.

'Cautious skiers? There is a place for them,' Hans said stiffly. 'Teaching the snowplough to *Kinder* on the nursery slopes. There has never been a woman skier like you.'

Elizabeth looked away before the tears started again. The dreadful thing was, she thought that too. Deep inside, she thought she was the greatest, could have been the female Franz Klammer. But everybody would forget her now, not right away, but soon. One single World Cup does not a legend make. Louise Levier was the gold medallist, and soon history would be rewritten. Savage took her world title by a hair's breadth. She lucked out once. She wasn't *that* good.

'Easy, when you have the best coach ever.' She tried to be British, brisk and impersonal. 'Anyway, I came to it so late. I've only been skiing for a few years. There are other things that I can do.'

Hans Wolf made a clear effort and agreed with her. Elizabeth smiled wryly; for the old man, life off the slopes was life hardly worth living.

'What will you do? Work for your father?'

'I don't think that's going to work out. He and I have fallen out. He won't let me do the kind of work I want.'

'I see,' Hans said. He looked at her with a fierce

protectiveness. He knows where I'm at, Elizabeth thought, he knows I don't have a degree or any experience outside of Dragon.

'There are many options for you. I can speak to the Swiss Sports Council. Or the FIS, they will be thrilled to have you market the sport. Not all of Europe reads the British tabloids,' Hans added, his wrinkled face creasing in disgust. 'Or Britain – Ronnie knows how bitchy are the lesser girls, and how hard you work. The British authorities can find you a place—'

'I don't think so. Thanks, Hans, really, but no.' She shook her head and Hans watched the hollow shadows under her eyes, the new gauntness in her face. 'Spend my life publicising slopes I'll never ski again, writing puff pieces about Karen's amazing reign as UK champion, or Jack Taylor's next World Cup?'

'You have not heard, then? Herr Taylor has retired from the sport. After this gold. In one year we lose both our brightest hopes.' Hans bent over and smoothed her coverlet. 'But what about him, child? I am not so old that I see nothing. You love him, he loves you. He is a rich, powerful young man, he can look after you.'

'Oh, Hans,' Elizabeth said, stroking his hand. 'It's all over between Jack and me, it has been for ages. He's got another girlfriend, Holly Ferrell.'

'The *Mädchen* who skis like a drill sergeant?' asked Hans, outraged.

'And anyway, I've had enough of being looked after. I'm going to take care of myself.'

Wolf looked down at his pupil. Under the misery there was something he had not seen in her before. A quiet fury, a cold chip of ice at the heart of her pupils. A certain foreboding mingled with his pity.

'You have a plan?'

'Something to start with,' Elizabeth said softly. 'Get on my feet. And get some answers.'

*

There were a lot of empty hours in the hospital bed, waiting for reflex tests and anodyne clinic food. Enough time to watch a lot of CNN or read months' worth of *Paris Match*. Or to brood.

Monica, Charles and Richard all paid dutiful visits. They weren't malicious like Tony, they just didn't care. Which made them and her about even. Ronnie and others asked for appointments but Elizabeth told Jopling to make medical excuses. She wasn't interested in other people. She was interested in Tony.

Elizabeth started to eat. She did intensive physiotherapy four times a day, against the doctor's advice. It was hateful, having to stand in between two poles, resting her weight on a foot that wasn't there. After years of instinctive balancing, her body was all out of kilter, every step felt like she was lurching drunkenly. And her foot. It was solid, plastic. She hated it. She thanked God she couldn't see her stump under the metal casings but she had nightmares about it, a hideous mass of red, nubby tissue at the end of her leg. Even though she was the same from the calves upwards, Elizabeth felt ugly, like her beauty had fled along with her hopes. But the cruellest dreams of all were pretty: soaring down the Hahnen-kamm, slicing through the mogul fields in Saas Grund, running barefoot over the clifftops at Caerhaven Castle. All the things she would never do again. Her body was changing too: from lean strength to slim, softer and weaker. It was the fashion model look and she hated it, she felt like a coathanger. But through all the pain and frustration, and the nightmares, Elizabeth never wavered. She ordered a new wardrobe and stuck it on Tony's account; clothes in smaller sizes and specially made boots and shoes.

She wanted answers. And she wasn't going to find them behind the walls of the clinic.

*

Jopling peered over the top of his wire-rimmed spectacles at the young woman sitting in front of his desk. Elizabeth's hair was washed and styled, newly dyed to a radiant blonde. She was made up in attractive shades of peach and gold, wearing a long Prada dress in moss green, a fitted jacket and chocolate leather boots. From the patient he knew in white hospital wraps to this sophisticated young lady was some transformation.

He didn't want to discharge her – the rehab period had been chopped in two by her exhausting schedule, but her ladyship resisted any attempts to slow down. Now she wanted out, and Jopling knew he was going to concur. Elizabeth Savage had arrived here a broken young girl and she was leaving a hardened woman. She had clearly done some fast growing up.

'Lady Elizabeth, you should really stay.'

'No, Dr Jopling, I should really leave. There are things I have to do.'

'Very well,' Jopling said thinly, scribbling her discharge papers. 'We'll send the account to Lord Caerhaven, if you could just sign here.'

Elizabeth initialled the bill and shook his hand.

'You do that, Doctor. Thank you. Goodbye.'

Well, she doesn't waste any time, Jopling thought as he watched the valet load her cases into the car. There was something about Elizabeth's attitude that made him very nervous.

Oh well; like father, like daughter.

Elizabeth had Mrs Perkins book her on a flight under a false name. Enduring the gushing sympathy of Tony's lapdog was worth it, if it meant she could get away in peace. The last thing she needed was paparazzi at Heathrow.

First-class was comfortably empty. Elizabeth took a glass of champagne, her first drink since that schnapps on the Gotschnawang. She took notice of the pleasant food served on real china, the luxurious seats and individual videos. It might be the last time she travelled this way. Since she was being compliant, Tony would send a limo to drive her up to the castle.

'I've thought about what you said, and I've decided to quit the company.'

'I'm glad, darling, I think that's probably best,' the clipped voice replied without warmth.

'Since the accident, I don't feel the same about things any more. If you'll give me an allowance, I can talk to Monica about finding something to do.'

'Fine. We can discuss it further when you get back.' Tony rang off.

Elizabeth felt her dull anger sharpen into a kind of strength. It was a vicious motivation, revenge. But very effective.

She made it through Heathrow in shades and a Burberry raincoat, so nobody recognised her except a respectful customs officer. He said he was sorry, and welcome to England. Elizabeth smiled bleakly. She got more goodwill from a total stranger than her own family.

It was raining lightly as the limo purred up the M4, water spattering over the glass so the traffic slipped by in a soundless blur. Elizabeth switched on the radio for privacy so she wouldn't have to chat to the driver. She had a stiff pad and a pen and immediately started making notes, letting the formless suspicions in her mind swirl into some kind of definite shape.

The Radio One news was all fresh to her. British troops had landed at San Carlos in the Falklands, preparations were stepping up for the Pope's visit, and the pound note was going to be replaced by a coin. It was another world, she had to adjust to it. Her reflection stared back at her from the glass, thin, blonde, fashionably lanky. She looked like a different person, and she felt like one too.

By the time they pulled in to the narrow country road twisting through gnarled hillside woods that led to Caerhaven, Elizabeth had an idea.

'Darling!' Monica kissed her. 'You look wonderful, so glad you're better after such a shock. And the hair, well, it's *very* dramatic …'

You hate it, you think it looks too good, you cow, Elizabeth thought. She smiled back. 'It's nice to be home.'

'Jenkins will unpack your bags, and there's a wonderful salmon mousse crying out to be polished off.'

'I don't feel that hungry, really,' Elizabeth murmured, petting Dolphin who was bounding all over her. 'I think I'll just have a bath, change, make a few phone calls.'

'Of course,' Monica said with perfect disinterest. 'Do whatever you want.'

In her room Elizabeth stripped and grabbed a warm sweater, her cowboy boots and some Levi 501s. They were hanging off her, but she fixed that with a thick buckled belt. Then she brushed her hair loose and picked up the phone. Joe Sharp, her old village boyfriend, had a brother who worked on the *Bangor Courier*. She hoped he hadn't moved.

'Hello?'

She felt a silly relief. 'Joe, it's Liz Savage.'

There was a stunned pause, then he laughed. His voice was a lot deeper, but it was definitely the same old Joe, redder than Stalin and a staunch Plaid Cymru man. She'd swear blind that Joe would still help her out.

'Christ! I haven't heard from you in years. *Shwd mae pethau?*'

'It's going OK, *iechyd da*, but could we stick to English? My Welsh is sort of rusty.'

'*Peidiwch troi i'r Saesneg* ... OK, OK, if you must. Not that your sort were ever really Welsh anyway.' The teasing changed to concern. She could just see his beat-up face on the other end as he gingerly approached the subject. 'Liz, I'm really sorry, I heard—'

'Thanks, but I'll be fine. Things happen for a reason.' That sounded unconvincing even to her. 'The stuff in the papers was all bollocks, but never mind about that now, I need a favour from Aled, as soon as possible.'

'Anything for you, *cariad*.'

'I want to check some old press cuttings. They've got that database up in the *Courier*, I need it to check something out. Family history.'

'That'll be no problem,' Joe said. 'I was going into town to meet a few mates. I could give you a lift if you like.'

'Now?' Elizabeth said, a bit startled. She checked her watch; it was still only three p.m. 'Sure, why not? Thanks, Joe, I really appreciate it.'

'Then I'll pick you up outside the front porch in ten minutes. Tell her noble ladyship not to set the dogs on the peasant boy.'

Elizabeth slipped out to find a black Mini Metro and a grown-up Joe Sharp. He was twenty-nine now, bigger and thicker, and the caterpillar fluff on his chin had turned into thick stubble. He was ugly as hell but very coarse and masculine. She could see why she'd been attracted to him as a teenage convent girl.

Joe whistled as she climbed in the front seat. 'You've dyed your hair, you look great.'

'How do you know that?' Elizabeth belted herself and turned round anxiously to see if Monica was watching them, but there was no sign of her.

'Come on, girl, you're all over the papers. I won fifty quid when you took the World Cup,' Joe said amiably, shifting fluidly into gear and speeding off down the gravel drive. 'First use a Caerhaven's ever been to anyone. God, will you look at this place.' They were passing the croquet lawn now and turning right past the orchards. A few horses were grazing in rolling meadows punctuated with landscaped oaks. 'Come the revolution—'

'I'll be first against the wall, yes, I know.' Elizabeth found she was grinning openly for the first time since the accident. 'Bloody Sharp the Mouth, I see nothing's changed.'

Bangor was relentlessly gloomy as ever, though by some oversight it wasn't raining. Elizabeth twisted around in the car. She always felt excited when they drove here. It was a relic from the time when Bangor was 'town', with real pubs and the Cannon cinema and Boots and W. H. Smith's.

'The *Courier*'s just down there. Aled knows you're coming in. I'm having a few jars with the lads, so come to the Royal Oak when you're ready.'

Elizabeth thanked him and climbed carefully out. A few people stared at her, then looked away again. The hair's confusing them, Elizabeth thought, and anyway, I won't be famous for long. She made it into the functional slab of grey concrete that was the local rag's office, home of the front-page lead on planning permission scandals, NUM fundraisers and village fêtes, and Aled Sharp came and met her at the front desk.

'My station's over here if you want to have a go,' he said, leading her to a beat-up IBM behind a plywood screen. He was blond and thinner than Joe, and he also seemed nervous. 'Just tap in the reference you want, press this, and then this to print it, er, Lady Elizabeth—'

'Elizabeth. Please. You're a lifesaver, Aled.'

'Well.' He smiled shyly. 'It's not strictly allowed, but seeing as how it's you ...'

'I just need half an hour,' Elizabeth said, then she had an idea. 'Look, tell your boss you did me a trade. Time on the clippings service, in exchange for an exclusive. I'll give you a great interview, really gory, I haven't talked to any national press. He can license it to the *Sun*.'

'Would you do that?' Aled's face pinkened with excitement. 'Oh, brilliant, terrific. I'll go and tell the editor.'

Elizabeth watched him go. Poor kid, it was probably the closest to a scoop he'd ever come. Quickly she entered into the database.

SEARCH PARAMETERS:

She tapped in EARL OF CAERHAVEN, and LOUISE, COUNTESS OF CAERHAVEN, 1956–60

CROSS REFERENCE:

LADY ELIZABETH SAVAGE

She thought a moment, then added one more name.

JAY DEFRIES

It took a little while for the computer to scroll and select. Elizabeth read it over. Double-checked to be sure. Then with a calm she didn't feel, she sent it all to the printer.

'He wants me to come over and interview you tomorrow,' Aled Sharp told her eagerly when he came back. He pointed to the wad of paper she was holding. 'Find anything interesting?'

'Yes, I did.' Elizabeth stood up to leave. 'I found the answer.'

'Oh yeah?' Aled ushered her out, smiling like he'd just won the pools. 'The answer to what?'

'The answer to everything,' Elizabeth said.

Chapter 37

Nina sat alone in her office.

London in April was a beautiful place to be. The scabby cherry trees that lined the street had burst into glorious froths of white and pink. It was sunny enough to set the cabbies whistling and bring out the ice-cream vans. Advances in the Falklands had united everyone here in a sort of friendly patriotism; dirty windows in the houses round about were covered with bright Union Jacks. Nothing like war to help you forget the recession.

It was not something Nina could forget.

She was only just realising how cocooned she'd been at Dragon. In a huge drugs company, the recession was just an idea. Boom or bust, people always got sick. Hospitals bought their drugs, institutions bought their shares, and the Robber Baron was cash rich. No wonder he'd been on such a shopping spree. Retail chemists and others were closing down everywhere. For bottom-fishers like Tony Savage, trawling for cheap market share, 1982 was paradise.

For everybody else, it was a nightmare.

Nina's premises were located on Wardour Street. Rent was high in Soho, but that was how it had to be. She had a tiny space in a good location. The office was two rooms, and it had come with peeling walls and filthy windows. Nina had rolled up her sleeves and repainted herself in a soothing apple green, then scrubbed the windows until everything gleamed. The front door was stencilled: 'ROTH CONSULTING'.

Roth Consulting. It sounded so grand. Six weeks ago when Nina registered at Companies House her head had been full of dreams of glory. She was going to start a bio-tech consultancy. Management consulting was the hot new business sector, and who knew more about European markets than her? Just a few contracts would let her hire staff ...

Nina realised certain doors were shut to her. The big companies wouldn't need her help, and word had gone round from Tony. It was the little fish she'd set her sights on: outfits with one product, or a single office in another country. Firms that Tony would never consider. Minnows.

Great theory. But lousy reality. The little firms she approached were too strapped for cash even to think about consultants. To them, it was a luxury. Meanwhile, the rent on the office, its equipment and her flat were eating up Nina's savings at a rate of knots. As she sat here looking out at the cherry blossom, tapping a pencil on her empty in-tray, Nina knew she was in big trouble. She needed a contract. And fast.

'Son?'

Jack tugged on the reins and turned round, his Arab stallion half-rearing in annoyance.

'You ain't been listening to a single word,' John Taylor said wearily. He pricked his mount forwards, breathing hard. Jack had ridden him right off the course today, flying over the ranch fields like he was riding for his life. Whatever Europe had done, it hadn't softened him.

Back to the States with a gold medal. Him and LouAnne had been right out there to see it. Watching their little boy stand up on that podium, taller and stronger than a Greek god, with the Stars and Stripes behind him, his hand on his heart as they played 'The Star-spangled Banner' – it was the proudest moment of their lives. The TV people and the papers made such a fuss, you'd fairly think the whole country loved Jack as much as they did. Even the movie people had come buzzing round like flies on horseshit, wanting to turn Jack into a picture. Like Robert Redford in *Downhill Racer*, but this time for real.

Jack should have been prouder than a white peacock. He wasn't. The one time he looked happy was when they looped that burnished disc around his neck. Saving that, he was moody and restless. Had the family lawyers serve injunctions on the Hollywood boys. Gave no interviews. Nothing like their Jack, the arrogant glory junkie. And he was moody back home; no interest in anything, even the ladies. The Dallas babes were queuing up for it. John had grinned a quiet male smile when he saw the bunch of females pressin' round his boy everywhere he went like they were in heat. When he was here a couple years back, Jack woulda bought a few rubbers and taken 'em on one at a time in a line-up, but he was real strange about it now. LouAnne had insisted he date Clarisse again – now that little lady was a perfect ten, a walking Barbie doll with sweet Southern ways. Jack had taken her out a couple of times. Probably got laid, too. But he did it by rote, and for Jack, that was acting like a goddamned monk.

Today their ride around the ranch had ended ten minutes ago, that was how long it took John to catch up with their son.

'Sorry, Pop.'

Taylor patted the horse's sweating flank. 'Boy, I don't need no shrink to tell me something ain't right. You'd better spit it out. I don't need no zombie round here.'

Jack looked down. 'It's Elizabeth.'

'Elizabeth? Her again? I thought that was all over. You're upset because she got into that accident? Hell, she'll be OK, her folks have money. You can't help her none by vexin' yourself, kid.'

'It's over, but I can't stop thinking about it. To come that close and then ... she'll never ski again.'

'There's worse things than that.'

'She wouldn't see me, you know? Her doctor said no visitors. I sent flowers, I called, but she never answered.'

'Dealing with it her own way. Now, Jack.' John dismounted and started to tether his beast to a post. 'I am mighty sorry for a girl who has something like that happen, don't get me wrong, but last time you spoke you were sayin' how you were through with her, what a stubborn, ornery bitch she was, how you couldn't even speak but you were gettin' into a fight. It's crazy how you're gettin' riled up. There's lots of pretty girls right here, and y'all know you got work to do.' He waved a leathery, suntanned hand around the rolling acres. 'The stud farm, the hotels and the land, it ain't going to nobody but you. You gotta start taking an interest.'

'Pa.' Jack looked down at him distractedly. 'I have to go and find her, tell her how sorry I am. In person. It's a skiing thing.'

'Back to Europe?' He snorted. 'Like hell, it's a skiing thing. Look, son, go if you have to, bang her again if that's what you gotta do—'

Jack frowned thunderously. 'Don't talk about her that way, Pa.'

'Hey.' Now John was mad. 'Y'all have had enough time for foolin' around. You want to waste thousands of bucks jettin' over to dry some chick's tears, be my guest. But then you get your butt back here.' He jabbed a finger at the stables behind him. '*This* is your future, Jack. Texas. Not London. You'd better have that real clear in your mind.'

The car came crunching down the gravel drive to park in

front of the house. Elizabeth sat at her turret window and watched it come, Tony's sleek Silver Phantom Rolls-Royce gleaming whitely in the warm spring sun. She was surprised he hadn't fixed a Dragon company flag to the front. Tony's monster ego suggested that was just a matter of time.

Now he was actually here, Elizabeth's calm deserted her. She felt the adrenalin surging through her as she watched Monica glide out and offer her husband that reserved, passionless kiss. There was none of the good, enhancing stress she got before a race, though. This was different, a sour mixture of anger and fear. But she knew she was ready; it couldn't be postponed.

Elizabeth picked up her folded set of clippings and looked at her reflection. She'd chosen an outfit Tony would hate: black CK jeans and a tight green T-shirt by Donna Karan. With her ankle boots and steel sports Oyster, it was aggressive and sexy. That had always bothered him; now she knew why.

She limped downstairs and walked stiffly across to Tony where he stood ignoring the ecstatic welcome of the dogs.

'Elizabeth, darling,' he said, his brow creasing at her new look. 'It's a bit too dramatic, wouldn't you say?'

'Not really. Look, why don't you step into the library, and we can have a little talk.'

Tony nodded his head towards Monica, busying herself in the kitchen. 'I was going to have a spot of tea first. You can wait?'

'If you like,' Elizabeth nodded with equal reserve, 'but I think you'd prefer to hear this now.'

He looked her up and down with that cold assessment that had been so hurtful before, but now just slid off her.

'As you wish.' Tony walked across the uneven flag-stones to the old library door, pushed the studded wooden door and held it open. Elizabeth walked into his green baize den with a flash of *déjà vu*. This was where they'd had their last confrontation, when she was sixteen years old, over Granny's will. His victory then had been complete, but that was not going to happen this time.

Tony sat at his desk again, comfortably, and glanced at her. He looked utterly self-possessed. Elizabeth shut the door firmly behind her and sat down herself. He thought she was crushed; her spirit as broken as her leg. At least she would have the element of surprise.

'You've always hated me, Tony. And now I know why.'

His Christian name. His eyebrows arched.

'Don't look so surprised.' Elizabeth smoothed out her list of cuttings and passed them over, seeing Tony's shock at the old articles. 'I never knew Mother, but I wish I had. She had you over six ways till Sunday.'

'Nobody had me over.'

'I look so like her, don't I? Nothing of you at all, Lord Caerhaven. Or of Jay DeFries, for that matter. But my, how awkward it would have been, for the Robber Baron we know and love.' Her voice was thick with sarcasm. 'Whispers at the Athenaeum. Jokes in *Private Eye* and the House. Tabloid fun at your expense. Of course, it simply wouldn't do, I see that. You had to take in the little cuckoo.'

'Well.' He did a creditable job of hiding the rage. 'You've become a PI, how inventive. You always were an unladylike little tramp, just like Louise—'

'A tramp? Because she wouldn't play dumb in the gilded cage like Monica? I can see just why she'd prefer Jay, even without money, or a title. I know I would have.'

'You cheap little bastard,' Tony said, with real viciousness.

'Well, that's the difference between us. I *know* you're a bastard. You don't know if I am.'

'You're no child of mine, Elizabeth. I have sons.'

362

'Lucky you, since we all know just what you think of females. Having been trampled by one of them.'

'She was a ball-breaking whore,' Tony snarled.

'I've always thought,' Elizabeth said slowly, 'that a man who could have his balls broken by a woman wasn't much of a man in the first place.'

'A pity your Mr Taylor didn't agree with you,' Tony said.

It was a direct hit. Elizabeth flushed, and the earl made an effort to settle himself. He pushed back into his armchair and looked at her coolly.

'What do you want? I think I should remind you, you don't have quite the same *cachet* you once did. The press think you're a spoilt, petty little brat. That you threw away a British medal.'

'I still have the capacity to embarrass you, my dear papa,' Elizabeth spat. 'We both know it. So if you still value your reputation—'

'To an extent. Don't think you have a blank cheque. I'd rather take my chances than have you back at Dragon.'

'I'm sure we can come to an arrangement.'

Tony steepled his fingers. He looked at her like she was something unpleasant he wanted to scrape off the soles of his handmade brogues. 'Then I repeat, what do you want?'

Elizabeth smiled. 'You'll like this one, Tony. I want out. Away from you, away from this freezing old relic, away from that vacuous bimbo in the kitchen, all your hypocrisy and high-class whores. I want enough money to look after myself. In exchange, I will always be Lady Elizabeth. A million pounds, that should do it. You won't even notice it.'

He shook his head. 'No guarantee.'

'You have my word.'

'Worthless. I might agree to a trust fund. A million,

paid at intervals over the next five years, conditional on your silence. You sign a contract; if you ever breathe a word, the money is repayable with punitive interest.'

'Fine with me, old man, but I want something now. My cases are all packed; I don't want to spend another night under this roof.'

Tony stood up and drummed his fingers on top of the grand piano.

'Fifty K and Walgrave Road.' That was a Dragon house, kept furnished for visiting executives, a beautiful mews in a villagey, tree-lined street tucked away in Earls Court. Elizabeth had stayed there once; it was a little jewel of a house, with a small walled garden out back full of roses and wisteria. The neighbours were an opera singer and a Saudi princeling. 'There's a housekeeper who will let you in, the lawyers will bring papers round tomorrow. That's the first year. It's worth two hundred grand easy.'

'Fine,' Elizabeth said. 'Go out and tell your chauffeur he has a passenger for town.'

Tony nodded. 'So, darling, I suppose this is goodbye.'

'I suppose it is, Father,' Elizabeth replied.

'You'll keep that promise or lose everything. You'd better realise that. I don't know what you think you're going to do with yourself, but I would strongly advise you to keep away from me.' He smiled thinly. 'You'll find out, Elizabeth – once you're outside, you stay there. I have a lot of enemies, and they all know the score. They hate me, but they don't mess with me. I don't think there's a soul in London who's prepared to risk that.'

Elizabeth left the room without replying. At that moment, she wanted revenge worse than anything else in the world. She would endure any humiliation to get it. And Tony's last bit of pomposity had put a name glowing into her mind.

The woman she'd disliked but respected. A blinkered

workaholic with a razor-sharp brain, a vicious bitch, maybe, but that was what she needed. Someone who had been close to Tony. Someone who might know a way to bring him down.

Nina Roth.

Chapter 38

Harry Namath slowly pulled off his white coat and looked over at Lilly.

'What?'

'I said she's left the company.' The older woman tried to sound casual, but it didn't come off.

Harry frowned as she sat there on their lab sofa, fag in one hand, sprawled out against the leather cushions. It was dark outside, three in the morning. They'd just come off a gruelling session of proto-lipid tests. Lilly was injecting her baboons while Harry ran complex computer models. He'd been seeing endless DNA strands revolve against his eyelids, double-helixes in purple and green spinning into his brain. But the tiredness melted away when she dropped this little bombshell. It was as bracing as a cold British shower. Harry sat up again and stared at Lilly. She looked worse than usual tonight: her skin was pallid and grey from fatigue, and she was ill tempered too.

'You're over-reacting. She got us the deal, she's gone, so what? Those corporate bods will get another suit to replace her.'

'She's a friend of mine, Lil. Why didn't you tell me?'

'I didn't think she was such a mate of yours.' This was so obviously a lie that Harry didn't bother replying. Lilly threw up nicotine-stained hands. 'OK, fine, but you hadn't been speaking, you hadn't seen her ...'

'We were in France working.' Harry's voice was cold.

'You were bummed out about her after that talk you had with Tony. So I reckoned it was all over.'

Harry pressed a hand to his aching forehead. He could feel the pincer-like claws of a migraine wrapping themselves round his skull. 'What would you know about that?'

Lilly sat up and glared at him. 'Tony talked to me too, all right? He told me the score. Little tramp. What would you want to hang out with her for?'

'Hey, bud, my friendships are my business.'

'She was bad for you.'

Harry paused. He couldn't believe what he was hearing. Lilly sounded really sour. '*Bad* for me?'

'That's right. I told Tony that too. He said he was going to can her, and I said good on him.'

'Lilly, you have no right to interfere in my private life.'

'Oh don't I?' the dumpy woman said bitterly. 'When I'm the one who's been your partner for years! When I'm the one who's doing the work they want! I'm the biochemist, Harry, they don't want computers. I could just have taken this whole thing for myself. But I carried you along with me and what happens, you run off with some floozy brunette, some career prostitute who slept her way—'

'That's enough!' Harry shouted, then calmed himself. 'Lilly, we hardly even socialise.'

'We're together enough,' she muttered.

Harry shook his head again. Lilly. She had a brilliant mind but she was squat, ugly and way too old. Yet somehow she had managed to delude herself that their working together was a relationship. She'd never said a word. Maybe she'd known inside that it wasn't gonna happen, she didn't want to spoil the dream. He remembered her disapproving looks at Nina. Harry thought it was the youth; now he thought it was the beauty. He had shattered her illusion like ice over a dirty puddle, and now she was sitting here screaming about betrayal.

It was worse because it struck a chord. Lord Caerhaven had reached into his heart and squeezed a burning fist around it. The words in that laconic English tone were almost more than he could bear: ugly pictures of Nina, screwing Tony, on her back for a promotion. Harry was already halfway in love with her. Making love to her had been incredible, he couldn't wait to hook up with her again. That memory had been tainted, corrupted with acid. Now he knew why she'd been so jumpy back at Dragon's office. She didn't want anybody to tell the boss that his mistress had her own bit on the side.

Harry had tried to shove Nina from his mind.

But he couldn't forget her. He thought about it every day. How could she? Was she really that cheap?

Harry decided to get an answer. That didn't mean anything – just curiosity. He wanted to confront Nina. To say all the things that were burning up his chest.

And now it looked like he wouldn't have the chance.

'When was she fired?' he demanded.

'How would I know?' Lilly asked sullenly. 'A few weeks back? Who cares?'

Harry turned away from her and started to pace up and down. He felt almost regretful; he would have been a millionaire in a few years.

'Sorry, Lil,' he said, 'I quit.'

'Don't be a jerk.'

'Whatever you think we have, we don't. I'm sorry. And nobody telling me about Nina Roth – I don't like being played for a schmuck. Or manipulated.'

'If you go,' Lilly said meanly, propping her fat torso up on her elbows, 'you're breaking contract with me. Your work on our research becomes my copyright, and you'll lose all your royalties and points from Dragon. Do you get that? You'll lose everything.'

'I'll lose this project.' Harry shrugged and reached for his overcoat.

'You're bluffing! What the hell will you do?'

He turned at the door and gave her a quick, dazzling smile. 'What I always do, Professor. Land on my feet.'

Elizabeth took the keys from the housekeeper on Tuesday night and signed the papers Wednesday morning. Tony's lawyers came by at nine a.m., on the dot. That was no surprise. She knew he was as eager to be shot of her as she was to go.

She had got Walgrave Road lock, stock and barrel, so she spent a morning checking it out. Dragon's corporate hospitality people were very efficient. There was everything a fat cat could wish for, from a power-shower to a study that came complete with IBM, home printer, copier and fax machine. There was a Quotron terminal in one corner of the room. Elizabeth checked the share price: up three points. Tony must be confident he could never be beaten. The garden was as pretty as she remembered, the refrigerator, freezer and wine cellar were fully stocked, and there was a small home gym in the basement. Elizabeth looked at it dispassionately. She could only use arm weights and a stationary bike now. If there was any point.

She arranged to have all the bills transferred to her name and called Coutts & Co., where a smug functionary confirmed the deposit of fifty thousand pounds. Then she went to the Lloyd's round the corner and picked up an account transfer form. Stuffy pomp and circumstance were behind her now.

'We'll handle that for you, miss,' said the teller. 'Name?'

'Lady Elizabeth Savage,' Elizabeth said, and smiled briefly as he gave her a quick, embarrassed stare.

'Yes, milady, right away.'

She wondered idly if that was really her name. Tony didn't think so. But Tony was wrong about a lot of things. In the end it didn't matter: Savage or not, she was out on her own.

Nina flicked through the pages of *American Scientist* and tried to pay attention. She knew she should use dead time to keep learning and improving, but it was no good. She dropped the glossy on to her desk and looked at her reflection in the switched-off computer screen.

Yesterday she'd gotten her first break. Peter Meyer, president of a small bottling plant, had returned her call. She'd had dealings with him at Dragon. Meyer had been impressed then and invited her in to head office. His firm was in trouble: one of their biggest clients was about to cancel a longstanding order, switching bottling function to their own firm. He knew Nina was a lateral thinker; maybe, he said without enthusiasm, she could come up with something. He'd tried every option he could think of – discounts, increased productivity – but their finance guys weren't going for it.

Nina hadn't needed asking twice. She had extensive notes on both Meyer and the client company when she'd showed up this morning, wearing her most businesslike charcoal suit and carrying a mobile phone and a briefcase. In a meeting with Peter and Linda, his secretary, Nina went over the options.

'In the short term, I can fix this,' she said confidently. 'In the long term, you'll need to diversify.'

'What do you mean?' Peter asked her.

'You can't die of hypothermia every time Tropex sneezes. They may want to cut costs again. You need other options.'

'And your firm can supply them?' Peter Meyer asked sceptically.

'We can indeed,' Nina said, ignoring the secretary's

sniff. 'If you're not satisfied, you pay nothing more than expenses.'

'Thank you. I'll think about it,' Meyer said.

She had gone back to the office on a cloud of hope. It had lasted all of two hours. That was when Linda called her back and said the board were minded to turn down the proposal.

'We'll give you a final answer by the end of the day, but I can't see them changing their minds.'

'I see.' Nina struggled to control her disappointment. 'Thanks for letting me know.'

Now she sat here facing the facts. The Meyer call was the first bite she'd gotten in weeks, and now the fish had almost wriggled off the hook. She'd offered him a no-win, no-fee deal and he still wasn't interested. If Peter Meyer didn't think it was worth the effort, even at zero cost, Nina stood no chance. She was going to have to give up. Pack in the office and take some menial job, entry-level like the ones she'd been offered before. If, indeed, they were still open. Or maybe she should go back to America ...

No! Nina thought. No! I can't let him win! She couldn't, couldn't quit! She jumped up from her chair and kicked the desk in a rage. There were no options, but she couldn't accept that. Her mind was dashing against the brick wall like a bee trapped by a windowpane—

There was a knock on the door.

Nina stopped dead. Somebody must have got the wrong address. Or really be looking for the psychic next door.

The knock came again, louder, impatient.

'Hold on,' Nina called. She walked over to the door and opened it.

Elizabeth Savage was standing there. She had lost the golden tan and about a stone, and she looked thinner and tireder than when Nina last saw her. She was still beautiful, skinny and tall, however, the kind of figure Melissa Patton and her cheerleader buddies had always idolised back at St Michael's. The startling blondeness of her hair framed the sharp cheekbones like a glossy halo. She was wearing tailored slacks, a close-fitting military jacket and a pair of heeled boots. Nina couldn't help but notice the boots, glancing down involuntarily.

'No, you heard right,' Elizabeth said wryly. 'I did lose a foot.' She banged her left leg on the cracked linoleum. 'Hear that? It's a prosthesis. Plastic.'

Nina opened her mouth to say something but nothing came out. Attack Savage? She could do that, but not to a cripple. It was like speaking ill of the dead or something, although Elizabeth, slim and blonde and designer top to toe, didn't look like your average zombie. Offer her sympathies? No way, that would sound as false as it would feel.

'Come in,' she said neutrally. 'I guess you had a reason for coming here, Elizabeth, unless you were in the neighbourhood and felt like dropping by.'

'You guess right.' Elizabeth walked into Nina's office and looked round.

'It's not the Stock Exchange,' Nina said defensively.

'It must rent cheap.'

'Well, that was the plan. Did you come here to gloat, milady? If so, you can just leave the way you came in. Or is it a message from Tony?' Nina's brown eyes glittered with distaste. 'Because the answer is no, no, and no. Whatever it is.'

'Neither one. Can I sit down?' Elizabeth asked, gesturing to a secondhand black leather chair.

Nina's eyebrows arched. She looked hard at the other girl. 'I'm busy, but you can have ten minutes.'

'Sure, you look busy,' Elizabeth wanted to say, but bit it back. 'Nina.' She sat down and brushed the hair out of her eyes. 'I don't like you, you don't like me. Fine, that's a given. But you've got something I really need, and vice versa. I was thinking we could help each other out. On a purely business basis. A pact of convenience.'

'Go on,' Nina said.

'I have fallen out with my father. It's been brewing for a while but now it's final. I've left Dragon – I was kicked out, or as good as. I've moved out of the family home. He expects me to live off the pocket money I've got in exchange for that, but I have other ideas. I want to make money myself and I want revenge.'

Nina laughed. 'You expect me to buy that? Why would he do that to you? You're family!'

'He hates me,' Elizabeth said intently. 'Look, I can prove it to you. He took all the Dragon Gold stock off the market. He incurred millions in losses just to spite me. I swear it's true.'

'I know it's true. I saw the memo,' Nina said slowly. Something about Elizabeth's face was convincing. The look in her eyes was one Nina recognised. She saw it every time she looked in the mirror.

'When I came out of recovery, he told me I could only work in Corporate Hospitality, Events Organisation, or Promotional Literature.'

Nina snorted. 'Might as well type the letters.'

'I said exactly the same thing. Come on, Nina, you knew him, you slept with him. He disliked me intensely. You must have been aware of it.'

'Yes, I was.'

'Then you should believe me. He destroyed my life.'

'He let you ski.'

'Because it suited him. Skiing was the one thing I did he could approve of – it fitted the great Robber Baron image. You used to hate me because I went to finishing school, I had no real education. I wanted to – you have no idea how much – and I wanted to work, but he wouldn't let me do either. That way he could control my destiny, can you understand that? No degree, no experience, I was qualified for nothing. Except winning races. The marketing skills I always knew I had, I studied in my spare time, I read *Campaign*, even those fucking boring stats you made me learn.'

Nina smiled suddenly, caught off-guard. It was so funny to hear that cut-glass limey voice say 'fucking'.

'Dragon Gold was *mine*. I made something of it.'

'You did. It was pretty gutsy, faking Tony's authority like that. He was so mad when he found out he dropped everything to fly home.'

'I'll bet,' Elizabeth said softly. 'You can imagine what that was like. He did the same thing to you, and you were his girlfriend.'

'Correction. I slept with him. When I no longer wanted that to continue …' Nina shrugged.

'Then help me.'

Nina stood up. 'Look, Elizabeth. I don't know what you think I can do. If I could have hurt him, I wouldn't have waited for your permission.'

'So. You've got the same problems I have. No credibility,' Elizabeth said shrewdly. 'Once you're out of Dragon, you're a non-person. And to start anything up, you need money, you need staff.'

'You got that right.'

'OK.' Elizabeth's green eyes narrowed. 'I'm not the president of your fan club, but I have money and I can sell this firm. You *know* I can, because you've seen me work. We could make something together.'

Nina stared at her. 'You mean that?'

'Every word.'

'Look, Elizabeth.' Nina sighed. 'It sounds good, on paper, but I can't take your money. There *is* no business. I got the first break I've ever had yesterday.' She explained about Peter Meyer. 'That phone's going to ring any second to turn me down, and it'll be the first and last bit of business I ever do. I can't afford to pour rent money down the drain any more.'

Elizabeth leaned forward urgently. 'Let me call them,' she said. 'I've got an idea. If you're going to fold anyway, what could it hurt?'

Nina shrugged. For a polished Sloany princess, she was certainly persistent.

'OK.' She pushed the phone across the desk. 'I guess you can give it a try.'

Chapter 39

'Come in,' Peter Meyer said expansively, ushering them both into his office. He smiled briskly at Nina and shook hands with Elizabeth. 'Nina, you never said Lady Elizabeth was on board with you.'

Nina nodded quietly. Meyer was grinning and bowing like a nervous butler. He had agreed to another meeting right away, because he was terrified of Tony Savage.

That little deception got Elizabeth through the door, but she'd need something more to get them any further.

'This won't take long, Mr Meyer,' Elizabeth said. Her voice was rather cold. 'I called as soon as Nina told me you were in negotiations. It's just a good-faith visit, really.'

'Good faith?' Meyer repeated. Under other circumstances, he knew he'd have been admiring the view across the desk – one young woman dark and lush, the other slim and blonde, both gorgeous – but he couldn't manage it. They were so well dressed, serious and relentlessly formal. Looks of twenty-five with an attitude of forty-five. It was unsettling.

'Yes. Lolland Jars have also replied to our pitch.'

Nina stiffened. Meyer sat upright and frowned. Lolland Jars were his biggest rival; they had narrowly lost out on the Tropex contract. Now he feared they were going to have their shot at it.

'They want to get their firm in shape for the future.' Elizabeth's smile was apologetic. 'Knowing how tough it is for independents out there. So, we'd be obliged if you could sign the formal "no" from your board and give it to us, so we'll be legally clear to start dealings with Rob Lolland.'

'Wait a second!' Meyer said anxiously. He hated Rob, the guy ate into his customer base a little further every month. What had he missed here that Rob had seen? 'You can't work for Lolland if you're in negotiations with me!'

'I'm sorry.' Elizabeth leaned back, an expression of confusion on her patrician face. 'I thought you were turning us down.'

'No, that's not correct. We were just trying to rejig the budget,' Meyer said hastily.

'I'm afraid we do need a fast decision. Mr Lolland needs an answer, one way or the other.'

Meyer glanced at Nina's briefcase. 'Do you still have that contract you brought round before?'

'Of course.' Nina unclipped her case and handed it across to him.

Elizabeth added, 'If you do want to hire us, we need expenses payments in advance. Two thousand for the first month.'

Meyer nodded and scrawled his signature at the bottom of the page. 'If that's your company account, I'll transfer the funds across at once. I'm afraid you'll have to disappoint Mr Lolland. Meyer Bottling got there first.'

Nina and Elizabeth exchanged a quick glance. Nina took the signed contract, and they shook hands.

'Good to have you with us. I'm sure with such a capable deputy you'll make very rapid progress,' Meyer told Nina with relief.

'Thank you.' Nina smiled back. 'But I should set you straight. Elizabeth is my partner.'

In the cab on the way back to Soho, Nina looked at

Elizabeth with amazement. 'Lolland replied to our pitch? They turned me down flat!'

So?' Elizabeth grinned. 'That's a reply!'

Nina streamlined Meyer's operations and cut costs, while Elizabeth provided them with a marketing prospectus for fresh clients. Tropex retained their account, and Meyer entered discussions with three more companies. Nina sent Peter Meyer pitching segments of the market he'd never even considered.

'How can you possibly know so much? You're so young!' he said, the night they toasted the Tropex renewal.

'Dragon teaches you fast,' Elizabeth muttered.

'I've been in this game for over seven years,' Nina said.

Meyer needed no convincing. He paid Roth Consulting, with a bonus. And he spread the word.

A month later, they had more work than they could handle.

Elizabeth and Nina found it hard going. They hired a secretary, a mature woman returning to work. She was cheap, but ten times more efficient than the gum-chewing teenagers with uninterrupted experience. Helen Potts kept them civil to each other: they couldn't snipe in front of her, although they were respectful of each other's talents. Elizabeth's effortless confidence and polished manners worked beautifully with clients, but they still got under Nina's skin, and Elizabeth hated the draconian way Nina ran the place: in at eight a.m., out at eight p.m. Plus, there was mountains of work, with little reward. All the money they saw went as fast as it came: hiring new equipment, moving offices to Hammersmith, paying lawyers and accountants as they set themselves up. Nor were their fees large. They were undercutting the big boys, and all their clients were baby firms.

However, they were too busy to snipe much. It was like scraping your way out of prison with a grapefruit spoon. At night they fell asleep when their heads hit the pillows.

It was a makeshift alliance, but bills got paid. Jobs got done.

They were in business.

'Mrs Potts, could you hold the fort for half an hour?'

It was a cold June morning, rain pouring down on Hammersmith Broadway. Nina could see it splashing on the red roofs of the buses that crawled past their windows. Elizabeth was silhouetted against the dull grey sky, her blonde head bowed over transparencies for a new brochure. Wellkin Pharmacies was their biggest client yet, but that wasn't saying much. They had six shops in the West End, a lot of clutter and no way to keep up with Boots. Nina was trying to persuade the chairman to specialise and Elizabeth was dreaming up a new look. The fee on this job was ten thousand – it would cover overheads for months.

'Certainly, Miss Roth.'

Elizabeth glanced up. 'Something up?'

'Let's go into your office a second,' Nina said. Elizabeth followed her into the orderly room she'd had decorated with framed ads, and settled into a chair. Nina seemed edgy and tense, and Elizabeth's guard flew up.

'I've got a proposition, but I need your consent for it.'

'I'm listening.'

'I think we're in the wrong business.'

'Oh! Is that all? Well, that's reassuring,' Elizabeth said irritably. 'Is this New York angst? You should leave Woody Allen on Manhattan, Nina. We have six jobs in hand and three more waiting.'

'Yes, but what are we getting out of them?'

'Money. OK? Are we done with the therapy session now? Because I'm really busy.'

'Jesus Christ, will you hear me out?' Nina snapped. 'We're not making *enough* money. We're keeping ourselves afloat, that's all, and since we can only handle so much consulting work, that's not going to change. We're just going to trundle along making a minor profit. We've been so busy we haven't looked at the big picture.'

'Can't see the wood for the trees? You're right, but I think we're working as hard as we can.'

'It's not about working harder. It's about working smarter. We need to advise bigger firms, and to do that we need something more concrete to offer them. Sterling Health don't need us to teach them how to suck eggs, but there's still a lot of wastage in their systems. If we can fix that, we can command *real* fees. Hire staff, expand—'

'But we can't fix that. You just said so.'

'Not on our own, no, but what they need is computer help. I can pinpoint market improvements – did it for Dragon *and* Dolan.'

'Yeah, but you never even graduated high school, you can't write a major computer program. It would take a genius like Clive Sinclair—'

'I know somebody. I think he'd go for it, but I'd have to offer him a partnership. Do you agree?'

'Providing our decisions have to be made unanimously,' Elizabeth said coolly. 'I'm sorry, but I'm not going to be outvoted by you and a friend.'

'Understood. Though I'm sorry to say he and I aren't exactly friends,' Nina admitted.

Elizabeth gave her a small smile. 'Hasn't hurt *us* so far.'

Nina used Elizabeth to track Harry down. She knew the numbers for Lilly's French lab like the back of her hand: she'd fought so hard with Harry over the location.

'I'm sorry, Lady Elizabeth, I can't help you.' Dr Hall's Australian accent was thick and rather sour. 'Henry Namath walked out of this firm months ago. Don't tell me Dragon has more business with him.'

'Absolutely not.' Elizabeth played a hunch. 'You sound as angry with him as I am.'

'You've got a beef with Harry?' Lilly snorted. 'He means nothing to me.'

'Actually, he owes me money. Quite a lot. I loaned him twenty grand when he moved to England.'

'Well, that's different. Twenty grand?' Lilly laughed meanly. 'I have an address here somewhere. Unless he's fled the country. Thirty-four Fount Street, South London. Phone number ...'

Nina caught the Tube to Charing Cross and picked up a cab at the station rank. She wanted to turn up looking successful. That would convince Harry to listen to her. She told herself she had to be strong, very dry and businesslike. It would do no good pleading with him to give her a second chance. Tony told him the truth and he was disgusted; that's why he didn't call or write when she was fired. She hadn't seen him since that Chinese dinner.

I was right the first time, Nina thought. I should never have let another man into my heart.

She was getting stronger all the time. She never let Elizabeth see she was unhappy, and she'd die before Harry got a chance to realise it.

For this meeting she had dressed with incredible care. Her raven-black hair was spritzed into neat submission with a burst of Elnett, she wore a dark green Jil Sander pantsuit, crisp and attractive, with Stèphane Kelian pumps and camel leather gloves. Simple gold studs in the ears, soft make-up, Mac colours and Shu Umera brushes. Nina wasn't going to hide away from him. She refused to apologise for being attractive. Dr Namath could take her or leave her.

The taxi pulled up outside his house. It was a quiet street near the Oval, a pretty mews house with a cherry tree in the front yard. She could see a light burning in the upstairs window. He was there.

She felt almost light headed with nerves as she paid the driver and walked up the steps.

Nina rang the bell. She was afraid she might run away, so she rang it three times, pressing really hard. The faint sounds of the Rolling Stones clicked off from upstairs and she heard him racing down the stairs. The door wrenched open.

'All right, all right, Jesus fucking Christ, what's the—'

Harry jumped out of his skin. He did a double take, then a triple take.

Nina tried to keep her impassive look but her control was deserting her like water sloughing off Vaseline. Harry was so surprised he hadn't said a word. It suddenly occurred to her he might just slam the door in her face.

'I do have a telephone,' he said slowly.

'I thought you might just hang up on me. I've got a proposal for you, Harry,' Nina said.

'Well.' Namath scratched his head and gave her a strange look. He was so attractive, he took her breath away. He was wearing a T-shirt, and it was plastered to him, sticking to his lean torso. His legs were covered in a black pair of workout shorts, black socks and beat-up sneakers. His chin was peppered with two days' stubble. His face was glowing; he'd clearly just been working out. Erotic images flashed uninvited into her mind: Harry doing push-ups, Harry laying into a punchbag. She felt the sudden pulse of lust all through her body. Like a hunger you didn't know you had until you smelt food.

'You're making quite a habit of it.' He lifted his T-shirt. 'I'm as unprepared as the first time. You can come in, but you'll have to wait while I have a shower.'

Nina went dry mouthed. She said, 'Fine, thanks.'

Namath stood back to let her in. His London house was an extension of the Swiss place, furnished minimally, with hardwood floors and exercise equipment stacked in a corner – a bench, heavy-looking dumbbells. Only a set of shelves on one wall, stacked with computer texts, spoilt the seamless line. It was a small slice of TriBeCa in South London.

'Kitchen's right through there. Coffee's freshly made,' Namath said. He bounded back up the stairs two at a time.

Nina went into the kitchen and fixed herself a coffee. It was so American, so recognisable it hit her in the gut. Coffee beans from Gloria Jeans, wafting cinnamon amaretto all round the kitchen. An empty Haagen-Daaz pot by the bin. Where did he get this stuff? She tried to take her time with the coffee, noisily opening cupboards and choosing a mug and switching off the machine. Trying to take her mind off the faint hiss of water coming from upstairs, trying not to think of him, standing there, with the water sluicing him down, pushing the soap across his armpits and his back …

She set the coffee down and leaned against the side, light with longing. It was bittersweet: he was so sexy and so close, and she had lost him. Did he have a girlfriend? He must have, by now. The thought made her wretchedly jealous, more pictures drifting through her mind like toxic gas. She felt physically nauseated. And sick with desire.

Thank God I'm not a man, Nina thought. It would be so obvious.

'So.' Harry's voice jerked her out of it. He was wrapped in a voluminous navy bathrobe and rubbing his hair with a towel. 'What's the story?'

'You broke the partnership with Lilly. Why did you do that?'

Harry reached over to the coffee pot and poured himself a mug, took a sip and gave her a cold glance. 'That's really none of your business. I guess you must have got this address out of Lilly. Don't ask her any more questions about me, Nina.'

She flushed. 'You're right. I apologise, I just needed to see you.'

'Why?'

'I want to suggest something to you.'

'Oh?' Harry dropped the towel on the floor and leaned back against the oven. He watched her neutrally, like he was trying to read her. 'Business or pleasure?'

If I said pleasure, would he kick me out of the house? Nina wondered miserably. Then she shoved that thought aside. She was offering Harry something she knew he'd be into, but she had to pitch it right. She squared her shoulders and looked him right in the face.

'Business. Strictly business. And believe me, Harry, this is perfect for you.'

Chapter 40

'There is a train strike. Please make alternative transport arrangements. Contact your local tourist information office.'

Jack grinned at the announcements crackling out of the Underground tannoy at Heathrow. Welcome back to Britain. Life sure was a lot easier in this country when you had money. He bought a paper, jumped in a cab and gave the guy directions to the Regency Hotel in Marylebone. *The Times* was the usual mix of optimism and outrage: victory in the Falklands, birth of Prince William, an IRA attack in Hyde Park. The photos showed Household Cavalry horses with their necks ripped from their torsoes. Sickening. Italy had just won the World Cup. They took soccer real seriously here: the sports pages were full of dissections. The US had come last in its qualifying group. What the hell, soccer was a limey game anyway. Jack flicked to the business pages.

He wondered how Elizabeth was doing. *What* Elizabeth was doing. When he'd called Dragon it was like butting into a wall. No, sir, they had no information, Lady Elizabeth had left; no, sir, Lord Caerhaven wasn't available; no, sir, under no circumstances could they release her address. Perplexed, Jack rang the castle. Monica Caerhaven had been vague but jumpy; she muttered something about Earls Court, excused herself, and put the phone down. Something was definitely up.

The British Ski Federation gave him her address with no trouble. Ronnie Davis, reduced to coaching third-raters like Karen and Kate, almost fell over himself in his eagerness to help.

'She's running some computer firm. Consultants ... they just changed the name. I got a number here, if you can ever get through. I keep trying to get her to come and coach, maybe do something with the youth programme, but she's way too busy.' Ronnie sighed. 'Gawd, I wish she would, great to have her teaching the kids.'

'You can't teach what Elizabeth had, Ronnie.'

'Bloody hell, mate, you got that right.'

In his room Jack unpacked, dropped to the floor and did fifty stomach crunches to shake off the lazy feeling he'd gotten from the flight. Then he dialled the number that Ronnie had given him. The company was out in Hammersmith, West London.

It was called Tall Poppies.

'Just one second, Mr Taylor,' Mrs Potts said brightly. She waved at Elizabeth, crossing to her office with an armful of ad layouts. 'Personal call for you on line two. It's a Mr Jack Taylor.'

Elizabeth froze. Then she said, 'Yeah, right, put it through.'

She put the layouts down on a nearby desk and shut her door behind her. The red light on line two was blinking silently at her. She felt herself break out in a sweat, a light dew of fear. Jack. He could still hurt her, and badly. What was he going to say? An invitation to a wedding? His wedding? The picture she saw in *Vanity Fair* last month had pierced her like an arrow. Jack, impossibly gorgeous in a tux, with Clarisse Devlin on his arm. Clarisse, his longtime girlfriend, revealed in the flesh to be just the daintiest, creamiest little piece of Texas honey you could possibly imagine, and Daddy probably owned two oil-wells with it. 'Olympic and World Champion Jack Taylor with Miss Clarisse Devlin at the

opening of the San Francisco Opera House.' She was sure
Clarisse would never argue with Jack or talk back to him.
She would be gracious and submissive and all the things
Elizabeth could never be. And would never be. No matter
what.

I've got no choice, I've got to talk to him, Elizabeth
thought. She steeled herself and picked up the phone.

'Jack! This is a surprise.'

'God, girl, are you ever hard to track down.'

'You could have tracked me down in the clinic,'
Elizabeth said angrily, then kicked herself. Great, where
did that come from? She could control her end of a
booming business operation but she still hadn't got a
handle on her runaway mouth.

There was a pause. Then he said, 'I've got to see you.'

'I'm really busy, Jack,' Elizabeth said negatively.
Talking to him was one thing; she didn't know if she
could handle a visit.

'Elizabeth Savage, I flew in from Dallas just to see you.
I fought like a bobcat with Pa to let me go.'

'Well, I'm sorry about that, Jack, but I never asked—'

'Elizabeth.' His exasperation as he cut her off was just
like old times. 'I am here and I am *going* to see you, if it
means campin' outside your door on the sidewalk. Now
do I come over there and punch out your security guards
or are you going to be a lady about this?'

'Be a lady about it?' Elizabeth chuckled despite herself.
'Jack, you don't know how to take no for an answer, do
you?'

'No, ma'am, guilty as charged.'

'Come to my house. Twenty-four Walgrave Road in
Earls Court. I'll be there in forty minutes, but I warn you,
I can only give you a little time.'

Jack smiled to himself as he hung up.

'We'll see about that, sugar,' he said.

*

He found the place without any trouble. It was a cute little house, tucked away in a tiny corner of village hidden in the heart of the city. Reminded him of their townhouse in Greenwich Village, New York, that Mom used for her shopping base. It struck him that he'd never been to any place of Elizabeth's before. They'd always met up on the circuit, in hotels or gyms. Apart from that one time in Sussex. That suddenly seemed so wrong and wasteful. Jack shook his head, smiling confidently. No more. Now he was going to rewrite the book.

He bounded up the small stone steps and hit the bell.

'Hey,' Elizabeth said. 'Did it insult your mother, or something?'

'And good morning to you too, sweetheart,' Jack replied.

She looked different. Real different. The athletic frame was gone, slimmed off her. No problem, she was beautiful either way. The competitive fire had also disappeared, but Elizabeth still looked tough and focused. He wondered what the new place was, Tall Poppies, that had given her a look like that. For Elizabeth, he'd have said you couldn't get it outside of a race piste. She was wearing a tailored pantsuit in dusty pink, cream leather boots, an ivory shirt and a gold bangle. Her hair was coloured a dazzling blonde, layered all round her face in a feathery cut. She blew Clarisse Devlin and all the simpering Dallas debs right out of the water.

'Come in,' Elizabeth said.

Jack stepped inside the house. It was sparsely but elegantly furnished, a few old oil paintings on the walls, rows of leatherbound books, the normal rich-limey clutter.

'Very nice. Your pop give you some spares?'

'I bought everything you see,' Elizabeth said flatly.

'Tony and I have split for good. The house was part of the settlement.'

Jack walked over to a far wall and examined a small pastoral. 'Looks Pre-Raphaelite. What is it, Burne-Jones?'

'Very good. I've started collecting.'

'Without the earl's help? Come on, Elizabeth, where would you get that kind of money?'

Jack settled himself in a deceptively plain leather armchair and found he was sinking into perfect posture. It must be orthopaedic. Eames, most likely. He took another look around the room, paying greater attention. Sure the décor was sparse, but everything here was top quality, costly stuff.

'I can't believe you, Jack.' Elizabeth sat opposite him and allowed herself to sound annoyed. That was simple, so much easier than actually confronting what she was feeling right now, a sort of dizzy joy combined with sick apprehension, the way she was desperate for him not to leave, how she was telling herself to get a grip and failing so miserably. 'You come over here, you drag me out of work, and all you can ask is how I pay for my decorating?'

'So you think I should ask you about your leg?'

'Shouldn't you?' Elizabeth demanded. He was totally wrongfooting her. She'd expected belated tears and hand wringing, and here he was, joking and squabbling with her like nothing had happened.

'Honey, there's nothing to say. You know how sorry I am. I know how it would feel.'

'Oh, you do?'

'Yes,' Jack said gently. 'Of all the people in the world, I do know what it would mean not to ski again. What it must mean to you.'

Elizabeth looked away before she started to cry. That was perfectly true. Only Jack, and maybe Hans, could have any idea. She swallowed hard to push down the dry lump in her throat.

'Think what it means to *me*, babe. You can't ski, so I can't collect on my bet. That would have been real intriguing. We'd both have got the golds—'

'You think I'd have won?' Elizabeth blurted out, then kicked herself. That was not the next thing she was planning on saying.

'There was never any doubt,' Jack replied. 'I wouldn't have let you bet me otherwise. When you had to come to my room and pay up, it had to have been at least a little interesting.'

Elizabeth pushed herself to her feet and rounded on him. 'For God's sake, Jack! I'm a fucking cripple and all you can do is fly over here to make sex jokes! Where were you when I needed a friend? Out partying with Holly Ferrell and all your stupid American groupies—'

'Hey. Hey.' He jumped up and grabbed her hands. 'You know I tried to visit. I begged to. Your father told me to get lost. And I never partied from first to last. Got the medal, flew home and tried to forget all about you.'

'And you couldn't?'

'I'm here, ain't I? And you're no cripple, girl, you're standing up like Lady Liberty.'

'But I've lost my foot,' Elizabeth muttered. 'I've got a plastic foot.'

'So what? It was never your foot I was interested in.'

'But what about Holly Ferrell? And Clarisse Devlin?'

Jack's hands had left hers and were cupping her face now, one finger delicately tracing the line of her jaw and her cheekbones. His touch on her skin was like an electric charge. Her stomach was melting into a liquid, shifting pool, she wanted him so badly.

'Y'all want the truth, or the PG version? PG, I never touched them, I sat in my room and pined like a dog. Truth is, I saw them both for a little while and I slept with them. I was mad at you, and you weren't there. It was OK. And then,' Jack added with a disarming grin, 'I sat in my room and pined like a dog.'

'Jack ... it won't work, it never does.'

'It won't work? Baby, you know we ain't ever tried it.'

'What about Sussex?'

'Not bad for a warm-up,' Jack said, reaching up to the ivory silk at her neck and undoing one of the buttons. Elizabeth knew this was her cue to push him off but she didn't. It was weird, like one of those running-in-treacle nightmares when you couldn't move. Except it didn't feel too much like a nightmare.

'But that's not a relationship, Jack ...'

'Yeah?' He breathed it, bending down to kiss her, just brushing her lips. 'That's just fine with me, sugar. I don't want a *relationship*.' Jack's tanned face was tight with scorn as he pulled her to him, one arm cradling the small of her back, supporting her whole weight like she was made of straw. 'I got a *relationship* with my cousin Sarah in Fort Worth. I want you. In case you're too blind mulish to notice. This makes twice I've flown round the world for you, and I'm not doing it again.'

'Jack—'

'Jack, Jack.' He kissed her again, briefly and impatiently. 'Is that all you want to say? Objections? Reasons we both should be somewhere else, right now? If you don't want me, Elizabeth, you just say so. Look me right in the eyes and say go.'

He tipped her face up to his. His eyes locked on hers were probing, intense. Elizabeth didn't say a word.

Jack pulled her closer still. Close enough to feel him hard up against her groin.

'That's what I thought,' he said.

It was wonderful. Elizabeth's fears and nerves couldn't withstand the hot longing for him that was racing through her. She let Jack undress her, because he wanted to and because she was trembling so much her fingers were all fumbling. When he peeled off her shirt and the filmy scrap of nothing over her breasts she was anxious, because she'd always been small and now she was flat, but Jack breathed in sharply at the sight of her, brushing his fingers over the pale-pink buds, then bending to suck them, until she was almost crying from pleasure. The feelings in her breasts distracted her from the way he was unzipping her boots and trousers, and then she was naked, and Jack took her left ankle in his hands, curiously, muttered, 'Poor baby,' kissed the flesh where her calf met the metal band, and moved right back up her leg, slowly, deliberately, kissing and biting the skin at the back of the knee, trailing his tongue up a little way and then stopping, his strong hands locking her in place; Elizabeth gasped at how he made her feel, she was squirming around under him, losing her control, it was all she could do not to moan out loud. Jack kicked off his shoes, tore off his shirt. Elizabeth heard the buttons thud on the carpet as he unzipped his fly.

'Your shirt—'

'Fuck my shirt.' He was naked now, leaning over her, his hands all over her, his fingers palming the slickness between her legs. It was broad daylight, pale sun streaming through her window, letting her see every inch of him: just like her fantasies, huge chiselled muscles, his arms were thicker than her thighs; not narcissistic like a bodybuilder, but about as big as you could be and still look like a normal man. Elizabeth knew girls that hated that look, said it was too big and too macho, and it was true, under him she felt as fragile as a reed; but it was painfully erotic, and she felt heat blaze through her like a forest fire. Something female and primal responded to that physical strength, that total masculinity.

'You're so beautiful,' Jack said. She saw him register

the hunger in her eyes. He smiled, but there was nothing of humour about it. It was pure sex, that smile; pure triumphant sex. 'You like?'

'You're huge,' Elizabeth said.

'And you like that.' Jack straddled her. He was like a Greek sculpture of Hercules. He lifted one knee and firmly, slowly, pushed her thighs apart. Elizabeth heard the breath wrenching out of her in a sob of desire. Jack pushed his knee up just a little, pressing into her, pushing against the wetness there, looking her right in the eyes so she could see he felt it. 'You like me to be a man. Admit it.'

'Yes,' Elizabeth managed. 'You know that.'

'You're right, sugar,' Jack said thickly, 'I do know that—' and suddenly he slid down the bed, cupped his two hands under the globes of her butt and pulled her up to his mouth, like she weighed nothing, burying himself in her. His tongue flicked over her in a light, sweet rhythm, sexy, relentless, ignoring her when she cried out. Her fingers twisted in his hair, and her fingernails dug into his back. Jack drove her forwards, until he felt her involuntary surrender. Her body melted against him, her back arched, and right at that second he grabbed her hands, pinning them back over her head, up against the bed-rails. She was open and waiting. Jack thrust right into her, all in a single motion, not gently, giving her exactly what she wanted, thrusting, as deep and as hard as he could go, automatically now because he couldn't wait either. Elizabeth rose to meet him and he was still pinning her there, it made the orgasm stronger. Their eyes were wild, locked on each other, as the white-hot scalding spasms broke over Elizabeth and her fierce clenching and releasing set Jack off, and then they were in each other's arms, drenched with sweat, fighting for breath, and kissing.

Chapter 41

'I can't believe it,' Jack said.

'Believe it,' Elizabeth answered. She showed him round the crowded offices packed with people, sixteen different programmers hunched over their workstations. Tall Poppies had taken over two floors of the Hammersmith offices. Downstairs was Elizabeth's own marketing division; a fancy name for a team of four people, but they were all rising stars poached from the big agencies, and the way things were going she might need to hire some more. 'Yesterday was the first day off I've had in four months. We're growing so fast I'm getting altitude sickness.'

Jack stared at her. Elizabeth did look frazzled, but she was happy too. 'We're stretched to the limit, but we're making a lot of money.'

'And it wasn't working before?'

'Oh, it was working, but in a small way. We fixed that when Harry came on board. He's a genius programmer. He creates the software, Nina applies it to the market, I spread the word.' She tugged at Jack's hand. 'Come over here, see the boardroom.'

Jack laughed. 'The boardroom? Oh babe, you're kidding.'

'Good morning, Lady Elizabeth,' said a middle-aged woman in a smart navy suit.

'Good morning, Mrs Potts. Jack, this is Mrs Potts, our executive assistant.'

'Good morning to you, ma'am,' Jack said politely,

trying to hide his disbelief. Elizabeth showed him into a small, well-equipped conference room, with a mahogany table and four chairs. Then she shut the door behind her and kissed him triumphantly on the lips.

'I'm not kidding,' she said. 'I'm deadly serious, Jack. This time it's working. And we're in charge. If it keeps up this way, I'm going to be a multimillionaire before I'm thirty years old.'

'Is Elizabeth still busy?' Harry asked, slightly annoyed.

'Is this about your new project?'

'Yeah. I'm done with the conceptual stuff. I need to know if we can sell it. I only have forty minutes before the Unilever meeting.'

'You're starting to sound like me,' Nina said, glancing across the hall. The boardroom door was still closed and she smiled. 'Elizabeth's got a lot of history with Jack Taylor. I think you should just let her alone.'

'It's going to mean working late tonight.'

'So what else is new? Success is tough,' Nina replied.

It was true. The addition of Harry had given them everything Tall Poppies needed. Nina's cold efficiency was offset by Elizabeth's warm English-rose persuasiveness, and the addition of the older American scientist banished any remaining doubts. The small companies they'd worked with before recommended them highly, but now they had something fresh to offer. Computerisation. What sci-fi writers saw as a sinister force, and Establishment fuddy-duddies regarded as a passing craze, was taking over. Namath's maverick code-jockeying now had a legitimate target. Tall Poppies became IT consultants to the UK drugs business. They were in demand right away. Nina made her first really big score, an efficiency programme for a division of Procter & Gamble. After that it was open season.

Nina was straining to go like a Dobermann on a leash.

She'd waited for this all her life. When Harry complained he was being pushed too hard, they hired more programmers, all the brilliant, unorthodox talents the hi-tech giants wouldn't touch. At Tall Poppies, staff wore Hawaiian shorts, Beatles T-shirts, anything they liked. And they kept their own hours, as long as the work got done. Soon Elizabeth needed marketing help too. They physically outgrew their surroundings, rented another floor.

Nina was now speaking to the landlord about a lease on the whole building, and they hired accountants and lawyers. Elizabeth arranged interviews in the business press.

'What do you feel about this overnight success?' the *FT* asked Nina.

'Overnight?' she'd laughed. 'It's taken me years.'

'Never mind my partner,' Elizabeth butted in. 'You have to speak fluent obsessive to understand her.'

The uptight, besuited journalist tried another tack. 'Female entrepreneurs seem to be the wave of the future – Anita Roddick at the Body Shop, Debbie Moore at Pineapple. Why do you think this is?'

'Well,' Elizabeth said, looking over at Nina, 'we women have to give ourselves a chance, because nobody else is going to.'

'And have you girls always been friends?'

Nina shrugged. 'We *girls* have always hated each other.'

The hack put his pad down. 'I don't understand.'

'Why not? I'm speaking English,' Nina told him curtly.

'And is that still the case?' asked the stuffy jerk, with a look that clearly said they were mad, hysterical females, and how the hell were they making all this money?

'No.' Elizabeth grinned over at her partner. 'We tried to keep it up, but the truth is, we were just too busy.'

'We understand each other better now,' Nina added.

'And the third partner? Dr Namath?'

'I like Harry,' Elizabeth said carefully, 'and our working relationship is terrific.'

He'd been satisfied with that because he had to be, Nina reflected. Elizabeth was too smooth to let anything slip out: how they worked together fine, but Harry and Nina fought all the time. Pushing. Yelling. Stand-up fights, blazing arguments the staff could hear through Harry's office wall, the two Americans jabbering at each other in a barrage of slang. Elizabeth acted as a bridge between them, and there was too much work and new business to have it get in the way. Nina knew it was mostly her fault, but she couldn't stop.

It was torture, having him there all the time. Watching him as he crouched over a computer station, his eyes locked on the scrolling numbers, his face lit up by a monitor. Sometimes they worked together late at night. Nina took care to keep out of his way. Otherwise, the urge to reach over and ruffle his hair might be too strong. She couldn't bear the way he looked at her sometimes, a guarded glance, like he was trying to figure out how he'd gotten her so wrong.

Every day she hoped he'd turn up and announce a new girlfriend. Every day she was terrified of it. When she had to be physically close to him, it was almost too much to bear.

But Nina couldn't do without Harry. His reputation grew every week. He was the engine for her revenge on Tony Savage, and for her and Elizabeth both, that was the absolute priority.

Elizabeth had told her what Tony said: 'You have to cut down the tall poppies.' Every job they landed, every new bill that got paid, was a slap in that bastard's face. Tony refused to comment on all the good-natured questions about his daughter's success. When Nina

imagined the journalists bugging him, it gave her exquisite pleasure.

And even better, they were hurting him.

Nina pitched Dragon sometimes, just to be spiteful,
and when they turned her down, she went to their
competitors. Dragon had its own IT people, but they
were hidebound, way behind Tall Poppies. In the UK, on
the Continent, rivals were chipping away at Tony's
market share.

The first day Dragon's stock dipped, Nina opened a
bottle of Cristal. Tall Poppies was still a small business,
but it wouldn't stay that way for long.

'Yeah, success is tough,' Harry said. 'Just like you.'

'Me?' Nina tried to smile. 'I'm just a marshmallow.
Look, is it really urgent?'

'Damn straight, it's urgent.' Harry ran his hands
distractedly through his hair.

'Then how about I go over it with you?'

'Tonight?'

'Not if you don't want to,' Nina said, blushing.

'No, it's OK. Your place or mine? Or does that sound
too much like a date?'

'Your place is fine. And no, it doesn't sound like a
date,' Nina said with a touch of bitterness. 'Don't worry,
I know better than that.'

'Let's go back to the hotel,' Jack said, kissing her
forehead and eyebrows. 'You're turning me on, sugar, I
swear.' He bent her back, both his arms resting on the
boardroom table. 'There's a desk in the bedroom, I
want to get you butt naked and push you down across it
and—'

'Jack!' Elizabeth pushed him off her. 'Jesus! Is that all
you ever think about?'

He grinned. 'Nope. Sometimes I think about having

you go down on me. Or getting you in the tub and washing you with a little bubblebath ...'

Elizabeth's creamy skin blushed a deep rose. 'Cut it *out*! This isn't some kind of sex-trip, Jack. This is serious, this is seriously my business!'

'I know that.' Jack stood upright, letting her wriggle out of his arms. 'And I'm totally impressed.'

'And surprised.'

He shrugged. 'That too. OK? I admit it. But come on, baby. You know things are changed now. You don't need to be worrying, y'all are going to get a whole lot of money for your share in this thing, and when we're in Texas you and me can—'

'Wait a second.' Elizabeth held up one hand. 'Back up. What did you just say?'

Jack shook his head. 'You're right, I'm all messed up. Going too fast. But I've had years of practice at that.' He dropped to one knee and took her hand in his. 'Elizabeth, you know I love you. And you love me, unless you're one hell of an actress. Will you marry me?'

'Jack ...'

His handsome face clouded slightly. 'Yes or no, sugar.'

'Maybe,' Elizabeth said.

Jack looked at her disbelievingly. Then he scrambled to his feet, frowning like thunder. '*Maybe*? You know, I had this scene all figured out.' He fished in his pocket and drew out a blue velvet box, flicked it open. Inside was a huge solitaire diamond, emerald-cut on a ring of white gold. 'Real romantic and all. I have to tell you, girl, *maybe* wasn't a part of it. Are we still playing games? Aren't we done with that?'

'Oh, yes.' Elizabeth nodded and blinked back tears. 'We're done with that. Which is why I say maybe. I do love you, Jack, I always have, and I want to marry you.'

'Then I don't see the problem.'

She waved at the busy offices behind them. 'That's the

problem, Jack. Tall Poppies. It's my thing and I'm not selling up. Not now. We're on the threshold of something extraordinary ... I've been waiting for this all my life, to be somebody in my own right. I can't give it up to go back to ... to *Southfork* and play at being Sue Ellen.'

Jack sat down heavily in one of the carved oak chairs. 'Sweetheart, I don't have a choice here. I'm an only child. I got hundreds of acres of prime Texas land, two hotels and a stable full of the best studs west of Arabia. I can't sell it.'

'You can do whatever you want.'

'You can come and help out with the business back home. I know how you feel—'

'No,' Elizabeth said. 'No, clearly you don't. Or you wouldn't ask.'

Jack scowled at her. 'Honey, get real! You're saying you want me to *live* over here, like a goddamn househusband? My business has been in my family for six generations.'

'And mine has been in mine for one generation.' Elizabeth blinked back a film of tears. 'Look, thank you for the offer, truly—'

'No!' Jack shouted. He caught her hand and pressed it on to his heart. 'You can't say no to me! We were meant to be together!'

Elizabeth looked at him. He was so beautiful, so perfect, and she loved him so much. She also knew if she gave up Tall Poppies to be with him, she would wind up resenting him so bitterly that love would turn to hate.

Sorrow clogged her heart so thickly she felt like she could hardly breathe.

'God,' she said, and one big tear trickled out on to her cheek before she could get a grip on herself. 'I thought so too.'

Nina left Elizabeth alone for the rest of the day. It was

strange, seeing Jack Taylor in the flesh; so tanned and Texan, he was Marlboro Man in the flesh. She couldn't imagine him on a pair of skis. Or ever dating a cool customer like Lady Elizabeth. He was real courteous when Elizabeth introduced them, said something about them being fierce enemies and fiercer friends, but Jack seemed distracted. That way they were matched: Nina was distracted too.

'Nice to meet you,' she said. 'Elizabeth, can you come round to Harry's house this evening, any time you can make it? We need to check out his new product.'

'Sure. Sure.' Elizabeth turned to go. 'I'm not going to be in this afternoon, is that OK? I'm going to drive Jack to the airport.'

'Whatever you need,' Nina said.

It was still light when she got to Harry's, the gold and pink streaks of the summer evening silhouetted behind the pretty Georgian houses in his street. London was a beautiful city, when you thought about it. Nina watched a pair of pigeons flurry on to Harry's roof, strutting around cooing to each other. The tree outside his front door was in full green leaf. She stepped up and rang the doorbell wearily. How nice it would be, just once, to have an evening off. She hoped whatever Namath had dragged her out for was worth it.

'Hey, come in, come in.' Harry led her into the kitchen where he liked to work at night. He had a terminal set up in the far corner, so he could programme and never be too far from the cookie jar. Tonight he was wearing grey sweats and sneakers; he looked relaxed and confident. Nina was wearing the same John Galliano she'd been in all day. She was frazzled from clients, and her neck hurt where the phone had been glued to it.

'You look tired.'

'You got it.' Nina rubbed the back of her neck. 'Can we get to it? I'd like to go over what you're proposing.'

'Something I've been working on,' Harry said. 'Proprietary software. I'm calling it Home Office.'

'Home Office?' Nina repeated. 'But we do consultancy—'

'And we still will, but this is going to take us to a whole new level. You won't just sell to big drugs firms, you'll sell to every small businessman in the country,' Harry said.

'OK.' Nina knew better than to laugh at Harry when he got that look on his face. 'Layman's terms, try and tell me what you've written.'

Over the next couple of hours he explained it to her. Nina tried to follow; she lost him in the jargon, but the concept was simple. Home Office was a software program you could sell in the high street. Disc-drive computers could access the full thing, smaller Spectrums and Amigas could run a mini-version on their tape recorders. It would centralise word processing, spreadsheet and inventory functions in one programme.

'What are we doing?' Namath asked enthusiastically, watching his partner with her head bowed and her neck aching, trying to read his graphics designs. 'We're reorganising all these giant firms to make them more efficient. Well, that's something *everyone* needs. The florist. The guy with the corner store. Didn't you tell me once you'd run a deli?'

Nina glanced up at him. That was the first time he'd ever referred to their time together before. But Harry didn't look sarcastic; he was just asking a question.

'Sure, South Slope, Brooklyn.'

Harry winced. 'Nasty neighbourhood. You ever have inventory problems?'

'Every week,' Nina agreed.

'Well, if you'd had Home Office, it would have done your inventory in ten minutes max.'

Nina looked at her watch. Quarter of eleven. 'Elizabeth's not coming, but I know what she's going to say.'

'She's going to turn it down?'

'She's going to love it.' Nina shook her head. 'It's brilliant, Harry, it's going to lift us to the next level.'

'But we'd need money.' Namath looked at her hopefully. 'To manufacture it, I mean. Unless you think I should license it?'

'Like hell, we'll do it ourselves,' Nina said firmly. 'That means a factory, sales force, packaging, the works. That means capital. And that means bank loans, or going public.'

'Which do you prefer?'

'A bank loan,' Nina answered. 'If we go public we'll get taken over, and we're not ready for that yet.'

'But if we go for a bank loan and it goes wrong, we've lost this company. My credibility. Everything.'

'That's right. So will it go wrong?'

'Not the code, sister,' Harry said with a grin.

'Then we'll do it,' Nina said.

Namath let out a whoop of joy. Then he came over and started to massage the back of her aching neck. He was strong, his fingers were pleasurable, she wanted to melt into it, just melt against him and let him take all her pains away.

Roughly Nina pushed him off. 'Cut it out, Harry,' she snapped.

'Right.' He lifted his hands and spun away from her. 'Business, I forgot. That's all life ever is with you, kid. Business. Is that it? Don't you want anything else?'

Nina got up to leave. 'It's a great idea, Harry.'

'Don't dodge the goddamn question.'

She turned at the door. 'You know what? You're right, they're all right. There's nothing but business in my life. I really don't see the point, because every time I've tried something else, I've always got burned.'

'By who?' Harry sounded furious. 'Tony Savage, the great heartbreaker? Are you going to pine after him for the rest of your life? Because he burned you?'

'Get this straight,' Nina snarled. 'If there's any burning between me and Tony, *he's* the one that's getting fried. And you can take that to the bank.'

She slammed the door behind her.

Chapter 42

When Nina woke up, it was a bright, cold morning, the early light crisp with the promise of great heat later on. For the first time in years, it reminded her of Brooklyn: summer on the Slope, when she'd woken up early in order to get a few moments on her own before Pop dragged himself out of bed to switch on the cable. But now her sheets were Irish linen, and her window had William Morris curtains instead of grimy slats. This morning felt significant somehow. And then she remembered. They were going to gamble.

A million things could go wrong. Her instincts, for a start. Maybe shopkeepers would be technophobes, maybe the village trader would as soon fly to the moon as buy a computer program. Tall Poppies was still small. If they blew several million pounds of financing, they were history. Like Elizabeth's skiing career.

This was the biggest stake she'd ever risked. For the first time in her life, she had something precious of her own to lose.

What the hell. Nina jumped out of bed and into the shower. She had never second-guessed herself. Make a decision, then go with it. Win or lose. Move to London, or sleep with Tony Savage. Start her own firm, or fall in love with Harry Namath—

Angrily she grabbed a towel from the rail. Bullshit, Nina thought, I'm *not* in love with Harry. I just find him attractive.

She went into the hall and phoned Elizabeth.

'Hey, kiddo, you awake?'

'I am now.'

'Come on, it's quarter of seven. No rest for captains of industry.' Nina teased her partner a little, but she could hear pain in her voice. Was she missing Jack already? You had to really know Elizabeth to hear anything under that well-bred Brit politeness. Elizabeth would have to be tortured before she complained about anything in public, still less something so private as an emotion. 'Get up but don't get in the car. I'm coming round. We need to have a meeting, I've got some great news.'

'Marvellous,' Elizabeth said, with a total lack of enthusiasm.

Nina reached Elizabeth's thirty minutes later. Her house near Green Park was direct on the Piccadilly Line, and that meant pushy, grouchy crowds of early-morning bankers facing another boring day with their caffeine and migraines, but she didn't care. Turning into Elizabeth's little tucked-away street she almost ran.

'You look happy,' Elizabeth said.

'You look terrible,' Nina replied. It was true. Her partner wore a defiantly pretty amethyst DKNY, and her blonde hair was gleaming, but she'd obviously been crying all night.

'I feel terrible,' Elizabeth admitted, then sank on to her chintz sofa and burst into tears.

Nina put aside her notes and finance projections and gave Elizabeth a hug.

'Jack and I are through.' Elizabeth explained what she could, in between sobs.

'But that's terrible. Did he fly back to Texas?'

'Just to Dublin.' Elizabeth was distraught, almost choking on her tears. 'He said he's got stud business there and in England ... God, if he comes back to London I don't think I'll be able to bear it.'

'London's a big city, babe, and he likely won't be here for long.'

'I don't know if that makes it better or worse,' Elizabeth said, wiping her hand across her eyes.

'Look, we'll buy you out if that's what you want,' Nina said bravely, wondering where the hell she was ever going to get the money. 'You should be happy.'

'But that's just the problem. I can't be happy in a gold cage. I should know,' Elizabeth said. She picked up the notes Nina had put down. 'Come on, tell me what's going on.'

'Are you sure? It's ... a pretty big deal. Do you want to look at it now?'

Elizabeth nodded. 'Don't worry, my head's still intact. It's just my heart that's broken.'

Outside Tony Savage's windows, all was calm. The sun glittered on the sluggish Thames, lambswool clouds bobbed across a periwinkle-blue sky, traffic flowed serenely across the bridge below them. Inside the office, things were not so calm.

'They're doing *what*?' Tony barked.

Frank Staunton recoiled from Tony's anger, the Terrier shrinking from its master's boot. 'Bank financing,' Staunton repeated. 'Maybe they suspect that going public would see them taken over.'

The earl got to his feet and started to pace around his office. The anger in his stomach was going to give him an ulcer. In the early days he'd kept tabs on Nina Roth's little adventure through a discreet but expensive private investigator; looking for the moment it got off the ground, so he could crush it. Then Elizabeth had hooked up with her. He had to hear that news twice before he believed it; didn't the silly little bitches hate each other? Evidently, not so much as they hated him. Tall Poppies! Elizabeth's long-distance insult, her arrogant slap in the face. And when they'd gone out and picked up Namath, that unshaven, unbusinesslike slob, Tony had fired three of his personnel directors in a blind fury. His company had discarded the programmer as so much excess baggage. At Lilly Hall's request, all Namath's royalties were sequestered; the bonus was eliminated; he'd got nothing. But Lilly's work was an expensive bust, while Harry Namath was already paying off. For a company that was turning into the London School of Dragon Rejects.

Yesterday at lunch Bob Cohen had teased him unmercifully. 'And you let them go, Tony! Talent like that?' The financier clearly enjoyed the joke as he speared his arugula salad. It had been a long time since the Robber Baron had looked this dumb.

'They're riding a craze,' Tony replied tightly.

'You think?' Bob shook his head. 'Home computing's not just Pac-Man any more. If this new venture is as hot as the money is saying, all bets are off.' Cohen lifted his Château-Lafite. 'Your daughter's company could be as big as yours in a year, Tony, it must run in the family. Good Lord, you must be busting with pride.'

Tony pleaded sickness and called for the bill. He couldn't deal with this, just couldn't bear it. All round the Square Mile they were whispering at him and laughing. He hadn't felt such powerful rage since Louise ran off with that prick DeFries.

'It *would* see them taken over. By me.'

I expect they know that, Savage, Staunton thought but didn't say. 'Of course, if the product fails—'

'They fail. So we must make sure it does.'

'I don't see how we can do that, sir. Dr Namath is a genius programmer, the Roth girl seems to know what she's doing and the banks are queuing up to lend them money. Lady Elizabeth has them mad with curiosity already. I must admit,' Staunton said admiringly, 'they move pretty fast.'

'There's a simple way to stop them,' Tony said. His manicured fists clenched on top of the table. 'There's always a simple way. Get out, could you, Frank, I need to think.'

Without saying a word, Staunton glided out of the room and shut the door behind him. Tony stared angrily into his Quotron screen. The Dragon share price was blinking down another eighth. In the dull glass screen he saw himself reflected: handsome, urbane, beautifully dressed. It didn't satisfy him. Nothing did that any more, not the limpid debs he was screwing, not his sons' bland obedience, nor the crawling of his corporate vassals like Frank Staunton. The explosion he had thought would catapult him into the really big time had fizzled out with a whimper. He wasn't ruined, but this felt almost as bad. Small stock dips. Loss of respect. *Treading water*.

And two young women laughing in his face.

They were laying themselves open now, though. All he had to do was see that this product failed miserably. Sabotage? No, too clumsy, and he didn't have the time. He recalled the smug face of Bob Cohen.

'Home Office. A tailored software package, a Filofax for the PC. Wave of the future, old boy, and Tall Poppies will be the first ones out there. Nobody can catch Namath, and he's immune to poaching.'

The earl caught his breath. It was so damn obvious, he was amazed he hadn't thought of it before. He lifted his Sèvres coffee cup in a toast.

'Bob, you're a bloody genius,' he said.

They divided up the tasks between them. Elizabeth toured the finance sources with the company lawyers, raising the money. Nina went round the country, inter-viewing software manufacturers for the subcontracting, and talking to sales reps. By the time Elizabeth had moved on to packaging and promotion, everything was in place. They were all waiting on Harry.

'Look, when I said it was ready I meant the basic code,' Namath said.

'You needn't talk to us like we're retards,' Nina snapped.

'Time out,' Elizabeth protested, holding up one hand. 'Isn't that what you Yanks usually say? Harry, just how far along are we?'

'Two weeks away from beta-testing.'

'Speak English,' Nina said.

Harry shrugged angrily. 'Hey, make your mind up, toots. Either you understand or you don't. Two weeks away from customer try-outs, a month away from production.'

'Who's in charge?'

'I'm doing the user interface – graphics, sound, cartoons, all the stuff that'll make it attractive to the buyers. Tim Paris is finishing up the platforms. John Cobb is checking the code, and Lee Reddy's troubleshooting.'

'We should be ready earlier,' Nina fretted.

'OK, Nina. You want to write the program yourself, be my guest. Otherwise it's one month. You must have business stuff you can do.'

'No.' Nina shook her head. 'The "business stuff", as you put it, is all done.'

'Then the only thing you can do is wait,' Harry said.

'Take a holiday,' Elizabeth said. 'Oh, don't look at me that way, Nina, just a week. Recharge your batteries. Like an investment in your energy.'

'I can't, you need me.'

'No way.' Harry grinned at Elizabeth. 'She's right. She's going ahead with the marketing and I'm writing. What I need is for you to get out of my hair.'

Reluctantly, Nina agreed to a holiday.

It was a mistake. She found she was scouring the business press every day, devouring Elizabeth's banner adverts and PR pieces. She couldn't relax with a book, knowing that her whole future was riding on this. She tried turning up to work on the Wednesday, but Elizabeth pushed her back out the doors again.

'But I'm going stir crazy,' Nina pleaded. 'I want to do something to help the company.'

'You really want to do something? Then you should go see Harry,' Elizabeth told her. 'Seriously. I mean it. When Home Office is launched, Tall Poppies will take off like a rocket, but the rocket will explode unless you guys sort yourselves out. Whatever the problem is, you need to talk it through. We're partners.'

'You don't understand.'

'On the contrary. I *do* understand. Look, Nina, if you and me can wind up friends, so can you and Harry. You're both adults.'

'OK.' Nina nodded. 'OK, I'll go round right now. We won't be friends, but … we can work something out.' She pressed Elizabeth's hand. 'How are you?'

'Me? Terrific, this is an easy sell.'

'I meant personally. With Jack. Is he still around?'

Elizabeth's beautiful face took on a tight look. Her smile no longer reached her eyes. 'Yes, but he's going home next week, so I'll be able to forget all about him.'

Nina smiled back and turned to hail a taxi. She knew neither of them believed that, but there was no point in saying so. Elizabeth was trying to get on with her life, and, as Nina knew herself, there was really nothing else for a woman to do. It was why she'd agreed to see Harry. To put the past in the past, and move on, like a grown woman.

'Hey, what a pleasant surprise,' Harry said wearily as he opened the door. He was wearing jeans and a faded blue shirt and he looked great, despite the red eyes and stubble. That's what you get, Nina thought, if you're shackled to a computer screen for days on end. 'What have I done now?'

'Nothing. Absolutely nothing,' Nina said, squeezing past him. 'Except work like a slave. It's OK, Harry, I've come to apologise.'

He looked at her suspiciously. 'Either this is a plot of Elizabeth's or I'm having caffeine hallucinations.'

'Right first time.' Nina went into the kitchen and reached for his coffee jars. 'See? I'll make decaf.'

She glanced around the pretty kitchen, taking in all Harry's chaos: drying clothes strewn everywhere, food left out on the side, running shoes kicked casually under the table. It was so homely and domestic. She fought the urge to mother him, to tidy up the mess. She had no right to do that. She had no true place in Harry's life. Elizabeth was right, this was a conversation she had to have. You couldn't fight with your partner all the time; it was bad for business.

But Nina was scared. She was about to face things she'd long since swept under the carpet.

'No way.' Harry followed her into the kitchen and Nina tried not to flinch at how close he was standing. 'You have some agenda, Roth, you're permanently on my case.'

'I came over to talk about that. To … apologise,' Nina repeated. Her mouth was drying up, this was a bad idea. She was feeling nervous. God, he shouldn't be able to do this to her. Not still. 'We're partners, we shouldn't be at each other's throats like hyenas. I think you're doing a great job.'

'You think I'm doing a great job.' Harry looked at her searchingly. 'Jesus. Do you have any idea how clinical that sounds?'

Nina shrugged. 'What do you want me to say?'

'I want you to tell me the truth.'

'Harry—'

'No. I want you to tell me the truth. You came over to clear the air, right?' Harry said mercilessly. 'So clear it.'

This was it. He's going to make me say it, Nina thought miserably. She couldn't stave off the confrontation a moment longer. It was so hard, though, with Harry standing there, looking so handsome, his gorgeous eyes with the thick black lashes staring at her so challengingly. He would never understand why she'd done what she'd done ...

'OK.' Nina took a deep breath. 'I thought it was easier to be aggressive than let you look down on me.'

'I didn't do that.'

She flushed. 'Come on, Harry. I know what Tony Savage said to you, and – it was all true.'

Harry nodded. 'I know that.'

'Then you must despise me,' Nina said, and to her horror she heard her voice break and felt her eyes film over.

'No. It's true, I wanted an explanation, but you made it very clear I had no right to one. You broke up with him, and I couldn't compete with some ghost. I hoped I might win you over, once we were colleagues again, but that hasn't exactly worked out.' He gave her a small grin.

'You couldn't compete? I *hate* Tony Savage.'

'So you must have loved him once, right?'

'Wrong! Are you insane?' Nina said. 'I hate him because he told you, he took you away from me!'

There was a moment's dumbstruck silence. Harry just stared at her. Then he reached forwards and grabbed her two hands in his.

'But you were having a relationship ...'

Nina tugged her hands away. 'No. I slept with him because I was young and tough, or I thought I was tough.

I didn't love anybody. I was new and hungry, and everyone assumed I was sleeping with him anyway, so I thought, what the hell? He can be of some use to me.'

'So why did you break up with him?'

'Because it didn't feel cut and dried like I thought it would. It made me feel … bad. I realised I was talented, I had promotions due me anyway.'

'And he didn't like it when you walked.'

'First he threatened me. Then he told you. Then he offered me rewards. And then he fired me.'

Harry Namath looked like a man processing a lot of information, Nina thought bitterly.

'But you did find him attractive.'

'Yes, at first I did, but I never loved him.'

'And I made you feel there could be something more to it.'

'Yeah, well. That was obviously another mistake. I should learn to trust my instincts. Look, Harry. I won't snipe at you any more, but I'll tell you right now,' Nina said, 'that's the way it was. I'm not apologising for it. You can judge me when you've walked in my shoes, and not before—'

'Jesus!' Namath said. He moved closer to her, lifted one hand and clamped it over her mouth. 'You know your trouble, honey, you never listen. I don't judge you. You don't love him?'

He lifted his hand. Nina muttered, 'No.'

'You never did?'

'No.'

'Then that's all I give a damn about,' Harry said, and he pushed her back against the cooker and kissed her.

Chapter 43

Nina didn't go into work the next day. Or the next. She moved her stuff into Harry's, and every moment he wasn't working on Home Office, they went upstairs and made love. She got that same thawing feeling she'd had in Switzerland, only this time there was no fear, no ghosts lurking in the darkness of her past. Harry filled in something missing from her life she didn't know was gone. In his arms she felt safe and relaxed. Except for the times when safe was the last thing she was feeling. Sometimes it was tender, but mostly it was harshly sexual, animal coupling, his hands twisting in her hair as she went down on him, their naked bodies writhing in front of the mirror, Harry talking dirty in her ear until she was half-maddened, and then thrusting savagely into her until she came. But there was no shame to that, no nasty, guilty tang in the mouth afterwards. It was the difference between having sex and making love. Nina climaxed effortlessly every time.

On the Saturday Elizabeth came round for a council of war and found them curled on the couch in their dressing gowns.

'Hey, don't mind me.' She held up a hand to block Nina's protests. 'It was always going to be when, not if. When's the wedding?'

'Whenever we have time,' Harry said, grinning.

Elizabeth looked horrified. 'You're going to wait that long?'

'So what's the news?' Nina asked.

'Thunderbirds are go, kids. The good news is the loans went through this morning. Our asses are in hock to the banks to the tune of four million quid.'

'I'm on schedule, despite the distractions,' Harry said calmly, 'if John Cobb and Tim Paris are ready.'

'Well, if not, they haven't said anything to me.' Elizabeth got up to leave. 'I hate to spoil the mood, guys, but maybe Nina should come into the office again. We need to be totally ready, and we can't afford to have Harry delayed.'

Elizabeth tried to analyse her feelings as she turned into Earls Court Road. She hadn't felt so upset in a long time. She was happy for Nina and Harry, wasn't she? They were two of her dearest friends now, and the atmosphere at work would be smooth as silk. But she didn't feel happy, she felt wretchedly miserable. It was too saintly to try and rejoice for other people when your own heart felt shattered.

She was glad the Tall Poppies situation was so urgent. It took her mind off Jack, off the dust and ashes in her mouth every morning when she woke up.

She parked the car and stepped out on to the sunny pavement. And stopped dead.

Jack Taylor was sitting on her steps.

Elizabeth's eyes lit up like floodlights. 'Jack!' She rushed over and hugged him. 'What are you doing here? I'm so glad to see you!'

He's changed his mind! He wants me, he can't stand it, he wants us to get married—

'You won't be, when you know why I've come,' Jack said.

Elizabeth pulled back and looked at him. He was grave. 'What's wrong? Is somebody dead?'

'No. Nobody's dead, but it's not good, sugar,' Jack replied. 'You're in big trouble. I'm real sorry.'

Elizabeth unlocked her door and took him inside. Jack told her everything he'd heard, and Elizabeth sat down, shakily.

'Are you OK?' He looked anxious. 'Let me get you a drink, or something.'

'No. Thank you,' Elizabeth said, distractedly. 'I need to call Nina, and my lawyers. Look – thanks for letting me know.'

'Hey.' Jack pushed the phone towards her. 'You call who you want, but I'm not leaving. Right now, you need a friend.'

Tony Savage walked into the lobby of the Dragon tower and smiled with perfect triumph.

Though it was a Saturday, the place was buzzing. Production designers had been recalled from their weekends, sales staff were busy placing calls and faxes, and Dragon factories were unlocking their gates for a little extra overtime.

'Your guest is waiting in your office, my lord.' The receptionist smiled deferentially. 'Good morning.'

Tony nodded. 'It is indeed.'

'They're going to do *what*?' Nina gasped.

'Put out a program of their own. "Executive Package." TV advertising starts tomorrow, a huge spend, commercials during the news and *Coronation Street*. Billboards in the City and the West End.'

'But that would cost millions!' Elizabeth said. 'It would swallow up initial profits—'

'He's got millions, and it don't look like he cares about profits,' Jack said. 'He just wants to be first. He's got all the machinery in place already. Factories. Sales forces hundreds of guys strong. Instant packaging expertise. And with the reputation of a big, cash-rich company behind it the analysts love it. They've seen the response to

417

your proposals, you see? They know people are waiting for this.'

'You mean to tell me we've just prepared the ground for Dragon?' Nina spat.

'Looks that way. I'm truly sorry.'

Elizabeth pushed her hands through her hair. 'If he takes the first wave of customers—'

'It could become industry standard,' Nina said dully. 'Nobody will buy a competing product from a baby firm.'

'But I don't *get* it,' Elizabeth said, jumping up and pacing around the room. 'Harry knows he was way in advance of the pack on this. How could anybody have overtaken Harry's team?'

The two women looked at each other.

'Oh my God,' Nina said. 'I can't believe it. That slimy prick. He's poached one of our team. He's creamed off Harry's work. It's the only answer.'

'If that's true, you got resources,' Jack pointed out. 'You can sue.'

'By then the horse would have bolted. And anyway, lawyers cost money,' Elizabeth said. 'It wouldn't do any good.'

'We need to call Harry. He's in the office, working on some last-minute stuff.' Nina punched in the number and Harry picked up right away. They talked quietly for a few minutes.

Jack looked at Elizabeth. 'If you want to hire lawyers, you can use my money, but I guess you wouldn't take it.'

'You guess right,' Elizabeth replied, 'but thanks, Jack. You've been a good friend.'

He nodded. 'I wanted to be a lot more than that.'

'Maybe you still will.' Elizabeth was on the brink of tears now. 'If my company isn't – if I turn into the most famous bankrupt in Britain, I wouldn't stick around out of pride.'

Jack lifted her hand to his mouth and kissed it softly. 'I hope you can believe I didn't want you that way.'

'But truly.' She smiled bravely at him. 'You must be pretty glad this has happened.'

He thought about that for a little while. 'No. I'm not,' Jack said finally. 'I can't stand to see you in pain.'

Nina hung up and turned round, shattering the moment. Her eyes as she looked at Elizabeth were bright. 'Harry and I have had a little chat. He doesn't think we should do anything. Just carry on as before. No statements to the press. No panic.'

'Pretend it's not happening?'

'John Cobb's gone,' Nina said. 'Left a message on Harry's answerphone. Tony hired him for over a million a year.'

'What?' Elizabeth's mouth dropped open. 'A million quid? We were paying him twenty-three grand! That's a hell of a pay rise! What does he have that's worth a million?'

'Experience.' Nina looked grim. 'He was in charge of checking Harry's code. He had total access to Home Office.'

'And Harry thinks we should just keep our heads down, carry on regardless?'

'If that's Harry's advice, we have to trust him.'

'You're right there,' Elizabeth said furiously. 'There's bugger all else we *can* do.'

It was agony to watch. The mighty Dragon sales machine swung into action with devastating effect. TV screens were bombarded with ads. The computer press ran profiles of both systems and concluded there was nothing to pick between them. Except for one key point. Dragon's was out first.

The press Elizabeth had courted were now hounding her wherever she went. If Tall Poppies had had a share price, trading would have been suspended. The hacks who'd loved them last week were now full of scorn. Trust two stupid bimbos to put all their eggs in one basket! Their bankers were on the phone every day, demanding clarification. When Tall Poppies' own campaigns, modest and well targeted, started to run, people poured scorn upon them. Scenting blood, the tabloids even got in on the act. The idea of a deadly rivalry between Tony Savage and his estranged daughter was just too delicious to resist. How stupid we were to criticise the Robber Baron, the papers crawled. Letting those three losers go was a great idea.

Lord Caerhaven gave a few triumphant interviews. Dignified pieces in serious organs: the *FT*, *The Times*, *The Economist*. Everybody feared him again. Dragon's stock took a massive ten-point jump.

Executive Package launched on the first of August in a blaze of publicity. Elizabeth and Nina stayed quietly in their offices, putting the final touches to Home Office. They took no calls from the press.

Sales for Dragon's package, as predicted, went through the roof. A super-efficient sales force was on hand to see huge piles of the beautiful box stacked everywhere from toy stores to stationers'. Initial stocks soon sold out and Tony switched two more factories to EP. More copies were rush-produced. Linguists produced interfaces in French, Spanish and German. For two weeks, Executive Package was the computer craze of the moment.

Tall Poppies bowed Home Office on schedule, but they were way behind. Lukewarm reviews said there was nothing wrong with the product, but so what? With its no-nonsense packaging, no sales discounts and lack of publicity, Home Office was a moth to Tony Savage's glittering butterfly. Their loans were due in two months. It looked like the game was up.

'He's won,' Nina said dully.

'Wait and see.' Elizabeth was defiant. 'I don't hear any fat lady singing.'

Exactly twenty-one days after the launch, Dragon took a call. A sweet shop in Birmingham complained of a bug. Instead of printing out its normal spreadsheets, Executive Package was typing a nursery rhyme. Over and over. Nothing they could do would stop it.

Tony called the customer personally. He thought it was a masterly piece of PR.

'Must be a faulty copy. What's the message exactly?'

The man sounded embarrassed. 'It goes, "I'm the king of the castle, and you're the dirty rascal," uh, milord.'

'What?' Tony coloured. 'Never mind. Just a glitch. We'll replace it right away.'

That same day, the Customer Service Department received ten more calls. The next day, twenty. By the end of the week, they were flooded.

'Jesus Christ!' Tony said, raging at John Cobb. '*Fix* this! Don't you understand, we have half a warehouse full of returned copies?'

Cobb looked helplessly at Frank Staunton. 'I can't fix it. It's programmed into the code. It, uh, appears to be a time-activated thing.'

'It prints the message three weeks after EP is turned on, sir,' Frank Staunton said smoothly.

Tony looked at his underling with loathing. The little jerk was enjoying this!

'If it's in the *code*, write new code! Change it!'

Cobb ran his hands through greasy hair. He looked like a man who hadn't slept. 'But I can't do that, milord. It was Henry Namath's code.'

'Get out,' Tony snarled.

Cobb scuttled out. Tony sat down heavily in his carved chair and stared at Staunton. 'I can't believe it.' The clipped tones were tight with humiliation and fury. 'It's a trap. The little bitches have trapped me.'

'We'll have to recall the entire line,' Staunton said blandly. 'I'm afraid the television stations are starting to pick up on it.' He tossed Tony a copy of that night's *Evening Standard*. Twin shots on the front page showed Tony and a computer screen, blurting out the EP message. The headline was, 'DIRTY RASCAL TO LOSE HIS CASTLE'.

'To do what?' Tony snorted. 'What are they talking about, Staunton?'

'I think it's this comment from Marcus Fitzallen, sir,' the Terrier said with undisguised pleasure, 'speaking as Chairman of the Board of Dragon. He says they want a word.'

Epilogue

'But he survived,' Nina said.

Elizabeth shrugged. 'Of course he survived. Men like that always do. My father knows too many people, he's spent a lifetime covering his back.'

They were in the office, sipping champagne and leafing through the papers at a celebratory Tall Poppies brunch. All around them was the chaos of last night's wild staff party. Friday morning, when Tall Poppies went public, the issue was an immediate success. After the bank loans had been repaid, they were all three millionaires, a few times over. Today they were looking at pictures of themselves in the financial pages, smiling broadly. Many of them were placed next to a grim-faced Tony Savage exiting his board meeting. The 'Rascal' fiasco had cost him a profits warning and a public reprimand.

'What made you suspect John Cobb?' Jack asked Harry.

He grinned. 'I didn't. I just didn't trust anybody. I booby-trap every programme I write against hackers.'

'Come on, sweetheart.' Nina stood up and beckoned Harry. 'Let's go home.'

'OK.' He reached over and briefly touched her cheek. 'I'll wait for you in the car.'

'Goodbye, Jack,' Nina said, waving to him.

'Nina.' He winked.

Elizabeth said, 'I'll walk down with you,' ran over and threaded her arm through Nina's.

'We did it,' Elizabeth said.

'We did the first part of it,' Nina replied, smiling softly. 'We've got a long way to go to get where I want to be.'

'Tony'll be back, you know? We hurt him badly, and we made him look like a fool.'

'Yeah, ain't life grand,' Nina said, her eyes sparkling. 'We can handle him, no problem.'

'It's true: he couldn't stamp us out when we had nothing …' Elizabeth grinned. 'Living well is the best revenge, but misery and humiliation's pretty good too.'

They hugged, and Nina slipped out to the back, to where Harry was waiting for her.

Elizabeth walked slowly back up the stairs. The place looked like it had been hijacked by a gang of marauding kids. Squishy cake on the steps and balloons drifting everywhere.

Jack was perching on the edge of her office couch, wearing jeans, cowboy boots and a thick blue jumper. He looked so gorgeous. Bittersweet pleasure, because now, Elizabeth thought, he's got nothing to stick around for.

She walked over to him and sat down. Don't cry, Elizabeth warned herself, as her exhilaration burst like one of the balloons. Don't ruin the happy mood by getting all emotional.

You know the score.

'So, I guess you'll be leaving soon.'

'Hmm. Maybe.' Taylor nodded. 'But first, I got a business proposition for you.'

Business. Right. Elizabeth tried to look enthusiastic. 'Sure, go ahead.'

'Well now,' Jack said slowly. His Southern accent dripped over her like honey, she hated how his voice turned her on. 'I spoke to Pop last night. Thought if y'all could make so much money with lateral thinking, we should give it a try. I was talking to him about property over here. The Viceroy Hotel.'

'The place on the river?'

'Yes, ma'am. We reckon it would look real good in the portfolio, but it'll need upgrading. We thought maybe Tall Poppies could do it.'

Elizabeth sat stunned. 'But that would take you—'

'At least six months. By which time, you'll probably need to open an office in the States.'

'Jack!'

He caught her left hand and pressed it to his mouth. 'Baby, I'll say it again. Will you marry me? We can be together, we'll work something out. Hell, you take all these dollar-and-cent gambles every day. Why don't you risk a little on something important?'

Elizabeth leaned up and kissed him. He tasted of sun and champagne and Texas, Jack, her Jack, absolutely the only man she had ever loved.

'Aggressive as ever.'

'Is that a yes?'

'Oh, yeah,' Elizabeth said, 'that's a yes, sugar.'